The Boy Sarah

The Boy Sarah

Grace Thompson

PIATKUS

First published in Great Britain in 1990 by
Judy Piatkus (Publishers) Ltd of
5 Windmill Street, London W1

British Library Cataloguing in Publication Data

Thompson, Grace
The boy sarah.
I. Title
823.914

ISBN 0-7499-0003-2

Phototypeset in 11/12pt Times Linotron by
Wyvern Typesetting Ltd, Bristol
Printed and bound in Great Britain by
Billing & Sons Ltd, Worcester

Chapter One

Sarah stood at the window of Houghton Hall and stared out at the sun-filled scene before her. To the distant right, she could see the figures of the farm-workers as they cut the rich hay. Flowers growing among the tall grasses gave a magnificent swathe of colour that grew smaller as the scythes advanced. The regular swing of the tools and the bending and rising of the women gathering the crop for stooking gave pleasure to her eye.

She had been in the field with them for a while, but when she returned, dusty and laughing, she had been reprimanded by her maid, Edith, for allowing her skin to be touched by the sun. She felt the warmth of her cheeks with her small hands and smiled. It felt good. What did it matter if it was not ladylike? This was not London.

Edith came into the room, disapproval still on her face.

'Miss Sarah, I want you to sit there with this raw potato on your forehead. It will help take away the burn.'

'Oh, Edith, must I?' But she submitted. In 1851 young ladies still obeyed their maid.

Sarah lay back on the velvet-covered armchair and wriggled down so that she could still watch the harvesters. She allowed Edith to place grated raw potato across her forehead and the bridge of her nose where the sun had caught her.

'I hope no one will come in and see me like this,' she protested, although she would have been embarrassed at being considered vain rather than at looking foolish. She smiled then, toppling some of the carefully placed potato, unable to be cross with Edith any longer. 'Oh, Edith, it was such fun up there in the fields. I went with the scullery maids and the odd-job boy to take the lunch basket. Cuts of meat and cheeses and a pie, fresh loaves and our own cider. It tasted so good, eating it out in the sunshine.'

'Watch for your father coming back, then I'll take the poultice off,' Edith said. 'Though why you won't sit in your room like any normal young lady, I don't know!'

'I find it impossible to behave like a normal young lady should,' Sarah said. 'I suppose I am too much like my mother.' She sighed. 'And soon we will be back in London.'

'Humph.' Edith put a great deal of disapproval into the sound. Her charge was a constant worry: the lax upbringing Sarah and her brothers and sisters had had made it hard to instill in her the behaviour and training of a wealthy young lady of society.

Sarah's father, Sir Jason Lindhurst Ayres, was a gentleman and his family could be traced back to the Conquest, but he had married a young woman from the music hall, much to his family's disapproval, and it was from her that Sarah, alone among the children, had inherited her waywardness. Edith thought that the desire to follow her mother, dance and perform acrobatics had been suppressed, but since coming to the country, she had often come upon Sarah cartwheeling, climbing trees or even standing up on the patient horse when she thought she was safe from discovery. Edith sighed again. Much as she loved Sarah, life would be far easier with a more conventional charge.

As Edith went about her tasks, Sarah continued to stare out through the curved bay window, envious of the workers and their freedom. A movement caught her eye and she turned her head slowly, trying to balance the potatoes. A horse rider was approaching from the east and appeared to be making for Houghton Hall. At once she called Edith, who came running at the urgency of her voice.

'I think we have a visitor,' Sarah said. 'Take this stupid potato from my face at once.'

A bowl was brought and, after discarding the beauty treatment, Edith washed her face.

'Fancy doing this in the drawing room, Miss Sarah,' she

protested. 'I don't know what gets into you sometimes, indeed I do not.'

'It seems I was mistaken. The rider, whoever he was, is not coming to Houghton Hall after all.'

They stood and watched as the horse and its rider passed the end of the long drive and hesitated a while, staring at the house, before turning and slowly walking back the way he had come. At the end of the drive he stopped again but did not approach the house. They saw him bend and pull up a passenger to sit up in front of him. It looked like a small boy.

'Should we send someone to ask if he is lost?' Sarah asked.

'There's no one to send. Everyone is in the fields. Your father and brothers are visiting Giles Hallam and your sisters are out for a walk with Isobelle's nanny.'

'Where is Renton?' Their coachman was rarely far from Sarah, since, as a child, he had appointed himself her protector.

'I sent him to walk with the women.'

'Perhaps you and I should . . .'

'No, Miss Sarah. I forbid it!'

Sarah chuckled and hugged her maid. 'Oh, Edith, you are so easy to tease!'

'Teasing maybe, but I know you could easily have meant it!' Edith said stiffly.

The rider passed the gates and picked up speed. He was soon out of sight.

'I wonder who he was?' Sarah frowned. 'It might have been someone looking for Father. A business acquaintance, perhaps?'

'Then he would have come to the door.'

'It's a pity he did not. It would have been a pleasant diversion to have met someone new.'

'With no one here but us? I would not have answered the door! Manners and behaviour are so lax here in the country. I shall be thankful when we are back at Sallis Close. London is so much more . . .' Edith frowned as she sought a suitable word. 'London is so much more orderly!' She clasped her thin hands and looked at Sarah's face, flushed and looking quite beautiful, although she would not admit how the touch of the sun had brightened her mistress's complexion and made her skin glow and the grey eyes sparkle. 'We need to get you back as soon as we can, Miss Sarah, before you forget completely that you have a position to uphold and it's not that of a farm-worker. Heavens above, you will ask permission to milk the cows next!' She could think of nothing more horrifying.

'Not the cows, Edith, I find them far too large and not a little frightening. I love to see them, and the sheep on the hills around us, but only at a distance.'

'I'm relieved to hear it.'

Sarah smiled and hugged her. 'Dear Edith, don't worry about me so. Once I get back to London I'll become what you think I should be, or as near it as I can.' She looked out of the window and unaccustomed envy touched her as she watched the group in the fields.

At Houghton Hall, behaviour was allowed to relax, but once back at Sallis Close she would have to fill the role of Miss Sarah, dutiful eldest daughter. No more riding bareback or using the barn to practise the exercises and acrobatics taught to her by her talented mother, while the rest of the household was still asleep. And no more secret wanderings with Renton, who, although born in the same house as Sarah and at the same time, was so knowledgeable about country matters.

Then she thought longingly of seeing Giles Hallam, whose country house was not very far from Houghton Hall, but whom she had hardly seen during the time spent in the country. In London, at least, he made regular visits to the house to talk with her father. As a business acquaintance of Sir Jason, he called almost daily when they had some scheme underway. She called Edith again.

'Edith, I think I will do as you say, and sit for a while with the potato on my face to cool away the effect of the sunshine.'

The horseman stopped once he was out of sight of Houghton Hall, and looked back. The place had seemed to be empty, no sign of a coach or of people present, but he had better not risk going to see. Pity. He would have loved to look at the house where Sarah Lindhurst Ayres lived in the summer months. He cuffed the small, red-haired boy in front of him and told him to stop wriggling.

'You'll get down and walk again if you don't stay still,' he warned. 'And head *down*, you're ruffling my beard!'

'One more good wriggle and I'm done,' the boy promised. He shifted so he could ease the tightness of the too small trouser leg which was cutting into his thin thigh, and gave a sigh of relief. 'There. I won't budge not an inch now, Jarvis.'

Jarvis King had come to see the old farm. It was tucked into a hillside not far from Houghton Hall. The farm was his dream. Not that he ever wanted to live there. No, the country was not for Jarvis, but knowing he had been conceived there, even if his mother had left before the birth, made it his roots, his only pretence at belonging somewhere.

When he was in difficulties and the future looked bleak, he would come to look at it, and the sight of the now ruined old building would renew his determination to succeed and show the gentry, who had thrown his mother out to fend for herself, that he, Jarvis King, was as good as, if not better than, they.

Today he had not gone inside the farmhouse, but had looked at it from the road. The day had been a long one and he was anxious to get back to the hotel where he had hired the horse and left his expensive leather bag. A bag that contained nothing but old paper to add weight, carried only to give the impression of prosperity.

In fact all he had in the world was a stock of clothes, including the uniform of the soldier he pretended once to have been, and the grudging permission to use the rooms of a few friends occasionally. Seeing the house again revived his confidence. The deals he had in motion were beginning to crystallise and soon he would be mixing with the likes of Sarah Lindhurst Ayres and considered fit company for her.

They passed the turning for Weatherby, the country house owned by Giles Hallam, but again Jarvis did not stop, only looked at the beautiful house and dreamed of visiting there as a guest. Soon, he promised himself. Soon. They increased their speed and when they neared the village inn where

Jarvis was staying, the boy darted into the stables to find a suitable place to hide himself. Jarvis handed the horse's reins to the stableboy and went inside.

Having eaten well, and supped some of the fine ale the inn provided, he retired to bed. But he didn't sleep. He lay smoking his pipe, staring up at the ceiling, dreaming dreams and making plans. When the inn had grown silent, he went to the window and whistled softly. The boy came out of the stable and climbed up to the window with the ease of much practice.

The clock in the room below struck three; the sound echoing around the silence of the building seemed deafeningly loud to the two who waited. When this failed to disturb the sleepers, Jarvis nodded and their night's work began.

Few of the inn's guests had bothered to lock their door and those that had would have been surprised at the speed with which the wooden barriers submitted to Jarvis's nimble hands. He opened the doors and the boy slipped in and found what money he could. Doors were closed and after a hurried tidy-up of their collection, the boy prepared to leave, again from Jarvis's window.

'Not this time,' Jarvis whispered. 'There's no one asleep below. Go out through the door and make sure you leave it open. Head for Will's lodgings. He's going to London in a day or so to deliver some rats for the rat killings. He'll see you safely back.'

'I wish I could go with you in the stage,' the boy said wistfully. 'A proper passenger, paid for an' all.'

'One day,' Jarvis promised, pushing him on his way. 'Now hurry. I have to raise the alarm before it's light.'

The boy left, and Jarvis moved to the window to watch him cross the cobbled yard and go through the hedge into the fields. A horse called softly to its neighbour and somewhere a mouse squeaked as a cat's paw held it down. The wind moved the leaves of a nearby tree, a branch moaned softly as it rubbed against another. To Jarvis, who was used to the constant noise of a city night, the place was eerie. He couldn't wait to get back to where the world was full of people.

The boy had been but a shadow, a part of the gloom and

stillness, and Jarvis only waited long enough to be certain he had covered enough distance not to be followed, before he gave a loud shout of rage and banged the wall.

'I've been robbed!' he roared, opening the door and, standing outside it, repeating his complaint until other doors began to open and sleepy figures emerged. Soon other voices were added to his and the landlord appeared, wearing a nightshirt and a long hat, a guttering candle in his hand. Jarvis showed him a coat from which the pocket had been cut open by the 'thieves'. Complaints were shouted as others discovered their losses. Jarvis was loudest.

'I am left penniless!' he raged. 'How will I get back to London without even my fare? And my best clothes have been ruffled so they aren't in a fit state to be seen in.'

Others added their lists of grievances and the village constable was sent for. It was morning before they admitted that nothing further could be done, and the inn settled into an uneasy quiet once again. Lists of stolen property had been written out, descriptions laboriously noted by the patient but unhopeful representative of the law. Few expected to recover anything they had lost. Except Jarvis, who continued to look more outraged than the rest.

'I paid money for a bed and expected to be allowed to sleep in it, not spend the night standing guard over my possessions! Where am I to find the fare back to London? And how do I eat? Tell me that!'

Others echoed his complaints. The landlord hurriedly supplied food and promised to plead with the coachdriver to accept notes of promise.

'If the coach is due this afternoon, I shall go to church this morning and pray for assistance in capturing the thieves.' Jarvis did not want to be the first to leave, that might be considered suspicious, and neither did he want to be the last. He thought his anger and actions were well judged when the constable took him on one side and confided that he thought the job was 'done from the outside' and the culprit 'long gone'.

Although Jarvis knew the road to take to the church, he allowed himself to be directed back to the hamlet through which he had ridden the previous day, not far from the old farm and Houghton Hall, and Sarah. The day was fine and he walked, passing others heading in the same direction, his long legs and tall figure taking him past the family groups with ease.

As a slight compensation for being robbed while under his roof, the landlord had given Jarvis's clothes to his cleaning woman to be pressed, and had polished the leather walking boots himself. Dressed in a brown woollen jacket with a shawl collar, under which a high-necked shirt showed off a long cravat in bright yellow, Jarvis felt pleased with himself. He wore a waistcoat of embroidered cotton and his brown hat had a band around it to match his cravat. He nodded slightly to those he passed, feeling superior to them all.

His beard and moustaches and the straightness of his tall, slim figure produced mutterings of 'army man, no doubt of it' from passers-by. Jarvis smiled. He touched his neat beard and hoped the glue would hold.

The church was a surprise. It was little more than a ruin: a long, low building with a square tower at the western end, which sprouted so much foliage through its cracks that it seemed to have grown there, and a porch on the south side that had lost most of its thatch. The roof dipped from the gables and on that, too, the thatch was in a poor state. When Jarvis stepped into the gloomy interior, the smell of mouldering wood and damp soil almost sent him outside again.

He looked around him at the earthen floor which improved slightly towards the altar, being pebbled with small round stones, probably brought from some distant beach. There were only two wooden pews and, for the rest of the congregation, an ill-matched set of chairs and benches.

What impulse had brought him to such a place? He had to wait for the coach but it would have been more pleasant to wait at the inn. Looking with apprehension at the seat on which he was expected to risk his fine worsted trousers, he stepped away to stand near the blocked-up anchorite's window to watch the proceedings. He was near enough to the porch to make his escape if the singing was too much to bear.

He was glad he was in the shadows when, with the small church almost full, silence fell and all bonneted heads turned towards the door. The rector, whom Jarvis had not seen until this time, entered, his Bible clasped in grubby hands, his clothes no less grey than the stone of the walls. Behind him walked Sarah, Sir Jason and the rest of the family.

He watched as Sarah and her father led the others to their pew. She was dressed in grey and lavender and Jarvis thought she had never looked more beautiful. The drab surroundings seemed brighter for her presence. She was tiny, looking like a child among the rest of her brothers and sisters. Only eight-year-old Isobelle was smaller and that not by much.

Jarvis did not follow the service. He watched Sarah, and dreamed of the day he would be introduced to her. The time was not far off. Perhaps one day he would stand in this church again and not in the shadows, but beside her in the family pew. But, by heaven, he would make sure the place was more habitable! How could people like the Lindhurst Ayres not give money to repair their village church? They had enough wealth to rebuild several.

People began to shuffle out and Jarvis brought his mind quickly back to the present. Staying in his corner and bending slightly at the knee to make himself less noticeable, he waited until the church was empty before stepping out into the clean country air. The congregation was gradually dispersing on small carts and on foot, some stopping for a word with neighbours before making their way homeward, where they would change out of their beribboned dresses or tidy trousers and smocks, into the work clothes of their various callings.

Sir Jason and his entourage of family and servants were walking back down the narrow road to Houghton Hall. Jarvis watched them go. One day he would walk with them. He would enter their lives and change them all. A lot of things would change once he, Jarvis King, entered the world of London's society. No more hiding in filthy church corners for him then!

He watched Sarah until she had faded from his sight. She was so small and dainty, so perfect. She was the wonderful bonus he promised himself once Sir Jason had been destroyed. Until then he would remain a secret admirer. The romantic thought pleased him and the hardness left his eyes. Sarah Lindhurst Ayres was his dream. The ruination of her father was rapidly approaching a fact.

Sir Jason sat in his wooden captain's chair, waiting. The office was filled with shelves on which large ledgers and reference books, dealing with many aspects of transport and trade, were neatly arranged. He sat behind a fine, leather-topped desk around which were set four extra chairs. In front of each chair was a blotter and a pile of clean paper. An inkstand with a collection of pens was in the centre.

Sir Jason wore a black suit and a lavender cravat and his tall silk hat was on the desk beside him. Although it was the month of June and very mild, a fire burned in the grate and he sat with his feet towards its warmth as he waited for the others to arrive.

He was frowning but the expression was a constant one these days. Since the loss of his dearly loved wife four years before, the serious and troubled face he showed to the world rarely changed. The deep-set eyes and the long, narrow nose gave him a haunted look and discouraged unnecessary pleasantries in those he met.

He heard the outer door close and guessed it was Topham, his secretary.

'Topham?' he called, and the door opened to admit a man of about forty years. He was carrying a sheaf of papers and there were ink stains on his fingers. He seemed unable to take his eyes from his work, and his head was bent in the study of it. He was hard-working and loyal, and irritated Sir Jason enormously.

'Have you found me a warehouse yet?' Sir Jason asked.

Most of the Lindhurst Ayres family money had been made through investment and the interests from ownership of land and property, but since his father had left the finances in his hands, Sir Jason had gradually become more interested in what his father would have disparagingly called trade.

He had been an importer and exporter of both ready-made items and the raw material for making them. His interest in fine glass and china had increased and he had become an expert in the quality market. Somehow the business had spread to include furniture and even veneers and wainscoting. Now he needed the use of a good, safe warehouse for a large consignment that was coming into St Katherine's Dock in less than two weeks. The meeting today was to approve and rent that storage. Every other warehouse he owned was crammed full.

Topham took so long to answer his question that Sir Jason tightened his jaw irritably. The man was cautious to the point of lunacy, chewing every remark he made before risking it to be caught by the ear of another.

'No, sir, I have not. But the three men who are coming to this meeting have promised to do what they can. In fact, one, a William Bartlett, seemed to have the solution to your dilemma, but he refused to discuss it until you were present.'

The men arrived and were offered coffee, which the errand boy fetched from the stall outside. Then they settled down to discussing the pros and cons of various storage accommodations. Most were rejected as too distant, others because of the impossibility of protecting the valuable consignment. Finally, Sir Jason looked at William Bartlett.

'I understand from Topham that you have a suggestion.'

Bartlett smiled. Sir Jason had the impression that the man had been waiting for all the other ideas to be discarded.

'If I may, Sir Jason, I would like to show you this sketch of a street not far from the docks.' He moved the inkstand to a safer place and opened a large sheet of paper across the desk. It was a street plan, and Sir Jason, Topham and the others stood to study it.

'I know this place,' Sir Jason said, his frown deepening. 'In fact, I believe I own it.'

William Bartlett nodded. 'So, if you should decide to demolish it, no one could forbid it?'

'Demolish it? I don't understand.'

'See here? And here?' Bartlett's slender finger touched the page and pointed to where narrow alleyways partitioned off groups of buildings and occasionally opened out into streets.

'I don't understand,' Sir Jason repeated. 'There is

nowhere here large enough to hold the goods. And certainly nowhere safe enough. This cargo is worth in excess of five thousand pounds, gentlemen.'

William Bartlett's finger pointed again. 'If the buildings between here and here were knocked down – and, from what I have seen of them, that would not take more than a few hefty kicks – the area between this wall – ' he slid his finger across the buildings shown – 'and this wall, with another wall behind it, would be ample for your requirements, Sir Jason. Tarpaulins firmly in place and a dozen reliable men to stand guard for the one day and one night would be cheap and effective.'

'But what are these buildings that would go?'

'Shabby housing. Overfilled with the worst of London's poor. I think you would be thankful to see them gone.'

'I can't see that it would work.' Sir Jason shook his dark head, his long nose closer to the paper as he considered the idea. 'Wouldn't it take a long time? There is so little time left.'

'A few hours to knock the places down, a day and, with flares, a night to dispose of the rubble – '

'Is there nowhere else in the whole of London?'

'I have the name of a man who says he has a warehouse which he will put at your disposal, but I don't know anything about him and hesitate to trust a stranger,' the quiet voice of the secretary put in. 'His name is Jarvis King.'

The five men all shook their heads. 'Never heard of the man,' Sir Jason said. 'Where did you hear of him?'

'He heard of us, or, at least, you,' the secretary explained. 'He said he had hired premises, then found he had no need of them. He knew you wanted storage and offered what he has.' Topham shuffled through the papers and brought out a letter. 'It sounds very suitable, but, not knowing the man – '

'Don't risk it,' Bartlett urged, and the others murmured their agreement.

'So for all our efforts, we have either to trust a man none of us has heard of, or do what Bartlett suggests and make a place of our own by demolishing a lot of buildings?'

'That would seem to be it, sir,' Topham said. 'I must say the latter seems a novel way of settling the problem, but a fresh thought often leads to more vigorous progress.'

'Who lives in these places?'

'No one who wouldn't thank you for eradicating their terrible conditions, Sir Jason. Giving them the impetus to get out and improve their lot – well, I think it would be a social blessing.'

'Very well. If you can be sure there will be no danger to the goods for the day and a night they have to stay, I'll agree. Will you see to the arrangements?' he asked Bartlett.

'It will be my pleasure, Sir Jason.' William Bartlett found it difficult to hide his smile. How easy it had been to persuade them to take down the buildings that were in the way of his newly planned housing! With the buildings gone, he had access to the area he owned and could not, until now, make use of.

'Dogs,' he said. 'We'll need a dozen fierce dogs. Don't worry, gentlemen, your cargoes will be as safe as houses.'

'Safer than the houses we'll be removing, I hope!' someone joked. The laughter that followed was somewhat nervous.

The meeting dispersed and Sir Jason went home, leaving Topham and William Bartlett to discuss the arrangements to deprive a few dozen families and their dependants of their homes.

'What about this Jarvis King?' Topham called after him. 'How shall I reply?'

'Politely, Topham. Politely. We might need even a stranger's assistance some time in the future.'

'But he wishes to meet you, sir.'

'Then say no, politely, to that too.'

Arthur was not a costermonger. Although he regularly pushed a cart laden with produce around the streets near the docks, he did not offer anything for sale. Under the cabbages, turnips and potatoes, he gathered stolen goods and transported them to the fence. For his helpfulness in assisting trade, he was rewarded by both the seller and the buyer and no questions asked. His own collection of stolen items was also carried about under the vegetables and fruit and disposed of in the same way.

He owned nothing besides the cart, which he kept in the small room where he slept, a room he occasionally shared with a woman. The cart, a few blankets and the clothes he stood up in were all he had in the world. In spite of large amounts of money earned he did not become rich, preferring to spend the money on drink and the company of others of a like mind. His thieving and housebreaking was a hobby and gave him enormous pleasure. The act of taking something that the owner had thought safe was the excitement that made every morning a promise of a wonderful day.

Ugly, feared and, for most of the time, alone, Arthur was a happy man. He ate in the streets, did his business in the streets and spent all he earned in the streets. What he wanted – and his needs were simple – he bought. What he couldn't buy, he stole. When someone annoyed him, his huge arm would come out with a speed that surprised, and knocked the offender down. Arthur wanted for nothing. He had been away from his home for almost a week and moved faster as he neared it, anxious for a long sleep.

Because of a close shave with the law, he had taken himself off to the country for a day or so, spending the time with his friend Will, who brought rats up from the country to sell for the rattings; pits where dogs were set against large numbers of the creatures, the winner – the dog who killed the largest number – often sold for two hundred pounds.

Arthur was not a gambling man, but he enjoyed hearing the tales that Will had to tell and a few days away from the noise and tensions of the city were a pleasant change. After a couple of days he set off back to his pitch. As he turned into the alleyway that led to his home, he stopped, frightened for a moment that his brain had been damaged. He had boxed for several years and this fear haunted him always.

He stood and looked around him. Everything had gone. The semi-derelict row of houses in which he had always lived was no longer there. In place of the houses was a huge pile of canvas-covered bundles, the numbers on them showing them to have arrived by ship. These were slowly being covered by sheets of tarpaulin by a gang of men, several of whom were accompanied by growling dogs.

Groups of men and women stood huddled in corners, watching them.

'What's 'appened 'ere?' Arthur demanded.

'Landlord took our 'omes. There was nothing we could do,' an old man wailed. 'In no time at all, they was gone.'

Arthur balled his fists, his powerful muscles tensed and demanding activity. 'Who?' he asked, his voice low and deceptively calm. 'Who did it?'

'That Lindhurst Ayres fellow. Pretends not to own us, but 'e does. Deals through others, but it's 'im all right.'

'I'll get 'im.' Arthur set off, his arms swinging from slightly stooped shoulders, to find Jarvis. He would know how best to deal with this.

Jarvis King stared at the letter which an errand boy had brought, for which he had given him twopence. The paper shook in his hand. His plan had failed. The note from Topham, Sir Jason's secretary, was brief, but it meant disaster to him and a serious setback to his plans for meeting Sarah.

Kind Sir,

Regarding your offer for the use of your premises. Sir Jason thanks you and asks me to convey his appreciation of your willingness to assist him. Unfortunately, he found a solution just prior to considering your offer.

Yours faithfully,
R.J. Topham

on the authority of Sir Jason Lindhurst Ayres

Jarvis stared at the letter, then screwed it into a ball and threw it from him. He was ruined: in debt, with nothing in the offing to help him out of it.

He had borrowed, robbed and cheated to rent the warehouse, having been told that the place was the only one that would suit Sir Jason's urgent needs. He had hoped to charge him an exorbitant rent for the two days and be formally introduced to the man at the same time. Now what could he do? Where could he raise money quickly and in sufficient quantities to save the situation? He was sitting despondent and low when Arthur found him.

When he had heard Arthur's story, his spirits began to rise. He touched his chin, now clean-shaven.

'Will you break into Sir Jason's office for me?'

'Break *'im*, too, should you ask me.'

'No, no violence, *yet*.' Jarvis looked at the heavily built ex-fighter; in his green eyes was a tacit promise. 'Not *yet*.' He began to think of a plan and, when he spoke again, he did not waste words. 'I need a few examples of Sir Jason's signature. I need some paper from his desk, carefully brought, not folded or crumpled. You will also bring me some pens, in case they are different in any way, and a sample of his ink.'

Arthur did not question the request, he just grunted and went on his way. Jarvis was no longer low, in fact he was smiling as his brain clicked over the necessary arrangements.

A few days later, a very ruffled Topham burst into Sir Jason's room without knocking.

'Sir Jason. Something very worrying has happened.'

'Sit down, Topham.'

'The consignment from Italy, the order for the hotel chandeliers and ornamental displays. They've gone.'

'So, they have been collected earlier than stated? As long as they pay for the original days of storage, what is the problem?' Sir Jason sounded irritated. Topham was an excellent secretary but he was inclined to fuss.

'Sir, they have gone. When the customer's man arrived to collect them they had already been called for. They've gone. The note claiming them seemed in order and they were handed over without question.'

'But how could someone have matched my note and my signature so accurately that a man who has worked for me for years could – the burglary! When the office was broken into a few nights ago and only a few worthless items taken we thought it was a child hoping for some money. But what if the object was simply to take my pens and note paper and find copies of my signature to be able to forge it?' Sir Jason sat down heavily. 'Last month we were robbed of two valuable cargoes from warehouses that were well guarded. Now this. What is happening to us, Topham? Are we being picked out for a deliberate campaign or is this a co-incidence that the goods stolen have lost me customers as well. Time for a replacement to be found is not always available, as with this order for a new hotel, the owners will not, cannot wait. These past few weeks have cost me a great deal of money and prestige, Topham.'

Topham was still trying to formulate a reply when Sir Jason left to go to his club a few minutes later.

Chapter Two

Sarah looked around the crowded ballroom, trying to prevent the disappointment from showing on her face. The long-case clock ticking ponderously behind her showed it was almost time for supper to be served and there was still no sign of Giles. The dance was to celebrate the eighteenth birthday of Giles's sister Caroline, Sarah's closest friend, and Sarah had been looking forward to the occasion especially because of the likelihood of seeing him.

Not that she disliked dancing. Sarah was full of high spirits and threw herself completely into every activity. In fact, she was constantly being reprimanded for being too enthusiastic.

'Please try to be a little more ladylike, Miss Sarah,' was the frequent plea from her chaperone, Great-Aunt Milly. Sarah looked across the room through the colourful dresses of the whirling ladies and the more sober suits of their partners, to where her aunt sat dozing gently, her head against the shoulder of another elderly lady, her puffed and red face moving slightly with every breath. Sarah grinned affectionately. Really, Great-Aunt Milly was more often asleep than awake these days!

'What are you laughing at, Sarah?' Caroline asked, seeing the smile on her friend's face.

'Only Great-Aunt Milly, asleep as usual.'

Caroline smiled as she too caught sight of the row of weary chaperones sleeping peacefully in the warm room. She leaned towards Sarah and began to snore in her ear. In a voice remarkably like that of the old lady, Sarah said, 'Don't you know, thoughtless child, that it's unkind to make fun of those less fortunate than yourself? You'll be old one day, then you'll be hard put to find the humour in it.'

The two girls laughed helplessly, the tension in Sarah, anxious for the appearance of Giles, making the joke seem hilarious. The amusement made their laughter continue through their next dance and they giggled at every attempt their partners made to be amusing; the two young men left the floor thinking they were very smart and witty fellows. It was fortunate for their confidence that they didn't hear the girls' discussion later, with more imitations from Sarah.

Sarah became aware of a young man in the uniform of a soldier who watched Caroline constantly. She guessed he was trying to summon the courage to ask her to dance.

Caroline was as fair as Sarah was dark. She wore her hair in thick ringlets, a bunch at each side of her neck, and her face had been coloured with lip and cheek rouge. She was vainer than Sarah and spent most of her time examining her appearance in any available mirror.

The fact that they were friends was, on the surface, surprising. But each had something the other lacked. Sarah had a daring and light-hearted approach to life, and Caroline the elegance and social accomplishments Sarah failed to achieve. Each envied the skills of the other, but without malice.

Sarah admired Caroline's beauty and knew she would never have the determination to compete. Caroline loved her friend's audacious disregard for accepted behaviour and her sudden bursts of acrobatic ability, which shocked the rest of her serious family. Sarah's high spirits were irresistible.

Sarah glanced at the clock as they waited for the musicians to shuffle their music and recommence. She tried to sound casual as she said, 'No sign of your brother yet, Caroline?'

'Business has detained him again, I expect,' Caroline groaned. 'Since Papa died he has hardly been at home. I do think he could have made an effort for my birthday, though.'

'Perhaps he will arrive in time for supper.'

The music began again and the friends parted, taking a new partner each dance until supper was announced.

Caroline danced with the soldier, and spent a little while talking to him.

Sarah was not hungry. The dancing had made her warm and she longed for a walk outside in the garden to cool herself. If only it had been summer, they would have had the large windows open and would have been able to spill outside onto the terrace. Once autumn came they had to keep the windows closed in this part of London because of the foul smells that came on the heavy, foggy air from the river Thames, which, at times, was only yards from the gates.

She tried to remember how it had been at Houghton Hall in the summer when she had helped with the haymaking. There was no need to pretend hunger then. Oh, the smell of the fresh bread, the cheeses made in the dairy at the back of the house, the beer made in their own still room! Once, when she had escaped Edith and had helped the maids with the preparation of the small beer, the second brew from the tub, she had become intoxicated with just the smell of it. And Edith had complained of it on her clothes for days.

She wondered at her restlessness. She loved London and the shops and visiting friends like Caroline, so why was she dreaming of Houghton Hall? To take her mind off the waiting for Giles? When he did arrive it was likely he would give her no more than a polite greeting before bustling off to his study to attend to his work, or perhaps he would stay for a while out of politeness to his sister and dance with some of the eligible young ladies who simpered at him, showed their full-blown figures and made her feel and look like a ten-year-old boy. She pulled down the neck of her dress and tried to coax her small breasts to swell. They only sank even lower and her spirits sank with them. How could she hope to entice Giles to take her seriously as a contender for his heart?

Through the doorway she saw Charles and Jeremy, Caroline's younger brothers, enter, and guessed they would be looking for her. Caroline would have sent them to escort her in to supper. She slid further into the heavy curtains in which she had partly hidden herself. She was small, only four foot nine inches, and slim, so she easily hid in the crush of people heading for the generously spread tables, and managed to stand between the curtains and the windows where the air was cold and the darkness a welcome privacy for her thoughts.

Great-Aunt Milly was still sleeping. Even the removal of the shoulder on which she had been resting her head failed to rouse her. As the dancers slowly disappeared through the double doors leading to the supper room, Sarah saw her aunt clearly; the pouted mouth emitted a faint puff on each outward breath, disturbing a loose curl and sending it waving gaily.

Through a short passageway, guests bearing loaded plates returned to sit in groups at small tables and chairs, laughing and chattering as they ate. Servants in black uniforms and white, lace-trimmed aprons and caps ran between them, refilling glasses and offering fresh food. Sarah slid behind the heavy curtains and stared out at the row of carriages, waiting for sight or sound of Giles's arrival. After a while she went back into the room, just in time to see her aunt waking at last.

'Dear Great-Aunt Milly, will you come and eat? There will be little enough to choose if you don't come soon.'

'You waited for me?' The old lady beamed. 'Dear girl!' With her weight shared between a carved and silver-topped stick and her companion, the old lady heaved herself up and walked towards the double doors, nodding at acquaintances as she passed.

Tables were filled with dishes of every kind of meat available, and included venison, mutton and hare as well as duck, swan and displays of songbirds decorated with the beautiful feathers of the tiny offerings. As dishes were emptied, more food was brought, and gradually, as the diners moved in and out of the room, the tables were changed to offer fresh courses. The flower arrangements changed with them until the white cloths were almost hidden under bowls of dried, painted leaves and flower seed-heads, candles and bowls of fruit, interspersed with plates piled high with cakes, fondants and sweetmeats.

Jellies, syllabub and junkets filled the room with delicate colours and delicious smells, but still Sarah did not eat. She deposited her aunt among the rest of the elderly chaperones with a plate filled with her favourite food, then slipped once more behind the curtain.

She pressed her face to the glass to look and, trying to ignore the noise behind her, listened for the sound of Giles's carriage.

'Where is Miss Sarah?' a voice asked, and she sank deeper into the thick folds of the velvet drapes. She held her breath but the call was not repeated and she relaxed, incurious as to the speaker.

She felt the curtain move and a voice, so close to her ear it made her jump with shock, asked, 'Miss Sarah?'

A young man she did not know stood there smiling encouragingly, one gloved hand holding back the curtain.

'Miss Sarah, allow me to introduce myself.'

Sarah registered a tall, fair-haired young man with an alarming scar running down his left cheek. He saw her startled glance and, fingering it, said;

'I am Alfred Cummins, a friend of Giles. Perhaps you have heard Caroline talk of me?' He spoke slowly and carefully in a rather deep voice which Sarah found attractive.

'Miss Caroline has so many friends,' she replied noncommittally. She glanced to where Caroline now sat with the soldier.

'I am also well acquainted with your father, Sir Jason.'

Sarah frowned. If he knew both Giles and her father it was likely he was a friend through an interest in the gaming houses, where her father could frequently be found, and, most likely, one that was owned and run by Giles. She stared up at Alfred Cummins coldly.

'Will you eat supper with me?' he asked. 'Supposing you have not already eaten. A time to talk and we might find we have no end of people and interests in common.'

'If gaming is your interest, I doubt we would have much to discuss.'

She wished this young man would go away. When Giles arrived she wanted to be free. It would be an unbearable waste of a rare opportunity to talk with him to be sitting with this Alfred fellow. She turned away and stared at the window, her eyes gradually making out the line of carriages lit by the street lights and the glow from the porch lanterns.

In spite of her rudeness, Alfred Cummins continued to stand beside her, getting slight and often offensive responses to his questions and remarks. He bent low to make himself heard over the chatter of the guests, most of whom had abandoned eating and were talking loudly, each trying to make himself heard above the rest. The flower in his buttonhole hovered close to her face and she coughed. Alfred took the flower from his jacket and gave it to her.

'Take this,' he said in a whisper, close to her ear. 'A fragrant flower to keep the air around you as sweet as yourself.'

It was a small, white chrysanthemum, but the scent was not the rather harsh smell usually associated with that flower; it smelled rich and heady. She frowned. He had sprayed it with perfume, French perfume.

Alfred bowed even lower as she accepted the flower. She looked over his shoulder and, through the gap in the curtains, saw Giles entering the room beind them. At once, Sarah moved to greet him, almost knocking Alfred aside in her haste to avoid a misunderstanding.

Alfred, his flower and deep, attractive voice were forgotten as she paused for a moment to look at Giles. He was standing just inside the door, looking around him. Not for me, she thought with regret; he is here to see Caroline. He was tall and powerfully built, lacking the fashionable slimness to wear the tight trousers and fitted jackets of the younger men. He was wearing his City clothes, and Sarah thought him the most handsome in the room. Almost by telepathy his dark eyes found hers and, forgetting the importance of ladylike behaviour, she ran to him and greeted him with obvious pleasure.

'Giles!' She smiled. 'I was beginning to think you were not coming. Caroline would have been disappointed,' she added quickly, suddenly afraid of appearing too forward.

'Good evening, Sarah. I see you have met my friend Alfred?'

'Yes, he has been trying to persuade me to eat supper, but I thought I ought to wait for you to save you eating alone.' Again she was afraid of being too forward. Why did her tongue run away with her? 'I thought that – as Caroline will have crowds around her on this special evening – you might . . . ' she finished lamely.

'I am sorry! I cannot stay. I have come to see my sister and wish her a happy birthday as I have not yet seen her today, then I must return to my business.'

'Giles sleeps while the rest of us are awake and is at his most active while we sleep,' Alfred laughed. 'Did you ever hear of a more topsy-turvy existence? It's no wonder he is still unmarried. What woman would stand such a life?'

Sarah felt her heart increase its beat at the thought. She would gladly give up any daytime pleasures to share her life with Giles.

'Won't you wait and have just one dance with me, Giles?' she pleaded, pouting childishly, her small face looking half her true age.

To make Giles notice her and be aware of her adulthood, Sarah had chosen a midnight-blue taffeta gown. It was tight under the bosom and cut daringly decolleté in a vain attempt to persuade her tiny breasts to swell. The result was to make her appear even younger, 'like a silly girl dressing up in Mamma's clothes,' Caroline's brother Charles had disparagingly remarked. Now, facing Giles and seeing him with his usual serious expression, so tall and mature, Sarah felt that the spitefully meant words were painfully true.

To her momentary dismay, Giles laughed. 'Oh, Sarah! Stop pulling that face. I have enough difficulty believing you are already nineteen as it is, without you making yourself look no more than ten!'

Sarah pulled herself up to her full height but failed to reach his shoulder. Yet in her beautiful eyes there was something adult and, to Giles, very enticing.

'I am almost nineteen and a half,' she said firmly.

'All right.' Giles took her arm. 'If you are that old, I think I ought to spare you an hour while you are still able to dance!' With a nod of dismissal to Alfred, he led Sarah proudly into the supper room.

She ate ravenously, appetite suddenly rediscovered. A frown of disapproval from Great-Aunt Milly did nothing to slow her enthusiasm. She saw that Giles had intercepted the look and she shrugged indifference.

'Why pretend not to be hungry when you are? Why pretend not to enjoy this delicious food that the servants have spent hours preparing?'

Giles laughed again and shook his head. 'Why indeed? It's a pleasure to watch someone enjoying food so well. Here, have another of these.' He added a saffron cake to the one already half-eaten. Sarah nodded her thanks with a wicked grin in the direction of her aunt.

'What a pity we have to pretend,' she said when the cake was finished. I'm expected to pretend indifference to the man I love, she thought as she looked up at him. I'm expected to sit still and not show my joy when I'm so happy I want to run and skip. Standing beside Giles, with the prospect of dancing with him once the supper break was over, made her very happy and she bounced on her toes, looking up at him, her grey eyes shining, her small features lit with delight.

'One of the nicest things about you, Sarah, is that you *don't* pretend,' Giles said. 'When you're happy, you make the whole room glow, and I don't think I have ever seen you otherwise.'

He stayed for more than an hour, and, with the exception of one dance which his siser Caroline claimed, he danced every one with Sarah. Great-Aunt Milly's protests went unheeded as other young men were sent on their way. The old lady sighed and sought sympathy from her friends before settling once more to doze.

'Regretfully, I must go,' Giles said at last.

Sarah lowered her head, disappointment showing clearly. 'Must you?' she asked boldly. 'It seems you have only just arrived.'

'My father's business gives me little time to spare as yet, but once I have completed some plans I have, things will be different.'

Sarah looked up, her eyes anxious. What could that mean? Was there hope that he at last thought of her as an attractive woman and not as one of Caroline's young friends? Bold as she sometimes was, she dared not ask that.

'Perhaps one day you will show me the place where you spend so much of your time?'

Giles shook his head. 'My places are hardly suitable for

young ladies like you, Sarah.'

'I meant when they are closed, of course,' she added quickly. 'I have no wish to meet people who frequent such places.'

'Even though your father is one of them?'

'Knowing that doesn't alter my opinion. There's so much tragedy, it seems evil to spend so freely on gambling and . . . ' She quavered to a stop. How could she be so stupid? 'I'm sorry, Giles. I didn't mean to offend you, truly I didn't.'

'It was my father's business and his wish that I continued with it. I have four brothers and a sister to educate, and I am trained for nothing else.'

He escorted her back to her aunt and said good night. He did not suggest calling on her, and Sarah was angry with herself. Why can't I learn to hold my tongue? she groaned silently. A wonderful evening had been ruined for the sake of a few impertinent words. I waited so long for the chance to talk with him and spent precious moments criticising the way he lives, she berated herself.

She was still staring at the door through which he had disappeared when Alfred returned and requested a dance. Sarah shook her head.

'Thank you, but I have to go and find our coachman. Great-Aunt Milly says it's time we were leaving.'

Alfred looked at the row of snoring chaperones and nodded understandingly. 'Yes, I can see she is very insistent,' he teased, unoffended by the obvious lie. 'Would you like me to find your servant?'

'Thank you, but I know where he will be.'

She walked away from the noise of the music and the chattering and laughing dancers and stepped gratefully into the cool of the entrance hall. As she went down the stone stairs to the servants' quarters, she felt the chill from the cold rooms below her. It wasn't until she opened the door into the large kitchen that she eased the shawl from her shoulders as the warmth from the huge fire hit her.

The room was large with a flagstone floor and a long wooden table almost half its length. The table was full of the remnants of the supper dishes and on another table, near the sink, two grey-aproned maids were washing and drying piles of plates and glasses.

The cook, in her frilled cap and white apron, sat on an armchair near the still-bright fire and watched critically as the kitchen was gradually brought back to order. Opposite the cook sat a long, thin young man smoking a warden's clay pipe. He rocked in his chair gently as he listened to the tales Cook was telling him of the events of the day and the gossip she had gathered from visiting servants. Behind Renton was Caroline's maid, Lucy.

When they heard the door open and saw Sarah standing there, they both stood up and the young man stepped over to greet her.

'Miss Sarah. You're leaving so soon?'

'Yes, Renton.' Sarah glanced at the glass of porter and the plate of sandwiches placed near his chair. 'But when you have finished your supper.'

Renton thanked her and drained his glass. He went to the back door and said, 'I'll get the boy to bring the carriage round to the front at once, my lady.' He opened the door and stepped out, immediately closing it behind him against the cold wind. Sarah heard him whistle; then he re-entered.

'Have you enjoyed the party, Sarah?' he asked as he escorted her towards the door to the hall. He spoke less formally now they were away from the others.

'Ye-es,' she replied hesitantly. 'But now my interest in it has gone.'

Sarah and Renton had grown up together, only hours separating their births. Renton's mother was the cook in Sarah's home and, in spite of her father's disapproval, they had remained friends, ignoring whenever possible the difference in their position.

'Didn't Giles come?' he asked quietly.

'He came, but only for a little while. He has gone back to his work so I thought I might as well go home.' She turned back to the servants. 'Thank you, Mrs Barnes.' She beamed at the cook. 'The food was excellent. You are a marvel! Good night, Mrs Barnes, and good night Lucy.' She nodded towards the others working near the sink and they curtsied politely. Sarah noticed a glance between Renton and Lucy as he said good night, and she smiled to herself.

Renton followed Sarah up the chilly stairs to the ground floor and sent a girl to fetch Sarah's and Great-Aunt Milly's wraps while Sarah went to wake her aunt. That good lady was already awake and in a terrible state. Unable to find her charge, she was convinced Sarah had come to some fearful harm, and her thankfulness at seeing her safe caused her to resort to anger.

'Really, Sarah! You have no concern for a poor body. I've been searching frantically, wondering where you were.'

'I went to tell Renton we are ready to leave, that's all, dear aunt.'

'How many times have I told you to send for him and not go wandering around in the servants' quarters where you've no right to be?'

'Just think of all the gossip we'd miss if I obeyed you,' Sarah whispered teasingly. She knew how much the old lady enjoyed the tidbits of information passed on by the servants. 'Servants know more of what goes on than your sleepy friends.'

Great-Aunt Milly tried to snort with disapproval but the chuckle of amusement was the stronger.

Sarah found Caroline to thank her and wish her good night and was introduced shyly to Bertram the soldier friend of one of Caroline's brothers.

There was no opportunity to talk to Renton on the way home, but on their arrival, Great-Aunt Milly was once again snoring softly, and Sarah called to him.

'So that was why you wanted to wait at Miss Caroline's house,' she teased. 'No wonder you encourage me to visit her so often!'

'I don't know what you mean,' he said, putting the steps down for her to alight.

'Lucy, Caroline's new maid, that's what I mean. How long have you known her?'

'Mmm, a week or two. I'm taking her to the music hall on Saturday.'

'Lucky you! I wish I could go, but Father won't allow it.' She sighed. 'Poor Father. He loved my mother so much, but never stopped being ashamed of her unusual beginnings.'

Sarah's maid came to the door, having heard the carriage, and she helped Renton carefully ease Great-Aunt Milly from her seat and up to her room, while Sarah followed.

'Stay and help her, will you, Edith?' Sarah asked, knowing Great-Aunt Milly's own maid was a little sharp and impatient. She kissed her aunt's puffy, soft cheek and went to her own room.

A fire still glowed in the grate and she sat for a while beside its comforting warmth and remembered the most enjoyable parts of the evening. Giles had been very nice to her before their stupid argument. Could it be a sign that he cared for her a little?

When she was warmed and finished with her daydreaming, she slipped into the next room, where her sister Margaret lay sleeping. Margaret was two years younger than Sarah and already betrothed. She lay with an arm outstretched to where her recently discarded embroidery was folded. Sarah guessed she had been sewing in the light of the candle that stood near it, hoping to stay awake and hear all about the party.

Her dark hair lay like a shining fan across the pillow. She's so beautiful, Sarah thought with wonder, unable to see the same beauty in herself. Both girls were dainty and had grey eyes surrounded by thick, brown lashes. Their features were neat and perfect and the only real difference was in their height.

Both girls were lively and glowed with vitality and the joy of life, and they were the best of friends. Sarah, however, had always been the wilder of the two. She bent to kiss Margaret's forehead and dreaded the day when marriage would separate them.

The next bedroom belonged to the two boys, Albert and Maxwell, aged ten and twelve. They were away at school. Sarah paused at the door of the empty room and smiled, thinking of how soon they would be home, filling the house with their noisy fun. At the last door on her corridor she tapped lightly and went in.

This was the nursery, where she had spent the first months of her life. Now it was the domain of Isobelle, her baby sister. When Isobelle was born, large and strong and lustily crying for food, her mother had died, her small frame unable to cope with the string of pregnancies. Two had produced stillborn babies and two boys had died when fever struck the family.

Edith's sister Hannah had been engaged as a wet-nurse for Isobelle and had stayed to care for her. Hannah was sleeping in a bed not far from the child, and roused and whispered good night as Sarah left the room. Isobelle would be four years old on the following Saturday and there would be another party, different from the one Sarah had just attended. She thought in vain for an excuse to invite Giles, and smiled at her own foolishness.

Edith was waiting for Sarah back in her room and began preparing her mistress for bed. Clothes were carefully removed and hung away, and water brought for washing. Sarah's long hair was painfully combed and plaited. It was a regular occurrence for Sarah to swear to cut if all off, and Edith did not even answer her groans and threats.

They talked in whispers about the party. As she told Edith about Giles's late arrival, Sarah lived again the moments when she had been held in his arms. Edith finally wished her 'God bless and good night' and Sarah was alone with her dreams of a future with Giles.

The room was warm, the fire made moving patterns on the flowered wallpaper and, although she was tired, sleep evaded her. The night was not silent. As well as the occasional noises from the fire as coals dropped and crackled, from outside came the sound of carts creaking past as sellers made their way to the markets far to the east of her. The clopping of a slow, reluctant reveller to his home seemed inexorably sad and she wondered what his life was like if he could not face returning home until the lonely night was almost gone. Disjointed bursts of song floated up from the man and Sarah recognised a song popular in the music halls, taught her by Renton.

There was faint music in the house as well. From far above her came an accompaniment to her strangely sad mood, and she recognised the strains of a love song. In his room under the roof Renton was also unable to sleep. Softly he played on a reed pipe. With a sigh, Sarah turned onto her side and tried again to sleep.

Much later still she heard her father return. Since his wife had died, Sir Jason was rarely home before dawn. He spent his nights at the gaming house that had once belonged to Giles's father and was now managed by Giles. Sarah knew of more than one family who had lost all they owned at the gaming tables and night houses.

She considered the thought that if Giles did fall in love with her and propose, she would have to learn to accept the life he led. She closed her eyes tightly, her mind refusing to dampen the excitement of her love. He was so handsome! She wondered if her lack of height would discourage him from considering her as a wife.

Caroline had told her he had never seriously courted a lady, and the thought pleased her. She would have been jealous even of someone who had once been a part of his life and was now gone. But perhaps he had no intention of marrying. Melancholy returned and her love of him was sad and doomed to be unrequited.

Sarah drifted into a daydream of dancing with Giles. His arms holding her gently but firmly so that she felt a part of him, they glided through an open window onto a terrace that was warmed by the sun. Down they drifted, through sweet-scented meadows, to the banks of a shining, softly rippling stream. She felt again his strong hands touching her spine, smelled his special manliness and imagined the touch of his face against her head as he bent down and enfolded her close to his beating heart.

Alone and with only the sound of the wistful music to be heard, she felt his lips on hers and smiled as she finally slept.

Her father was already seated when Sarah went in to breakfast a few hours later. She ran to hug him and wish him a good morning.

'Good morning to you, my dear child,' he said, extricating himself from her tight embrace. 'I didn't expect you to be abroad so early after a party. Did you enjoy yourself?'

'Yes, Father, it was great fun. Such a crowd of people! Giles was there for a part of the evening and I danced with him for an hour. Do you think we looked foolish, me being so small?'

'Of course not. It flatters a man to have someone towards whom he can feel protective.' A memory stabbed his heart. 'Your dear mother was no taller than you and I loved to dance with her. She was so light on her feet and always so happy and full of merriment.' He paused and Sarah held her breath, hoping he would continue. She loved hearing about her mother.

'You know, of course, that when I announced my engagement to your mother, my family were angry? It was weeks before they would come and meet her, yet even they, so determined not to accept her, were won over by her. I was not the only one to cry like a baby when she died. Loving someone blinds you to the doubts and enhances the joys. I never regretted for a moment defying my friends and family to marry her.'

He shook off the momentary display of his loneliness and grief, still fresh after four years, and smiled at his daughter, bringing out a reflecting smile on her face, so similar to the one he had lost. 'Tell me, who else was there last evening? Did Great-Aunt Milly sleep through it all as usual?'

'No, she did not sleep through it *all* – she woke in time for supper!' Sarah was pleased to see laughter lighten the look in his deep-set eyes. 'Giles is a splendid dancer, Father,' she said, unable to keep her mind from the hour she had spent with him.

'So he should be, with all that has been spent on his education.'

'There was a man there called Alfred. Alfred Cummins. He was rather bold and came unannounced and introduced himself as a friend of Giles. He said he knows you too.'

'Yes, I know him.' Her father frowned. 'I wouldn't like you to foster a friendship there, my dear. There's a bit of a mystery about that young man. He hints that he is an ex-army man, but he changes the subject very suspiciously when someone attempts to discuss the troubles in Portugal, or even the possibilities offered to a young man who wished to make the army his career.'

'If Alfred Cummins calls I will be out, Father.' Sarah

bowed her dark head.

'That would be best, Sarah, my dear.'

Sarah stifled a smile. Obedience, when it was over something of no importance, gave a favourable impression.

'That scar on his face looks suspiciously like a duelling injury,' she said, finishing her dish of fruit.

'Oh, Sarah! Duelling, indeed!'

'Do you think he would be brave enough for such a thing? His hands are very smooth and he seems to have a fondness for perfume.'

'Eat your breakfast, young lady.' He failed to hide a smile.

'The fruit will suffice for the moment, Father. I think I'll wait for Margaret. She will want to know all about Caroline's party. Such a pity she couldn't come.'

'Margaret has done with flirting now that she is betrothed, and I suspect that was how you spent your evening.'

'Father!' She hid her face in mock embarrassment. 'As if I would!'

Sir Jason stood up and prepared to leave. He kissed his daughter. 'Here,' he said, taking out his wallet. 'Take yourself shopping. Buy yourself something pretty.'

'Thank you, Father! You are the kindest of men!' Sarah jumped up and kissed him.

When he had gone to where Renton was waiting with the carriage, Sarah ran into the large drawing room which overlooked the street. She sat on the window seat to watch as he left for the City office where he spent most of his days. She waved him off and watched as the carriage disappeared into the gloom of the autumn morning.

She stayed for a while in the large, elegant room where the family did most of their entertaining. It was decorated in gold and a rich blue. The walls were covered with silk and cotton, chosen to match the gold in the carpet. The blue in the Aubusson carpet had been carefully matched in the covers of the gilt-framed chairs. A piano stood near one of the three windows, a small table close to the sofa. Festooned curtains were identical in shade to the walls and to the background of the raised pattern of the cornice. In the centre of the ceiling a glass chandelier hung, glistening with a thousand facets. Fresh candles had already replaced those used on the previous evening both in the great chandelier and on the wall sconces.

Sarah studied the room with a deep interest although every item was well known to her. She imagined what it would be like to furnish a home of her own. Most of the contents of the room she would value and love to use in that imaginary house of the future, but some things she would change. Lighter, flowery prints and fabrics, she decided, thinking of the newer decoration in Caroline and Giles's home, where the work was more fashionable. Forgetting ideas for furnishings, she allowed her thoughts to drift back to the previous evening, or the only part of it worth remembering.

Renton returned from taking her father to work and she went back to the dining room to wait for her sisters and the excuse to talk about it all over again. Margaret walked in with a calm grace, leading Isobelle by the hand.

The four-year-old still had the features of a baby, full cheeks, soft full mouth and large eyes but already the similarity to her father was beginning to show. She sat eating enthusiastically, listening to the chatter about the previous evening, how many engagement presents Margaret had received and how her future mother-in-law would be taking her house-hunting as soon as Christmas was past.

'Please can I say something now?' the little girl said at last.

Her sisters turned to her.

'Please can I go shopping with you this morning?'

'How do you know I'm going shopping?' Sarah asked.

Isobelle pointed to the small, partly concealed door in the corner which the servants used to tend fires and candles.

'You mean you've been listening at doors and using the servants' stairs again?' Margaret accused.

'So did we not so long ago!' Sarah laughed. 'But no, you cannot come shopping, you have your lessons.'

'We'll take you on Saturday and you can choose something for your birthday,' Margaret promised.

'How many days till Saturday?' Isobelle wanted to know, putting up her plump fingers to be shown. Holding out three fingers to be able to tell Nanny, she went happily off to the schoolroom.

Sarah wondered how Isobelle could accept the imprisonment of the schoolroom so willingly. Sarah as a child had protested loud and long at the waste of time. She had always hated every moment spent indoors at her books, especially during the summer months.

Renton drove the carriage, which had returned from taking Sir Jason to his office. At the sisters' request, he headed for the shops in Jermyn Street. Before they reached their destination, Sarah asked him to stop beside a shabbily dressed flower-seller on a corner, next to a woman selling hot chestnuts.

Renton helped her down onto the mud-splattered pavement and she walked to the flower-seller. The girl, who was younger than Sarah and blue with the cold, smiled hopefully as she saw Sarah approaching, and offered her large basket for her to choose the flowers she required.

When Sarah returned to the carriage with the bunches, she saw Renton wave at the flower girl. As he helped her to her seat, Sarah grinned at him and said, 'So Lucy isn't the only girl who takes your fancy?'

'That's Emily Tilt, Miss Sarah,' he explained. 'She's my cousin. You must remember her?'

Sarah thought back to the ragged child who had sometimes visited Renton and his mother when they were children. Then, ignoring a disapproving frown from Margaret, she waved at Emily, determining to buy from her whenever possible.

The sisters shopped first for material, planning to have dresses made for the winter season of parties, and for Christmas a day dress that needed to be warm and full as the holiday would be spent at their country home. Sarah used the money her father had given her on perfume and they spent a long time choosing in the House of Floris. It was late afternoon before they had completed their shopping, exhausted and happy.

Leaving Renton and a houseboy to carry in their purchases, they ran up the steps of their home to be met by

Edith.

'You have a visitor, Miss Sarah.'

At once Sarah's tiredness left her. Her first thought was that it might be Giles, but in that she was disappointed, although disappointment eased when she saw Caroline.

'Caroline! I hope you haven't waited long. I'm so sorry we weren't at home.'

'Ten minutes only, I swear. And the fault is mine. I should have sent a note, but I was passing your door so decided to call.' She smiled and added, 'I believe you've been shopping. I hope you have some interesting things to show me?'

Caroline's maid was sitting patiently on a chair. Remembering Renton's interest, Sarah suggested she went to the kitchen and took refreshment. When Renton appeared with the packages, she asked him to escort Lucy, and looked at him with a raised eyebrow. After requesting that tea be sent in, she returned to her guest.

For a while the three girls discussed the clothes they would have made, and the material that was on its way to their dressmaker. Then Caroline came to the purpose of her call.

'We are all going to the country for a long weekend,' she explained. 'Giles has some business acquaintances to entertain and, as there is some work that has to be arranged on the outbuildings of Weatherby, we have suddenly decided to make it into a weekend party.' She looked pleased at the prospect. 'We all hope *you* can come, and that your fiancé can join us too,' she added to Margaret, 'if he can get leave.'

'We'd love to, if Father has no objection – ' Margaret began.

Sarah's reaction was less formal. She quickly glanced around to make sure they were alone, then, with a shriek of delight, did a cartwheel across the room, ending up in a heap of petticoats against the far wall.

'Stupid clothes!' she grumbled as she untangled herself.

'Sarah!' Her sister laughed, covering her mouth with her hands. 'If Father saw you – '

'But he didn't, did he? And I'm so happy, it's the only way I can show it. Oh, Caroline, thank you! It will be fun. Father won't have any reason to forbid it, will he?' she asked anxiously.

Margaret shook her dark head. 'Of course not. There's nothing to prevent us from having a lovely country holiday. Except,' she added thoughtfully, 'for Isobelle's birthday.'

'Oh, but she won't mind if we postpone her party, will she? There's plenty of time.'

Sir Jason agreed. Isobelle was promised two parties – one on her birthday and a second, larger one during the following week – and was perfectly content for them to go.

Chapter Three

The morning they were to leave for the weekend in Weatherby, Sarah dressed with impatient speed and ran to her sister's room.

'Margaret, aren't you ready?' She was surprised to find her sister still in bed. 'Have you forgotten that today we are off to the country?'

'I'm afraid you'll have to go without me,' Margaret whispered painfully. 'I have a fever and a sore throat.'

'Then I won't go. I'll stay and keep you company.'

'Of course you must go. It wouldn't be fair to disappoint Caroline. You go, and have a lovely time! I'll look forward to hearing all about it when you get back. You always make things more fun in the telling.' Margaret insisted, and Sarah reluctantly agreed.

'But it won't be as much fun without you,' she said sadly.

'Not even with the handsome Giles there?' Margaret teased.

'Not even then!'

As Margaret was not going, the two friends were travelling together. Renton drove the large two-horse carriage to Caroline's house soon after breakfast and, while he helped Edith and Lucy arrange wicker baskets and boxes of luggage, Sarah and Caroline drank chocolate. Giles was there and Sarah, for once vain about her appearance, was glad she had worn her new saffron-yellow blouse and the dark-green skirt with the matching cloak.

If only she were allowed to travel with Giles instead of Great-Aunt Milly, Caroline and Edith! Why was everything pleasant and natural forbidden? But there was some pleasure in being helped into the warm coach by him and having a blanket tucked around her knees by Edith, with a hot-water bottle placed at her feet and foot and hand muffs to make sure they were comfortable.

The seats were not covered in cold leather, but in soft, deeply quilted material, warm to the touch, and in a shade of blue much liked by Sir Jason. The edges of the seats were decorated with fringes of the same colour, as were the windows. A mirror above their heads and an oil lamp, should their journey be prolonged into the dark hours, added to the sensation of comfort and Sarah felt the surge of excitement always present when she began a journey. At least she knew Giles would not be long after them.

The day was misty and, as the journey progressed, the mist increased until they were hardly able to see the hedges that bordered the road. Caroline became anxious.

'These roads out of London are notoriously dangerous, even in the clearest weather. How much worse they must be when highwaymen and thieves can hide so easily and pounce on the unwary traveller!'

'Renton is with us, so don't think of such things.' Sarah frowned and glanced at the old lady sitting opposite them with Edith. Caroline realised that Sarah did not want Great-Aunt Milly frightened and quickly changed the conversation to lighter things. But she continued to stare out into the now swirling fog.

Several times the carriage had to stop to allow a farm cart to pass, and once they had to back in through the gate of a field to enable a wagonload of root crops to pass, when it was obvious that the young boy in charge of the wagon was unable to move from their path without losing his precarious load and blocking the road completely. Each time, Sarah and Caroline watched through the window, afraid it was a trap to be sprung by highwaymen who would rob them of all they possessed, perhaps even their lives.

It was much later than they had planned when they finally alighted at the porched entrance to Giles's family's country home. They stretched stiffly after the long and tiring journey and went into the drawing room, where a huge fire blazed cheerfully and refreshments were quickly offered.

'I hope Giles and the others will arrive soon,' Sarah said anxiously, when she and Caroline were momentarily alone. 'The fog is getting worse by the minute.'

As she spoke they heard the sound of a carriage coming up the gravel driveway and they went quickly to the window and peered out into the night. Lamps, made hazy by the fog, showed ghostly figures stepping down from the vehicle and hurrying towards the porch, while servants bustled around them, gathering the piles of luggage from the back and top of the carriage. Although the light was poor, Sarah knew none of the new arrivals was Giles.

Carriages began to arrive frequently. For a while the girls stayed in the drawing room and were introduced to the guests when they came in and received refreshments, but as each coach unloaded its occupants and Giles was not among them, Sarah and Caroline became worried.

'Come, Sarah,' Caroline said firmly. 'We will go up to our rooms and change for dinner. It will take our minds off worrying, and when we come down, my brother is sure to be here.'

Regretfully they left the fire-warmed room and hurried up the long, cold staircase to their bedrooms. The house was full of activity now most of the guests had arrived, and the staircase bustled with chattering ladies and busy servants.

Their clothes and toilet necessities were set out for them and, in a short time, Sarah was ready and waiting impatiently for Caroline to call her to go down to dinner. She was shivering in her new satin dress with the pelerine, around which she had draped a shawl to warm her while she waited. It had a full skirt and sleeves that were full from the elbow down, and the colour was apricot. She wished it was wool and had its own coat, and that she could wear high boots with it instead of the white buckram slippers.

The fire in her room was reluctant to burn and there was more smoke issuing from it than either flame or warmth. She began jumping up and down, doing some of the exercises her mother had taught her for warming up before a performance. Then Edith had to reset her hair.

Dinner was set out on a long table in the panelled dining

room. The table was highly polished and Sarah saw that it was in fact four separate tables. Two were square and the two at the ends were D-shaped so that accommodation could be arranged for a variety of numbers of diners. On this evening there were places for twenty, and most had already found their seats when the girls made their entrance. A footman in green and red livery escorted them to their seats. Red-faced table maids were poised ready to begin serving at his command.

Sarah saw that the seat at the top of the table was empty. Giles had still not arrived. The seat beside her was also unclaimed and, not having a neighbour to talk to, she sat admiring the beautiful room. A chandelier as large although perhaps not as fine as the one in her drawing room at home sparkled above and at least two dozen candles added light from around the room. The sideboard was full to overflowing with dishes waiting to be served and she noted with amusement how anxious the servants were with their constant glances from the door and back to the stern face of the footman.

The chatter was so loud it was no longer possible to hear a carriage arrive, but each time the front door opened and closed, the candles guttered in the draught and ladies pulled their stoles from the backs of chairs and replaced them on their shoulders. She guessed that the servants had not been sent early enough to get the house really warmed. Tomorrow it would be better. She hoped her bed was not damp.

Giles came in, still in his travelling cloak and carrying his hat. A walking stick in his hand and a glow to his cheeks made him seem perfectly attired for the role of country gentleman.

'My apologies, ladies and gentlemen. I am sorry for my delay. We had a bit of trouble on the road, I am afraid. The only carriage available in my own stables was a barouche and hardly suitable for a cold winter's night, so I hired one instead. Not a wise choice!' He said this in such a way as to cause laughter to begin to ripple. He walked around the table taking the hand of each guest to shake or to kiss, according to sex. As he moved, he continued his tale of how the coach had lost a wheel it becoming caught in a deep, mud-filled rut.

'We were instructed that unless we preferred to spend the night where we had stopped, we were all to climb out and assist with temporary repairs. This we did, each unwilling but, there being no alternative, with reasonable good grace. That is, apart from one young man, who could not face the destruction of his new boots. In spite of our entreaties, he remained in his seat, being rocked about by the rest of us trying to fix the wheel.

'The coach tipped and tilted and his hat fell through the doorway and was trodden on. He himself was thrown from his seat into the straw, and when he finally had to face the prospect of walking the last five miles, he attacked the guard! He felt more than a little foolish, knowing that he would have fared better if he had helped us from the first.'

Most of those present had suffered similar experiences and felt a sympathy for both the young man and his new boots and for the rest of the passengers who had the right to expect his willing assistance. By the time he reached Sarah, the guests were laughing and wiping tears from their eyes.

He placed a hand on Sarah's shoulder and said, 'Now, please excuse me for a few more minutes while I relieve myself of these filthy travel clothes, and I'll rejoin you.'

Conversation and laughter broke out anew and seemed to set the mood for the evening.

During the meal, the talk was mostly about the difficulties of travelling in autumn and winter when the ground was often thick mud and a passenger had to be prepared for long delays and might even, as had happened to Giles, have to walk. The new macadam surfaces were talked of with enthusiasm and the gentlemen wondered if these would ever be widespread enough to ease the problems of mud and the large number of holes that frequently discommoded an unwary driver and his passengers.

Sarah sat quietly, allowing the buzz of a dozen conversations to flow around her, adding a word at times to Caroline's comments and helping Great-Aunt Milly to more food. Giles sat at the head of the table and seemed able to command the attention of anyone he wished to address. Silent in the noisy gathering, Sarah wished, not for the first time, that she were a man. Life would surely be far simpler.

'It's so unfair!' she whispered across the table to Caroline. 'We aren't expected to add anything to the discussion, although we have plenty to say; we have to just sit and look charming.'

'Thank goodness for that,' Caroline replied. 'I have a fear of saying something stupid. Besides, I'd rather be free to concentrate on eating. I swear Giles hasn't managed more than a mouthful of this delicious goose, he's so keen to repeat his story.'

When the long meal was over, Sarah and Caroline followed the other ladies into the drawing room to take coffee and leave the men to their port. They sat demurely listening to yet more conversation, this time on ladylike subjects like sewing, dancing and the latest fashions, which Sarah found even more tedious than the state of the roads. She wondered what the men were talking about in the room across the corridor.

A loud knock at the door surprised them. They stopped their chatter to listen and discover who the late caller could be. Sarah could not sit and wait to be told. She slipped from the room and looked into the wide, mosaic-floored hall, shivering in the cold draught. To her surprise, Alfred Cummins stood there, looking dishevelled and exhausted.

'Alfred?' Puzzlement was in Giles's exclamation. 'I thought you had refused my invitation? Come, my good fellow, warm yourself while the servants make up a bed and find you some food. Which will be first, a wash or food? Please do as you wish. We have no desire to see you clean but unconscious with hunger!'

'Thank you, Giles. I'll survive a little longer without food if I may strip off my wet clothes. But I will have to borrow some. I'm afraid my luggage has been lost.'

Giles brushed aside the questions about what had happened to cause the man to arrive in such a distressed condition.

'Later he can tell us his adventures. First we must make him comfortable.'

Caroline gave up her room to the late arrival and moved her things in to share with Sarah. In all the rearranging and excitement, the story Cummins eventually told was not heard by the girls until the following morning at breakfast.

Alfred sat in a dressing gown far too large for his tall, slim figure and explained that the coach in which he was travelling had been attacked and that he had had to run for his life across fields and through hedges. It was a tale well told, but without the humour of Giles's story of the evening before. Sarah did not believe a word of it.

He answered all the questions ably enough but there was something about the words that gave Sarah the impression that he had invented it all. She thought of the children's story that had been one of her favourites, 'Puss in Boots', in which a man who was not a gentleman was able to convince people he was a nobleman, after pretending to have had his fine clothes stolen while taking a bathe. His own shabby garments had been hidden. Perhaps it was something similar with Alfred Cummins? Perhaps he had no other fine clothes and only pretended to have lost them to convince Giles he was something he was not?

But why? What had really happened? His green eyes were glittering and he was obviously enjoying being the point of interest during the meal. Unaccountably she shivered. What was he running from that had forced him to arrive unannounced at Giles's door? The law?

The fog had cleared by the middle of the morning and the day was mild and sunny.

'Let's take out a picnic lunch,' Sarah suggested.

'At this time of year?' Caroline laughed. 'Really, Sarah, what an unpleasant idea!'

'But think, it might be our last fine day before winter closes in completely.'

'Very well, I'll ask. But don't expect Mother to agree. She so fears the damp air these days.'

Sarah remembered that Caroline's father had died of a fever, brought on, so the doctors thought, by damp, foul-smelling air. 'Then please don't ask her. I'm sorry, I had forgotten how sad she must be. I mustn't distress her by making her worry for us.'

'Don't ask her what?' a voice demanded. Sarah turned

and saw Giles, dressed in thick woollen trousers and jacket, his hair combed forward and allowed to curl on his forehead. His dark skin seemed to emphasise his clear eyes, dark brown with whites that seemed lit from within. He looked pleased with himself and Sarah was suddenly unable to speak. He was so handsome. What a fool she was to even imagine him loving her when he could choose from the many available women he must meet.

'What were you two discussing when I came in?' he asked with a smile.

Caroline told him of Sarah's suggestion of a picnic lunch.

'But that sounds an excellent idea! I'll ask the others.'

Sarah's eyes sparkled, the momentary shyness forgotten. She loved anything that broke the monotony of repetitious days that contained so many hours of boredom. This late autumn picnic with Giles would be something to remember and to tell Margaret about when she got home.

'Thank you, Giles! If only Margaret were here, everything would be perfect.'

'Don't thank me yet,' Giles said. 'I have only agreed to discuss it with the rest.' His gaze lingered a moment on the happy, laughing face looking up into his.

'But I know you will persuade them.'

He smiled and shook his head. 'You, Sarah, are a very determined young lady!'

'Thank you again, Giles,' she replied with a slight curtsy, taking the half-concealed criticism as a compliment.

The picnic was a success in spite of complaints from the older members of the party. Unable to sit on the grass, which was wet and muddy, they all ate at tables set in and around the summerhouse, facing the lake and half sheltered by trees. Afterwards, Giles suggested a walk to warm themselves and the party separated into small groups, varying the chosen walks to suit their ages and inclinations.

'Will you walk with me, Miss Sarah?' Alfred asked. In a panic, Sarah looked around for Giles.

'Just a little stroll around the shore of the lake?' Alfred pleaded.

'No, I . . . er . . . ' Thankfully, Sarah saw Giles nearby and waved at him. 'Giles! Didn't we plan to walk to the top of

Hare's Hill?'

'Of course.' Giles offered his arm and, with a sigh of relief, Sarah nodded at Alfred and turned towards the steep slope at the end of the lake.

'You don't like my friend Alfred?'

'I would prefer to walk with you. He suggested a little stroll around the shores of the lake. I feel the need to stretch myself after the cramp of living in town all these weeks.'

'You really want to climb Hare's Hill?' There was amusement in his eyes as he gestured towards the hill to the east of the house.

'Yes, and I will reach the top before you!'

Great-Aunt Milly was appeased by the reassurance that they would be in her sight the whole time, and she sat contentedly in the summerhouse, well wrapped in blankets and rugs, prepared to watch them climb the grassy hill on which sheep grazed. She was asleep before they had skirted the lake.

Sarah was filled with excitement as she walked up the slope beside Giles. It showed in her eyes and in the lightness of her step. Although she was not interested in Alfred, he was rather handsome and it would surely do no harm for another eligible bachelor to show an interest?

The view from the top was over miles of farmland. Weatherby House and the lake looked lost in the wide expanse of small fields. From little houses smoke rose gently in the still air.

'This is wonderful!' Sarah breathed, looking to the horizon where the mist was already threatening to enclose them again. She looked down on the mere dots that were people standing around the summerhouse and waved, hoping that some of them were looking, although she doubted her moving arm could be seen.

'You say it's wonderful,' Giles said thoughtfully, 'but what about living in the country all the time? Would you still think it wonderful through the dark winter, when there's snow and ice and when rain beats down day after day so you cannot leave the house? I can't imagine you accepting such confinement. Town is manageable in extremes of weather; out here, it would not be easy.'

'Why do you ask?'

'It seems that everyone who spends a pleasant few days here in Weatherby says it's heavenly. But they are only too thankful to leave once the holiday is over. Most cannot bear being away from the shops and theatres, the visiting and the gossip that town offers.'

'I like shopping,' Sarah admitted. 'To come home and unwrap my purchases and rediscover the pleasure of new clothes and small treats is something I would hate to lose. But as for the rest, no, I would not be broken-hearted to leave it. We spend Christmas in the country at Houghton Hall and I am always the most reluctant to go back to London.'

Giles turned to face her, his dark eyes close to hers as he stood on lower ground. 'Could you really leave London and the comforts of town for a place like this?'

Sarah's heart began to race, the nearness of him throwing her mind into a heady turmoil. 'Without a moment's regret.'

He moved away from her and they walked back down the grassy slope. Giles's hand was held out for her to take when the ground was slippery or steep. She had no need of it but took it happily. She was giddy with excitement. The need to run began to make the sedate walk impossible and when they reached the stream which fed the lake, she suddenly leapt over it. She pulled a face when she saw her tiny shoes were covered with mud.

'Sarah!' His mouth tightened a little in disapproval but his eyes showed a suspicion of laughter.

Was his question about her living there what it sounded? Was he really considering her as his wife, with Weatherby as their home? She had been honest about leaving London. The only doubt was not seeing Margaret. Could she move away from her and accept seeing her only on rare visits? Yes. Margaret herself was likely to move away once her future husband had decided where they would live. But it was hard to imagine life without her dear sister to share every thought and idea with. She looked up at Giles again. Better be separated a little from Margaret than from Giles, if there were ever to be a choice.

She looked at Weatherby with greater interest as they

approached the remainder of the luncheon party. It was larger than Houghton Hall and newer, but the grounds were smaller. The garden was still in a state of development and there were few trees higher than ten feet tall. To Sarah, it lacked the ageless beauty of Houghton Hall, but living here with Giles would be perfect. She even began imagining flowerbeds cut out towards the lake, which would be seen as they walked out on summer evenings. And dogs. She would be able to have a couple of spaniels and exercise them on Hare's Hill.

That evening after dinner, several of the guests sang or played an instrument. Alfred surprised them all by singing a sweet love song and, to Sarah's embarrassment, he seemed to be looking more at her as he sang it than at anyone else. Then Giles sang, his voice not so deep as Alfred's, and he too chose a love song. He only glanced at her, but she was certain he meant it only for her. The words spoke of a man afraid to declare his love for the beauty who had stolen his heart.

For her part in the evening's entertainment she recited, never having succeeded in mastering the piano. With the excitement engendered by Giles's presence, she performed well. Giles applauded long after the rest and Caroline looked from one to the other, seeing the gleam of admiration in her brother's eyes.

'What were you and Giles talking about on Hare's Hill?' she demanded of Sarah when it was time to retire.

'Giles talked about his love for this place,' Sarah answered evasively. 'That was all.'

'Was it?' Caroline tilted her head as she stared at Sarah in disbelief, smiling to coax further comment.

'Oh, how infuriating it is to be sent to bed while the men return to their discussions!' Sarah hastily changed the subject. She wanted her memories of the brief conversation on Hare's Hill for herself alone. Only to Margaret would she disclose her hopes of winning Giles's love. 'They are probably discussing those awful gaming houses.'

'Awful they may be,' Caroline rebuked, 'but they have given me a good and happy life. My grandfather was a moneylender and by sheer determination bought land in

London for his son to inherit. My father spent all his life improving our situation. I'm rather glad he did.'

Sarah immediately regretted the comment. It had nothing to do with Caroline how her family became rich. But she did wish Giles had inherited a more wholesome way to earn his wealth. And that has nothing to do with me either, she thought sadly. If I marry him I will have to accept all of him and that includes the unsavoury night-life businesses.

She hugged her friend. 'I'm sorry, Caroline. I'm being thoughtless and extremely rude to you, my dear friend. Tell me about Bertram. You seem to have a great liking for him.'

The brief disagreement forgotten, they went upstairs to their room.

The room was bitterly cold, the fire still refusing to draw. Sarah thought again that the servants had been negligent or had not been given sufficient time in advance of their arrival to make sure everything was prepared for them. They were unable to sleep until they agreed to share a bed to warm themselves under the double share of blankets.

'I'll ask Giles to get the chimney cleared tomorrow,' Caroline promised. 'It's probably blocked with a bird's nest. The fire won't have been lit since last winter.'

'Our servants at Houghton Hall are instructed to light fires at least one a week.'

'My mother takes little interest in Weatherby. She is only happy in the town,' Caroline explained. 'And Giles has so many calls on his time.'

'Will there be a man and a boy to clean it?'

'The servants do it usually, with a few boughs of holly.'

'I will enjoy watching that,' Sarah said slowly as sleep claimed her.

Several of the house party gathered outside the following morning to watch the chimney being swept. Others, like Great-Aunt Milly, stayed in their beds and complained in whispers about the carelessness and mismanagement of having such a thing dealt with while guests were present.

Those servants who were not involved with either cleaning the rooms or clearing up from breakfast stood at the corner of the buildings and watched with quiet amusement the peculiar London people following the quite ordinary happening with such fascination.

Sarah noted how easy it was to see which of the servants came from London and which were hired locally; the local girls had a high colour, the city inhabitants were pale and, for the most part, thinner.

A young boy climbed out onto the roof from a high window, carrying a long rope to which a stone was tied. This was lowered down the chimney and the boy shouted instructions to an unseen assistant in the room below. Giles came and stood beside Sarah and Caroline and explained what was happening, although little was necessary as the boys dealing with the chimney shouted loudly enough for them to hear.

They saw the boy on the roof haul out a surprising amount of nesting material before lowering the stone into the room below. Then from the house another boy ran out and, after whistling furiously to attract the roof-boy's attention, shouted, 'You got the right room first time.' The roof boy's face appeared from the chimney and he waved a hand in acknowledgement.

'I'm ready to pull,' the second boy called. 'You'd better come in and help me.'

'I'll tie the holly on first, stupid.'

The boy made his way slowly to the window from which he had emerged and was handed a large branch of holly, which he attached to the rope. Someone inside pulled and the holly slowly began to disappear.

'It's too big! It will get stuck!' Sarah said, but the branch slid into the chimney with little delay.

A second branch followed the first but this one did get stuck and the roof-boy climbed up to tug at it. A branch moved suddenly and sharply and the boy lost his hold. Sarah saw him grab for the rope; his hands flailed wildly and he slithered down to rest on the gutter.

'Don't move, boy!' Giles called. He turned and gave orders swiftly and without panic. 'Fetch ladders! You ladies, will you all go inside? The fewer distractions for the boy and his rescuers the better.'

Servants scuttled indoors to spread the news. The guests, all craning their necks to see until the last moment, walked back inside. Only Sarah and Caroline did not move. They watched, frozen, as the boy teetered at the edge of the frightening drop. The only barrier to a disaster was the weak, wooden guttering at the edge of the roof.

The fact that the ladders were too short was apparent even before they had tried them. When they were opened and set against the wall, there was a gap of more than six feet between a man's reach and the boy hanging on to his precarious anchor.

Sarah knew she was the one to save him. Holding her inhibiting skirt daringly high, she ran inside. When she reached the soot-filled room, she stepped over the debris of the sweeping and removed her skirt, handing it to the bemused, tearful boy who stood wailing for the fate of his friend on the roof.

'Tie that rope firmly to the bed,' she commanded. As he obeyed, her sharp tone bringing him out of his daze, she fixed the other end around her small waist, with plenty to spare beyond. Then she was on the windowsill and leaning out to judge her best route.

Giles burst into the room as she slid onto the slates.

'Sarah!' he called, but then, as he was about to beg her to come back inside, he sensed it was too late, and the best way he could protect her was with support and encouragement. To call her foolish and tell her she would fall was a sure way to reduce her confidence, and confidence was all that would keep her from falling to her death. He took hold of the rope gradually snaking over the windowsill, and called to her softly.

'Sarah, I have hold of the rope. You are quite safe, my dear.' His heart was pounding but he forced himself to speak calmly, as if she were engaged on a daring prank on a garden wall, not at roof height with a paved area to meet her, should she fall.

Sarah pressed herself flat against the slates and moved slowly down to where the boy held on to the gutter. Resting her weight cautiously against a drainpipe, she reached over and slipped the rope end around him. Using the slack she had allowed herself, she climbed slowly back to the window.

Giles reached over and helped her in with a huge release

of pent-up breath. His voice was far from calm as he held her and said, 'My dear, my dear, I was never so afraid in my life.'

Sarah relaxed into his arms and left it to others to pull on the rope and guide the boy back safely to the windowsill.

Shouts outside and in congratulated her, but there were others who shook their heads in disapproval of such behaviour. If ladies acted so headstrong and with such blatant disregard for appearances, how would the working class ever look up to them for example? Great-Aunt Milly had to be given a glass of brandy before she could even speak and she tried to prepare some explanation for Sir Jason when he heard about the escapade. Few thought of the life saved.

Sarah's arms began to shake and her whole body trembled by the time the soot-black boy stood beside her. He stuttered his thanks. Sarah stayed in the comfort of Giles's arms, delaying the moment when he released her. She looked at the doorway where several faces stared in, including that of Caroline, drawn and wide-eyed.

'I hope someone will clear up this mess before we are expected to sleep here tonight,' Sarah said lightly. Then she cried.

It had been the intention of most of the party to go to church but no one seemed able to shake off the fright of the near accident.

'It seems so much has happened since breakfast,' Sarah said, much later, when she had bathed and dressed and was sitting with Giles, Caroline and a still-tearful Great-Aunt Milly. 'I feel sure it must be time for luncheon.'

'Why, what has happened?' a voice asked. They turned to see Alfred, dressed in heavy coat and strong boots. 'I've been walking and seem to have missed something.'

Sarah left it to the others to explain what had happened, but was surprised at the vehemence with which Alfred criticised Giles for allowing Sarah to take such a risk.

'Giles could not have stopped me,' Sarah protested. 'I was already out on the roof before he knew of it.'

'You should have pulled her back, man. You were holding the rope!'

'Do you think I did not want to? Can you believe I was less than terrified? I couldn't risk a struggle up there. I had to help her. It was the surest way to disaster to argue with her at such a time, when she needed all her concentration.'

Sarah listened to the two men and smiled at Caroline. Now the danger was over and the shock of it leaving her, she couldn't help enjoying the unusual excitement of having two such presentable men arguing over her.

'I think we should go to church as we planned,' she announced. 'Not least to give thanks for the happy ending to a dangerous situation.'

The church was five miles away in the small village of Dymbank. Renton drove Sarah, Edith, Caroline and Lucy. Giles, Alfred and some of the others rode on horseback.

Renton was very upset. He whispered to Sarah as he helped her into her seat.

'Sarah! *I'm* your partner in danger. You should have called for me. I don't trust anyone to look after you like I can. How could you have taken such a risk without me there?'

'You were nowhere to be found. There was no time. I had to go alone or the boy would surely have fallen.'

'Promise me, never again. Whatever it is, I'm your partner. Promise me, Sarah!'

'Is anything the matter, Miss Sarah?' Alfred Cummins approached and looked pointedly at Renton, standing close to Sarah.

'I was just telling Renton what happened.'

'I'm sure the servants will give him any gossip, even though it is none of his business. He is hired only to drive the coach.'

Sarah was about to raise her voice angrily when Giles said, 'Alfred, please leave this to me. Is everything all right, Sarah?'

'Perfectly, Giles. I wanted to explain to Renton what had happened this morning.'

Giles nodded at Renton, waited while Sarah was settled into her seat by Edith, and rode off. Sarah smiled at Caroline. She did not find herself drawn to this Alfred Cummins, but she was very glad he had come.

On reaching the pew allotted to the Hallam family, Sarah was pleased to be sitting between Caroline and Giles. His fine baritone voice added to the pleasure of the well-known hymns. The sermon was particularly interesting, being on the theme of consideration for the wrongdoing of the less fortunate; a very novel idea. It was certain to be the topic for discussion over dinner and Sarah was determined to take part.

Alfred sat behind Sarah and during a slight pause in the service, when the vicar dropped his papers, asked, 'Miss Sarah, is this the church you attend? I understand from other worshippers that there is another church, closer to your own country place, Houghton Hall?'

'Yes, we do have a church close to Houghton Hall, and it is in a poor state, as you undoubtedly also heard. My father intends to refurbish it as soon as he has time to discuss the plans.'

'But,' Giles added, 'I think it will have to wait until the present rector goes. He is not a man to accept upheavals and the work will be extensive.'

'I must walk over to see the place one day,' Alfred said.

Sarah and Giles ignored the hidden invitation and returned to face the altar, where the vicar, made nervous by the large number of important and beautifully dressed people in his congregation, was ready to resume.

'Would you like to walk the last half-mile?' Giles asked when they began to fill the carriages for the return journey. Sarah and Caroline agreed. The day was chilly, but clear and very bright. Giles led his horse and walked with the two girls and their maids along the rutted, muddy track towards Weatherby.

Stopping at a farm gate, Sarah looked up at a large but obviously disused building nestling in a slight hollow against the foot of a sloping field.

'What is that place?' she asked. 'Is it part of your land, Giles?'

'Sad, isn't it?' Giles replied. 'It was once a beautiful home, but when the farmer and his wife disappeared, no one wanted to live there. It's been empty since I was a boy.'

'Can I explore it?' Sarah pleaded.

'One day. But not now,' Giles said firmly. 'I think you've had quite enough excitement for one visit.'

From what Sarah could see from the road, the house was built in three sections around a courtyard. The entrance looked as if it had once been very grand. The wall above the gateway bore a crest or an elaborate design. Although it was difficult to judge the height accurately from the distance, Sarah imagined that the gates that had once filled the opening must have been enormous.

'A farm, you say?' she queried.

'It was owned by a wealthy man who, besides his activities in town, enjoyed the life of a farmer.'

'A pretend countryman?'

Giles shook his head. 'From what I've learned about him he was a countryman at heart, who needed to spend his time in town from the necessity of earning a living to feed his family.'

Sarah wondered if Giles considered himself of a like mind. His face was quite serious, but then, it usually was. Only occasionally did his features break out into laughter or smile in pleasure.

'What happened to his family?'

'No one knows.' Giles shrugged. 'One day they were there, the next the couple had gone. Most of the furnishings are still inside, damp and mouse-nibbled.'

'How strange!'

Giles clicked to his horse, who had taken the opportunity to graze the poor, damp grass on the verge, and urged them on. 'Come on, or we'll have Renton coming back to search for us. I suspect, Sarah, he doesn't trust me to look after you.' There was a gleam of amusement in his eyes. Perhaps, Sarah thought, he understands the strong friendship between Renton and me.

Sarah followed the rest but kept turning back until the derelict farmhouse was no longer to be seen. The land had begun to rise and there were hills now on either side. She realised that they were rounding the foot of Hare's Hill.

'Surely you aren't tempted to climb Hare's Hill again today, Sarah?' Giles had noticed the direction of her gaze.

'I would love to. But I suddenly feel tired.' She said it without emotion, but Giles was at once concerned. He cupped his hands for her to mount his horse and insisted on her riding the rest of the way.

'This afternoon you will rest,' he said firmly, and for once, Sarah was not inclined to argue.

She lay on the bed in the thoroughly cleaned room and tried to sleep, but although she was aching with the tension her body had suffered during the rescue, she remained wide awake. When Caroline came up to see if she needed anything, she sat up and admitted that she would prefer to go out for a last look at the fields.

'It will be months before we can walk in the grass again. At Christmas it's rarely warm enough for us to venture out. Shall we go for one last walk? Persuade Renton to come with us, we needn't tell the others.'

Caroline agreed. Avoiding the rest of the party, who, for the most part, were dozing after a heavy lunch, they found Lucy and Renton and set off.

They walked through tangled woodland, where carpets of bluebells would give a magical display in the spring, and through more orderly coppices from which thin branches were regularly cut to supply the needs of the basket weavers and fence-makers on the estate. Renton explained something of the property, which had more than a dozen farms. He admitted to having gleaned the information from the servants.

Renton always surprised Sarah with his knowledge of the countryside. He had always lived in London and left the streets only for family holidays and the occasions when work on the property was in progress and he was needed to assist Sarah's father. He pointed out the remains of bird's nests, the flattened grass where a hare had rested and the huge warren from which a cartload of fresh rabbits was taken to the London markets twice each year.

The trees tempted Sarah, although she was still feeling rather stiff and aching. She glared down at her dark-green, woollen skirt, so smart, but so inhibiting. If only she could wear more practical clothing, like a boy, she would have been able to show her skills of climbing and standing upright in the highest branches. She was sure-footed and confident at any height and could climb and walk a tightrope or a high wall with a complete lack of fear. Her mother had taught her to juggle and do many of the acrobatic tricks that needed a perfect balance and coordination. Sarah's only dismay was that, before today's rescue, she had found no occasion to display her talents. With Renton as accomplice, she practised in secret.

Thinking of the rescue, Sarah felt a flood of shame. How could she have cried? She guessed that the difference was knowing the boy depended on her for his life. That, plus the anxiety of those around her who were afraid for her, added to the tension and resulted in tears.

Seeing her staring up at a huge beech, Renton knew how frustrated she felt. He smiled and she knew his thoughts were with hers. Leaving the tempting tree unclimbed, they walked on until they reached the lonely, neglected farmhouse. They were a long way from Weatherby and the sky was already losing its light, so they did not stay long. They peered in through the dirt-grimed windows and tried the door. It gave easily under slight pressure, but the smell drove them back. The exploration would have to wait for another day.

They returned to Weatherby, washed, and changed their clothes and went down to tea. Great-Aunt Milly was just rousing from sleep and complaining of being neglected.

Giles left early the following morning. Sarah was deeply disappointed at not being up early enough to see him at breakfast. On the long drive home she clung to the memories of the time they had spent together. She delved repeatedly into every word to find some hidden meaning, wondering about the old farmhouse, imagining more than politeness in even the most formal remarks.

'You're very subdued, Sarah,' Caroline remarked. 'I hope you haven't caught Margaret's fever.'

'No, I'm well and so happy.' She hugged her friend impulsively. 'Thank you for inviting me, Caroline. It's been a perfect visit.'

Caroline leaned closer to whisper, 'If my brother is the

cause, then I'm happy too.'

Sarah smiled and gazed out of the carriage window. There was another pleasure in store; telling her sister Margaret all about the weekend. That way she could relive it and warm again to the memories of the moments she and Giles had spent together.

'I'm sorry Margaret didn't come,' she said. 'But it will be fun telling her all about it. She won't be too pleased to hear about the rescue, though. I'll have to make light of it. Margaret is a gentle person and she worries so.'

The day was clear and, with no fog to slow them, they made good time in reaching Caroline's home, where they stopped for tea. Darkness had fallen before Sarah and Edith prepared to go. They watched from the window as Renton lit the carriage lamps and put hot bottles ready for their feet. It seemed a long time before he finally stood waiting to assist them into their seats, and Great-Aunt Milly was becoming impatient.

'I rather think Renton is serious about your Lucy,' Sarah confided to her friend.

'Oh, dear,' Caroline wailed. 'I hope he doesn't take her away from me just yet. I do so hate training a new maid.'

'I wish I could ride up there with you, Renton,' Sarah said as he helped her into the carriage. 'There's so much to see and the night streets are as far from my understanding as a foreign country.'

'I'll leave the flap open and we can talk,' he said. 'I'll tell you of anything interesting I see.'

On the short route through the darkness of the town, lit occasionally by gas lamps, the streets seemed alien, gloomy and somehow threatening after the quiet of Weatherby, where the nights were completely black without a single spark of light anywhere. The lamps throwing a brief pool of illumination onto the empty pavements added to the dark and Sarah tried to imagine the ordinariness of daytime, but could not. She shivered. Ordinariness went with the light. Hidden in the blackness were untold horrors. She allowed her imagination to people the streets with danger and dreamed of being rescued by Giles. The horses picked up speed as they turned into Sallis Close and they were soon in sight of home.

But something was wrong, and this time the danger was not imagined. Lights were showing through the mistiness, adding patches of colour through the gloom. The doors of the house were wide open and people were milling about. As they drew closer, they could hear voices wailing and shouting. Sarah held her hands to her mouth in fear as she could make out the uniforms of many policemen.

Her father was standing at the iron gates and, as she stepped down, he saw her and beckoned to her. With Renton beside her she ran to him. As she reached the gates, a procession began to make its way down the steps from the house. A litter was carried, a still figure on it. Behind it came another, and the person on this one was so small it could only be Isobelle.

'What's happened?' she demanded in a voice unlike her own.

'Margaret. And little Isobelle. I fear they are . . . ' His face was contorted and the words would not come.

Sarah stared at her father. His dark face with its long nose and deep-set eyes looked like that of a stranger. She saw it crumple as he sobbed and reached out to hold her in his arms.

'Sarah, my child! How will we survive this?'

Chapter Four

Sarah stared at the people who were lifting the litters into the hospital wagon. Renton stood beside her, gripping her arm. She thought she was hallucinating, had allowed her fanciful thoughts to take over her mind with her fears what the darkness held. Margaret couldn't be seriously ill. She had only had a slight soreness of the throat. She asked Renton as she had asked her father, 'What happened?'

'Edith, wait with your mistress while I go and find out.' Renton led Sarah back to the carriage. The horses were snorting, impatient to get to their stable and their feed. Sarah felt Edith's arms around her and she sat shivering while Renton walked to one of the policemen, spoke briefly and returned.

'Come on, Miss Sarah, we'll take you indoors now.'

'Renton, please tell me!' She looked up into the lean, strong face and read the distress there. 'Margaret, Isobelle – what happened?'

'The house was burgled. Margaret – she must have been remarkably brave. She probably tried to stop them harming Isobelle and was . . . attacked.'

'How badly is she hurt? Tell me, Renton.' She looked from Renton's hollow-cheeked, sorrowing face to the sagging expression on that of her father. 'Tell me!' she shouted.

'Sarah, prepare yourself for the worst news.' Renton was almost crying. 'Your Margaret is dead. And there is fear for the life of little Isobelle.'

'But how could there have been a burglary? The house is full of servants.' Her mind refused to accept what she was being told. 'No thief would have broken in in broad daylight with a house full of people!' She looked at his face, in deep shadow with only the gate sconces and a gas lamp to give illumination to the scene. His eyes were downcast. There was something more. 'Tell me everything. Please, Renton. My father cannot speak of it and I must know it all. I couldn't bear to have the story in parts. Let me know the worst at once. What happened here?' She turned then as the hospital transport reached the corner. 'No! I must go to the hospital with my sisters.'

Renton held her back. 'No, Sarah. Your father needs you first. Then I will take you and stay with you until we know that Isobelle will recover.'

Edith came and put an arm round the girl's shoulders. Her sister Hannah had gone to the hospital with the injured child.

'I must know what happened before I talk to my father.' She glared at Renton. 'Tell me the rest of it.'

Renton still hesitated, then said, 'The police are sure it happened last night.'

'But where was my father?'

'He has only just returned. One of the servants finally managed to untie himself and sent for him and the police.'

'You mean Margaret lay there injured and no one found her for hours?'

'Perhaps I have it wrong, that was why I did not want to tell you.'

But Sarah knew he was not wrong. Her father had stayed out all night and had gone from some woman straight to his office. If he had not, Margaret might have been saved. 'Giles and his night houses!' In her grief, she hated him, her father too. How could they be so careless of others?

Renton guided her inside and she felt that the house was different, no longer the comfortable, warm home she had left a few days before. She sat on a chair and stared at her father, who had been assisted inside by a footman and thc housekeeper. She was unable to speak to him, aiming all her anger and unhappiness on his bent shoulders.

A footman announced Mr Henry Bannerman, a detective from the police station, who was a friend of Sir Jason and his family. He began by offering his sympathy, then explained as fully as he could what they surmised had happened. He was a burly man, with hair that curled somewhat wildly around his face and head. His presence seemed to make Sir Jason smaller and more shrunken by comparison.

'There's a new kind of criminal operating of late,' he began quietly, 'bold and extremely dangerous. He probably knows he is for the gallows if he's caught, so he isn't afraid to kill to protect himself. Got nothing to lose, you might say.'

'Was this the work of one man?' Sir Jason asked incredulously.

'Oh no, a gang. He gathers a group of like-minded villains and they burst in, wielding fearsome weapons and hitting out at anyone they meet. They soon have the household cowed or unconscious and then ransack the place and take what they came for. Yes – ' He anticipated the next question. 'These raids are planned, and that's our main difficulty. The men who carry them out aren't the ones who plan them. They work for whoever will pay them.'

'But where would they get the information about the contents? And how do they get in?'

'Getting in is easy. A knock at the door, then, when it's opened, they push past the servant and begin to terrorise the household.'

'And knowing what to take?' Sarah asked.

'It's easy for someone to gather knowledge that would be useful to thieves. Idle gossip in coffee houses, night houses and anywhere people gather to relax and talk freely with their friends. Women receiving beauty treatments, visiting hairdressers, dressmakers and the like, all let information slip in conversation. Telling your friends you will be away for a few days is often enough. Servants are rarely brave when it means their life compared with a few valuable pieces, and who's to blame them?'

'Margaret was to have come with me,' Sarah said. 'If only she had!' Her hands tightened as she added, 'If only my father had been here! But he was out all night. Giles Hallam earns his money in a way no less evil than the thieves!' She stopped Henry Bannerman's protest. 'It was probably there that the details of our weekend were overheard. It would be easy to discover my father's whereabouts on any night!'

'Try not to blame anyone, Miss Sarah. I have a few ideas and I feel sure we'll find those responsible.'

'I *know* who's responsible!'

'Miss Sarah, the best way you can help is by making a list of all the items missing. I don't want you to think about it now, but tomorrow, if you could go through each room and take a good and careful look. Will you do that?'

'I want to do something more positive than count up their *haul*, as I believe it's called.'

'I need that information and the sooner I have it the more chance I have of catching the men who did this to your sister.'

Sarah looked into his face. Kindness and concern showed in the faded blue eyes. His chin was rounded and pock-marked, his nose slightly out of true, but the features were familiar and appealing to Sarah, to whom he had been a favourite uncle since she had been born. But behind the sympathy she saw a mind that was sceptical and doubting, seeing everything and believing none of it.

He gave her a hug before taking his leave.

'Where were you, Father?' Sarah asked when she and Sir Jason were alone.

'At the house of a friend.' He looked away from her as he replied.

At once she accused, 'You were at one of Giles's night houses.'

The distress felt by them both caused him to ignore the rudeness. Unrepentant, she went on.

'You were away! Most of the staff had been given leave of absence. You stayed away, leaving a sick Margaret and Isobelle in the care of the most idle of the servants.'

'I stayed out for company.'

Sarah stared at him. He looked older than his fifty years and she saw for the first time how lost he still was without his wife, whom he had dearly loved. Anger at his neglect faded and in its place came sympathy for his loneliness. He had never attended the gaming houses or the supper rooms when her mother was alive.

Sarah hugged him. 'Oh, what will we do without them all?'

Isobelle was unconscious for several days. Sarah spent all the hours she could at the hospital, sitting beside her, watching anxiously for the first hopeful sign. Giles called to see her but she refused. At Margaret's funeral she had given him nothing more than a polite nod. She had forgiven her father for the hours he had spent seeking company, but she could no longer ignore the part played by Giles in making such places available and enticing.

Another visitor was Alfred.

'I won't stay long, Miss Sarah, but I had to come and say how sorry I was to hear of the tragedy you suffered. I hope the little one is improving?'

'Isobelle is still unconscious. We don't know yet if she will recover.' She stood up to hide the tears that threatened. 'Would you like to visit her?'

'Thank you, but I think not. This is a time for families. But when she is well again . . . '

Sarah thought she saw sympathy in his greeny-grey eyes. He was pale and the scar more visible.

'I did not know your sisters were at home while you were in the country,' he said.

Sarah didn't pause to wonder what he meant by such a remark. She was fascinated by the greenness of his eyes and the stillness of his features as he watched her. He made her feel strange, vulnerable and in need of his concern. His deep voice warmed her. At this time there was a need for a friend in her life. Was it possible Alfred could fill that need?

'Margaret became unwell at the very last moment,' she said, answering him at last.

'Miss Sarah, is your father at home? I would very much like to see him if that is possible. Business, I'm afraid. Sir Jason has been absent from his offices for several days and . . . '

Sarah pulled the cord and, after polite farewells, Alfred was shown into Sir Jason's study.

As he left, Sir Jason and he were still discussing their arrangements for some sort of delivery.

'So, as soon as you have the list of what panels you need, you will let me know?' Alfred was saying.

'Yes, and if the deliveries are as efficient as you promise, we shall do business together again,' Sir Jason replied.

Sarah stepped out into the hall as the heavy door closed behind Alfred.

'Have you changed your mind about Alfred Cummins, Father?' Sarah asked.

'No. But,' he added, 'I am too hard-headed a business man to refuse a good offer on the grounds that I dislike the man making it.' He looked at her and frowned. 'I thought you had promised me you wouldn't receive him?'

'It was difficult to refuse this time. He had called to ask about Isobelle, and, as he had been a guest at the weekend party at Weatherby, it would have been very rude. You wouldn't want me to appear rude, would you?'

'No, I suppose not.' Still frowning, he went back to his study.

A few days later, Jarvis King was sitting in a dark lodging house. The place was gloomy, with most of the windows broken and boarded up; what light there was came through the door. It was a regular meeting place for a number of criminals, and Jarvis, in one of his many disguises, was waiting for one in particular.

The place was popular because of its many entrances and exits, and because the landlord, who was standing close to the fire, had a poor memory for those who used it. He would hold out a hand to be filled with coins and turn back to face the fire without looking.

Jarvis sat in a dark corner. When a heavily built man came in and offered his contribution to the silent landlord, Jarvis coughed and the man came over to sit beside him.

'There are two addresses for you,' Jarvis whispered. 'Number 3 Belmont Square, where you'll find the cupboard where the silver's kept unlocked. And take what else you fancy for yourself. The other is more difficult. I want three pictures for a customer.'

In a low whisper that went unheard by anyone other than the large man, Jarvis described the items he wanted and for which he had customers. The large man, whose breath whistled slightly down a fight-damaged nose, waited for a while after Jarvis had left, then followed without further attention to the landlord at the fireplace.

Ten days after the attack Isobelle opened her eyes fully, and it was soon clear that she had undergone a change. The truth finally had to be faced. Isobelle, Sarah's beautiful, happy little sister, was going to live, but with a damaged mind.

Sarah stayed in her room for days, crying for the sisters who were lost to her. The house was silent; everyone talked in whispers and tiptoed about as if afraid of disturbing ghosts. No visitor called to bring a breath of the outside world to the mourning family.

At night, when the house was silent and Sarah lay waiting for sleep to ease away her troubled thoughts, she could hear very faintly from far above her the sound of Renton's pipes and knew he too was filled with grief. She could imagine him up in the attic room, lying on his small bed and staring up at the ceiling, and she longed to go to him for comfort. Everyone grieved in a different way; her father was once again visiting the night houses and several times he did not come in until dawn was showing its reluctance to begin another day.

For herself, Sarah filled her days so there was no time to sit and think, apart from this time just before sleep. The days since the terrible attack had first kept her fully occupied with arrangements for the funeral. She had gone out with only Edith to advise her to buy drapes for the windows, which were still in place, and mourning clothes for herself. There were appointments to be cancelled and other members of the family had to be contacted to tell the sad news. Writing on black-edged paper, she had spent a whole day on that task alone.

Her young brothers had returned home from school but thankfully had stayed only a few days before being sent back. Then there was the daily visit to see Isobelle. Each time she went to the long hospital ward, which her father had never seen, she hoped for a slight improvement. But when the little girl finally opened her eyes they were those of a stranger.

At breakfast, after another almost sleepless night, Sarah sent for Renton.

'Will you come with me today? I want to see Henry Bannerman. Perhaps if we call he will have something to tell us, some news of the men who . . . '

'I'll take Sir Jason to his office and come back for you,' he promised. 'But wrap up warmly. That office is chilly, with people always going in and out.'

They rode through streets filled with crowds busy with their shopping. Christmas was approaching and all along the dirty pavements sellers were offering everything from home-made sweets, wrapped in bright paper and representing the traditional shapes of the season, to branches of holly rich with berries.

Renton smiled and told her the berries were probably hawthorn, fastened on to trick the ignorant. 'We'll find plenty of real holly if we go to Houghton Hall for Christmas.'

'I hope my father doesn't change his mind and stay in London.'

'He might. You are in mourning.'

'I think he needs to get away or he will never recover.'

'Then begin persuading him now,' Renton advised.

This exchange had taken place while the traffic was at a complete standstill. Carts and wagons were pushing their way through from all directions, horses were being pulled, shouted at and beaten in an attempt to clear the snarled confusion. An elderly woman on a small cart shouted abuse at the driver of a wagon containing pigs, and the man jumped down and pulled the woman from her seat. They were soon fighting, rolling around on the ground, while the crowd made a circle around them, shouting encouragement. Soon, supporters in the circle took offence at those shouting for the other side, and smaller scuffles broke out.

Renton dismounted and tried to lead the horses out of the fray, but it was not until several of the fighters had been carried away, bleeding or, in some cases, unconscious, that there was room for them to pass. Sarah had drawn the curtains in the coach but, with Edith tutting disapproval, watched excitedly through the crack.

The man who had begun it all had lost his pigs. Sarah had laughed delightedly as the three porkers had pushed between the legs of the watchers and spilled a row of them before running between the carts, wagons and coaches down the main street. As they drove away she saw one standing looking confused, as if unable to decide how to deal with his new-found freedom. Two men were sitting on a bank of earth near a lamppost when they saw the pig, unaccompanied and obviously looking for a home. They ran for it and succeeded in guiding it into an alleyway, dreaming of a pork joint for every day until Christmas, no doubt. But, the pig suddenly turned and charged them and ran off. The two men recovered their balance and, holding on to their hats, gave chase.

Sarah was in a lighter mood when she arrived at the detective's office. Henry Bannerman was expecting them. Renton went in with her.

The room was cluttered and dusty. Shelves were filled with piles of papers, ledgers and boxes labelled with unreadable, spidery writing. Around the walls that weren't covered with shelves, notice boards hung. Papers of various size, colour and age were stuck to the surface with pins. Everywhere there were lists. Some were of names, others described articles stolen, or found and unclaimed. While Henry Bannerman arranged for them to be served with biscuits and mulled ale to warm them, Sarah and Renton studied the fascinating collection of cases past and present. There were letters from many countries, showing how wide the net was cast in attempts to find those guilty of crime.

'What have you discovered about the men who killed my sisters, Uncle Henry?' Sarah asked, when she was settled comfortably in a large wooden armchair close to the fire.

The policeman looked shocked. 'You mean that Isobelle is – ?'

'Isobelle is still alive, but she is not the sister I knew. I sometimes think it would have been kinder if she had died with Margaret. Father is talking of sending her away. So I have lost both of them anyway.' She felt her throat tighten with grief.

'We are still searching for information, Miss Sarah,' Bannerman said. 'All we know for certain is that there were three men and a boy, who must have been their "crow", their lookout. The men were heavily built, probably known to us and with little to lose. Bursting in and attacking anyone who challenged them was the act of desperate men.'

'There has been no sign of the items stolen that night?' Renton asked.

'Nothing yet. But we haven't given up hope. Time passes and we remain diligent and hopeful, while they will become more confident and careless.' Bannerman stood up and touched the shoulder of the small figure on the wooden armchair, toasting her feet near the fender. 'Miss Sarah, you know how fond I am of you and your family. Your father and I have been friends – er, acquaintances – for many years. We went to the same school although our social position was hardly the same. I knew your dear mother. I watched you all grow up. It was like losing a member of my own family when Miss Margaret died. And as for young Isobelle . . . ' His voice faltered.

'If father would let her stay with us, I wouldn't feel she was lost to me too,' Sarah said. 'If she lived in the place she knows, where she had always been happy, I am sure she would recover.'

'If what you say is true,' he said gently, 'she has been – damaged, and the doctors can hold out no hope of any great improvement.'

'Father is arranging for her to go to the country, to a farmhouse where she will be cared for by strangers. I will be able to see her, of course.' There was defiance in Sarah's voice, a refusal to accept that Isobelle's mind was permanently broken.

'But not too often,' Bannerman said quietly. 'There's no use distressing yourself.'

Bannerman talked to Renton for a while, leaving Sarah to sip her drink and gaze thoughtfully into the coals. He wished he had news of an arrest to tell her. It often helped to ease the grieving when the culprit was captured and no longer free to benefit from his crime.

When she stood up to leave, Bannerman went with them into the outer office. As he ushered Sarah and Renton to the door, a policeman handed him a small item. He suddenly called them back.

'Would you kindly wait a moment, Miss Sarah?' Henry discussed something with his officer in a low voice and examined the item carefully before turning to her again. 'Do you recognise this?'

'Yes!' She showed it to Renton, who also nodded. 'It belongs to my father.'

It was a small snuffbox with a head of Queen Victoria decorating the lid. Made of silver, it was lined with glass and very beautifully crafted. Sarah stared excitedly at Bannerman.

'This is one of the pieces stolen that night. Where did you get it?' she asked the constable.

The young man glanced at the superintendent for permission, then said, 'It was offered for sale in a shop that deals in second-hand goods.' He half turned to Bannerman and added, 'From the description of the man who brought it in, it was Arthur.' He pointed to one of the posters decorating the wall of the outer office. Sarah stared at the artist's drawing, which showed a burly one-time prize fighter.

'It's as we guessed from the information given by your servants and others.' Bannerman pointed to another poster, showing a heavily built man with a jutting jaw and small, half-concealed eyes. 'That one usually accompanies Arthur. Will the Ratman they call him.'

Sarah looked at the faces of the two men and shuddered at the thought of her gentle sisters being at their mercy.

'They are so clever at gleaning information, aren't they?' she said sadly. 'Someone wanted something of ours so they set a dangerous man like that – ' she pointed at the ugly face of the one called Arthur – 'on to innocent and defenceless people like Margaret and little Isobelle.'

'As I've explained, Miss Sarah, information is cheap. For the price of a pipeful of tobacco, sometimes even less, a man will give details of the contents of a house and of ways to enter.'

'In places like gaming houses?' she said with a hint of

bitterness in her voice.

'They're a very good source. Men talk without a thought when they believe themselves to be among friends. Women, too, are good at gathering details and are frequently paid for information they impart. They are expected to listen and take little part, and men are inclined to trust them, even to forget they are there.'

Sarah's thoughts flickered to Giles and his businesses. If his places were not such a magnet to men like her father, the disaster might not have happened.

'Servants or friends,' she said thoughtfully. She took copies of the posters of the two men from a pile on the wooden counter. 'I'll show these to the servants.'

'We already have.' Bannerman smiled.

'I'll take them anyway.'

'Don't be tempted to make any enquiries of your own, will you?' Bannerman warned as he opened the door to the noisy street. 'Any ideas you have, bring them to me and my men at once. These men don't play polite games.'

'Thank you very much for your time, Uncle Henry,' Sarah said, not replying to his warning.

Edith was waiting in the carriage. Irritation showed in her face as she greeted Sarah and Renton on their return. She would have liked to go in with them.

'Did you think we had been arrested, dear Edith?' Sarah teased.

'We need to call to collect more embroidery thread before we go home, and we are already very late for luncheon,' Edith said stiffly.

That night was another sleepless one for Sarah. She lay restlessly imagining how she could hurry the process of finding the frightening Arthur and Will. She was lonely in the quiet house, missing Margaret and sad for Isobelle.

The music could still be heard from the attic room, and she gave up trying to sleep and reached for her gown. If anyone saw her she would be in trouble and create problems for Renton, but the thought did not stop her. She needed to talk and there was no one else. She knocked softly on the dark wooden door and whispered softly, 'Renton, can I come in? I need to talk to you.'

The door opened and revealed, in the light of a guttering candle, the tall figure of her coachman in an ankle-length nightshirt with vertical stripes and a tasselled hat.

'Sarah! What are you doing here?' He hurriedly pulled her inside and closed the door. 'If you want me to lose my post, this is a good way of going about it!' He was angry and frightened, but his expression softened when he saw her distress. 'Let's get dressed and go out the way we used to and meet in the stables. It will be warm there.'

Sarah went back down the cold staircase, stepping carefully on each tread for fear of being heard, ashamed now of her thoughtlessness in coming to visit Renton. She dressed in as many clothes as she could comfortably wear. Using a small hatch through which groceries and vegetables were delivered straight into the cold storeroom, she went out into the dark night.

Renton had already arrived when she opened the small door in the larger sliding doors of the stable and slipped inside. She turned and leapt backwards up onto the manger which sloped from the wall and held sweet, country-scented hay for the horses now standing quietly against the far wall. Above the manger, in the ceiling, were doors to the hayloft through which the food was dropped. These doors hung open and she heard the soft whisper of greeting and saw dark shadows move as Renton crouched before dropping down beside her.

'It's such a long time since we did this, Renton. It was such fun, wasn't it? Each of us sneaking away from the life we had to live and pretending everything was different. Do you think disobedience is necessary for children?'

'It certainly was for you!'

'Because my life was so confining, I suppose.'

'Because you were a rebel!'

'Remember how we used to dress up in ragged clothes and go out at night when we were children?'

Renton's soft chuckle breathed against her ear. 'I remember! In some of my oldest clothes you looked every inch a boy. What about the night when you worked as a sweeper and earned fourpence?'

Sarah remembered. They had found a broken broom and tied it with ribbons that had held her hair back. Daringly she had brushed the dirt and horse-droppings aside to allow a daintily dressed woman to alight from her carriage and enter the theatre with her satin slippers unsullied. The woman's escort had thrown down a handful of coins and Renton and she had been knocked down by urchins appearing from nowhere to grab them. The next carriage came and they were ready. Renton, her champion, had fought like a tiger while she had gathered the pennies.

'Chased us for miles, those boys, declaring we'd stolen their pitch,' Renton said, his thoughts on a line with Sarah's. 'We were lost for a while, and with the darkness and the fog, we imagined walking straight into the river.'

'And we got back by riding on the back of a carriage after hearing the passenger ask for Covent Garden.'

They were still laughing at the memories until Sarah, suddenly serious, asked, 'Renton, do you think I could still pass as a boy?'

'Yes, I reckon you could, being so small, and – *no*! Sarah, *no*! I wouldn't let you. I'd tell your father in an instant if you were foolish enough to try. Bannerman wasn't joking. Those men are without pity. They'd kill you and enjoy it,' he warned as she leapt from the manger.

'I am going to search the streets for those men.'

Renton jumped down. He looked at her face anxiously, recognising the determined set of her pointed chin, and knew he was in for an argument.

'Come or not, but I'm going out tonight. I'll find the men who deprived me of my sisters. Or die in the attempt,' she added lightly.

She was grieving deeply for her sisters and for the dream of marrying Giles. Death did not seem so frightening since the attack. She missed Margaret, who had shared her secrets, and the little girl who had been Isobelle. She felt the loss of Giles as fiercely as if he too had been a victim. Blaming him for the disaster, however unfairly, she mourned for the love she had longed for and that was now lost to her.

The grief went back to when her mother died. Loving and

losing seemed impossible to cope with. If she could avenge her sisters, perhaps she would prevail upon fate to treat her more kindly in future?

Renton pleaded with her, threatened her, bullied her, but nothing would alter her mind. In the end, he agreed to go simply because he knew she would go anyway, and without him she was as good as dead. The London streets at night were no playground where children could have a bit of timorous fun before running back to the safety of their privileged homes any more.

'Please, Sarah.' He made one last effort.

'We'll meet at ten-thirty,' she said firmly.

'Reluctantly,' he said.

In a pair of ill-fitting trousers and a ragged jacket, Sarah slouched along the pavement while Renton, similarly attired, followed some distance behind. They made their way towards the theatre area where there would be most activity at this time of night. Crowds streamed out of the ornate playhouse entrances and headed for the long line of carriages and cabs, anticipating supper and dancing, or entertainment at one of the less savoury night places.

The noise of horses pulling an assortment of carriages and carts, the voices of vendors offering every imaginable item for sale, and the shouting and laughter of the crowds bent on having fun, threatened to deafen them. The smell was a mixture of rotting food, excrement, animals and overcrowded humanity. The sight, showed by the light from carriage lanterns and torches, was a kaleidoscope of colours and drabness. People wearing bright dresses and sparkling jewellery passed in and out of the light, now a blue dress, then a gentleman in dark grey, a flash of white fur and the glitter of a necklace. All seen for a moment, then gone as the torches flickered on their passing.

Prostitutes leaned casually against walls, or strolled to meet their friends to sip coffee or take a glass of something to keep out the cold. Even in the spasmodic light they were different from the ladies in both dress and manner. Their dresses were too gaudy, their skirts too short and the catlike eyes were watchful, waiting for a hesitant customer who needed a little encouragement. Sarah, with Renton, watched it all in wonder and fascination.

At the corner of a street where she had seen her before, Sarah noticed Emily Tilt, Renton's cousin who sold flowers. She wouldn't be stopping to buy from her tonight. As she watched, she saw that the girl was glancing repeatedly at the corner of the nearby building, as if she were expecting someone.

Taking Renton's arm briefly, Sarah walked through the slowly dispersing crowds, listening, looking, hoping to pick up a sight or a word to lead her to the men she sought. After two hours they went home. Nothing had been achieved, but a start had been made.

Chapter Five

Emily Tilt straightened the basket of flowers. Clutching the handle into her waist, she leaned back to ease the aches in her body and legs. She was tired and the basket seemed heavier tonight. The crowds had thinned; there was no point in wandering around in the hope of catching a customer who would buy the last of her flowers. She returned to her corner and, with a sigh of relief, dropped the basket onto the bottom step of the drinking fountain and straightened.

' 'Ere, love, warm yerself on one o' these.' With a laugh, the little old woman selling chestnuts threw one to Emily, who caught it with a shout.

'Thanks, Maggs! Cold tonight, ain't it?'

'Yes, thank goodness I've nearly finished.' Maggs sighed. 'Me old man'll be back soon, then I can go 'ome and get the kids to bed – *if* I can find 'em!' she added with a laugh.

The people passing on their way to their late-night entertainments moved faster as the numbers diminished. Emily began to feel the nervousness she always suffered when she thought the man would soon come. She knew it was almost time for him to stride around the corner and push his way through the throng to buy his usual buttonhole from her. She had no way of knowing the time except when she heard the distant sound of a clock chiming out the hours and quarters, but she always knew when he was due. In the few weeks he had been buying his evening flower from her, his short visit had become the highlight of her dreary day.

She watched the corner where the theatre-going crowd bustled past in their splendid clothes, while, darting among them, shabbily dressed urchins begged pennies or tormented and teased those whose lives were so different from their own. Carriages rattled along the road, making people jump out of the way, horses sending sparks from the stones on the frost-hard street.

Although she never took great risks, through the evening Emily would occasionally steal a trinket or a silk handkerchief when the opportunity was too good to miss. She handed the results of this secondary activity to a small boy, who returned a while later with money.

Watching for the chance of an easy snatch and for a prospective customer for her flowers, she continued to glance at the corner, waiting for the man. She nervously straightened her hat, tucking her unruly red hair into place. When she saw him come towards her she felt the usual shyness, and a mild anger with herself. What was she doing, thinking and dreaming about a well-dressed gentleman like him? Ridiculous!

She smiled as he walked towards her, pushing past the groups buying chestnuts. 'Evenin', sir.' She handed him a flower.

His hand held hers for a moment before taking the flower and putting two coins into her palm. His eyes held hers with a certain longing, but he said nothing more than, 'Thank you, it's perfect.'

He always stood for a moment, watching her. She admired his lean, handsome looks, the grey-green eyes above the luxuriant moustaches and beard. When he turned to walk away, he went slowly, glancing back occasionally as if he too wanted to prolong the moment. She felt the drop of her heart as he vanished in the jostling crowd. She knew she loved him although they had never met except for the regular evening transaction.

After he had gone, she stood for a while, stamping her feet and blowing on her hands to try to ease the pain of the intense cold. In her basket were only a few flowers so she decided not to wait until the crowds returned. The posies were fresh and might sell the next morning. She waved good night to Maggs and turned thankfully towards the overcrowded lodging house she called home.

In a dark corner she stopped and, making sure she was not being observed, transferred her takings into a bag strapped around her middle. She left out twopence only, the price of her lodgings at the Nethersken for the night. Before going there she first went to a public house called Peg's Palace, but she didn't buy. She asked for and was refused credit, and waved with the enthusiasm of a drunk to some acquaintances. She stumbled around noisily, bumping into a group in the doorway. Some silk scarves and a wallet found their way into her pocket as she passed a party just about to enter. Waving an empty gin bottle she had picked up from a table, she left.

Outside, she raised the bottle to her mouth and smeared the dregs around her face. Swaying and singing, she staggered homeward through the tumble of connected buildings, over bridges and under foul-smelling archways into the collection of derelict and overcrowded dwellings around St Giles. She stepped warily around a deep pit full of stagnant water and human excrement arranged for the unwary Peeler foolish enough to enter the area in search of a wanted man.

Pulling her hair out of its pins and holding the twopence tightly in her hand, she staggered up to the owner of the Nethersken and paid her rent. Laughter greeted her entrance.

' 'Ere she is, drunk again!'

'Emily, what would yer father say, supposin' you 'ad one?'

'Never got no money and works all the hours she can find.'

' 'Angs on to 'er rent though, never loses that.'

Emily gathered her heavy, mud-splattered coats around her and curled up to go to sleep. The noises drifted over her as she dreamed of the man who bought a flower every night, and of the house she would one day own. Through sleep-heavy eyes she saw hands slyly slipping into the pockets of sleepers and she smiled to herself. No one bothered Emily Tilt, not as long as they believed she spent all she earned on drink.

Sarah had been shopping. In an attempt to coax Isobelle to

play, she had bought some baby toys and, as a treat for the little girl, some jellies and other sweets. With a few small packages on her arm, and others being carried in by Renton, she ran up the steps to where the parlour maid held open the door.

'You have a visitor, Miss Sarah,' she was told. Dropping her packages on the hall table, she went into the drawing room. She thought it might be Caroline, but it was Giles who stood up from the deep armchair near the fire.

'Please, Sarah, don't go,' he said as she hesitated in the doorway. 'I must talk to you.'

'Then please be quick. I have to go to Isobelle.'

'I have seen her myself only moments ago. She is sleeping and is quite comfortable. Hannah is with her.'

Sarah's shoulders drooped. 'And that is all we can do for her now, keep her comfortable until she recovers.'

'Sarah, my dear, Isobelle will not recover. What your father suggests is for the best. Isobelle would be well cared for and the country air would at least give her good health and a happy life.'

'To send her out of our lives? How can you say that is the best?'

'Not out of your life. The place your father has chosen is near Weatherby. You can go there as often as you wish. Sarah, for your father's sake, you must agree. He is destroyed by what happened and he takes the guilt on himself. That guilt is increased each time he looks at her. He has lost your mother and two young sons, then Margaret and Isobelle, and he feels estranged from you, his dearest child. Help him. He is alone and can be saved from his misery. The dead are beyond us.'

'Isobelle isn't dead!'

'Of course she isn't. But what life will she have if she stays here? And what of your father? With her a constant reminder of that tragic day, he will never recover.'

'Is that why you came?'

'Partly. I cannot bear to see you and your father both grieving for your sisters apart from the comfort of each other. Partly it was that: the hope that I could persuade you to think more kindly of him. But mostly because I wanted to see you, to tell you how sorry I am that the happy weekend ended so tragically. I have not found the opportunity to talk with you since. I almost believe you are avoiding my family.'

There was no response from the sad little figure standing near the door.

'If there is anything, anything at all I can do, you have only to ask and it will be done.'

'You can find the men who did this to us! Or, better still, you can forbid my father to visit your night houses! He shouldn't have been out that night chasing – '

'I cannot tell your father how to live his life, Sarah,' Giles said quietly. 'And,' he added, 'have you considered that if he had not gone out that night, he too might be dead?'

Sarah gasped and ran from the room. How *could* he remind her of that possibility?

'Sarah, listen to me . . . '

Sarah covered her ears as she ran up the curving staircase, knowing she had spoken foolishly and was acting like a child, running past her own room and the one that had been Margaret's. On, up a second staircase to the room where Isobelle lived. She stood at the door, tears flowing for herself and her sisters. She was still a little in love with Giles but could not accept a life that depended for its comfort on the activities he represented.

She did not go into the room, but ran lightly down the stairs again to where she could look over the banisters to the hallway. Giles stood at the door of the drawing room and her heart twisted at the sight of him. He was dressed in a dark suit with an embroidered waistcoat. He wore his hair fashionably short and combed forward, allowing it to curl on his forehead. From her present view, high above him, his face was in shadow and it was possible for her to cast him as a villain.

She watched as he finally gave up hope of her returning. She wanted to run down the last flight of stairs and tell him she was sorry she had been so unkind. She felt a desire to be held in his arms, to receive the kisses she had only dreamed about, and tears seeped to blur her vision. But she stayed silent and unseen as he took his hat and gloves from the maid and walked out through the door.

Sarah collected her parcels and, when she had composed herself, went into Isobelle's room. The little girl woke as she entered.

'I'll stay for a while,' she told Hannah. 'Go and take a rest.'

Hannah curtsied. 'Thank you, Miss Sarah.'

Isobelle was looking around the room, frowning and talking in a strange, unintelligible language to imaginary people and things around her. She raised a thin arm pointing to unseen delights and greeted them with eerie laughter.

'I'm here, Isobelle. Sarah is with you.' Sarah took one of the hands and sat talking to the child, watching, hoping for an intelligent response, willing her sister to recover. This, she said to herself, is where my life ends until I find the men who did this to her. Shutting Giles out of her heart, she sat beside the bed and began reciting some of Isobelle's favourite nursery rhymes.

Giles sat in his carriage on his way home for the few hours' rest he allowed himself, before returning to the places he managed and owned. A frown darkened his serious face. He had been a fool to think he and Sarah could have a life together. He was too old for her; she was still a child and needed someone less staid. Even if there were not the years to separate them, her opinion of him was too low ever to change. Yet he doubted that he would ever find another woman to take to his heart.

If she would only accept his friendship and support! His frown deepened. Since the loss of her sisters, it seemed even that was denied him.

With Renton watching over her, Sarah spent hours out in the streets, searching for a clue to the men she knew only as Arthur and Will. They often saw Emily Tilt with her heavy flower basket, and one night Renton asked her to help collect information about the men they were trying to trace.

'Who's 'e?' Emily asked, pointing a thumb at Sarah, who was standing some distance away.

'Just a friend. He thinks he might be able to help me find Arthur,' Renton explained.

‘ ’Ardly big enough to ’elp anyone, is ’e?’

‘Not big, but he’s fast.’ Renton grinned. ‘And he can get into places that I can’t manage.’

Emily laughed at him. ‘You ain’t that big yerself,’ she jeered. ‘Tall you may be but big you ain’t. You’re as thin as that flower stalk,’ she said, holding up a chrysanthemum. ‘Turn yer sideways an’ you’d disappear.’

Renton chuckled as he walked back to Sarah.

He hoped that, as the days passed and the robbery began to fade into hard, cruel memory, Sarah’s enthusiasm would wane, but he was wrong. She had even gone out without him on occasions, when he was working or, off duty, visiting Caroline’s maid Lucy.

Sarah had inadvertently let slip her solo forays when she mentioned seeing Giles with an elegantly dressed woman on his arm. Renton rounded on her angrily.

‘Sarah! How could you let me down so badly? You asked for my help and, although I did not approve and thought the idea was both dangerous and stupid, I agreed. At least for that you owe me honesty.’

Sarah was contrite. ‘You’re right and I’m sorry.’

‘And you promise you won’t ever go out on your own again?’

‘I promise.’

It was in Renton’s mind to say the game was over and he would not go out with her again. It seemed a chance to end the dangerous search, but he knew Sarah. If he did not support her, she would continue alone.

She must have sensed what he was thinking, because she said, ‘I promise, but only as long as you continue to help.’

‘*I* will make the rules,’ he said firmly, and she agreed.

One Saturday night they were making their way back home through some of the meanest streets, when the sound of a scuffle was heard. Sarah ran towards the scene. Renton tried to stop her but she ducked under his arm. Where there was trouble there was likely to be an unguarded word.

A wealthily dressed man, who had obviously been visiting one of the prostitutes in the house in the darkest corner, was chasing a young woman. The young woman was Emily Tilt.

‘Come back! You promised you’d do as I say,’ Renton

growled as he ran after Sarah. But Sarah ran after the girl, whom Renton had not recognised. Emily lifted her skirts high with one hand and, holding on to her flower-decked hat with the other, charged towards the narrow alleyway which led to the safety of the crowds.

'Emily!' Sarah called in a coarse accent. 'Come this way!'

Emily saw the figure of a small boy and followed him down a poorly lit alleyway. Sarah darted between posts set to prevent carts from using the access, and through dark passages between factory walls. At the other end, the way was blocked. Sounds of pursuit were clearly heard as Emily caught up with Sarah. At once, Emily began to shout abuse.

'You stupid little fool! Now I'm trapped! Why didn't yer leave me alone? My friends would've 'elped. Never been trapped before, I ain't.' She raised a hand to clout Sarah but the hand was clasped, and Sarah pulled Emily closer to the wall.

'Stay there,' she instructed. With a bound that surprised Emily into obedience, Sarah pulled herself up on the high wall and, lying across it, reached down and offered her hands to Emily. Bracing herself with her feet, Sarah slowly hauled the girl up beside her. Sarah jumped lightly down on the other side, landing with knees bent as her mother had taught her, and motioned to Emily to do the same.

Emily wailed softly and shook her head. 'I'd rather be caught than killed.'

After a bit more coaxing, made urgent by the imminent arrival of the group supporting the man, Emily gingerly held on to the wall and lowered herself down to where Sarah's hands reached up to help her.

'You're only a couple of feet from the ground, I promise you,' Sarah whispered. 'Let go and don't stiffen yourself. Be a rag doll and you won't be hurt. But hurry!'

Sounds of feet and angry voices were all around them, as the man who chased her had gathered enthusiastic onlookers. At the end of the blocked alleyway, the footsteps had stopped, then receded. Sarah knew they were making their way around by another route and it was only moments before they were found. She wondered where Renton had got to. She was angry at herself for not waiting for him and angry that the extra time she had found for them was being lost by Emily's fear.

If Emily had jumped when Sarah pleaded, there was no doubt they would have got safely away, but the delay had given time for the man to get help from the law. As Emily picked herself up and straightened her floppy hat, two policemen ran towards them. In panic, Sarah ran straight into the arms of a third. Renton arrived in time to see her being led off, kicking and struggling, her voice the coarse copy of the tones of Emily Tilt.

'What can I say to you, Miss Sarah?' Henry Bannerman stared at the captive, now without her boy's cap, her dark hair flowing across her shoulders and framing her angry face.

'Just say good night and let me go home!' she demanded. 'This girl was being wrongly accused of stealing and I went to her aid. That's all there is to it. The man was a bully and tried to take advantage of one of the weaker sex. Now, tell Renton I am ready to go home.'

'Would you wait here for a moment, please? I'll have some tea sent in for you.'

'And for Miss Tilt!'

The two girls looked dishevelled and flushed. Sarah wore a haughty expression that hid her anxiety and fear. Her hair was tangled and she pushed it back in a nervous gesture. Emily's hair too was in disarray. Thick, red and curly, it fell about her face and no amount of coaxing would persuade it to lie neatly. They looked at each other and began to smile. Nervous tension made the release of pent-up emotion difficult to control and soon they were holding on to each other, helpless with laughter.

When Bannerman returned, he noticed the tears in Sarah's eyes and was gratified.

'I'm glad to see you're upset, Miss Sarah. Perhaps this will teach you a lesson. You could have been badly beaten by those men tonight. Your tears show me you're aware of what a narrow escape you've had.'

This was enough to send the girls into paroxysms of laughter, but, with her face hidden by her handkerchief, Sarah hoped it looked like remorse.

Bannerman left the tea and disappeared again.

'What a laugh!' Emily spluttered. 'You bein' a girl an' a lady at that! Fancy!'

'What a laugh, me bein' a girl, an' a lady at that. Fancy!' Sarah mimicked, and the laughter burst out anew.

'Should be on the 'alls, you should, an' no mistake.'

In spite of their superficial hilarity, Sarah waited anxiously for Henry Bannerman to come back. Time seemed to drag and she began to wonder whether he intended to keep her there until her father could be found. She had pleaded with him not to tell her father but he had been evasive in reply. Renton had not appeared. She had not seen him since he had tried to prevent her from assisting Emily. She hoped he had gone home and she had asked Uncle Henry to send someone there to fetch him.

'There's someone here to see you, Miss Sarah,' Bannerman said quietly as he re-entered the room.

Sarah looked up, hoping to see Renton. The welcoming smile faded to surprise as Giles followed Bannerman through the door.

'Giles! What are you doing here? How did you know?'

'Can I speak to Miss Sarah alone?' Giles asked.

The policeman nodded and, gruffly telling Emily to follow him, left the room.

'How did you know I was here?' Sarah repeated.

'Renton came for me. He explained what you were doing and that he had promised you not to tell your father. Sarah, this has to stop! It's much too dangerous. Think of your father if you won't think of yorself. He's already lost his wife and Margaret, and seen Isobelle destroyed. He couldn't bear to lose you as well.'

Sarah felt disappointment that he hadn't pleaded for her safety on his own behalf. Why couldn't he have said how he would feel if she were dead? Did she mean nothing at all to him?

He seemed to read the question on her small, anxious face, because he lowered his voice and added, 'And what about me? I would not have you even slightly harmed. I – I'm fond of you, Sarah. Surely you must know that?'

She thought of him with the beautifully dressed woman only a few nights previously and there was anger in her voice as she replied, 'I cannot ignore the tragedy of Margaret. We were such good friends as well as loving sisters. I miss her terribly.'

'I can understand how you feel. Believe me, I can. My feelings are almost as strong, but you cannot continue to face such dangers. Promise me you won't do anything as foolish as this again.'

'Will you persuade Uncle Henry not to tell my father?'

'I will try. But what about this woman, Emily Tilt?'

'What about her?'

'The man's watch is missing. Bannerman can't let her go, she's a thief.'

'She isn't! She's Renton's cousin.'

The illogical remark, coupled with the look of outrage on Sarah's face, caused him to smile. 'Being related to Renton does not make her immune from charges of thieving. There's enough evidence in her deep pockets to keep her in prison for years.'

'That man had been with a street woman. *She* must have taken his watch!'

The smile left Giles's face in an instant. 'Sarah! How do you know of such things?'

'Well? Was his watch found on her?'

'No . . . '

'And she has an explanation for the other things?'

Giles did not answer. His face had returned to its usual seriousness.

'Then you must help her. Please, Giles.' She appealed to him with all the guile she knew. The look she used on her father with such success also softened Giles's heart. She looked wild and elemental in the firelight: the weird dress and the untidy hair reinforced the urgency of her pleading.

'You will try?' she repeated, lowering her voice.

Giles nodded. 'For you, Sarah, I will try.'

Renton was waiting for them when they finally went outside. Giles's carriage took them as near to the house as they dared go, and slipping through the gardens they ran back into the house via the loosely fixed window just as the household began to wake.

* * *

Sarah sank into her soft bed gratefully. She was tired in every bone and muscle. She wondered if her father was in and for a while she tried to stay awake to listen for the sound of the hansom bringing him home, but her eyes became heavy and as soon as she closed them she slept.

She was woken soon after by loud, angry voices. She recognised the authoritative tone of her father, used to giving orders and making speeches, his voice boomed through the house insisting on being heard. She sat up in bed, wondering what was happening, and for a moment she feared some new catastrophe had struck the household. She began to reach for her gown, then memories of the night's escapades raced back to fill her mind with dread. She put on her night coat and sat on the edge of the bed. With only a cursory knock, her father marched into her room as she was lighting a candle.

'Where have you been?' he demanded.

Sarah stared into his angry face, almost unrecognisable in the shaking light of the small flame. He knew! Somehow, in spite of Henry Bannerman's promise, he had discovered what had happened. She groaned softly. Now it would be almost impossible for her to continue her search. She blustered for a moment, trying to deny that anything had happened, but soon saw it was hopeless.

'I came to see you when I got home,' he said, more calmly. 'I need to reassure myself you are safe these days. When I found your bed empty and your maid knew nothing, I went straight to find Henry Bannerman. Sarah, I was devastated!'

'I'm sorry, Father. I didn't think of you being frightened by my absence – '

'My daughter arrested!' The anger was back. With a shaking hand he lit the gas light on the wall and blew out the candle. 'My daughter, in the company of her coachman and a common thief! Well? What have you to say?'

'I've been trying to find the men who killed Margaret,' she said in a tremulous whisper. She began to cry. Slow sobs forced tears to trickle down her cheeks. 'I loved her so, and little Isobelle. I had to do something. Don't blame Renton. I *made* him help me,' she added as the thought of him being punished occurred to her.

'That I can believe!' Sir Jason snapped. 'Well, you've cost him his job. He no longer works for us. How do you feel about that?'

'Father! You can't!'

'I already have. He's packing at this moment.'

'But he's been with us all my life! I was brought up with Renton. He's like a brother. Please, you can't dismiss him. I am the one to be punished.' She lowered her head as she recognised the adamant tightening of her father's jaw. She was ashamed and angry with herself for the trouble she had brought to Renton.

She pleaded and cajoled, using every guile to persuade Sir Jason to change his mind. When everything failed, she made one request.

'May I ask one favour, please, Father?'

'Why should I even consider it?'

'Because you love me.'

'What is it?'

'Buy Renton his own cab. You owe him something, or at least I do. It's my fault he's lost his place. He only came to look after me. If he hadn't, who knows what might have happened? He's a loyal and true friend and because of those qualities he's lost his place. He risked it to watch over me.'

Her pleading finally had its reward. Renton was sent from the house, but a stable with a room above was promised to him and he was to be given the means of earning his living, a cab of his own.

'Father, you are the most kindly and generous of men. I love you and I'm so proud of you.' She hugged him.

Sir Jason stroked her hair, his eyes showing his pleasure at her genuine affection and love. Sarah's eyes glowed more brightly than his. She was already planning how she and Renton could use his cab for further escapades.

She lay wondering how her father had found out. He did not make a habit of looking in at her when he came home in the early hours, of that she was fairly certain. Henry Bannerman had promised to keep the affair from him. There was no possibility that Renton had talked to him. There was only Giles.

After a late breakfast, Sarah sent Edith with a note to Caroline, telling her she would call and take afternoon tea if that was convenient. Edith returned with the reply and at three-thirty they set out to walk the short distance to Hazelgrove Road, hoping, at that most likely time, to find Giles at home as well.

'My father found out what happened and now Renton has been dismissed and I've lost my friend,' she concluded, as she sipped tea and ate the thin coconut biscuits Caroline offered.

'Thank goodness he did!' Caroline had listened to the story in horror. 'It's a miracle you're still alive to tell me about it!'

'Is that why you told him, Giles?' Sarah asked sweetly, 'for my own safety?'

Giles could see no point in trying to deny it. 'Yes. I'm sorry, Sarah, and very sorry that Renton has been dismissed. But it's far too dangerous to you to continue.'

'Your honesty and concern cost Renton his place!'

'You'll get another coachman.'

'I don't want any other coachman!' Sarah was angry at his lack of understanding. 'Renton and I have been friends all our lives.'

'But he is only a servant . . . ' Caroline spoke hesitantly, aware of her friend's affection for Renton.

'He's more than that. When I was a child he stayed for lessons with me when I wouldn't work alone. He helped me when I couldn't understand. We used to meet in the garden and stables, he would go over and over the words with me, keeping me interested where no one else could.' She smiled at the memory and continued, 'I had music lessons but I never did become proficient at any instrument. Renton learned to play the pianoforte just by helping me with my lessons. So you see, it's him I am hurt for, not simply the loss of a coachman.'

'Your father has been exceptionally generous,' Giles said.

'My father is a generous and kindly man. And he knows how little Renton was to blame for what happened. It was my fault. All of it. And because my father was *told*,' she emphasised, 'I have lost Renton's friendship.'

'Renton is the son of your cook. Nothing more. Hardly a suitable companion for you,' Giles said stiffly, hurt at the strong criticism in defence of someone of the lower orders. 'I'm sorry, Sarah, but I still think what I did was right.'

Sarah stared at him but did not reply. He looked uncomfortable and she at once decided she had made enough of the subject.

'Has your Superintendent Bannerman any clues?' Caroline asked to break the uneasy silence.

'Uncle Henry thinks that gangs like those who killed my sister work on information given to them by someone who knows the movements of the family and the contents of the house, so the thieves know exactly where to go to find what they want to steal.'

'That seems likely,' Caroline said. She shuddered. 'Who knew we were all going away that weekend?'

'Servants,' Giles said firmly, trying to score on the previous argument. 'Everyone knows how unreliable servants are. They're a race apart.'

He blames Renton, Sarah thought, but she did not argue. Best if she said no more but let him think she had lost heart and would forget her search. Otherwise she would be so carefully watched that getting out to meet Renton would be impossible.

'Giles has suggested we go riding on Sunday morning after church. What do you say, Sarah?' Caroline asked. 'It's an age since we did.'

Sarah's eyes lit with pleasure. Horse riding was something she did well. 'I would love to.'

Arrangements were discussed and, as Edith and Sarah stepped out to walk home, Giles looked at Sarah, staring deeply into her eyes. 'I shall take you in the carriage. It is not safe for you to walk even the short distance between our houses so late in the day. And Sarah, as for that other matter, I hope we have an end to it. Will you give me your promise?'

His nearness and concern made her want to shout with joy, and she lowered her head so he could not see the excitement on her face. Giles thought she was being contrite.

'Perhaps the men will be captured soon,' she said, evading

a promise. 'Uncle Henry says they have a few ideas and plans. It's only a question of waiting for the men to come out of hiding, he said.'

'Let the police do their work. Henry Bannerman is a good man.'

Sarah nodded and gave him a devastating smile before he led her to where the carriage waited for her. The smile did not fade. The prospect of his company on the short journey home was a happy one and it was easy for her to forget how strongly she disapproved of him and his business.

Giles talked with obvious pleasure of the prospect of their Sunday-morning ride. Sarah's smile widened ever further as she imagined his horror and alarm if she used the opportunity to display some of her talents – if she stood on the horse's back or did any of the dozen tricks her expert equestrian mother had shown her. Giles believed her smile was pleasure in his company and he was warmed by it and even allowed his own features to soften a little.

Chapter Six

The ride with Giles did not take place. On the day before they were to have taken their horses through the park, Sarah and Sir Jason took Isobelle down to the country to her new home. The four-year-old was bundled up in blankets and, together with her favourite toys, put in the coach with Hannah, Edith, Sarah and her father.

Boxes and travelling trunks filled the luggage space at the top of the carriage and a basket of food was put in the back just in case of a breakdown. It was the middle of November, and to be caught in the lonely lanes without food would be distressing if not dangerous.

Hot bricks were wrapped in woollen cloth and stone bottles in which lemonade had been sold were filled with hot water and these were placed at their feet to help keep them warm. A tin in which a rag smouldered was surreptitiously handed to Isobelle by Mrs Baxter, the cook, to warm the child's hands. She smiled as she remembered giving Renton the same comfort when he had to sit in the cold church on winter Sundays.

Isobelle clutched the warm tin, snuggled down in the layers of warm blankets and looked around her. She seemed content but almost unaware of where she was. Her eyes were dull as if what she was looking at had no relevance for her. What went on in her head seemed to give her more pleasure than external things.

'I'm sorry I will have to leave her,' Hannah said, as she cuddled her charge. 'But I cannot live away from the town and I would be too unhappy trying to teach a child who, sadly, can no longer learn.'

Sir Jason did not answer. It was Sarah who said she understood, although she did not. How could Hannah, who had lived with Isobelle from her birth, abandon her?

'Your skills will be better used with your new family, Hannah,' Sarah said, seeing the sad and guilty expression on the woman's face.

The new coachman was old. Whiskers grew out of every pore, giving him a wild look, which was reinforced by his gruff, complaining voice. Only the hair on his head seemed to have lost none of its youthful vigour. It sprouted in all directions so his head was a furry tangle, through which blue eyes and a pink mouth were glimpsed.

Sarah hated him. She hated him because he was ill-mannered and grumpy and she hated him because he wasn't Renton.

The route they took to Houghton Hall took them towards Weatherby for a part of the way. Then they left it and turned in a more westerly direction at a place where the roads crossed. Sarah looked down the remembered road and thought of the weekend party, of climbing Hare's Hill with Giles, and of his vague mention of living in the country permanently.

Sir Jason was silent for most of the journey. Only when they stopped at a farmhouse for food did he relax and talk easily to them. But it seemed to Sarah that it was an effort to be polite and sociable. He seemed relieved when they all returned to their seats and he could sink once more into silence.

The farm where Isobelle was to stay was not large, but Sarah noticed that the yards were well brushed and the fences around it were sturdy and well kept. The house and the cattle sheds were all one building. As she stood looking about her, a movement caught her eye and she saw a young boy peering at her from the corner of the cowshed. She called good day, but at once the boy vanished.

'Peter?' a rather harsh voice called. The boy popped out again and looked towards the door of the house. 'Fetch a freshly drawn pail of water! These ladies and gentlemen will need a good, warming cup of tea.'

Once more the boy disappeared, and Sarah heard the sound of water rushing into a pail.

Inside, a huge fire burned in the flagstoned kitchen and gave a welcoming warmth after the cold journey. From hooks in the ceiling, a ham and several lengths of fat bacon hung. Herbs were also suspended in bunches to dry. A pantry adjoining the kitchen was filled with jams, pickles and preserves, all neatly arranged in rows. Everywhere was clean and shiny and attempts had been made to make the functional room pretty with a frill of fine cretonne around the mantelshelf, cushions in the wooden armchairs and curtains of flowery cotton over the window.

The fireplace, with large armchairs pushed close to the warmth, was the centre of the place, where all the cooking was done. Although there was a small room called the sitting room, with a few chairs and a table on which a bowl of daffodil bulbs sat, Sarah guessed that it was in the big kitchen that the occupants spent their spare time.

'Occupants? Bless you, my lady. There ain't no other occupants, only me,' said Mrs Brandon, her ample bosom held supported by two brawny arms. 'Farmer and farmer's wife, you might say. There's only Peter to help when times is extra busy. Most days there's no one to talk to but my animals. That's why I'll be so glad to have your little maid to keep me company. A child is the best company of all, so's my experience.'

The black kettle began to spout steam and Mrs Brandon bent over to pour water into the teapot, her large body blocking out all sight of the fire. She stood up and hollered for Peter. Sarah felt the impulse to cover her ears against the noise.

'While the tea's a brewing, would you like to have a look around at the farm?' Mrs Brandon offered. 'Leave the little maid with me, give her a chance to get to know me. Ice is soon broken between me and children. Off you go. Peter?' she shouted again, and instructed the still unseen boy to act as their guide, changing his name at times to Pigpen.

The long building had two storeys and there was an opening two thirds of the way along it. But this, as Sarah and her father discovered, did not separate the house from the cattle. The gap was a storage area in which turnips were piled up and partly covered with a tarpaulin.

'It's where we does the winnowing, come harvest,' Mrs Brandon said as she followed them, still calling at intervals for Peter.

The farm was mixed, some fields producing cereals, some planted with food for the cattle. There was a small herd of cows, and hens and a jaunty cockerel ran around the yard. Sheep roam the hills sloping up to the west and a stream filled a pond on which a few ducks lived.

'You manage this all alone?' Sir Jason asked. 'It seems to be enough for several men.'

'I employs men, but only on a temporary arrangement,' Mrs Brandon said. 'That way it's much cheaper, so's my experience.'

They were offered ham, potatoes boiled in their skins, and some vegetable which Sarah suspected was the same as that fed to the cattle. Then they were invited to look at Isobelle's room.

Sir Jason was still very quiet. Sarah saw him watching Isobelle and looking around him as if assessing the suitability of the place, and perhaps, she thought, trying to convince himself it was the best thing for her. It was certainly cleaner and brighter than she had expected, but she still hoped her father would change his mind and take Isobelle back to London with them.

Isobelle's room was painted yellow and had two windows around which bright floral curtains hung. One window overlooked the front yard and in the distance, the road. The other, to Sarah's surprise, looked down on the cattle.

'Young people like animals, or so's my experience.' Mrs Brandon smiled a fat smile. 'Always happier when they have the care of a few animals. Isobelle's sure to want to help me feed the cows of a morning, and help me find the eggs, won't you, my precious maid?'

Sarah nodded, but she thought the woman was crazy. Who would want to look out and see cows? Huge, smelly creatures! It would be like sharing a room with them. She looked at her father, but he seemed unaware of the discussion. He was staring at Isobelle as if drinking in the sight of her to remember once he returned to his home without her.

'If she doesn't like looking at those – animals,' Sarah said, 'you will find her a different room, won't you? Now if it were horses she could see – '

'Horses?' Mrs Brandon laughed. 'We don't have no horses, my dear. It's bullocks we use round here. Less trouble they are; stronger and less cost to feed. And food when they're finished.'

Sarah found the oxen more horrifying than the cows, but Isobelle seemed to enjoy touching their thick, warm coats and put out her hand to allow their steamy breath to touch it. Isobelle also responded to the cats. There seemed to be dozens of them. The little girl stretched out to stroke their coats and for the first time they saw some animation in her face. At home they only had one cat and that one was confined to the kitchen.

Sir Jason had arranged for them all to stay overnight, and Sarah found she had a room high up in the attic with a window jutting out from the tiles. The bed was large and stuffed with hay. Unable to sleep, she sat on the windowsill looking out into the black night.

She wished Renton were with them. Unrecognisable noises, which he would have been able to explain, unnerved her. This was a different life and she began to think about Giles's remark about town people always being thankful to return to the lights and noise of their homes.

The next morning Sarah dressed and rose early, not waiting for Edith to attend to her, and went to the kitchen where already the fire roared and a kettle sang on the hob. She was offered bread and milk, which she ate hungrily before going outside. The boy Peter was scraping ice from the pond and Sarah saw for the first time how ragged his clothes were. His boots were broken and tied with string. He sensed her presence as she approached him, and turned. Then she recognised him. It was the boy she had rescued from the roof. He must labour for several places, she decided, but how and where did he live?

The coachman had been given a blanket to sleep in one of the barns and he was not pleased. Sarah and Edith, who had joined her, heard his complaints long before they saw him emerge from the hayloft.

'Never slept a wink,' he groaned.

'I slept in the barn next along and he was a-snoring fit to rattle the timbers as soon as he lay down,' Mrs Brandon whispered. 'Folks who say they never sleep is usually the best sleepers of all, so's my experience.'

'Where does young Peter live, Mrs Brandon?' Sarah asked when they were all sitting down to breakfast. 'I thought I recognised him from when I stayed at Weatherby, a few miles from here.'

'Pigpen, we calls him.' Mrs Brandon smiled. 'He lives in my barn mostly. Does work here, there and anywhere. I do fancy he worked a while at Weatherby, but that's only occasional, like most places. Rich people like them only come down here for visits, so there's no regular work.'

It was very different from the home farm at Houghton Hall, which was Sarah's only other experience of the country. There they employed a large number of people and they all lived in small, well-kept cottages and slept in beds, not in barns. Houghton Hall was a large estate and there were several farms included, but Sarah had never explored them. Perhaps there were others as small and poor as this one. Although, from the sight of the well-stocked larder and rafters, Mrs Brandon was adequately fed. She hoped the boy was included in the comfort of a full belly.

'Father, before we go, can I climb the hill behind the farm and look at the view?' Sarah asked.

Sir Jason agreed, and decided he would go as well. They changed into walking clothes and, with a stick to help them, climbed the steep, muddy hill where sheep wandered and chewed thc damp grass. The weather was chilly and rain threatened, but they enjoyed the exercise.

At the top, Sarah stared in amazement. They were on Hare Hill, and looking down on the house and lake belonging to Giles.

'I had no idea we were so near Weatherby,' she said.

'Neither had I, but you recall Giles saying he would be near enough to call and enquire after Isobelle, and invited you to stay as often as you wished.'

'I wonder if anyone is there.'

'We haven't time to call, Sarah.'

She pointed. 'Look! I can see carriages arriving. What an odd time to come, in the middle of Sunday when most are preparing to leave.' They watched as boxes were unloaded from the coaches but saw no one apart from the drivers alight. 'How curious!'

'Come on, Sarah, we mustn't show our inquisitiveness so boldly.'

Reluctantly Sarah turned away. It would have been nice to have seen Giles. Perhaps his carriage would meet theirs and they would have company on the journey home.

Taking a packed lunch – bacon, and sausages cut from strings hanging beside the ham and cooked on the fire in an enormous frying pan, and some freshly baked bread – they set off. Leaving Isobelle was distressing, but Sarah held back tears, knowing her father needed help to cope with the parting. Isobelle was standing in the yard beside Mrs Brandon and was nursing a tabby cat, oblivious of the near departure.

It began to rain almost as soon as they started off, and their last sight of the farm was gloomy because of it. All the way home, the coachman drove the horses at an unfair pace and complained about the dangers of highwaymen and the difficulty of finding his way in the semidark. Sarah ignored his voice after a while and, trying to forget the loss of her sister, began dreaming about Giles. She kept glancing back, ignoring groans about the cold draught as she leaned out, hoping his carriage would accompany them through the dangers of the empty lanes. It must have been Giles's carriage she had seen from the top of Hare Hill. Who else would be visiting Weatherby at such a time?

The London house seemed larger and emptier than when they had left it. Sarah went to her room and changed from travelling clothes with the assistance of Edith, and bathed and dressed for dinner with a heavy sadness on her.

She stopped on the way down to dine and looked into Margaret's neat, cold and empty room. All her belongings had been dispersed: some given to the servants, others to be sold for a charity that provided an occasional dinner for the poor of the city.

She thought of the posters and could see the men's faces in her mind's eye without having to look at the artist's impression. She would know them when she saw them. Finding them was going to be her sole occupation. She was tired, and if it was not for the thought of her father dining alone, she would have asked for a tray to be sent up. Tonight she needed sleep, but tomorrow she would find Renton and they would make plans for renewing their search. The loss of Isobelle had reinforced her determination.

When the carriage had left the farmhouse which was Isobelle's new home, Mrs Brandon took the child upstairs to the room in which her trunk of clothes had been placed.

'Come, my precious maid, time to change out of those fine clothes of yours and dress like is proper for a country girl. That's what you are now and clothes have to be fitting for what you are if you want to be happy, so's my experience.'

Isobelle's beautiful clothes were taken off and replaced with a simple linen smock and a bonnet. Shoes made of rough leather, which buttoned up to reach her knees, took the place of the soft slippers she wore. All the time, Mrs Brandon spoke softly to her and the little girl allowed her to change her clothes without complaint.

When Isobelle was dressed in the country clothes Mrs Brandon had made in readiness for her, she was sent to play downstairs and the clothes she arrived in were carefully folded and wrapped in pieces of old blanket before being placed in piles on the floor. Isobelle's trunk was emptied, the contents sorted into piles, and the whole lot was carried downstairs and piled onto a handcart.

'Tomorrow,' Mrs Brandon said aloud, 'I'll take that lot to the market. Get a good price for most of it. People'll always pay for quality, so's my experience.'

'Taking her now, are you?' Peter asked, tilting his head to where Isobelle was playing happily with the cats.

'Yes. No point feeding her when I'm paying another to do it, now is there?' she answered amiably.

She threw a thick shawl over her hefty shoulders and found another, smaller one for Isobelle.

'Come, my precious, come and meet some new friends. You'll enjoy Mrs Starkly, she's got cats too, bigger than ours, though not such good ratters.'

She chattered away, not expecting or receiving any response, and led Isobelle across fields, through a long stretch of woodland, over a stream to a small cottage, some distance from the farm.

'Mrs Starkly? You at home?' she called, poking her head around the door, which stood open to let out the smoke.

A neatly dressed woman with grey hair folded into a bun at the back of her head, came to the door and smiled a welcome.

'Mrs Brandon! Do come inside. Will you take a small helping of ale?' Mrs Starkly smiled and offered a hand to Isobelle, who looked around the tiny room, searching for the cats she had been promised.

'Cats?' Isobelle asked in a low, grating voice. 'Cats?' Peering through the smoke she looked around her, stepping further into the room.

A quarter of the single room was taken up with a bed, around which curtains hung. Below it, a truckle bed showed, neatly covered with blankets crocheted from many-coloured wools. At the far end a fire burned smokily on the floor; there was no hearth. Above it, a fire-crane dangled a kettle over its sullen heat, and all around it were the tools needed to cook. There was little furniture and what there was had been roughly made from wood. A wooden settle stood near the fire and on the solitary cushion sat a large tabby. Isobelle walked up and began stroking him. He arched his back against her hand and a soft, growling purr issued from his pink mouth.

At the door, Mrs Brandon refused the ale.

'Thank you kindly, Mrs Starkly, but I have to get back. There's all the animals I borrowed, and all the fine curtains and drapery to take down and return to their boxes. That boy Peter won't do half of what he's supposed to if I'm not there to push him on.'

Mrs Starkly nodded in sympathy and held out her hand. 'If you'll just be paying me for the girl's keep, I'll let you go.'

Digging deeply into the pocket of her shawl, Mrs Brandon took out two shillings in small coins and counted it slowly into the offered hand. 'I'll bring you more as her father sends it, Mrs Starkly,' she promised. With a wave at the little girl, who was still playing with the cat, she left to hurry home and drive the cows and sheep back to their rightful owners before it was too dark to see.

When he had finished the chores he did for Mrs Brandon, on the following day, Peter walked to Mrs Starkly's tiny cottage to see the girl. He was curious about her. From conversations between the two women, he had gathered she was mad. He had never seen a mad girl before. He watched her as she sat outside playing with the cat. The animal was old and past playing with the string and balls of mud the girl offered him, but occasionally it would leap, grab the toy and kick with its back legs, and Peter heard a noise he recognised as low laughter.

She saw him, and stared in a way that made him feel uncomfortable. Backing away from her, he ran back to the barn in Mrs Brandon's farm he looked upon as his home.

Gradually, over the following days, he became less afraid and they began to spend a little time in each other's company, Peter talking and, occasionally, Isobelle responding. She was more like a puppy than a girl, he thought with a grin. But something about her drew him back and soon he was spending most of his spare moments with her and the tabby cat, who was her constant companion.

They began to walk around the fields and explore in procession. First Peter, then Isobelle, and then the cat. Peter chatted to her all the time, the pleasure in her companionship strangely satisfying. He explained about the work on the farm, and the state of the countryside, and gave a picture of what it would be when spring revived the flowers and leaves. She did not speak but would occasionally turn and make soft murmuring sounds towards the cat, as if she were trying to pass back the information as Peter had done. Peter was very happy. Isobelle seemed, as far as he could tell, quite content.

* * *

The wind blew across the corner where Emily stood with her basket of flowers. She shivered and pulled her coats and shawl more tightly around her shoulders.

'Why don't yer call it a day, Emily? You look perished,' Maggs said. She threw a hot chestnut for the girl to catch. Emily was so stiff and chilled she missed it and had to bend down to rescue it from the ground.

'I suppose I might as well, I don't think there'll be many hanging about tonight.' Emily couldn't tell Maggs that she was waiting for the man to come. She had had quite a good day, selling small bunches of holly besides her flowers. If it wasn't for the disappointment of not seeing the man, she would have gone home long ago.

The man had continued to come each evening to buy his flower and occasionally Emily had seen him during the day. He would stand for a moment before bowing and walking on. But tonight he was late and she began to realise he would not come. She became more anxious as the time passed and glanced continuously at the corner around which he usually appeared.

She held out her last few bunches and the solitary buttonhole until at last, hope gone, she decided to go home. The bottom of her feet felt like pieces of slate and the numbing cold reached up her legs, making her knees stiff and unwilling to function. As she bent to pick up her empty basket and drop the last flowers into it, Maggs said:

'Shame 'e ain't come. Never mind, there's always tomorrer.' She laughed and added, 'Don't think I ain't noticed. But 'e's not fer the likes of you, Emily. A gentleman like 'im wouldn't take up with a girl who drinks, and sells flowers fer a living. Dreamin',' she went on in a low warning voice, 'dreamin's dangerous.'

A voice called Emily as she set off with her basket against her side, but she hurried on. Then she heard footsteps running and the voice repeated, 'I say, you, young woman. Just a moment.'

'No chance, mate,' Emily shouted back. 'Yer luck's out tonight.'

The young man caught up with her and touched her arm. Emily shook him off angrily.

'Just you leave me alone or I'll shout fer the Peelers!'

'I have a message for you. It's from Jarvis.'

'Oh yeh?' Emily sneered. 'And who might Jarvis be, supposing I care?'

The young man hesitated. 'I understand he buys a flower from you every night.'

Emily's heart lurched and she turned to look at the young man, staring at him curiously.

'I didn't know his name.' She took the flower from her basket. 'I saved his flower. Here, you take it for him.' She thrust the flower into the young man's hand and turned to go. She longed to ask why Jarvis hadn't come. Was he ill? Or was it the end of his regular visits? What was the message? She was too nervous to ask anything of this rather pompous young man.

'Don't you want to know his message?'

'If you like.'

'He asked if you would like to deliver his flower to him, as he is too unwell to come to collect it.'

Suspicion flared in Emily. 'What? At this time of night? What d'you take me for then?'

'Oh no. Not tonight, he wouldn't dream – er . . . he thought perhaps tomorrow. Look, here's the address, and the name is Jarvis – er, Williamson.' The young man seemed to hesitate over the name, a point Emily's sharp mind noticed. 'He said he would expect you at eleven.'

Emily stared at the paper as the young man hurried away towards the more brightly lit streets, anxious to leave the shadows of the side street down which Emily had led him. She couldn't read the address under the poor lighting so she put the piece of paper in a pocket and hurried on home, her thoughts in turmoil. She blessed the time she had spent in the workhouse, for without the teaching she received there, she would have been unable to read it.

The address was a room above a shop. The same young man showed her up and she grasped her cloak nervously as she climbed the stairs. Her sharp eyes noticed the clean and comfortable furnishings on the landing and also the plate which proclaimed it to be the residence of a Dr Flint.

He was lying on a sofa and was obviously in fever. His face

was flushed, his expression was one of fatigue, and she thought how beautiful he was. His eyes opened and he smiled a greeting. The servant helped him to sit up against cushions and then he held out a slim, smooth hand for her to take. She hesitantly proffered her red and swollen one before quickly hiding it again in her pocket.

'Forgive me for bothering you like this,' he said, and his voice was quiet, as if he were very tired. 'Today I have been ill and I thought if you came to see me, I would soon be well again.'

Emily was still standing, wondering what to do. Should she take a seat or wait until asked? Should she remove her cloak or just loosen it?

'No trouble,' she said. 'I wondered what had happened to you when you was late.'

The servant placed a chair beside the sofa and left the room. Nervously, Emily sat down. She looked around her at the expensive desk and upholstered chairs and more books than she had ever seen in her life. Like a bookshop it was.

'You read all these books, have you?'

'Most of them. Some are factual books, there to refer to when needed.'

They sat for a while and Emily gradually relaxed. Jarvis asked her questions about her life and she gave him a carefully edited version, making sure she pronounced all her aitches. She didn't know much, but she was aware that gentlemen considered it important.

'I missed seeing you, Emily,' he said, and she saw the longing in his eyes, now fiery with fever. 'I would be sad not to have our transaction to look forward to each evening.'

Jarvis watched the flush of pleasure spread over her young face. She will do, he thought, inwardly smiling. Yes, Emily Tilt, flower girl, will do very nicely. Besotted with me as she obviously is, she'll be easy to manipulate and persuade. And short-term, she will be a pleasant diversion.

Emily had been there for about half an hour when the servant returned and, coughing politely, announced it was time for a posset and perhaps a little rest. Emily jumped out of her chair, embarrassed at the thought she had overstayed her welcome. Then she was angry with herself for jumping up so quickly and showing she had no idea how to behave in company. One day I'll learn, she promised herself.

Going home after the visit, she wondered about the man who called himself Jarvis Williamson. From the pictures, the furniture and the rooms themselves, complete with servant, she thought he must be a man of importance. But there were niggles of doubt. There was the doctor's plate in a different name, for instance. He could have just moved in and not had a chance to change the plate, or he could be simply borrowing the rooms for a while. For a fleeting moment the thought occurred to her that he might be using the room dishonestly, while the real owner was away. No. How could she think it for a moment? What would be the point? He didn't have to do that much to impress Emily Tilt, flower girl!

After several days, his visits began again. Although he stayed for a few moments after buying his flower, he again said little more than 'thank you'. She decided that he loved her but realised the position was a hopeless one and would gradually fade from her life. But one day they met in circumstances that changed their relationship completely.

Jarvis was the victim of a pickpocket. Not only was his pocketbook with all his money taken, the thief having slit open his jacket to relieve him of it, the bunch of keys had also gone. He had an appointment with some people from whom he intended to make a lot of money, but he could not go without cash to buy drinks and food, nor could he meet them in the clothes he was wearing.

He could break into the house in which he had a temporary room, but at this time of day, it would have looked suspicious, and he had no desire to attract any attention to himself.

His clothes and his spare cash were out of his reach. He would have to resort to something he had not practised for several years. He hoped he had not lost the skill. He was furious. He, who had lived on what he could take from the pockets of the rich since he had been a child, had been robbed. If he ever discovered who it was, he would enjoy teaching him never to do it again.

He began to move to where the crowds were thickest, looking for a likely mark. His heart beat wildly. How stupid if all he had worked for was lost by this foolish situation.

A crowd were gathered around a shop window and Jarvis walked slowly, casually, to join them.

Emily was walking through the Seven Dials district towards Covent Garden, where she went to buy her flowers each morning. But instead of carrying her basket, she was draped in a voluminous cape, in which her hand was poised, hoping to relieve some unwary shopper of a purse or a wallet. The wish for a house of her own had become an obsession. She had been patiently saving for years, but now she felt it was urgent. Her thoughts of Jarvis had emboldened her to believe she *could* win the love of someone like him, once she was secure and confident enough. So the hand which had usually been cautious became more daring in her determination to make the dream come true.

She joined crowds around a street fight and around shop windows, where passers-by had been attracted by a new display and were less intent on protecting their own valuables, making it easy for Emily to dip a few pockets.

As she walked away from each successful theft, she wriggled around in her clothes and transferred her collection to a pocket deep within the layers of dresses and coats. As her steps turned to the Nethersken, where a dealer would be waiting to exchange her goods for cash, she heard shouts of 'Thief!'

'Pickpocket!'

First one voice, then several, and the shouts changed to calls for police. The voices, and then the sound of the Peeler's whistle being frantically blown for assistance, chilled her blood. Someone must have seen her last dip and found a policeman.

Her mind sharpened and her eyes flashed about her, deciding on the quickest and safest escape. The area was one she knew well and as she made her way, slowly at first, to the tumbled-down alley that would lead her to the jumble of buildings in which the Nethersken was situated, she realised the sounds were not coming any nearer. Although her instincts still told her to get away, her curiosity was roused. Glancing back from the shelter of a doorway, she saw a man who was obviously the cause of the excitement. Tall, thin and poorly dressed, he was struggling with two men, while the tall hat of a Peeler could be seen above the crowd as the lawman made his way towards them, blowing his whistle to attract help. Emily picked up a few stones and pelted them at the tall hat, as others were doing. Then she realised the man being chased was her man – Jarvis Williamson, or whatever his real name was!

Ignoring the danger of being caught with her pockets full of stolen goods, she quickly made her way towards him, shouting and screaming and pushing at the tall uniformed man as he tried to get hold of the struggling Jarvis. Other people, seeing Emily's concern, joined in the scuffle and soon Jarvis was able to escape. Emily ran back to the alley-way as soon as she saw he was safe.

She waited in the shadow of a wall while the crowd that had gathered held the Peeler in a game of teasing, blocking his escape when he tried to get out of the circle of jeering faces. The laughter and shouting grew louder as the Peeler became angrier. The crowd danced back as he hit out and danced in again as he tried to push his way to freedom.

Emily found Jarvis hiding in the bushes around a half-demolished shed. At first he began to bluster and make excuses, denying any attempt at thieving, but Emily just stared at him and smiled. She led him swiftly through the maze of walls, bridges and buildings back to St Giles's. He was a thief! She laughed with happiness. As a thief he was no longer out of reach. Fine clothes or not, he was not a grand fellow from a grand house. That room with the doctor's plate! There was no doubt in her mind now that it was borrowed without permission.

Jarvis's excuses became lamer as he saw the smile on Emily's face widen. When they were far enough away from the Peeler to feel safe, Emily drew from a pocket a small object which she slowly dropped into his hand. He recognised the Peeler's whistle.

The smile on Emily's face was reflected in his and he gave up all pretence. They looked and they knew, and threw their arms about each other and met in a long-awaited kiss.

Chapter Seven

The street was dark and wet. Fog moved over the drab buildings, causing people to cough and bend forward in an attempt to avoid its stifling odours. The colour changed as it moved, the yellow lights from shop doorways shining weakly through its fingers. Apart from the soft footsteps of an occasional passer-by and a news-sheet-seller's cries of the latest killings and robberies, there was little sound.

Most of the shops had already closed, and as Sarah watched from the dark interior of the cab, she shivered at the thought of walking in these dark and dangerous places. Renton had heard that one of the men they sought frequented a coffee stall nearby, and from Henry Bannerman they had learned that the stall owner was suspected of passing information between thieves and fences.

'There he is,' Renton whispered. He pointed to the man he had seen selling the gold tie pin. The man was large, and his shoulders were slightly rounded so he walked with arms swinging loosely from his shoulders.

They had seen the man three times before but had failed to follow him to where the police could find him. Renton knew the streets well but even he was lost in the maze of buildings when trying to learn where the man slept. He suspected there was more than one home where he could find a night's shelter and no explanations needed.

Renton, having driven Sir Jason's carriage for several years and, before that, worked as an errand boy, was well known to all the hansom-cab owners and to the coachmen of most of the big houses. Through his network of spies he had gleaned a great deal of information about their quarry, but, slippery and with a strong instinct for personal danger, the man had always eluded them.

Renton stood beside his cab, where he was able to talk easily to Sarah waiting inside. She looked across the street and saw the man disappear into the fog-shrouded churchyard. They waited until a small boy appeared and in the light of a gas lamp they saw him stealthily creeping along the pavement following the man they knew as Arthur. He was keeping to the shadows and it was obvious from the way he was turning his head he was looking for someone. Sadly, Sarah recognised him as a boy who had once worked for them and whom her father had sacked for stealing. Perhaps he was the one who sold information? It was a moment's thought, but she felt a relief that perhaps Giles was not responsible after all.

Renton waited silently, watching until the boy slipped into the churchyard entrance between shops, and then he followed him. Sarah waited a few moments, then stepped out of the protection of the hansom cab and went after him.

She ran first to a young child selling news-sheets and with a half-sovereign persuaded him to part with the pile. The child felt the edge of the coin suspiciously to make sure it was not a doctored farthing before releasing his hold on the pages. Sarah ran across the road in her boy's clothes, a cap hiding her long hair, and, in the abrasive voice of the seller, shouted the headlines and pretended to chase a prospective customer.

In the churchyard, a short whisper from Renton stopped her.

'I'll lock him in the cab until we get back. Take care. Don't take any chances, Sarah.' He had the boy who had followed Arthur held firmly, and was tying him up to prevent him shouting. Sarah did not reply. She ran on in the gloom and danger of the churchyard, calling, as if to sell her papers was her only thought.

The lights were far behind her and the possibility of a policeman was slight. She slowed and began to notice the uneasy quiet and the unrecognisable shapes that loomed up near her in the swirling fog. She stifled a scream with difficulty as a huge figure appeared at her side, jumping from the shadow of a gravestone with a suddenness that seemed to stop her heart.

' 'Ere, where you goin'?' The bruised and battered face of Arthur bent close to her own as the man peered at her.

'I'm Jim Slater's mate. 'E sent me to 'elp you 'cos 'e's 'urt himself.'

'Got sharp eyes an' ears, 'ave yer?'

'Yeh, an' fast feet,' she answered boldly.

'All right, I'll try yer.'

It took them twenty minutes to reach their destination. All the time, Sarah kept up a constant chatter. She told Arthur of her varied if imaginary career, hoping her boy's voice would carry far enough for Renton to hear and follow. Her companion cuffed her from time to time and warned her to be quiet, but she paused only a moment before continuing her stories.

The temptation to glance behind to see whether Renton was following was strong, but she knew that one wrong move and she would be killed without being given a chance to explain. With a death sentence hanging over them, criminals like Arthur usually left no one to talk.

Another man appeared silently beside her. With one dangerous man on each side, Sarah was unable to suppress a shiver of fear, recognising the face of Will the Ratman.

'I think we're bein' followed,' the newcomer said.

Immediately Arthur grabbed Sarah's neck with a large hand. 'What are you up to, boy?' he growled.

'Nothin'. I ain't done nothin',' Sarah wailed in an aggrieved voice. 'I didn't get us followed, I swear. Let go! If you 'urt me I can't work and I don't eat if I don't work, do I?' She hoped the words would help Renton if he was in hearing distance.

'I don't trust you.'

'I don't trust you neither. Blamin' me for everyone what walks through the churchyard. Public path, ain't it?'

'What d'yer think?' Arthur asked his companion.

'I won't do nothin' to bring the Peelers. I can't take no more prison. Please, I need a job. Please!'

The face of Arthur was close to hers and she could smell

the stale drink on his breath. She hoped he couldn't smell soap on her skin. Thank goodness she had used soap from the kitchen. Her heart was racing and her inner voice was praying that Renton was able to follow. She had always hated fog, because it brought the stench of the river and inhibited visibility, but tonight she was thankful for its help in hiding Renton.

The men held her and held a whispered discussion, then they both nodded.

'Come on, and don't play no trick or you'll never 'ave a chance to play another!'

She walked on between the two men. Although not reaching their shoulders, she tried to walk jauntily, hiding her fear. They stopped at a large detached house called Greenfields. No light showed, and the two men quickly opened a ground-floor window that had obviously been left unfastened for them, and slipped inside. Leaning back out, Arthur whispered, 'One call for a cab, and two for a walker. Right?'

Sarah nodded. 'I'm goin' to be the best crow you ever 'ad.'

The silence after the men had disappeared inside the house almost unnerved her. There was not even the distant sounds of horses hooves. The fog seemed to blanket her completely from the rest of the world. She coughed carefully, twice, then an echoing cough came from out of the darkness. Renton appeared beside her and she rested a hand on his arm in relief.

'I'll follow a while longer. Then, when we know where they live, I'll go for help,' he whispered. But before he could be swallowed up once more by the night, a hand grabbed his arm and he turned to find his way blocked by a burly man. Renton at once aimed a blow at the man's stomach but Arthur didn't flinch. Turning to face the same way as his captor, Renton kicked back savagely at the man's shin with his heel and this time the man relaxed his hold.

Sarah stayed where she was until the men, who had gone off in pursuit of Renton, came back empty-handed.

'I didn't see 'im in time to whistle. Came at me quiet, he did. But 'e only wanted to buy a sheet.' Sarah showed the news-sheets she still carried. A blow to the side of her head made her eyes close on a bevy of stars such as London had not seen for years, and with a sickness filling her stomach, she fell to the ground.

She woke to the strange sensation of being carried under a thick, muscled arm, her head and feet almost dragging the ground. She had no idea how long she had been unconscious but guessed from the familiar area that it had been only a few moments. They were still in the garden of the house they had robbed. Arthur's partner had disappeared and of Renton there was no sign. She hoped he was safe and able to fetch help.

She remained slack and relaxed in her unusual position, thinking that if Arthur thought her still unconscious, she was safe. They passed through silent streets, narrow and dark, and eventually a door creaked open and she was carried through a large, warm room full of the smell of unwashed people and stale food. From the room, they went into a dark passage. She was at last set on her feet and made to walk along the stinking, slippery floor between damp walls, lit by the candle the man had picked up in the room as they had passed through.

'It wasn't my fault,' Sarah complained, still in her young boy's voice.

'Maybe it wasn't, maybe it was,' her companion growled. 'You'll stay here 'til I decide.'

She was pushed roughly through a doorway and fell on the floor. The door closed and a heavy bar dropped into position. She knew there was no way of opening it and from the brief glimpse she had had before the candlelight had been lost, she was in a coal cellar. As her eyes became accustomed to the dark, a dim light showed through a grating high overhead. The floor was slimy and Sarah curled her mouth at the filth on which she lay.

Her head ached and the sickness she still felt made her weak, but she forced herself to stand up and explore her prison. There was a small pile of coal, but not enough to enable her to climb up and reach the small grating temptingly showing above. Without much hope, she coughed once, then twice, and waited for a response. To her surprise and relief an answering cough echoed her own. The dim light darkened as Renton's head appeared in the grating.

'I'm sorry, I couldn't go for help. I thought it more important not to lose you.'

'Then go now. I don't expect they'll be back before morning. Please hurry, Renton.'

Once she knew Renton had gone, fear wrapped itself around her like a choking blanket. The cellar, its corners utterly black, seemed to threaten her with all the ghosts and devils she had ever imagined. She was completely alone and the only person to help her was gone from her.

She stood, hardly daring to breathe, her ears tuned to catch the slightest sound, her heart drumming. She began to shiver and knew it was fright rather than the cold making her limbs tremble.

Why was she here? She thought longingly of her warm, safe room with Edith within call, and of the love that had always surrounded her. What had dulled her mind so much she could end up in a sordid place like this with a man like Arthur likely to open the door any moment and treat her with who knows what cruelty?

The idea of helping Margaret was unbelievably stupid. How would it help her or little Isobelle if Sarah were to die as well? And what of her father? How would he survive another loss? Tears were near but she deliberately forced them away. She was Sarah Lindhurst Ayres and would get out of this somehow. But, she thought as she glanced up at the round coal hole above her, I hope Renton comes back soon.

She forced herself to sit down on the floor, trying not to imagine what was there, and tensed and relaxed her muscles, determined not to be unprepared when the time came for action. She wondered what her father would think if he could see her situation; dressed as a boy, locked in a cellar in the middle of the night and perched precariously on a pile of coal lumps to avoid the mess on the floor. It seemed years since she had attended afternoon teas with Caroline, wearing a smart tea gown and with her long hair carefully arranged by Edith, not stuffed under a scruffy cap. She knew there was a strong possibility she would never spend an afternoon with Caroline again.

Unless Renton could find help quickly and convince someone of the truth of his story, she believed Arthur and his companions would kill her. Sadly, she wondered whether Giles would care. She deliberately forced her mind to imagine herself and Giles being betrothed. She built up the scene in her mind, invented his words and her own response. Then cold began to stiffen her limbs and she let the daydream slip away, and began to exercise again to drive away the damp chill that threatened to disable her and weaken her chance of escape.

It seemed like an hour before Renton returned. The darkness with its mysterious sounds that could be rats, mice, or the cautious re-entry of Arthur filled her with tension in spite of her determined exercising. She felt her strength draining with every movement she heard.

At last the dim light showed a shadow and Renton was back.

'I brought two constables, but one is going back for reinforcements,' he whispered.

'How much longer will I have to wait?' She tried not to allow her voice to waver.

'They shouldn't be long, sonny. Be brave for a while longer,' the slow, reassuring voice of the constable told her. She smiled in the dark at the assumption she was a boy. Thank goodness Renton had done what she had asked and continued with the pretence! She felt optimistic now that the adventure might yet end happily.

She could face danger – her determination to avenge Margaret and Isobelle gave her the necessary strength – but the thought of trying to explain to everyone was something she dreaded. 'I'm not scared, only a bit cold,' she answered the constable. But it was Renton's head at the grating.

'Move away from the middle of the floor,' he whispered. 'I'm coming down to join you.'

'No. Please, Renton! It's dangerous for us both to be trapped.'

'We aren't alone any longer. I'm staying with you until you're rescued.'

Accepting his decision, she scrambled away from the grating, leaving the centre free.

'Remember to keep your knees bent when you land,' she whispered. She pressed her ear to the door as Renton prepared to jump down. There was no sound of anyone approaching.

Renton lifted the grating with the aid of the constable and lowered himself over the edge. It was simple for someone as thin as Renton to wriggle through until he was hanging down, his feet still some distance from the floor. He let go and gave a stifled groan of pain as he landed.

'What is it?' Sarah ran to him, bending down to comfort him.

'It's my ankle,' he whispered through tight lips. 'It was farther than I thought. I twisted it on a piece of coal.'

'How bad is it?'

He moved it gently in her exploring hands. 'Not broken, but bad enough if we have to run for it.'

'I thought the police were on the way?'

'They are, but we don't know where those men are, do we? If they are out and see that constable sitting on their coal hole, there's no knowing what they'll do.'

'That's why you came down to be with me in case of – trouble?'

'We're partners, aren't we?'

'Thank you.'

They curled up together and waited silently. Renton was content. In spite of the danger he was with the one person he loved best in the world and she needed him. There was no thought of sexual love, but it was love nevertheless that filled him and it was greater than the danger they faced.

Renton heard it first; the shuffling, limping gait approaching the door of the cellar. He helped Sarah to her feet and they stood, wondering what would happen next.

'Get into the corner,' Sarah whispered. 'I'll try and shield you from their sight.' She helped the injured Renton into the farthest corner. She was worried by the way he leaned on her as he walked. As the light showed around the edge of the opening door, she stood facing it and began to cry the wailing, moaning cry of a child with no tears left.

‘I want to go ’ome!’ she said between sobs. ‘There’s spiders an’ rats, an’ Gawd knows what in ’ere.’

Albert caught hold of her and pushed her roughly against a wall.

‘You an’ I ’ave an appointment with the riverbed.’

To Sarah’s dismay, he lifted the lamp he carried and looked around the cellar. He made no comment, but walked over to where Renton was curled up and kicked him savagely time and time again. He pushed Sarah out into the passage and locked the cellar door. ‘Thought I ’eard voices.’

She was pushed in front of him until the passage opened out into the large room through which she had been carried. A huge fire burned in the grate and the remains of hastily left meals on platters were strewn about the floor. A plate overturned and she saw a rat dart across the floor, leapfrogging over the bundles of rags that were the still-sleeping tenants. A fat man dozing in a wooden chair close to the fire opened his eyes and threw a bottle at the rat, then nodded to Arthur and closed his eyes again.

Sarah couldn’t cry out. Arthur’s hand was pressed firmly over her face. She struggled to breathe and each intake gave her a sick feeling as the dirty hand across her mouth and nose released its stale, unsavoury smell.

Once in the street he took the hand away and she stopped and took a deep breath. It was early morning; the fog still rested on the buildings but the sun was already easing it up and away. There were a few people about, some on their way to market and pushing empty carts. Others were making for the coffee stalls and public houses that opened at five, to accommodate the market traders. A policeman passed close by as they neared the market and Arthur held her tightly.

‘If you so much as breathe in his direction, you’ll take a long time a dying and your friend’ll die first, in front of your eyes.’

‘I’ll do what you say. I ain’t done nothing. Why don’t yer let me go?’ Sarah wailed. Her eyes were frantically searching for a chance to escape. Where were the policemen? What had happened that they had taken so long?

‘You walk ahead of me past this Peeler without doin’ nothin’ to attract ’is attention. If ’e asks, you’re meetin’ yer dad what works in the market.'

'Right.' Sarah sobbed and it was not all pretence as she acted out the part of a frightened boy.

They approached the end of the road and she saw a boy appear with his brush ready, offering to sweep the crossing for them. Sarah was trying to control her fear by remembering who she was, and how able she was to outwit someone as stupid as Arthur. She was Miss Sarah Lindhurst Ayres and Arthur was no match for her.

When the boy saw the burly man and the small boy, his face dropped with disappointment; no chance of a few pennies here. To his surprise, Sarah signalled for him to sweep. Her mind was so full of the need to escape, and the thoughts of her superiority over her captor, she forgot her role for one brief moment. The sweeping boy stared; the man at her side saw the gesture and the look, and stopped.

'Used to 'avin' crossin's swept for yer?'

'No, course I ain't. What would I want with a sweeper with shoes like these?' Trying to brazen it out, Sarah bent to show her old, broken boots. Arthur, aiming a blow at her shoulder, hit her head instead and her hair fell out of the cap and down about her shoulders. This time it was Arthur who had the shock. A gentleman's son he might have expected, but a lady he did not!

Given the slight hesitation, Sarah ran. Fortunately it was an area she knew well, very close to where Henry Bannerman lived. It was to his home she went.

Although it was very late, Henry Bannerman was not asleep. He was sitting in his study reading reports of various robberies and making notes of similarities in his neat writing, trying to build up a picture of the gangs who carried them out. A map of the London streets was spread across his desk and on this he marked each investigation with a pencil.

There was quiet in the room, only the gentle hiss of the gas light on the wall beside him and the occasional dropping of the coals in the grate. His wife and sons were asleep upstairs and, after bringing him a last drink, the servants had also retired.

He enjoyed the peace of the house at night. Days at his

office were sometimes frantic when every hour was different from the last. Mealtimes were noisy with his young sons and harassed wife and servants – he thought the boys were naughty but refused to cow them into what was called good manners. These moments alone at the end of the day, with no one to descend on him with more stories of disaster and trouble, were balm to his mind.

He had married later than most of his friends and envied those who had grown-up families. He thought of Sarah and a smile lit his face. Sir Jason and he had both determined not to insist on the usual seen-but-not-heard approach with their children and he wondered idly if Sir Jason regretted it. Sarah was the most unconventional of his children; pity she was a girl. What an adventurous boy she would have made! But with a girl perhaps Sir Jason should have been stricter. Still, he decided, someone would appear in her life soon and tame her into the role of mother and wife. He wondered if her children would be brought up with as much freedom. It did not always follow.

He put his work aside and stretched his long legs. Time to go to bed. As he was about to leave the room, he heard the gate creak. He groaned quietly as he stood waiting for a knock on his door. He should have slept when he had had the chance.

The knock was loud, insistent and repeated. A servant hurriedly dressed and opened the front door. Bannerman heard a familiar voice.

'Call him at once! This is urgent!' Sarah did not wait for the startled man to reply but pushed her way inside, meeting Henry in the doorway of his study. 'Uncle Henry, please hurry! Renton is in danger.' She tugged at his arm, pulling him towards the still-open door.

'Not again, Sarah! You promised me!'

'Please hurry! We can save Renton and catch one of the men if you hurry.' She was almost crying with impatience.

Henry removed his smoking jacket and reached for the heavy overcoat his man had already brought. In little more than a minute he was following her out through the door.

They ran first to the police station for reinforcements, then back to the house where she had been held. As they ran, Sarah explained. Bannerman added what he had learned during his brief call to his office.

'It seems the constable you left on watch gave up waiting and went to see where his colleague had got to. Then he couldn't find the right house.'

'The fool!' Sarah panted. 'What happened to the first?'

'He couldn't convince the men on duty that a boy was in danger and when he did finally get back, the other officer had gone and he thought he was the victim of a hoax.'

They reached the door of the house. Leaving men on guard, Sarah and Bannerman ran to the coal hole to call Renton. It was difficult to find. She at once understood the reason for the delay in the constable's return. She tried several times without getting a response and began to fear for Renton's life. The kicks she had seen aimed at him as he had been led away filled her mind and she began to imagine him lying unconscious and helpless, unable to answer her call.

Desperately she tried to visualise the walk along the dark passage and relate it to the street. There were so many coal holes, some for houses that no longer existed. How could she find the right one? She couldn't go down them all and time was running out. It would soon be morning.

Throwing away all pretence at being a lady, she opened her mouth and shouted, 'Renton? Where are you?' The cockney voice penetrated the alleyways and echoed between buildings. They listened, and in the silence that followed the raucous shout, heard:

'Sarah, I'm over here!'

Renton called a few times and then began to whistle to guide them to him. Bannerman prepared to slide into the coal hole. He tied a length of rope to a nearby tree and tested it by tugging firmly.

'Can I come down with you?'

'No,' Bannerman said firmly. 'You wait here and at the slightest sign of trouble, *run*!'

'I'd feel safer down there with you and Renton,' she said. Although the thought of returning to the foul-smelling cellar was dreadful, it was only slightly better to wait on the pavement alone.

'Here, you'd better take this.' He handed his truncheon to Sarah. He blew a series of blasts on his whistle, which was the signal for his men to enter the house, and, with a last squeeze to force his hips through the hole, he disappeared. Sarah dropped to the ground and tried to see into the darkness below. But all she could make out by the faint illumination of Bannerman's torch was distorted and unrecognisable shadows.

She sat down against the tree on which the rope was tied and watched the entrance anxiously in the growing light. The constable had gone to assist his friends at the front and rear of the house and she was alone. She held the truncheon in her hand, prepared to protect Renton even if it meant using it. She wished she were taller.

She was so intent on watching the hole and the rope that lay still beside her, and listening for a sign that all was well with Renton and Bannerman, that she did not hear the softly padding footsteps approaching. Arthur had followed her, and anger at the way he had been deceived was boiling inside him. His anger was so great he had followed her to seek revenge rather than going to warn his friends.

He was breathless with rage and with running to keep up with her, and his ragged breath gave her a second's warning. She rolled over and the heavy bar he had picked up for a weapon hit the ground where she had been sitting. He turned to make another swing at her as she darted behind the tree. The truncheon was in her hand but she knew she was not tall enough or strong enough to hit him over the head.

Instead, she swung at his knees. The heavy stick did its work and the man stumbled and bent to rub the offended part. She hesitated for a moment. It was possible that if things went wrong inside the house, Renton and Bannerman would be coming out through the coal hole. She had to get the man away from there. A blow from that metal bar as they began to show themselves, and they would be done for.

Arthur was rising, his face purple in the morning light. His eyes glittered as he ambled purposefully towards her. If he should get a hold on her there would be no escape. She had to get him away from that coal hole. Renton's head might appear at any moment.

She turned and ran towards the passageway between two houses. Arthur followed, his hoarse breathing close behind her. Too late, she realised her mistake. The passageway led nowhere. The houses were built around a courtyard. Doors and windows there were in plenty, but no exit.

She ran from side to side, trying doors and windows, with Arthur lumbering after her, fast, in spite of his size and weight, and closer all the time. She tried zigzagging in the hope of getting behind him and out once more through the passageway, but he outguessed her each time. Then she slipped on some rotting vegetables and fell. In a second he was over her, the metal bar held aloft, his breath foul on her face.

'Led me a proper dance, 'aven't yer?' He leered. 'But no more. This is the end of yer.' He raised the bar higher and a satisfied smile transformed his ugly face as if the act of destroying her was a beautiful thing. His feet were on each side of her, making it impossible to roll away from the murderous weapon, but there was one thing she could do. She sat up. Suddenly.

It took him by surprise and sent him slightly off balance, and he tottered back on his heels and fell awkwardly. Taking her chance, she leapt up and, taking the bar that had fallen from his grip, brought it down on his head. The sound of the blow made her close her eyes in horror, but she reminded herself of what he had done to Margaret and Isobelle and what he had intended for her. She raised the bar for a second blow if it was necessary, her lips tightly pressed as she steeled herself.

She opened her eyes slowly to see Arthur sprawled on the ground, and Renton and Bannerman approaching through the passageway.

'Are you all right?' Renton hobbled towards her, holding out his arms.

'Of course I am,' she said, and in a trembling voice, added, 'but I don't know about him.'

'I'll go and fetch my men,' Bannerman said. He left Sarah, Renton and the unconscious body of Arthur and went once more into the passageway.

'I can't stay here with him, even lying there helpless. I'm scared,' Sarah said, clinging to Renton.

'Come on, we'll start moving towards home. It doesn't seem as if he'll be going far.' Renton, limping heavily, led her back to the entrance to the alleyway. They walked slowly, Sarah shaking with shock and Renton in difficulty because of his painful ankle. But, frightened as she was, Sarah could not resist a glance back into the silent courtyard. She gave a gasp. It was empty.

It was difficult for Sarah to get back into the house unseen. The servants were up and about their morning work and when she eventually climbed the stairs, she found that her bed had been made. Edith was probably looking for her.

She was aching and felt as if her limbs had been beaten with clubs. Hurriedly hiding the old clothes she had been wearing, she climbed into bed. When Edith came bustling in, scolding her for disappearing so early in the morning, she explained weakly that she had gone for an early walk. Then, as Edith fussed over her, she fell asleep.

She stayed in bed all that day, and in periods of wakefulness, when she was too lethargic to rouse or even sit up, she lay thinking about the man called Arthur who had seen her and probably knew where she lived and who she was. Her life was in danger now and so was Renton's, and for that she felt guilt. Perhaps she could go into the country for a while, stay at Houghton Hall and pretend it was in order to see Isobelle. She tried to think of a way she could take Renton with her. Surely there they would both be safe?

When she left her bed on the second day, she went at once to see Mrs Baxter, their cook and Renton's mother. When she learned that he was laid up with an ankle injury and unable to work, she sent Mrs Baxter to his lodgings with a parcel of food. Mrs Baxter's appreciation made her feel even greater remorse.

A note from Caroline on the third day asked if she could call. Sarah sent a reply, and, to her surprise and delight, Caroline arrived with Giles. Sarah saw at once that he guessed the reason for her 'illness'. He looked at her and there was strong disapproval in his dark eyes.

'So sorry to hear you're not well, Sarah,' he said. 'And I understand that Renton too is laid up with some injury.'

Sarah was sitting on the couch in front of the fire, and she hoped that her blushes would be explained by the heat.

'His mother told me he had turned his ankle,' she replied. 'I do hope it isn't serious. He doesn't eat if he doesn't work. But I sent a parcel of food round as soon as I heard.'

'You're so kind, Sarah.' Caroline smiled. 'Renton is lucky to have you as a friend.'

'You look flushed,' Giles said, and there was a quizzical quirk to his eyebrow as he added, 'I hope it is only the warmth of the fire that makes your cheeks burn so?'

'I have been indoors too long,' Sarah said. 'Why are doctors so afraid of fresh air?'

'Fresh country air is just what you need,' Caroline said. 'What a pity it isn't the time of year to enjoy a visit to the country!'

'Soon it will be Christmas. Father thought we might go to Houghton Hall,' Sarah said. 'We are still in mourning, but we must have the usual Christmas for the sake of others – no parties, of course.'

'The country? For Christmas?' Caroline shuddered delicately at the thought. 'I have been invited to stay with Bertram's family.' It was Caroline's turn to blush. 'They are anxious to get to know me better and, by good fortune, Bertram's regiment will not be away.'

'I like the country,' Sarah said and glanced at Giles. All thoughts of hating him or even blaming him for the absence of her father and the death of Margaret seemed childish and utterly unfair now she sat near him and felt the attraction of his powerful presence. Whatever he did for a living was a part of him and she would have to accept it or deny her love for him, and that she could not. Oh, what a muddle life could be!

'Will you be at Weatherby?' she asked Giles boldly.

'I too love the country,' he said, smiling.

'And Bertram and I may be there for a part of the holiday, too,' Caroline said, 'if his parents can bear to part with me,' she added coyly.

Sarah privately thought it unlikely that Caroline would want to tear herself away from Bertram's family, whom she hoped to impress. 'How marvellous! We can all meet. How long will his leave last?'

'Long enough for us to plan our engagement! Oh, Sarah, isn't it exciting?' She moved nearer to her friend and hugged her. 'Will you come shopping with me as soon as you're well? There are so many things to buy and I need your guidance, Sarah dear.'

Sarah frowned. The thought of wandering in the busy streets frightened her. She wondered if she would ever be free of the fear of Arthur. If only Bannerman would send her a message to say he had been caught!

'I don't think I'll be able to come for a while,' she said. 'But not because I don't want to. It would be such fun helping you choose your clothes and discussing furnishings and drapery. Perhaps in a week or so?'

They talked of the preparations for Christmas and of the cooking already taking place below stairs, which was issuing tempting smells as fruit and spices were made into puddings, mincemeat and cakes.

'Renton's mother is such a clever cook!' Caroline sighed. 'Far better and more imaginative than our Mrs Barnes. How lucky you are, Sarah!'

'But our new coachman is a horror!' Sarah said. 'He grumbles about everything. It's too wet, or too dry, or too cold. Or he doesn't know the way, or the way lies through places too dangerous to travel. It's too late for decent people to be about or too early for respectable people to be abroad. Nothing has yet pleased him, except my being unwell and confined to my room. Oh, how I wish Renton were back!'

'You were too friendly,' Giles admonished. 'It's best that he has gone.'

'You don't understand,' Sarah began, and she thought to explain how close she and Renton were, but she sighed. What was the use? Giles would never understand.

'You have to grow up some time, Sarah,' Giles added softly. 'He may have been your companion in your childhood, for foolish games, but it wasn't fair to the man to treat him differently from the other servants. He forgot himself at times, and embarrassment was the result, for him as well as those he spoke to with too much familiarity.'

'Where does he live?' Caroline asked.

'He has a room over a stable where he keeps his cab and horses.'

'And a poor room it is, with nothing more than a few blankets and a fireplace that won't take a fire, because of a chimney that is blocked with fallen bricks.'

Sarah looked at Giles in surprise. 'You have seen Renton?'

'Yes. I called to see that he is managing, and I use his cab whenever I have need of one.'

Sarah smiled, her face glowing with pleasure. 'Thank you, Giles.'

'I did it only partly to please you.' Giles smiled back. 'He is the most reliable and trustworthy man.' As he guessed, that pleased her even more.

When her guests got up to leave, Sarah's face had lost its drawn look and the brightness was back in her eyes.

Giles had been watching her closely, and she was not surprised when he managed to talk with her alone, while Caroline collected her cloak and muff from the maid.

'You and Renton have been out again, haven't you?'

'Out? What d'you mean, out?'

'You promised.'

'Will you excuse me, Giles? I feel far from well and I don't think I can indulge in puzzles and games today.'

Sarah sighed. If only he had shown concern and not disapproval! Why couldn't he say he cared for her and worried for her safety, or that he would be devastated if something happened to her? But all he showed was hostility and reproach as if she had let him down, no concern or – she sighed – any attempt to discover from her what had happened.

If only he would offer to escort her! She was feeling much better, but still shivered at the prospect of walking out in the streets, where Arthur was undoubtedly waiting for her. With Giles she would feel utterly safe.

None the less she had to see Renton for herself, to know he was well and recovered from his sprained ankle. Tomorrow she would go out and brave the streets; her fondness for Renton would give her the courage. But she shivered a little at the thought of Arthur's eyes watching for her.

Chapter Eight

On the following morning, Sarah pleaded with her aunt to go with her to visit Renton. The new coachman grumbled as usual that his back was playing up and he would find it almost impossible to climb up to drive the horses.

'Very well,' Sarah said, and she saw the relief cross her aunt's face that the outing was being cancelled. 'We shall go on the omnibus.'

Great-Aunt Milly's sigh of relief turned to horror. 'Sarah, you can't consider it!'

But Sarah, having decided to brave the streets, would not be discouraged.

The distance was not great but the journey took a long time. The streets were crowded with vehicles jostling to get past, and traffic was trying to move in every direction. Drivers shouted in rage at their inability to move and, amid the confusion, the opportunist pedlars were offering their goods for bargain prices and pestering the weary passengers to buy. Ignoring the danger, they walked past and even under the horses to cross the road, so progress on the crowded omnibus was slow.

Looking through occasional doorways, Sarah saw counters selling tobacco and beer, clothes and jewellery, and coffee shops where people sat and watched the frantic bustle. All along the sides of the road were carts offering meat and vegetables, oysters and fish. Cats and dogs were being sold, and prospective buyers were promised a good ratter or a good mouser. Books, china and odds and ends of second-hand furniture, as well as boys offering the latest news-sheets and music sheets, all added to the din.

Every vendor shouted his wares, every cabman and coachman yelled in rage at the delays, and every child shouted jeering comments at the rest, so the result was pandemonium. People left their vehicles to attack others who teased them. Sarah constantly watched for a sight of Arthur. Great-Aunt Milly clapped her hatbrim over her ears and held it there, releasing it occasionally to hold her vinaigrette against her nose when some of the worst smells permeated the coach.

'I think this is a foolish idea, Sarah,' she complained. 'There's no knowing what will be the result of it. This area is not for the likes of us!'

Sarah hoped that Arthur would think the same and not be watching for her on an omnibus on the wrong side of the river.

They reached their destination at last and stepped out of the omnibus, bringing down hay from the floor as they did so. From the top deck, some youths clambered down the stairs, knocking the oil-lamp from its hook in their haste. The conductor jumped down and, bidding Sarah and her aunt a good day, retrieved the lamp. Holding on to his strap, he stood on the step and signalled to the driver. The horses, snorting with impatience, walked on and Sarah and her aunt were left to find Renton's new home.

It was in a dingy street and Sarah felt her fear returning. A rag-picker's yard was on one corner, and there was a large warehouse with a riverside landing stage. Renton saw them coming and came down the stairs to greet them, his ankle obviously painful.

'It's very different from your room at the top of the house,' Sarah said sadly, when he had shown them in and offered them a seat on the low bed.

'I miss you more than the room,' Renton said. 'I have no one to talk to.'

'You will have soon. The coachman will not be with us for long, I am sure of it. Even Father finds him a trial. If we get a new coachman I will still need a cab often. You know how impulsive I am – when I want to go shopping I have to go that very moment. Father will soon see the sense in having you back with us.'

Great-Aunt Milly tutted and pulled her cloak around her. She shuffled her skirts to make it clear she was uncomfortable, and Renton rearranged the blankets he had made into a cushion for her. She just looked around the almost empty room, disapproval on every line of her old face. Now and then she would glare at her charge, hoping for a sign they were leaving. After a few loud sighs and groans of discomfort bravely borne, she leaned back against the wall and slept.

'I'll come back again tomorrow with your mother, Renton,' Sarah said, when they had quietly discussed their plans for another attempt to find Arthur. 'We have a few things we no longer need – if you don't object to taking them?' she said teasingly.

'Your unwanted items wouldn't include a chair?' he asked hopefully.

'Two, in case you have a visitor. Which reminds me, how is Lucy?'

'Well . . . I think we will be marrying soon.'

'Renton! I'm delighted! In that case I had better make sure there are two of everything.'

'Thank you.'

'Does this mean you won't be able to come out with me any more?'

'You know I could never stop looking after you, or give up our search.'

It was Sarah's turn to say, 'Thank you.'

They heaved Aunt Milly to her feet and the ladies went home.

The following day a cart arrived at Renton's home with a carefully packed load. Renton's mother had been allowed a day off to help him, and together they unpacked rugs, cushions, china, bedding and also a large bed, a table and two chairs.

Mrs Baxter filled her son's cupboard with home-made pickles, jams and potted meats and some eggs and a piece of bacon which Sarah had persuaded her father to donate. Bread and cakes were included and the transformation was complete. The area was still an unsavoury one, but once through his door, Renton was as comfortable as Sarah could make him. Once Lucy moved in, his happiness would be assured.

A few days later, Renton was well enough to work, and he called for Sarah in order to take her to visit Caroline. It was only a short distance and she could easily have walked but, using her recent illness as an excuse, she went in Renton's cab. Now was the time to ask a favour.

'Renton, I want to go out again tonight, before I lose my nerve completely.'

Renton nodded agreement. He was afraid not to; he knew he had to be with her or she would go alone.

Dressed in boy's clothes different from those she had worn before, Sarah followed the usual trail to where the theatre crowds were filing along the pavement on foot from their carriages. It was bitterly cold and she soon wished she had added extra layers of clothes under her disguise.

She felt the warmth of the carriages as their occupants spilled out onto the pavement outside the brightly lit theatres and music halls, and envied the laughing, cheerful crowds that filled the thoroughfare. Some were singing songs learned at the music hall and, on impulse, she decided to visit one.

It was easy to find a discarded piece of paper among the litter outside the gaudy entrance. Folding it, she informed the man at the door that she had a message for someone inside. She chose her moment well; a crowd of people had just arrived and the doorman was so busy, he just flicked his head to give her permission to go in.

The sound of many people talking and the clatter of cutlery on plates was a surprise. It was deafeningly loud. Somehow Sarah had expected to see an attentive audience sitting silently and watching the stage. The tables, large enough for ten or twelve people, were set in rows around the room, and the noisy diners were eating their meals with only an occasional glance at the stage, on which an unfortunate man was singing a comic song. He was having to shout rather than sing, in an attempt to make himself heard over the din. His act finished and he went off to a few desultory handclaps.

Sarah stared around the large room with its bright chandeliers and decorative mirrors. The audience was mostly men, the few women there were for their benefit. Male hands lingered on female thighs and satin-covered hips, while the women laughed and ate. It seemed to Sarah's shocked mind that they were all there for selfish enjoyment, the women to eat and earn themselves some money, and the men to make sure they had value for their payment. The poor entertainer was no more important than another flea bite in a low boarding house.

The band gave a loud chord and drums rolled to announce the next act. A waitress running across the floor was tripped, the food she had been carrying spread across the floor and howls of laughter rose. Drums and cymbals increased their insistent proclamation and when the noise had subsided to an acceptable level, a woman came on the stage. She stood for only a moment before getting the attention of all.

She was dressed daringly in a skirt that showed her legs and a blouse that teased the audience by its hint of what was beneath it. She moved slowly and provocatively as she sang a saucy song. It was irresistible to Sarah, who, by the second chorus, was finding it difficult not to join in. She was not embarrassed by the spectacle. Her mother had sung and moved in a similar way as she had told her daughters stories about the time she had spent on stage.

Sarah stood transfixed, the present blending with memories of her mother's reminiscences. The singer brought the often repeated stories to life, adding colour to scenes never before seen but described so vividly in her childhood. It was at a place like this that her father had watched an acrobat perform and had fallen in love with her, later defying his family to marry her. Sarah felt the loss of her mother but also felt closer to her than she had since her death nearly four years before.

As the singer finished her song, Sarah began to look about her. She was partly hidden by one of the large pillars which supported the balcony and she moved from side to side of the smooth column to survey the diners. She wished Renton were with her. This was something she needed to share: the atmosphere, the beautiful performer and the way it brought back the years when her mother was alive. They had all been so happy then.

The faces were a fascination to her. They were rapt in admiration now and respectful of the woman's ability, so different from when the previous act was on. There was something very special about this woman. Sarah wondered who she was but dared not ask; to bring attention to herself was certain to result in her being thrown out.

Then a face she knew spoilt the occasion and made her wish she had never succumbed to the temptation of entering the forbidden place. Giles sat at a table not far away from where she stood.

She slid carefully around the pillar away from his sight. She thought it doubtful that he would even glance in her direction. He was watching the singer in rapt attention. When her performance was over, he stood up and walked to the stage to help her down. Sarah's heart gave a sickening jolt of jealousy and despair.

Giles escorted the beautiful woman through the admiring crowd and up the stairs to the balcony, where they would probably eat supper together and walk while she waited until the time for her second act. What chance did she have of winning Giles's heart when there were worldly-wise and beautiful women like the singer so readily available and so much a part of the life that he led and she, Sarah, hated? She grieved for her lack of beauty, talent and height.

She could not leave. There was a chance of seeing Giles again and perhaps of seeing the singer with someone else. So she stood as still as she could and watched as act after act walked onto the stage, some to receive applause, several to catcalls and even missiles thrown at them until the offenders were stopped and escorted out.

It was after midnight when she saw her father. He had joined Giles and the singer and the three of them were walking towards where she stood. Instinctively she darted away from them, although she would surely not have been recognised by either Giles or Sir Jason. The move was her undoing.

As she stood upright again, a stinging cuff under her ear

sent her reeling and she landed against the wall. She stood up immediately, holding back with difficulty the haughty retort that sped to her tongue. She faced her attacker and almost sighed with relief. In the split second before he spoke, she had thought it might be someone who knew and recognised her. She was faced by an angry doorman.

'Get out, you little pest!' he growled. 'Want to get me the sack, do you?' He aimed another blow, but Sarah ducked under his arm and ran through the crowds still pressing in through the entrance, and out into the street.

There was no sign of Renton. She darted one way, then another, until at last she saw his cab at the end of a line evacuating their bejewelled and colourfully dressed revellers.

'Sarah! Thank goodness! I had to take a fare or be thought a villain up to no good. What happened?'

'Nothing. I was curious, that's all, thinking of my mother. My father was there,' she added. She could not talk about Giles and the beautiful singer.

'Where now?' he asked.

'Towards Seven Dials.'

Emily Tilt was at her usual spot, calling her wares, impatiently offering the last of her bunches so she could go home where there was at least a warm fire to ease the chills and aches from her young body. Maggs threw her a chestnut and Emily peeled it with stiff hands. She took the kernel to her mouth, tossing it from side to side until it cooled enough to chew.

' 'Ow long you been standin' 'ere, young Emily?' the old woman asked.

'Six years. Since I was ten,' Emily replied.

'You must be tough, gel.'

'My dream keeps me going,' Emily said, and the old woman laughed.

'You still think you'll 'ave a 'ouse of yer own one day?' She shook her head. 'Not the way you knocks it back. Never seen you go back to the lodgin's without staggerin' on rubber legs. Pack up the gin and maybe you'll get a room of yer own, but I can't see you managin' without yer booze. Got you hooked good an' proper, it 'as.'

'One day I'll surprise you.'

'Well, I suppose you 'ave to dream or there's no sense goin' on.'

Emily didn't reply. Her dream was a private thing and it was safer to let it stay that way.

Maggs's husband arrived to take the last night turn, and Maggs went home, grumbling about how long she had waited. Emily's eyes began to watch the corner. Jarvis was late tonight, too.

When Sarah sidled up to her and laughed at her surprised expression, Emily hissed, 'What are you doing out? Trying to get Renton into even more trouble, are you?'

Sarah was startled at the lack of friendliness. She had after all, saved the girl from almost certain prison.

'Go on, go back to your fancy home!' Emily went on. 'You think you can get away with anything, people like you. Ain't you caused enough harm, Renton losing his place and all?'

'I want to find someone,' Sarah tried to explain.

'Don't we all, dearie, don't we all?' Emily's eyes were darting repeatedly to and from the corner. The anxiety in her expression was only partly concealed by anger, which appeared and faded as the flickering light played on her features. Sarah sidled back out of sight and waited.

A man appeared at the corner and stood looking at the flower girl. From Emily's attitude Sarah knew he was the person Emily had been waiting for.

It was too dark for Sarah to see the man clearly, the red glow from the brazier distorting rather than assisting, but he had the attitude of a gentleman. There was such poignancy in the thought of the poor, uneducated flower girl being in love with a man obviously out of her reach that it was Emily whom Sarah watched and not the man.

The man slowly approached Emily, who stood as if spellbound at the sight of him. He spoke softly, close to Emily's cheek, and a few words were passed between them before the buttonhole Emily offered was accepted and paid for. They stared at each other for a moment longer, then he disappeared, swallowed up by the night.

Sarah saw the girl's shoulders droop with dismay that the long-awaited moment was over. She watched as Emily moved to the chestnut-sellers brazier and saw her face glow red as the chestnut-seller poked the fire into a sudden glow. Hands partly covered by woollen gloves were warmed over the heat before Emily lifted her basket onto her hip and prepared to go home.

A hissed warning from Renton made Sarah look around. To her consternation, she saw Giles walking towards her in an impatient hurry. She was so sure he had recognised her that her knees all but gave way. After all, he had seen her dressed like this before. She stood there, hoping her dirt-grained face would be sufficient disguise. A black streak across her cheek and another over an eyebrow distorted her features. Emily ran off through the dark streets towards the Nethersken and Sarah stood waiting for the challenge from Giles Hallam.

'You! Boy! Get me a cab.'

Sarah almost laughed with relief. 'Renton, take him. Find out where he's going,' she whispered urgently. When Renton began to argue, she added, 'I'll go straight home, I promise. Please, Renton.'

Renton spoke to Giles and gestured towards his cab, which was waiting at the kerb in the charge of a small boy.

'Evening, Mr Hallam. Can I take you somewhere?'

'Oh, Renton. Take me home, will you? I've had quite enough of this rabble for tonight.' He threw a coin to Sarah, who scrabbled in the dirt of the roadway to retrieve it.

Sarah wavered between relief that Giles was not enjoying the company of the beautiful singer, and disappointment that, as he was going home, she would not learn anything of his activities. With a wave to Renton, she ran home, clutching the coin thrown by Giles. One day, she hoped, she would show it to him and explain how she had received from him her first present.

In the cottage on the opposite side of Hare Hill from Weatherby, Isobelle sat in a haybarn watching for Mrs Brandon. She had no idea what day it was, but knew that it was the day for Mrs Brandon to visit the cottage where she lived.

This morning she had been woken and coaxed out of her bed and down the ladder to the living room by Mrs Starkly and dressed in a clean smock and forced to put on the hard boy's boots that hurt her feet and made them bleed.

Mrs Brandon arrived soon after breakfast and, as usual, did not stay long. She examined the child and seemed satisfied she was well. The poor clothes and the rough, too large boots she ignored. Bruises and cuts didn't kill children and as long as the girl was fed and reasonably clean she was not bothered.

Isobelle watched as Mrs Starkly held out her hand for the coins and waved Mrs Brandon on her way. Then she went willingly to have the clean smock changed for an older, well-mended one, and thankfully removed the hated boots.

She returned to the shed and watched as the figure of Mrs Brandon grew smaller and finally disappeared from sight. Sometimes the farmer widow brought some cakes for her for a treat, and these she saved for when the boy came. Today there had been none. She didn't dwell on her disappointment; there was always next week.

Isobelle stared at the place where Mrs Brandon had vanished from sight, dreaming lazily about how she would spend her day. She usually wandered through the woods, gathering any pretty stone or interestingly shaped piece of wood she spotted, until hunger led her back to the cottage and supper.

On special occasions, Peter would come. She wished he would come today. Staring at the trees from which he usually appeared, and where Mrs Brandon had recently faded from view, she saw a movement. Was it Mrs Brandon coming back with her cakes? She felt her mouth fill with water at the thought of them. No, it was Peter. Standing up and stumbling towards him, she began calling his name in a growling voice only he understood.

'Peer!' she called excitedly. 'Peer! Peer!'

'The missus forgot your cakes. Left 'em on the table. I've brought them for you. Would you like one now?' he asked as they met on the path.

Isobelle held out her hands and took the cloth-wrapped food. She sat down on the dirt and ate one, offering one to Peter with an unusually clean hand. Peter held her hand against his own, laughing at the smallness and pinkness of it resting on his brown and callused paw. They ate contentedly, then, taking the rest of the cakes, went back to the cottage, where Mrs Starkly relieved them of the remainder.

'Walk back with me a little way?' Peter asked.

For answer, Isobelle trotted ahead of him, and he ran to catch her up. They both skipped on the hard earth until they reached the grass of the hayfield, then walked towards the wood. Isobelle walked awkwardly, leaning to one side, and she was silent, but Peter waited for her patiently and chattered to her as they went. She seemed to understand, although her efforts at replying were mostly incomprehensible. Only occasionally would a word come out clearly, and when this happened, the boy patted her back and praised her until she laughed.

One clear word was 'walk', and he knew that meant she felt the need to go farther than usual, to stretch her legs and break out of the monotony of her surroundings. He always agreed, even though it meant a hiding when he got back to Mrs Brandon. This morning, she said, 'Walk' and looked at him with such pleading in her full, moist eyes that, although he began to shake his head, he eventually agreed. There was a pile of wood to be chopped, and the sheep and pigs still to be fed. But he wilted under her repeated, 'Walk, Peer. Walk, Peer, walk.'

The ground to the north of them was marshy and they turned southwest and walked towards the base of the hill that lay nearer to the road. When they reached the derelict farmhouse which Sarah had seen on her walk with Giles, Peter went inside. Isobelle followed without hesitation, clapping her hands to show her pleasure.

The building smelled of decay and everything in the first room they entered was covered with a layer of damp dust. Isobelle sank to her knees and began rubbing the film from a fallen chair. Using her full-skirted smock, she rubbed until the wood glowed. Putting the chair upright, she sat on it and pretended to warm her hands at the iron oven-range. Dragging another chair forward, she cleaned it before offering it to Peter, who sat and repeated her pretend gestures.

They explored first upstairs, then through passages that took them into rooms now empty of everything except the evidence of wild animals who had found shelter there. Chewed-up paper in a cupboard showed where mice had nested. Bones where a fox had eaten his supper were in a corner of the dairy.

Peter talked to Isobelle all the time, explaining what they had found, and making up games of grand ladies and gentlemen living in the once fine old house. To his delight she began adding words to her gestures, repeating some of the simpler words after him. He praised her when she did, and said nothing to criticise her when she did not.

One of the downstairs rooms was padlocked. Isobelle took hold of it and pulled and struggled in a futile attempt to free it.

'It's no good. It won't open.'

'Open. Peer, open.'

'Good girl. But it won't open. It's a strong new lock.'

'Open.' She pointed at the lock.

This was another surprise. She was using a word, not just repeating it. This time he didn't show excess delight, afraid it would discourage her.

'It won't open from here. Shall we try from the outside? There may be a way in through the window.'

They ran out and round the side of the house. Peering in through the dirty glass, they could make out a number of boxes. Isobelle pointed and demanded peremptorily, 'Open!'

The frame was rotten and it was no difficulty to force the window up, breaking the weak clasp right out of the wood. They climbed inside.

The boxes were a disappointment. When the children's busy fingers unfastened the top of one, it contained heavily padded packages, slotted in side by side and filling the box with what appeared to be nothing more exciting than brown paper. Scraping at the fastened end of one of the flat packages revealed silver foil and under that was what Peter declared to be baccy for pipes. Disappointed, they rewrapped the containers and slotted them carefully back in the boxes.

They walked around the base of Hare Hill, stopping briefly to look at the lake in the grounds of Weatherby, crawling through the long, straggly, wet grass in case they were seen from the house. Ducks sheltered in the reeds that grew near the feeder stream and for a moment Peter was tempted to try and catch one. A mallard might save him from a hiding when he got back.

'Best I don't,' he said aloud. 'Might cause them in the house to see us and that would mean a worse row.'

To skirt the marsh they climbed the hill and headed back down to the cottage, but here, Isobelle didn't leave him.

'Walk!' she insisted.

'I got to go back,' Peter said anxiously. 'There's work waiting, and a smack on the arse and no supper if I don't be quick about it. I've been gone too long as it is.'

'Walk.' Isobelle ran on ahead of him to where Vale Farm came into view.

'Go back now,' Peter pleaded. 'It'll be dark and you'll be lost.'

Isobelle pointed at the farmhouse. 'Walk.'

'You want to see Mrs Brandon?' He was startled by the idea.

Isobelle put a finger to her lips, suggesting a secret.

'You want to go in and no one knowing?'

'Walk.'

He searched around to find out where Mrs Brandon was working but the place seemed deserted. He shrugged. 'Why not?' He led the way to where a small doorway opened into a storeroom. From it a stone staircase led up past the bedroom and into the roof. Isobelle followed, her finger still sealing her lips.

Once inside the house she made for the little room which had been her bedroom for the first night after leaving London. Her trunk was in a corner, with the wooden boxes that had contained her clothes and belongings. She lifted the lids, one after the other, but they were all empty. She turned to look at Peter, a frown on her face. Peter looked about him and spread his arms to show he too was puzzled. Then he saw a paper carrier and in this he found a china-faced doll dressed in frilly underskirts and a beautifully embroidered dress. Isobelle snatched it and ran down the stairs.

'No!' Peter groaned. 'Isobelle, you can't take it. My mistress'll want to know how you got it.'

Isobelle turned to face him, tears in her large eyes as she held on to the doll he was trying to take from her. Her face was pudgy and plain, less alert than she had once been and without the sparkle of a bright intelligence, but to Peter she was beautiful and he could not refuse her.

'Very well,' he sighed. 'Although it'll get me a row and a good hiding when the mistress finds out it's gone. Our secret, eh?'

When Mrs Brandon next called at the cottage with the coins for Isobelle's keep and some cakes, the girl was nursing the now rather grubby doll.

'Where did she get that from?' she asked Peter later in the day. 'I know it was still up in the yellow room a day or so ago.'

'She's been got at by the pixies, hasn't she? They do things others don't understand, pixies do.'

'Some pixie! A pixie called Pigpen!' She aimed a clout but asked no more questions. She was doing well out of the girl. What if she had stolen her doll? The rest of the deal was going well. She thought about all the changes she had made for the first visit. Kept her busy for days, but well worth the effort. Gave the right impression and likely they wouldn't be calling again for a long time. Yes, a very satisfactory arrangement was little Isobelle Lindhurst Ayres.

The days were short and although there were the usual routine jobs to be done, Mrs Brandon allowed Peter more freedom than at other times of the year. Soon the work with the sheep, followed by the planting of the crops, would mean they were both kept busy from dawn until darkness drove them indoors, but for a few weeks she could be lenient.

She made sure she did not put the easing of his workload into words. No point creating a precedent, but while he was still a boy, it wouldn't harm him to give him a bit of time to himself.

Peter and Isobelle often went to the old farmhouse. They

noticed that the boxes went and others came in their place, but they didn't bother to investigate again. Each time they went to play their games of pretend, and make the food they had scrounged into picnics, they were careful to replace everything much as they found it, even overturning the chair in which they sat wrapped in sacks trying to keep warm. They never saw anyone and, so far as they knew, no one knew of their visits.

Isobelle was still strange and, to Peter, fascinating. To his delight, she began to add more words to her vocabulary. Like an infant, she seemed to have stored words and understanding but had been unable to speak them. Now, each time they went to the farmhouse, her word power increased. Sentences were stilted and lacked the modifying words to smooth out conversations, but she was more of a companion than ever and Peter longed for her presence as the most important part of his day, as he had once longed for a real bed and a fire to warm his feet. She was more necessary to his happiness than anything else in his life. He had never been cared for with love in his memory, he was just a part of the farm's livestock. Having someone to care for was an excellent substitute.

Jarvis sat in Sir Jason's office. Spread out in front of him was a plan of a section of the area owned by Sir Jason, which had once been a jumble of streets, alleyways and derelict warehouses.

'I do see what you mean, Sir Jason,' Jarvis was saying. 'This area alone would go a long way to improving the number of rooms available for letting to the workers. But, although I know you are doing it mainly for them, you really must consider making a sensible profit.'

'I intend to. I have to remember how quickly a building can deteriorate when it's inhabited by people who aren't used to decent housing.'

'Yes, you are wise to remember how unfortunate these people are.'

'If the costs you have listed are accurate, then I shall get a reasonable return for my investment and still be able to put aside a regular amount for the care and repair of the property.'

'Oh, be assured they are accurate, Sir Jason. I have checked them all myself. I trust no one when the business-man concerned is a personal friend.'

Sir Jason almost protested at that but swallowed the retort. The man was audacious, but he was useful at the moment. Once the lodging houses were built, then would be the time to discourage him. He satisfied himself by glaring.

Jarvis sensed he had gone too far and smiled to himself. What did a few unspoken insults matter? He would soon have Sir Jason where he wanted him.

Topham entered, after knocking on the door.

'Sir Jason,' he said apologetically, 'is there anything you need me to look over? I thought that if the plans for the new area are here, I might as well examine them and cast an eye over the whole thing.'

'No, Topham. I can deal with this, thank you.'

Jarvis was amused at the sharp way Sir Jason dealt with the man. The hawklike face was lowered and he glared at the secretary, who, after a brief moment of defiance, backed out.

Old fool, Sir Jason thought to himself. I really think he is past his best. Time to replace him, perhaps.

Jarvis walked home well pleased with himself. He had fixed the idea of the lodging houses in Sir Jason's mind and allowed the man to believe it had been his own. The flattery, telling him he was thinking first about the homeless, was almost impossible to say without laughing; really, these people were so easy to gammon! Their vanity made them believe the most unbelievable things.

He decided he deserved a treat, and went into one of the inns where he would be sure of a pleasant evening. A good meal, entertainment and female company, perhaps even a room for the night. He deserved it for spending hours telling Sir Jason what a wonderful man he was. He smiled briefly, imagining how different Sir Jason would be when the roles were reversed and he, Jarvis King, was the one with the money and position. How he would enjoy making Sarah's father squirm! He sang softly as he entered the inn.

Chapter Nine

Sarah was embroidering a cushion cover. Needlework was not something that came easily to her, and every evening, after she had put it aside, Edith patiently unpicked the worst of the stitches and resewed them. As Christmas drew near, Sarah's impatience with the work increased but she was determined to have it finished in time for Renton's engagement to Lucy.

Three days before Christmas Eve, when most of the servants had already left to begin their preparations at Houghton Hall, Sarah snapped the last thread with a huge sigh of relief.

'I'll see that it's pressed and ready for you to take tomorrow, Miss Sarah.' Edith smiled, thinking that the cushion cover would need a few hours' work that night in the light of a candle before it was presentable.

'We'll go tomorrow morning and, if Renton is to be found, he can come with us when we call on Caroline and give it to Lucy.'

'And what about Miss Caroline? Isn't she becoming betrothed to her soldier at Christmas? There will be a present needed there, won't there?'

'All these celebrations and we are still in mourning! It's impossible to withdraw into a shell of grief without ruining things for others.'

'Official show is important and right, but Margaret will always be mourned, so don't be afraid to feel joy for others,' Edith said softly.

'At least having the usual Christmas at Houghton Hall will

be an opportunity to spend some time with Isobelle. I wonder if she has improved?'

'Without any teaching, Miss Sarah?' Disapproval showed clearly on Edith's serious face.

'Father did what *he* thought was best for Isobelle,' Sarah admonished quietly. 'He took all the available advice, and the country, far from worries and without the stress of forced learning, was the best choice for her. The kindest life for her.'

'I'm sure she will love the dress you bought for her.'

'And the doll you so patiently made, Edith.' Sarah sighed. 'You're so clever with your hands. What can I boast of? Nothing.'

'Making people happy seems a grand skill to me. Everyone is happier for seeing you, and it's been that way since you were a baby.'

'Dear Edith! What a lovely compliment!' Sarah hugged the aging lady who had been her constant companion, then said brightly, 'It's very cold, and I fear there might be snow on the way, but could you bear to come shopping with me?'

'Of course. I'll send the boy for Renton, shall I?'

'Yes please. I'm sure the coachman is nowhere to be found!' They both laughed at the mild deception.

When they set off for the country two days later, the carriage was full and the coachman groaned and complained at all the carrying to and fro of parcels, trunks and boxes. The outside of the vehicle was soon full and Sarah, Edith, and Sarah's brothers, were squeezed into their seats, surrounded with brightly wrapped gifts pushed in around them.

Sir Jason had business meetings and would follow later, and a few boxes were left in the hall to be brought with him.

'Havin' to go there and 'ere, there and 'ere. Enough to snap my poor back in half it is, all this 'ere heavin' and shovin' and to-in' and fro-in',' the coachman muttered.

Sarah imitated his complaining voice and her brothers added their comments, and the coach finally set out with the passengers, at least, in good humour.

They stopped once for refreshments and arrived at Houghton Hall when there was still some daylight, to find the servants lining the steps, all holding boughs of holly bedecked with red and green ribbons. Lights shone out through windows and open doors and Sarah felt the excitement of the holiday tighten in her throat.

Sir Jason and his manservant arrived on the following day and, to Sarah's delight, Giles was with him. She had hardly recovered from the surprise of this when Mrs Brandon brought Isobelle to join them. Sarah ran to her sister and picked her up, but the little girl began to cry and pull away.

Sarah put her down. Isobelle clutched the skirts of Mrs Brandon while that woman apologised.

'So long since she saw you, beggin' your pardon, Miss. I'm sure it's only that. Such a short memory my precious has.'

'I'm sure you're right, Mrs Brandon. Perhaps you will stay a while until she has remembered me.' Sarah was upset, but tried to prevent her sister from seeing her disappointment.

Isobelle was much fatter and her face was barely recognisable as the pretty child Sarah expected to see. Her memory of her sister was from the time before she had been attacked; the damage to her had seemed like a bad dream. This little girl with dirt-grained hands, chilblains and ill-fitting clothes was a stranger.

'What has happened to her clothes?' Sarah asked.

'In ruins they were in no time at all. My precious is such a one for climbing, you'd never believe. Ladies is usually so ladylike, or so's my experience, but my precious is always climbing and crawling in places where you'd never dream she'd want to go. Have to keep replacing them, all the time she keeps me that busy sewing.'

Sarah glanced at Giles, who was smiling at Mrs Brandon's expertise in ladylike behaviour. She tried to ignore his amusement but failed, and shared his smile.

When Mrs Brandon left, Isobelle had to be restrained by Sarah and Edith. It was a long time before the child was comforted, and only Giles's suggestion of sweetmeats and a few gifts to unwrap finally subdued her fears. Sarah insisted on sharing a room with her sister, to make sure she was not frightened in a strange room in a strange house, because it was clear that Isobelle remembered nothing of her life before the attack. It reminded Sarah of how lax she had been during the last weeks in her determination to find the men who destroyed her.

'I know what you're thinking, Sarah,' Giles said, when the little girl had been led off by Edith to be settled into her bed. 'I too cannot forget what happened. I have men searching for the gang who did this, but whoever organises them is clever and keeps changing their base. But we will catch them. I promise you.'

Sarah was surprised to learn of his involvement. She thought that, like most, he had allowed the shock to recede and the urgency to fade from the search.

'You are really trying to find them?' she asked, staring up into his dark eyes and wilting under their concern.

'There is nothing we can do to help Margaret, and all that can be done for dear Isobelle is being done by your father. But for you, Sarah, I have employed men to seek out the men responsible. I'm doing it for your peace of mind. I know you will not be content until they're punished. You are very important to me, Sarah.'

She did not know how to reply. It was what she so wanted to hear, but suddenly she was unable to think clearly. Did it mean he really cared for her? Or was his concern simply because she was the daughter of an influential business partner? She was saved from making the wrong response by the gong announcing dinner.

'Thank you, Giles.' She smiled demurely as he offered her his arm to walk into the dining room. He looked hard at her as if waiting for more, but she could not read his expression.

They entered the dining room, larger and rather shabbier than the one at Weatherby but, to Sarah, more elegant and splendid, although it lacked the brightness of the new furnishings of Giles's home. The chandelier gave a warm glow with its dozen candles and stands containing four and six long, fat, candles added to the richness of the setting around the oblong room.

Because the family was still in mourning, the table, instead of being gaily dressed for the celebrations, was set without any of the usual trimmings. The Christmas tree was in its usual place near the foot of the staircase, but even that was decked only in ribbons of dull shades.

'I have a surprise for you,' Giles said as he helped her into her seat, next to her father. 'Bertram had a desire to experience a country Christmas. He and Caroline are at Weatherby now. We are having a party to celebrate their engagement. Will you come?'

'I shall ask Father,' she said. 'Perhaps he will not refuse, but I can't wear my prettiest dress.' She looked down at the sombre black gown she wore, and felt guilty at the momentary regret at the need for mourning clothes.

'You will look lovely whatever you wear,' he said gallantly.

'Do you think it was the household all wearing such dark and gloomy clothes that frightened Isobelle?' she wondered.

'If that is so, she will soon overcome it and enjoy her stay with you,' Giles said. 'Who could not be happy in your company?'

When Sarah arrived with her family at Weatherby on Christmas Eve, she was surprised to see Lucy, Caroline's maid.

'Lucy? I thought you would stay in London. Aren't you and Renton being married at New Year? You haven't quarrelled, have you?' she asked anxiously.

'No, Miss Sarah. Renton is here, too. Mr Giles decided he would need extra transport for his guests so he hired Renton for a few days. We'll be back in time for our wedding.'

'That was kind of him,' Sarah said, her grey eyes sparkling. She was twice pleased: because Renton was there and because he came on Giles's instruction. Giles must now know how much she valued Renton's friendship. She looked around for Giles to thank him. He must care for her. This gesture was surely more than casual concern. He was demonstrating how much he wanted to please her.

In the small garden room leading off the hall, a Christmas tree had been set up and decorated with coloured baubles. Beneath it were assorted parcels, each bearing a gift label. Stopping to examine them, and touch and squeeze and guess the contents, Caroline declared she couldn't wait until the morning of Christmas. 'Besides all these, there are the gifts for my engagement to dear Bertram,' she said. 'You must come and look at them as soon as we have eaten.'

A large parcel caught Sarah's eye and she knelt down to read the label. It was addressed to her and signed Giles. Caroline went on talking about the excitement of her gifts, but Sarah's mind shut off from her chatter. She dreamed of opening the parcel and showing Giles how thrilled she was with the contents. She just knew that this Christmas would be the beginning of all her dreams coming true. He cared! He really cared. He had shown it by talking about the farm and about living permanently in the country, and by using Renton's cab when it must be more convenient for him to use his own coachman. And best of all, Renton was there, only a few miles from Houghton Hall, where he would be safe. She wondered if he would be able to leave his Lucy and meet her to talk.

Dinner was announced and people gradually began to move into the dining room, where the table was dressed in festive mood with each place given its own arrangement of holly and candles. Sarah looked in, but decided she must wait for Giles. He would surely expect to take her in to dinner.

She waited near the tree, imagining how she would walk in on his arm and sit beside him. They would all be congratulating Bertram and Caroline, but she and Giles would be exchanging glances that would tell the observant that another engagement would be announced as soon as this one had been allowed its excitement and importance.

She looked at her reflection in a mirror and saw that her cheeks were rosier than usual, and the glow and the rich dark-blue of her dress seemed to add to the colour of her eyes and make them shine. Shining with happiness was more than a fanciful phrase, she decided, content with her looks. Giles's love had made her almost beautiful. She smiled at her reflection with unaccustomed vanity. She went to the door and saw Giles coming out of the study.

He was talking, and she saw that her father was with him. For a moment her nerve went and she stepped back towards the tall Christmas tree. The doorbell rang and Giles hurried past her in time to greet the latecomer. Sarah waited in the small room for him to return. He must surely look for her, and for a moment she had the childish impulse to hide from him. But that was not the way she must now behave. She pretended to examine the gifts beneath the tree, trying to recognise the voice of the new arrival.

She heard the tinkle of happy laughter and the rich voice of a woman, followed by Giles's laughter, and felt the first pang of unease. She looked into the hall and saw an elegantly dressed woman with her hand on Giles's arm. She turned, and Sarah recognised the singer from the music hall.

Maids scurried around, taking the woman's clothes and escorting her to her room, while Giles stood at the foot of the stairs, obviously waiting for her. Sarah felt sick. She was trapped in the room, unable to escape and join the others without passing Giles and having to explain why she was alone.

Her first reaction was dismay. The second was relief at how close she had come to embarrassing herself and Giles by a show of affection he did not share. Pride was a strong antidote to despair. She waited in an agony of fear in case one of the servants saw her skulking in the garden room when everyone else was in the dining room waiting for their host. It was a relief when Giles called a greeting and the singer came down the stairs to join him. As he led her in and announced her as Miss Marie Mackworth, Sarah slipped through the door and found her place next to her father. On her right sat Alfred Cummins.

She greeted him more enthusiastically because of her disappointment over Giles. She laughed up at him and seemed to enjoy his company in a way she normally would have found impossible. She avoided looking towards the head of the table, where Giles sat with Miss Mackworth. If Giles looked at her she was certain he would recognise her unhappiness and know himself to be the cause of it.

Everyone must know, just by looking at her. She increased her flirting with Alfred. She felt vulnerable and hurt. Analysing her feelings, she decided the sensation was similar to being found naked. Connotations of that thought had her blushing.

'I have been to Paris lately,' Alfred was saying when her

mind returned to him. 'I took the liberty of buying a small gift for you, which I placed under the tree.'

'Thank you,' Sarah purred, gazing into his quite remarkable green eyes. He really was rather handsome. Flirting with him to heal her wounds might not be so difficult. 'That was most kind.'

Alfred bowed his head. Half hidden by him, Sarah risked a glance towards Giles. She sighed. Although older and far more sober and serious, it was Giles who made her heart flutter. She turned back to Alfred more determinedly bright than ever.

'I'm looking forward to the dancing, aren't you?'

'If I can hope for you to partner me, Miss Sarah, it will be the happiest part of the evening.'

The party gathered in the spacious drawing room after dinner to hear the announcement of Caroline's engagement. Bertram was a soldier and wore his uniform proudly. He was a rather earnest young man on whom the bristling moustaches of the warrior sat uneasily. He stood tall and, apart from the nervousness in his eyes at being the centre of attenion, looked quite impressive. Only when he spoke did the illusion fade. He stuttered and constantly apologised.

The many parcels were unwrapped, the gaily coloured paper and ribbons falling in a heap on the floor to be swiftly gathered by the servants. There were glasses, dishes and an enormous pile of linen. Ornaments of every imaginable size and subject and a set of Italian glassware for Caroline's dressing table, which had been given by Sir Jason and his family.

Sarah, who had of course seen it before, still gasped as the sparkling bowls, trays and candlesticks were revealed to shine in all colours of the rainbow in the lights playing on them from chandeliers and candles.

'They're beautiful,' she murmured.

'The very best I could obtain for Sir Jason,' Alfred said.

'You?' Sarah frowned.

'I deal in import and export and your father and I work together on many things,' Alfred explained.

Sarah was curious, wondering why her father dealt with Alfred, yet told her not to encourage him. Surely he must be an honourable man if Sir Jason shared business involvement with him? But honour was not enough to allow the young man to be accepted. He dressed well and was reasonably comfortable in the company of Giles's guests, but he was not a gentleman. A pity, really; she was beginning to find him rather fascinating.

When all the gifts had been admired and the couple wished all the happiness and success the future could possibly hold, the dancing began. For Sarah, it was the best part of the evening. Unease about how close she had come to embarrassment with Giles had spoilt the meal, and even the obvious admiration of Alfred could not blur that. The dancing was more anonymous. She could lose herself in the crowd and enjoy the music and the movement, unnoticed by the rest.

Dancing with Bertram was fun. He was so nervous she had to pretend a lack of skill to stop the constant stream of apologies that his clumsiness provoked. She looked up at him and saw he was searching the crowd for Caroline as if he were completely happy only when she partnered him. Sarah was a little envious and her eyes sought the reassuring admiration in Alfred Cummins's green eyes.

She watched anxiously between dances for Giles to approach her, wanting to dance with him, but knowing she would be gauche and ill at ease with the singer there.

Miss Mackworth was sitting at the piano, talking with the musician who, together with a violinist and several others, had been engaged for the evening. She seemed to be discussing the music sheets he had spread across the top of the piano. Perhaps she would be persuaded to sing for them.

Alfred had disappeared. Then she saw Giles leaving the room with her father and guessed that even on an occasion like this, they were unable to forget their business matters. She sat watching the rest, moving a little closer to the piano and the beautiful Miss Mackworth.

It was only minutes before the men returned, and they were discussing a meeting which they would hold at Weatherby on the day following Christmas. Sarah watched them enter; her father looking tired and a little worried;

Giles taller than the rest and the least concerned; and Alfred, who was decidedly anxious. She went to Sir Jason, when he had moved away from the other two.

'Father, is something wrong?'

'My dear, of course not. Only a few business problems.'

'Problems?'

'Perhaps that was the wrong word. I have a decision to make about taking on a new line. It will mean stretching myself but – ' He stopped, as if suddenly realising whom he was talking to. His eyes had been vague and were now sharp. 'What am I thinking about, worrying you, and at such a time? Sarah, my darling child, I'm sorry. My plans are challenging and I'm fired with enthusiasm for something new. There's nothing seriously wrong and I assure you they don't affect you at all. Now, go and dance and enjoy yourself.'

'Will you dance with me, Father?'

'Perhaps later, my dear.'

She watched him walk through the laughing crowd, a sombre figure among the colourful throng, and she had a sense of fear. Whatever he had said to reassure her, there was something not quite right in his life. She wondered how Giles fitted into the picture, and whether Alfred was a part of the problem.

Staring into space, trying to guess, without any real information, what was wrong, she was startled out of her reverie by Giles. Doubly shocked, she scowled at him.

'Don't frighten me like that, Giles!'

'Sorry. I did not realise you were so far away from us. Is something not right? Can I help? You are well, I hope?'

'Perfectly well, thank you.' She still spoke sharply.

'Good, then you won't refuse me a dance.' He led her onto the floor and partnered her in a lively polka, which completely took her out of her anxious mood. She forgot Alfred, forgot her father's worried appearance, forgot everything around her except Giles and the excitement of his touch. The room seemed empty of others, there were only she and Giles, and the music. It was like waking from a particularly wonderful dream when the music ceased and she was abruptly returned to reality.

He left her then and she saw him walk over to the piano.

'Friends,' he announced. 'We are fortunate tonight to have for ourselves the talents that have driven London audiences wild with excitement. Ladies and gentlemen, I am delighted to introduce Miss Marie Mackworth, known to us all as Merry!'

The piano tinkled an introduction through the applause and Merry began to sing. Sarah's jealousy faded and she sat enthralled as the songs of the music hall were performed with skill and irresistible joyfulness by the talented woman. She was unaware of Alfred sitting beside her until she heard his deep voice adding to the praises and the calls of 'Encore!'

'She is truly wonderful, is she not?' Alfred said. 'How I envy someone such a talent, and the determination to develop and display it! She must be a remarkable woman. I hear she was born into abject poverty and has grown into the fine performer she is by sheer hard work and doggedness.'

Sarah thought of her mother, whose early beginnings were a shrouded mystery but whose lowly background was undisputed.

'Sorry to disillusion you,' Giles's voice said with a laugh. 'But Merry is a wealthy woman, whose family were embarrassed by her chosen career. Abject poverty was not her life; she is a lady and she is constantly amused by the newssellers' inventions.'

The information did not make Sarah feel any better. Talented, beautiful and of good family – what more could Giles ever want? She wandered back through the hall to the small garden room and the Christmas tree. Behind the open door she sat fanning her cheeks, wishing she were back in London. The celebrations were out of tune with her mood. Apart from the difficulty of knowing how to treat Giles, she was constantly reminded of Margaret. Her engagement party was not so long ago, and she imagined how her sister would have enjoyed sharing this one. Under the tree would have been several presents bearing her name.

'You look sad. Is this all too much for you so soon after your loss?' Giles's voice asked.

Sarah stood up, wondering where the voice came from.

'Giles?'

'I'm being very ungentlemanly and watching you through the door-crack.' His voice had a laugh in it and she poked her head around the door at the same time he did. Their cheeks met, and his arm steadied her. 'Sarah. I wish you the happiest of Christmases.'

'And for you, Giles, everything you wish for yourself.' Her cheek tingled where they had touched and it seemed he felt a similar sensation, because his hand came up and stroked his cheek while he stared at her, his dark eyes glowing and seeming to envelop her in warmth.

'Don't stay so far from the fun, Sarah. Shall we go into the dining room? I think the servants have finished their work there.'

He led her through the crowd, nodding to acquaintances over the heads of most, giving a word of greeting here and a teasing remark there. Sarah felt she was floating as he escorted her, his hand holding hers.

There were several other couples in the room, where tables had been cleared and re-set for supper snacks. In corners, the chaperons sat talking in low tones, glancing at their charges between confidences. Great-Aunt Milly was not there. A chill had made her rest at Houghton Hall.

Giles offered Sarah a glass of wine and a small biscuit, and they sat looking out into the dark garden, where a few torches lit the area directly in front of the large french windows.

'Will you allow me to take you and Isobelle for a drive tomorrow morning?' Giles asked. 'Once the presents are opened and discussed, there will be a lull before luncheon. I suspect Isobelle does not enjoy much variety in her life; it would be a treat for her. And an even bigger treat for me,' he added.

'Thank you, Giles. I look forward to it.' She wondered anxiously if Merry would stop him from going.

'You haven't had further news of the villains who robbed you, have you? Bannerman hasn't learned anything new?'

Sarah shook her head. 'He says the trail has gone cold and, although he once came within an inch of capturing Arthur, he escaped. I think we may never find them.'

'I go to see Bannerman occasionally and I've offered a reward. He has not given up hope of bringing them to justice.'

'That is generous of you. Thank you.'

'It's better to offer money than risk your life, Sarah, as you and Renton were doing. These men are already liable to the harshest penalties and have nothing to lose. They would kill without a moment's regret, even someone as lovely as you, to prevent themselves being caught.'

The compliment was lightly given but Sarah was heartened by it. She was in one of her constant dilemmas where Giles was concerned. When she was near him she wanted nothing more than to stay, but when they were apart, her capricious heart wavered and her mind warned her of the impossibility of loving and marrying a man with his lifestyle. She vacillated between joy and despair every moment she thought of him. Now, sitting beside him looking out into the winter garden with its dead flowers and evergreen foliage, quite beautiful in the flickering lights, all doubts faded. He was showing her more attention than ever before and she could not think beyond the moment.

When most of the forty or more guests had gone, the two families went to the garden room and opened the parcels. Sarah watched jealously as Merry opened a silk scarf, a gift from Giles, and was none too pleased to find an identical one in her own parcel. She thanked him politely but found it hard to smile. He laughed at her, and pointed out another parcel, almost hidden deep in the branches. She reached in and took it out. The wrapping was beautiful with gold-coloured paper, lace, and a band of yellow ribbon ending in an enormous bow. Small imitation pearls decorated the bow and made the shape of another bow.

'It's too lovely to destroy by opening it,' Sarah whispered.

She paused to look around to make sure the others were occupied in unwrapping their own gifts and exchanging thanks before gently pulling at the ribbon. The box inside was covered in small jewels and inside that she found a necklace set with sapphires. She gasped at the beauty of it, and looked at her father. Would he allow her to accept such an expensive present from Giles?

Sir Jason had been watching her and, as she looked up, he nodded and smiled.

'I asked Sir Jason's permission before buying it for you, Sarah,' Giles said softly. 'If you would accept it, my Christmas joy would be complete.'

'It's beautiful!' She put it around her neck.

'And so are you.'

The rest of the evening went like a dream. Caroline hugged her and whispered, 'Perhaps my greatest wish will come true and you will be my sister. Oh, Sarah, it would make me so happy!'

'I couldn't wish for a nicer sister to take Margaret's place, Caroline, but it's too soon to think of such a thing.' But she thought of nothing else as they drove back to Houghton Hall in the crisp, cold night of Christmas Eve.

Her father travelled with her and he too seemed in a happy mood. Whatever business discussions he had planned seemed less of a worry. Perhaps the beautiful singer Marie Mackworth was somehow the reason for his change of humour. He had danced with her several times and had stayed near her the rest of the time. Could he be taking a more than musical interest? she wondered. She took hold of his hand and smiled up at him.

'Although the ache of sadness for Margaret and Isobelle will always be with me, I do feel that the rest of my heart is happy, Father,' she said. 'I hope it is that way with you, too.'

'Thank you, child. My heart is a patchwork of good and ill, but we are coming out of it, aren't we? Together. That is most important. We are together in our loss.'

The happy mood lasted until they went upstairs to bed. Sarah walked with her father to her room, but instead of calling a final 'good night' to her father, she screamed. The room was empty. Isobelle's covers were thrown back on the abandoned bed, her clothes were in a pile ready for the morning, but of the little girl there was no sign.

Chapter Ten

Jarvis hated the country. The weather was harsher, and the air so cold he could hardly contemplate walking out in it so early in the morning, but he knew he had to go.

The sky, which had been so clear on the previous evening, was low and as grey as old pewter. The houses and even the trees reflected the same drabness and he was sure there would be snow before many days had passed. In town, he always remembered how oddly different the roofs looked before snow fell and guessed the same effect was showing here in the openness of the empty fields, as the sky spread its grey light over them.

The house he was silently leaving was still, but he knew that the servants would soon be about, even though they had been so late to bed the evening before. He dressed in his suit of tweed and wrapped around himself the thick woollen cloak he had obtained specially for this visit. His boots reached his knees and he hoped they would withstand the wet and muddy fields. He shuddered at the thought of all that mud on the fine leather.

Slipping out of the house unseen was easy but he gasped with the cold as he closed the door behind him and was tempted to go back inside. It was barely daylight and he did not try to conceal himself as he crossed the courtyard and hurried down the long drive to the road. He glanced back once and the place was still in darkness. Only beyond the green baize door would there be any lights burning.

He kept to the road for a while but, as the day lightened, he set off across the fields, curling his face with disgust at first at the squelching mud underfoot. He stopped several times to remove the build-up of soil and hurried on, determined to get to the farmhouse before anyone saw him. There were few houses in the vicinity, only a couple of farmhouses, and these he skirted. The only sign of life he met was a covey of partridges which he disturbed at the edge of a field.

It was impossible to walk briskly and keep warm, and by the time he reached the old farmhouse he was shivering. He struggled to get the key from his pocket and into the lock, then found that the door opened without it. He must have forgotten to lock it on his last visit. Another key was necessary for the padlock, however, and he stamped his feet as he forced his stiff fingers to turn it.

The house was cold and offered no relief from the outside chill. He would stay only long enough to check that all the goods were there and ready for his customers.

The packing cases were standing innocently in rows against the walls. Sliding out the foil packages, he examined each one before slipping it back into place. The tobacco was all correct. Then he carefully eased away the lining of the boxes and slid his hand into the opening. Wrapped in slim parcels of cotton wool were the real contraband articles. Tearing aside the wadding, he nodded approval as jewellery glinted dully in the gloom. He wrapped everything as neatly as before and put it back. He looked around as he reached the door to make sure everything was as carefully concealed as he could make it, then he checked the window and saw the dust that had been released when the window was open. With a curse he fastened the damaged clasp, but it would no longer hold. Searching through the house, he found pieces of wood and with these he jammed the window firmly so it could not be shaken loose. Locking everything up, he left.

When his shadow had crossed the window of the sitting room of the old building, other shadows moved. Slowly, Isobelle and Peter crept out from the cupboard where they had been hiding. They removed the wood with which Jarvis had jammed the window. Isobelle growled.

Alfred Cummins shivered in the bed. The fire had long since

gone out and it would be some time yet before the servant girl came to relight it. These huge old houses were fearfully cold. He wondered how elderly people like poor Great-Aunt Milly stood it. He was pulling his night-hat down over his ears when he heard shouting. Reluctantly he rose and added a greatcoat to the nightgown and smoking jacket he already wore, and opened his door.

'It's Isobelle, she's missing,' Giles explained as he ran along the passageway. 'We're organising search parties. Will you help?'

'Of course.' Alfred dressed and, when arrangements were being made, agreed to search to the east of them. Once out of sight, he slipped back into the haybarn and allowed the warmth of it to thaw his frozen feet. Let others search; their enthusiasm would keep them warm. He could not imagine why anyone would want to spend the best hours of the morning on a fruitless hunt. If the child had run away, then she clearly had somewhere to go. He spread his blanket and made himself comfortable.

He felt a sudden pang of guilt when he went back into the house to where mulled beer was being served. Sarah was white with fear. She really did care for the simple sister.

'I walked until I came to an abandoned farm,' he lied. 'I saw no sign of her. I'm so sorry.'

'She was probably looking for me,' Sarah said. 'I shouldn't have left her. The house is strange to her now.' She called to Edith. 'We must go back to Houghton Hall.'

'Don't worry, Miss Sarah,' Alfred said firmly. 'We will all search until she is found. I'm sure she will be safe. No one would refuse to shelter her in such bitter weather.'

Sarah nodded and went back into the house. She had been strictly forbidden to help in the search. But, in fact, it was she who saw her first.

The men had been given torches although it was early in the day. Clouds hung low and the day was gloomy. The sight of torches might attract attention and encourage Isobelle out if she was hiding, and show the farmers she was being hunted if she had found a safe place. Sarah stood at the drawing-room windows of Weatherby, wishing she had stayed at Houghton Hall. She felt sure that if Isobelle did wander back, it would be to her home, not here, where she would remember no one.

Watching for the line of torches, she did not at first realise that two figures were approaching. They seemed almost unreal in the grey air, wrapped up against the cold. She was startled when she finally recognised them. Then she ran to the door, calling for servants and calling her sister's name.

Mrs Brandon held Isobelle's hand and it was clear to Sarah that the child came with her unwillingly.

'Come on, my precious,' Mrs Brandon was shouting and there was irritation in her voice. 'Come on and get us out of this cold wind, do. Cutting me in half, it is.'

Sarah ran to Isobelle and bent down to comfort her but her sister seemed frightened by her reaching arms.

'Peer!' she wailed. 'Peer, Peer!' She struggled to escape.

'What is she saying?' Sarah asked.

'Peter. She wants that Peter, him that works for me on times. Following behind he is, like the cow's tail.'

Sarah coaxed them inside, where servants waited to warm them. Lucy and Caroline were holding shawls to wrap the little girl, but all she seemed to want was her friend, 'Peer'.

There was a shawl wrapped around her small body that was large enough to drag on the ground, but underneath it she was wearing only a thin muslin dress, filthy now and streaked with farmyard mud. There were torn shreds hanging from the hem and only holes to show where there had once been daisies sewn on the skirt. Over the dress and under the shawl was a boy's waistcoat, a few rushes poking out of a pocket like a forlorn buttonhole. Her hair was tangled and only partly held back by a boy's flat cap.

'Peer,' she pleaded.

While servants took Isobelle off to be bathed and dressed in warmer clothes, Renton went outside and fired a shot with Giles's flintlock, to tell the others that the child was safe. The procession, which had grown as farmers and cottagers had joined in the search, returned and they were all invited in to take a warming drink. In the kitchen, the cooking of Christmas dinner, which had been abandoned, recommenced.

'Where do you think she spent the night, Mrs Brandon?'

Sir Jason asked. 'Could she have been trying to go back to you?'

'Bless you, sir, if she had come back she'd have been straight up to my bed. The door is never locked. No, I think my little precious got herself lost and some cottager took her in. Not being very good at talking, she probably didn't tell them when she decided to find her way back. Peter found her and brought her to me.'

'Didn't he say where she was found?'

'Says little enough, does Pigpen.'

Renton found Peter outside the window and brought him inside. Alfred tried to persuade the boy to tell him where he had found Isobelle.

'An old building, perhaps?' he asked softly, in his melodious, deep voice. Sarah was impatient but he explained that the information might be useful should a similar situation occur.

Isobelle was brought back down, cleaned and warmed and dressed in clothes that had once belonged to Caroline. Pink satin knickerbockers and a dress with several petticoats of lace made her look more forlorn than before. Even Sarah's soft heart was jolted by her plainness.

Isobelle looked around the room at the family, whose silence at her entrance contrasted strongly with the merriment rising up from the kitchens, where celebrations at her safe return were enthusiastically continuing. Then her swollen face rose and she looked at Alfred. She pointed at him and the growl in her throat made him step back.

There was embarrassed laughter as Peter explained that the young maid did not like men. 'Excepting of me,' he added, and the laughter became more genuine at the idea of the undersized, poorly dressed and dirty ten-year-old describing himself as a man.

Sarah and Sir Jason took Isobelle out to the coach and took her home. She settled to sleep against Sarah's shoulder, but intermittently she woke, sobbed and called for her friend. Behind the coach, straggling farther and farther away from it, the servants with their relighted torches walked to Houghton Hall, singing and laughing, pushing and teasing. Even when they were back in the house, it was a long time before they were able to resume their duties.

Sir Jason ate alone. Sarah had a tray sent to Isobelle's room and she spent an hour coaxing her sister to eat. But Isobelle was tired and could not be roused enough to eat, and she was put into bed. Sarah sat with her long into the night and finally slept in the chair beside the bed towards dawn. When she woke, the bed was empty once more and Isobelle had gone.

This time they went straight to Mrs Brandon, where they were met by voluble excuses for the lack of comforts.

'Sir and lady, I'm ashamed of my poor home. I took the opportunity of my little maid being away and put all my fine flounces for washing. What will you think of me, so shabby the place looks? Forgive me, but I thought – '

'Mrs Brandon,' Sir Jason interrupted. 'My daughter has gone missing again. I simply want to know if she is here. I cannot think about curtains and cushions at such a time.'

'Can you ask Peter if he has seen her?' Sarah asked.

Mrs Brandon looked shocked. 'If he's the cause of your fright, I'll kill him!' All pretence and gentle voice once again disappeared and she went to the door and called, 'Pigpen? Come this instant! What have you done with her? Pigpen? I know you're there somewhere. Come out!'

There was no movement and, although Mrs Brandon proceeded to search the barns, there was no sign of either Peter or Isobelle.

'If they turn up here, I'll come with her at once,' Mrs Brandon promised. 'But she's a law unto herself, my maid, goes where and when she wants. Best to give her time. She has no memory, thinks of you as strangers, I reckon – if you'll pardon,' she added, looking down in embarrassment.

'I think you're right,' Sir Jason said. 'I think we are wrong to disturb her and expect her to welcome a visit to her home.'

Sarah was about to protest, but a memory of the sad face in the ridiculously fancy satin clothes held her tongue. Isobelle did not belong with them any more.

The servants from Houghton Hall, having failed to find the child in the vicinity of Weatherby, called on Giles's household to help.

Alfred hurried off as soon as the alarm was raised.

'I'll search to the east,' he offered. 'Best you concentrate between here and Houghton Hall as before.'

Alfred was pleased to see the grateful smile Sarah bestowed on him and decided that a long, cold walk over muddy fields would be well worth it for the appreciation she would feel and certainly remember. He hurriedly moved off before someone was allotted to accompany him, and set off with great enthusiasm across the ploughed fields towards the old farmhouse.

In the cupboard at the farm where Isobelle and Peter spent many hours, they sat, wrapped in old sacks and a blanket, which Isobelle had brought. They were nursing some mice that they had tamed. Peter chatted to her but, although she stared at him, her eyes glowing with pleasure, she made little attempt to reply.

From his pocket, Peter pulled a paper bag. Isobelle snatched the bag and, taking out the cakes and sweets, began to arrange them on the broken saucers which were their plates. The picnic had begun. She left the cupboard to go to the pump over the sink to fill their jug with water, but as soon as her hand touched the wooden handle, a noise sent her scurrying back to Peter.

The door opened, and the heavy breathing told them someone was in a hurry. Pulling the cupboard door tightly closed, they waited silently as Jarvis ran through the rooms.

'Where did you leave the jug?' Peter whispered when the footsteps had faded upstairs. Isobelle's eyes filled with tears. She had left it at the sink. Peter guessed what she had done and, warning her to be still, crept from his hiding place. He placed an old broom handle through the banisters, close against the rise of the fourth stair. Crouched in the darkness he was sure he would not be seen as Jarvis hurried down. He counted as the feet touched each stair and when Jarvis was on the fifth from the bottom, raised the stick.

With a shout of rage, Jarvis lost his footing and fell to the floor. Peter had slipped away and the silence convinced Jarvis of his own carelessness. Limping painfully, and using the stick as a crutch, he left the house.

* * *

On the following day they took Isobelle back to Mrs Brandon. It was clear as soon as they reached the yard that it was what the child wanted. She ran in her stiff-legged way straight to the barn and came out hugging the cat. They heard her calling for 'Peer' and accepted that this was where she was happiest.

'Thank you, Mrs Brandon,' Sir Jason said. 'My daughter seems so content here, she no longer needs us.' He was sad as he spoke and Sarah too did not smile.

'But we need her,' she added, 'and I will come to visit as often as I can.'

'Of course,' her father agreed. But Sarah sensed that, although he regretted the failure of Isobelle to settle for the holiday at Houghton Hall, he was embarrassed by his simple child and would be glad to get away.

They left all the new clothes they had brought for her and the toys which had been wrapped and placed under the Christmas tree.

'Seems she likes cats and all manner of wild things better than toys,' Mrs Brandon said. 'That fine doll you brought with her, it's ruined, though I've mended it so often there's nothing left of what she started with. No, my precious is happy with country things. Children aren't all the same, so's my experience, and it's best to let them be how they'll be.'

The celebrations were so disjointed that everyone seemed unable to recover the excitement of the holiday. They tried to revive the mood but there was a numbness over it all.

Sarah sat one morning, staring out of the window, thinking of Isobelle and wishing she had shown signs of improvement. But she admitted that, although she had become fatter and decidedly grubbier, she seemed content. Mrs Brandon and Peter were her family now.

She became aware of voices and, stepping into the hall, realised they were coming from the garden room. Opening the door, she saw that a table and several chairs had been taken in. Papers were in neat piles around the table and her father sat with Giles and Alfred, obviously preparing to discuss some business plans.

'Giles! I did not hear you come.'

'My apologies, Sarah. I did enquire but no one knew where to find you.'

'Sarah was sitting in the drawing room staring out of the window,' Alfred said. 'But she seemed too wrapped in dreams for me to want to disturb her.'

'I cannot stay more than a few moments,' Giles explained. 'I have to return to town in an hour.'

'Oh, what a shame! Not Caroline too?' Sarah asked.

'Bertram will come back with me, but Caroline will stay, and she'll need your company with all of us leaving.'

'Your brothers too?'

'Unfortunately, yes.'

'Tell her I will call and bring her back here, if she will stay.'

'Will you please excuse me, Sarah, my dear?' Sir Jason asked. 'We have so much to discuss and little time.'

'Excuse *me*,' she said, a little sharply. 'Forgive me for interrupting matters that cannot wait.'

Sir Jason smiled at her disapproval, and shared the smile with Giles.

'We have no secrets, Sarah,' Giles said. 'I am opening a new kind of club in the spring. A club for gentlemen, where they can sit and read, talk or play some mild-mannered games, and eat luncheon or dinner, and' he added slowly, 'where no women are allowed. Not even women servants.'

'Who would attend such a place? Surely it's the company of a certain class of women that persuades men from their homes at night?'

'There will always be accommodation for such needs. But I want to provide a quiet, peaceful ambience for business-men and politicians to rest between their activities. To discuss in pleasant surroundings matters of interest, and exchange views on the political scene.'

'And your father,' Alfred interposed, 'is importing much of the furnishings.'

'I see. And you, Mr Cummins? Where do you fit?'

'In the transporting of it, Miss Sarah. I have undertaken to collect the consignment from the ship, deliver it to Mr Hallam's premises and unpack it.'

'So you are all involved in this new project of Giles's?'

'I have the good fortune to be able to assist, yes,' Alfred replied. 'In fact, I'm off to Paris again next week to make sure the items are packed as thoroughly as Sir Jason would wish.'

'Then I will leave you to your discussions.'

Sarah closed the door and returned to stare disconsolately out of the window. Christmas had been a disaster. The disappointment over Isobelle's estrangement and her running away from them had overshadowed everything. She had seen little of Caroline, who was wrapped up in her plans for her future, and had hardly had a chance to speak to Renton. The loss of Margaret, with whom she had been able to discuss her every thought, was a constant, aching void. She tried to behave normally in front of others but it was a hard act to sustain. She sighed. The sooner they were back in London, the better. It was grey and the clouds were threatening snow. Yet another reason to hope for an early end to the holiday.

Chapter Eleven

Emily Tilt was standing at her usual spot, leaving her flowers occasionally to warm herself at the brazier where hot chestnuts were offered. Her hands were stiff with the cold and her fingers remained curled long after she had put down the heavy basket. The remnants of snow lay on the ground, dirty now and, where people walked, wet underfoot.

She wore woollen stockings, having taken money from her savings to buy them. Chilblains had made her legs red and swollen and they were raw where her fingernails had raked them, attempting to ease the discomfort. The stockings were held up with circles of thin elastic and these bit into her thighs. She felt for them through her thick skirts to try to alter their position and had to put her hand down inside her skirts to do so. It was warmer there and she stood for a while with both hands inside her navy serge skirt, allowing the pain of the new discomfort to show on her face as they thawed.

'Snow again before midnight, I bet yer,' Maggs said. 'What say a tanner on it? You likes a bet, don't yer?'

'Only a fool bets against a certainty! I can feel the first flakes on me face already!' Emily retorted. Then she laughed as she saw from her friend's face she had been joking. 'Oh, Maggs, what a way to live!'

'Cheer up, love, 'ere comes your gentleman. 'E's early tonight, ain't 'e?'

Emily looked at the corner and, sure enough, Jarvis was standing there watching her before approaching, as he always did. She saw him no more frequently than before the night she had saved him from the police, but now, instead of a few moments during which he bought a flower, he sometimes took her to the stall and bought her a coffee. Today he bought his flower, then, to her delight, gestured at her to go with him.

'Go on.' Maggs waved her away. 'I'll keep an eye out fer yer flowers. Don't reckon to try and sell none, though, so don't be long.'

Jarvis walked with her but did not take hold of her elbow to guide her as she hoped. Perhaps one day, when she was dressed proper, he would walk with her instead of just near her. He disappeared once as a carriage disgorged its passengers nearby, reappearing only after it had gone. He's ashamed of me, she thought, but I don't blame him for that. She thought of her reddened nose and cheeks, and eyes rimmed red by the frost. Her hands were swollen and cracked. These she hid under her cloak. There was nothing she could do about the rest.

Jarvis bought the coffee and she sipped it thankfully. Waiting for him to begin the conversation, she examined him admiringly. His clothes were expensive; an embroidered waistcoat under a fine wool jacket, a cloak with an extra shoulder cape, a cravat covering his neck, and slim-fitting trousers slid into good leather boots.

'I have a favour to ask you,' he said when she had swallowed the warming liquid. 'I need your help.'

'Anything.' Emily waved her arms to describe how wide was his choice. She parted reluctantly with the still-warm cup and looked at him expectantly.

'I need someone to act as my maid servant for an hour or two. Would you do that for me?'

'I ain't got no clothes. I 'ardly look the part in these, do I?' she protested, her voice slipping from the attempt at ladylike speech.

'I'll see to the clothes.' He slipped an arm around her, but with the layers of thick clothing he could only guess at the slim waist underneath.

'When?' she asked, confused by his touching her.

'Tomorrow evening, about seven-thirty.'

'What? That's into me best time. Sorry, I couldn't do

that.'

'I have a boy who will watch your pitch for you. I'll pay him. It will only be for a few hours.'

'A couple of hours? You sure? It ain't going to be one of them all-night larks, is it? I don't bother with none of that.'

Jarvis laughed delightedly. 'Oh, Emily, you are a real character! Of course not!' He leaned closer and lowered his voice. 'Any night larks, and it will be you and me, in our own place. And, if you help me with this little transaction, that day will be closer than you think. Imagine it, Emily, you and me in our own little house!'

'Room, you mean.'

'House I said and that is what I mean. Emily, if this deal comes off, you and I will be able to buy ourselves a house.'

'Come off it!'

'I am not teasing. This business deal will buy us a house, and you some fine clothes so you can visit the coffee shops with all the ladies. You'll look a lady, Emily Tilt, when you have the clothes.'

Emily held out her red, swollen hands. 'Think so, do you?' She knew a daydream when she heard one.

To her surprise he felt in his pocket and dropped five sovereigns into her grubby hands. 'That's for you to visit a doctor and get creams to soften your skin. And that is only the beginning.'

'You mean it? You really mean that you and I will rent a house?'

'No, we will buy one.'

Emily still frowned, unable to dare to accept what he was saying. She looked at him, and the frown and the flicker of hope gave her a childlike expression. Jarvis closed her fingers over the coins.

'Put it away before some unsavoury character knocks you down for it.'

Emily handed them back. 'Jarvis, you mind them for me. I can have them any time I ask, can't I?'

'They belong to you, and you can have them when you ask.' It was a declaration of trust.

'Now, what d'you want me to do?'

* * *

They met the following evening at the address he had given her. When Emily arrived he was waiting, a wicker case in his hand. Shushing her greeting, he led her down the sloping lane behind the well-kept houses of the street. There was an extra row of windows at the back as the yards were lower than the street. Tall brick walls separated the lane from the yards. He opened a gate and pulled her inside.

'See that window?' he whispered, pointing to a sash window where no light shone. 'I want you to climb in that way.'

'Not bloody likely!' She tried to push past him and ran back into the lane. 'I ain't getting caught for breaking in and robbing! I knew there was a catch. Ain't there always?'

'I don't intend to rob anyone.' Jarvis held her in his surprisingly strong arms. 'The room belongs to a friend who is away at present. I'm going to borrow the place, that's all. I promise.'

Her struggles ceased and, after a few more reassuring words, she agreed.

The window was not difficult. The clasp was loose and, following Jarvis's instructions, only needed a few shakes to persuade the semicircular catch to slide around and allow Emily to push the window up on its cords. She climbed in, and offered him a hand.

'No,' he whispered. 'Go round to the door and let me in.'

It was eerie walking about in an unknown room, lit only by the street lamps. She started back in alarm on reaching the hall door as a shadow loomed over her. But it was only a large plant that threw its leaves in the shape of a threatening figure. She held her breath against the squeak as the door opened and let it out with relief when she saw Jarvis standing there. He slipped inside and went into the room.

After closing the curtains, he found and lit the oil lamp.

'Hurry and get into these.' He opened the wicker basket and gave her a dress and some fine leather shoes. She was tempted to stand and exclaim over their excellence but Jarvis was impatient. 'My friends will be here soon. Admire them later then they've gone.'

The dress was grey and peacock blue and the neck was daringly low. In the pocket of the dress was a fine pendant which Jarvis hung about her throat. A lace cap was in the basket too and this went over her long, richly red hair. She waited for him to admire her but he was too busy setting out papers, bottles of ink and pens to notice her.

The room had a smaller room leading off it that was little more than a cupboard. There they found glasses and plates as well as food and drink. Jarvis showed her the Madeira wine he had brought and some biscuits and small cakes no larger than a florin. These they put on plates and she was instructed to serve them with the wine. While she busied herself exploring the tiny kitchen and examining the beautiful china and glass, Jarvis sat puffing his pipe and filling the room with the pleasant smell of his tobacco.

Emily used the time that was left to comb out her long, thick hair. She went and stood in front of him, wanting his approval. He was unable to withhold a gasp of amazement.

'Why, Emily Tilt, you are a beauty!' He stood up and stroked the long, curling hair that she had washed with such care that morning under the tap in the street near the Nethersken. Her hair had been mostly hidden from him before under the hats she wore. Now, with the curls falling in a sea of golden-red waves down her back, she was a different woman. Her figure, too, was a revelation. The bundled-up flower-seller was hard to imagine as he stared at her in the revealing gown.

He took her hands in his, saddened by the coarseness of her skin. The cracked surface was like handling ashes from a dead fire.

'Soon we will buy gloves for you and creams,' he murmured. 'You will be a truly beautiful lady then.'

Emily pulled her hands away in shame. 'Take more than gloves and a bit of cream, they will!'

There was a knock at the door and she wanted to run.

'Jarvis, I can't do it! What will they think I am, eh?'

'They'll know you are a beautiful lady.' He touched her brow with his lips. 'Go now and remember what I've taught you.'

There were four men. Although they were dressed in clothes as costly as those worn by Jarvis, Emily knew they weren't gentlemen. In years of watching and learning about the great and varied public, earning a living first by scrounging and stealing and later by selling her flowers, she had become an expert at judging a man's income. These were tricksters. She looked at Jarvis anxiously. Did he know? How could she warn him?

She sat down in the kitchen and put on the dainty lace cap Jarvis had instructed her to wear when she served drinks and food. She tried to listen to the conversation through the door but the men spoke in whispers and when words were clearly spoken she failed to understand them. When she heard Jarvis say loudly, 'And now, gentlemen, I think a glass of wine would not go amiss, eh?' Emily stood up and tried to calm herself to begin her duties.

She opened the door and stepped into the room with a tray of glasses and the wine. Placing it on the small table as he had told her, she went back to fetch the cakes specially bought in Fortnum & Mason. These she handed round after serving each man with a drink. She smiled politely and, in spite of nervousness, began to enjoy the novel experience.

As she closed the door to the kitchen, she could hear the men complimenting Jarvis on his lovely maid and making ribald remarks about her duties.

Three bottles of wine were consumed and then the four men left. She closed the door behind them, accepting their thanks with a polite nod of her head and the hint of a curtsy, as if she had had years of dealing with such occasions.

'Emily, you were perfect!' Jarvis said as soon as his guests had departed. 'How did you learn to act so well?'

'I don't know, it just sort of came.' She smiled.

'I think I am about to make a lot of money,' he said, pulling her towards him, pressing her body against his. 'You and I will be rich. What d'you think of that, Emily Tilt, one day to be Mrs Jarvis King?'

Emily gasped. If only he were serious! She felt the pain of his deceit; the boy who came when he was ill had called him Jarvis Williamson.

'Now,' she said, deciding to risk all. 'If you were to tell me I'd one day be Mrs Jarvis Williamson – '

For a moment she regretted the words. His green eyes darkened and a frown crossed his face, the mouth tightening as anger ran through him. Emily stepped away.

'Who have you been talking to?'

'I don't know how it was said,' she wailed. 'I thought I overheard someone calling you Williamson, that's all. I was mistaken.'

'No, Emily. You were right. The truth is, I have several names for several occasions. I'll be honest with you. I intended telling you but the time passed and . . . ' His expression softened and he pulled her close once more. 'Emily Tilt, soon to live in a fine house with her husband, Jarvis King. There, will that name please you?'

Emily did not reply. She stared at him, her eyes glowing.

'The clothes.' He touched the front of her dress. 'I borrowed them from a friend. You can keep them. In a few weeks there'll be more. In the meantime, we'll have to find a place to keep them, won't we?' He looked into her bewildered eyes. She wanted to believe what he was saying but was afraid of being thought a fool. 'Tomorrow, my Emily, or soon after, you and I will be going to see a little house I have chosen. If, and only if, you like it too, then we'll buy it.'

'For you to live in, with me?'

'I wouldn't want to live in it – or anywhere else for that matter – without you. Emily, I love you. You and I will make such a wonderful partnership.' He lowered his face slowly, looking deep into eyes that were dark with longing, and when they closed in a fluttering surrender, he kissed her.

The first time with her was disappointing. She stared up at him, transfixed like a rabbit by a stoat; unmoving and uninvolved until the very last moments. She did not smell as sweetly as he had hoped, and for a moment, he thought that even for a temporary arrangement he had made a mistake.

'Jarvis, I want to wash,' she surprised him by saying. 'I've been thinking about it ever since I've been here. That kitchen, there's a sink. I ain't never had a wash in a proper sink, not since I left the workhouse, and even then it was shared with half a dozen others.'

Jarvis was offended. 'Didn't my lovemaking give you more exciting thoughts than sinks?' he said harshly.

'I couldn't enjoy it. I was frightened and I felt ashamed. A gentleman like you is used to sweet-scented ladies, and I

. . .' She turned away from him. At once he felt better about her attitude, flattered almost and pleased at the prospect of teaching her.

'I'll wash you,' he said.

They went into the small kitchen. Taking the glasses and plates out of the sink, they filled it with water and made a lather with the bar of soap from the dish. Together they washed her body and, although the water was cold, Emily felt nothing but warmth.

The second time they made love it was wild and imaginative and Jarvis wondered if she had experience after all. It was early morning when they finally left the house, Emily wrapped warmly in Jarvis's cloak. They parted soon after, and Emily made her way to Maggs's room where she could change back into her ordinary clothes.

For the next few days Emily was in a daze. The lovemaking and the promises whispered in the dark of that borrowed room filled her thoughts. The prospect of a house to share with Jarvis seemed one moment an impossible fancy, the next she believed it would come true. Even when two, then three days had passed, she still hung on to her dream.

She continued to sell her flowers and each night she went back to the Nethersken and pretended to be drunk; she was too wily to risk losing her precious savings at this late stage. But during the night, as her chilled body thawed in the warmth of the crowded room, she imagined the luxury of not having to listen to the snores, groans and complaints of the people with whom she had shared the dark hours for all the years she could remember.

Weeks went by without Jarvis calling for his flower. Her hopes were fading. He had used her, just as all the other girls had warned her. Sharp Emily Tilt had been made a fool of. She was thankful she had not confided her dreams to Maggs; they were hard enough to come to terms with alone.

Then, when she had given up looking towards the corner, Jarvis appeared. He offered the money for his flower, leaned close enough to whisper a brief apology and led her to the coffee stall. She stifled her anger.

'Emily, my dear. I'm sorry I had to leave you for so long. I had to go down to the country. A business arrangement that the snow delayed.'

'I thought you'd – '

'I can't stay. Tomorrow I will meet you at the corner where you sell your flowers, and this time I want you dressed in the clothes I gave you. We are going to look at the house I've chosen.'

'Jarvis!' She breathed the word, still a little shy of using his name, but determined to live up to his expectations of her. She said the name again, louder. 'Jarvis, I can't wait! What's it like? Does it have a place for me to have a bed? And a mantel for a clock?'

Jarvis smiled at her. His face was shadowed and mysterious in the torches on the stall. 'You'll have to wait and see, my pretty flower girl.' He smiled and stroked his beard. Then he walked away, leaving her hugging the hot coffee cup.

He was excited at the thought of sharing a bed with her, but deliberately slowed down his thoughts. Emily was only a temporary diversion, a brief, albeit pleasurable, moment or two of low respectability. He was bound for far higher things than a bed with Emily Tilt.

He had just returned from Weatherby, having secretly borrowed the place for a few days while the stores from the old farm had been collected. It was risky, but he had been careful to change even his walk and had not been seen except when wearing the old clothes of a country labourer, his face hidden by a floppy hat.

He had a dream, but, unlike Emily's, his was on the grand scale. He would own Weatherby and live there, once Giles had been ruined, with Sarah. She would teach him how to be a gentleman, and Sarah would be a delightful teacher. He imagined for a while the ecstasy of taking Sarah's small and perfect young body, then smiled. Until then, Emily would do.

Emily had difficulty sleeping that night. She had nightmares each time she dozed, and dreamed that her fine clothes had been stolen or burned. She would wake with a start, convinced the dream was real, and look around wondering if she had spoken in her dreams the words that would put one of her sleeping companions on the scent of either her money or her clothes.

She rose early. She took a pinch of coffee from her pocket and, with water from the large, blackened kettle that was always simmering beside the fire, made herself an insipid drink. Most were still asleep when she went out into the cold streets to wake Maggs and reassure herself that her precious clothes were safe.

When she wore her normal, drab clothes with several layers hiding her shape, she felt almost invisible. She was so like many of the passers-by that she was confident she would be impossible to describe, should she fall foul of the law. People would not notice a shabby, poorly dressed woman of unguessable age and unremarkable features; her red, curly hair was always hidden under hat and shawl.

Today, wearing the dress given to her by Jarvis, she felt glaringly obvious.

The dress was not warm enough for the February chill but she had nothing to cover it that was suitable, except Jarvis's cloak, which she carried over her arm to return to him. A dress of this quality and neat leather shoes would look very odd if she wore an unravelling shawl of dirty grey, which stank of the many nights spent in the Nethersken. She had washed her hair and, with a comb she had stolen many months before, had removed all the tangles. Now when she unpinned her beautiful tresses they would fall in glorious waves down over her shoulders and almost to her tiny waist.

It was her slimness that made her feel so different and made her wonder if she could walk past even Maggs without being recognised. Feeling very self-conscious, she held her head up and forced a smile as she sauntered through the dingy streets from Maggs's room to her corner.

She had left her own old clothes in a corner of Maggs's home; a room which measured only seven by seven feet and in which a family of eight lived and slept. A ragged curtain hung on a line across the room at night and was the only attempt at privacy.

It was behind this that Emily had disrobed, washed and put on her fine clothes. She had taken her time, relishing the feel of the fine material on her skin and the new sensation of being young, slim and feminine.

The eyes that appeared occasionally at the holes in the curtain, she ignored. A half-dressed woman was no new spectacle to the small, wide-open eyes, there would be very little they had not witnessed many times before.

Now, on the way to meet her man, she did not hurry. She strolled as if it were a summer's day, determined to act the part Jarvis had offered her. Reaching her corner she slowly looked around for him, seeing as if with different eyes the corner where she spent so much of her life. The fire to cook chestnuts was already alight, and Maggs was sorting out the small paper squares from which she made the bags to hold the hot snacks.

Impishly, Emily strolled closer. She would give Maggs a surprise. The clothes had been wrapped and hidden in a flour sack and had not been seen by her friend. Would she treat her like a lady? She had reached the edge of the pavement when Maggs, without looking up, said, 'Fine feathers! Bleedin' perished you look, my girl.'

Emily contained her laughter with difficulty and replied, 'Don't you use that tone with me, my good woman!' before the laughter escaped and she had to hide her face with her gloved hands.

'Good luck, gel!' Maggs whispered. 'Come an' tell me what's new, won't yer?' She gestured with a slight tilt of her head and added through the corner of her mouth, 'He's 'ere. Get off with yer!'

There was surprise and admiration on Jarvis's face as he saw her. She stood still and waited for him to come to her, sudden shyness adding colour to her cheeks and brightness to her blue eyes. She was unsure of herself; had he been serious when he made all those promises? She looked into his eyes and they shared a look of such intensity that everything else faded. The noises of the street – the shoppers strolling past, horses dragging an assortment of carts, cabs and coaches – now seemed not to exist. They were alone in a silence of perfection.

Neither could speak. He took her hand and threaded it through his arm and they walked off, watched only by Maggs, whose hard features had softened and whose eyes bore a suspicion of a tear.

Irrelevant thoughts fluttered through Emily's mind. Thankfulness for the gloves that hid her ugly hands. The coldness of the pavements through her small slippers. The flecks in his clear eyes which changed them from grey to green. The need to press her nails into her palms to convince herself this was real.

She was jerked out of her daze by Jarvis suddenly changing direction and hurrying her down a small alleyway. She guessed he had seen someone whom he didn't want to meet while he was with her. She was only slightly hurt. Soon they would be married and she would meet all his friends.

They walked for a while without talking. When the bustle of town had been left behind, Jarvis said, 'I think you should still keep your flower pitch, but for a while we'll need the addition of some pocket dipping. You're good at it, Emily, and it will help us to buy the furnishings we need. I want to have a place where we can entertain my friends, a servant perhaps, once my dealings are complete.'

'Dipping's dangerous, the thought of prison – ' She shuddered. 'I've only done it now and then, when my savings needed a bit of help.'

'Your savings?'

'I've been saving so I can get myself a house. It seemed a hopeless dream, but it kept me going.'

'Perhaps you won't have to work the crowds for very long, if you have something for us to make a start.'

'I'll do it for a while but I'll be careful and only take something when I'm sure it's safe.'

'My friends will help you. A boy will come with you and watch, to see you aren't spotted, and create a diversion if you are. And I have a fence who'll be generous. And,' he added with a pat on her arm, 'if you need them, I have some bullies who work for me on occasion and they will easily sort out any problems for you.'

They turned at last into a narrow street with houses on one side only. Opposite them was a stretch of waste ground and, beyond it, the railway. The dwellings were small and all looked the same. She guessed they would have two rooms up and two down and perhaps a yard at the back. Excitement grew in her, feeling they were close to their destination.

Instinctively she looked around her for escape routes, yards where she could run if necessary. She gauged the height of walls and marked trees and bushes that would assist her in an emergency. There would be times when she would have to move fast; Jarvis had not offered her an end to her thieving, just a partnership in crime.

He stopped and pointed to a house in the centre of the row, and they walked to the door. The rest of the houses were well cared for but this one was neglected and dirty. Emily pushed open the front door and they stepped inside.

It was dark. The windows were streaked with dirt and remnants of curtains barred the daylight. A partition had been built separating the room from the draught from the door and this swung as Emily touched it. She gave it a push and it fell with a clatter, raising clouds of dust and sending several beetles scurrying from its shelter.

There was a door which led into a kitchen, where blue and red quarry tiles were just visible under a layer of dust and rubbish. Outside there was a shed, leaning at a crazy angle, which showed signs of being used for coal. Emily examined the iron fireplace with its oven and the swivel on which a rusted kettle stood, forlorn among the splattered soot and coal dust. Behind the door leading to the narrow strip of garden was a curving wooden staircase. Emily looked about her and sighed.

'It's lovely.' She went to the window in front of which stood a sink. She patted the sink and gave him a saucy wink. 'Perfect.'

There were two rooms upstairs and Emily squealed with pleasure as she ran from one to the other, looking out of broken windows and remarking on the views.

'Oh, Jarvis, we'll be so happy here!' She impulsively hugged him.

'Can you get it cleaned? I'm afraid, unless you're willing to lend me some of your savings, that the furnishings will have to wait a while.'

'We're a partnership, aren't we? Of course I'll furnish it for us. I'll find my cousin who has a cab, he'll drive me around and help bargain for stuff in the markets.'

'No rubbish, though. I want us to have nothing but the best. And, on a temporary basis, can you let me have enough to pay completely? It will save us such a lot of loan fees.'

Emily happily agreed, excited at the prospect of shopping for her own home at last.

She looked down at her dress. 'I'll need to change first if I want some bargains. I won't do to look for bargains in these clothes.'

'Don't change just yet, Emily. I want you to help me entertain some friends this evening. The same place as before. Will you do it?'

'Just serve wine and food?'

'Of course. Just wear that dress and look your beautiful best.'

It was a disappointment for her that she could not start at once on the cleaning. The house was like a sick person who needed loving attention, and Emily was aching to begin treatment. But she was persuaded, and as soon as her carroty-haired assistant had been settled into the flower pitch and given his instructions, Emily set off for the borrowed room.

This time she examined it more closely, thinking these were the kind of furnishings Jarvis was used to. She particularly admired the gold and marble clock on the mantelpiece, and told him so.

It was not the same four men who arrived. The door opened on Giles Hallam and Sir Jason Lindhurst Ayres. She knew them from seeing them with Renton and from serving them occasionally with flowers. She lowered her face and hoped that her changed appearance would make them fail to recognise her. Of the two, it was Sir Jason she thought the most likely to know her, as Renton had mentioned that she was his cousin on more than one occasion, hoping he would be a regular customer for her.

When she served wine, her little lace cap set on her long hair, she doubted if she could be compared with the shabbily dressed flower girl who was a part of the nightly scene. The surroundings were different as well as her clothes. They showed no sign of recognising her and she thought it unlikely she would have to make any explanations.

When the men had gone, Jarvis sat for a while going over his papers, adding columns of numbers and scribbling copious notes. Emily washed the glasses and plates and, when they had been dried and put back where they belonged, eyed the sink full of soapy water with interest.

When he finally put away his papers, he opened the door to the kitchen and burst out laughing. Emily was sitting in the water, her knees almost touching her chin, soaping herself. She offered him the bar of soap. The smile faded and desire showed on his face as he began sensuously to smooth her pale, creamy skin.

When they left, as dawn began to break, Emily asked, 'Can I start cleaning our house today?'

'I'll see the solicitor this afternoon. Thanks to your savings, which you added to mine, by tomorrow the house will be ours. Can you bear to wait until tomorrow at midday?'

'It will be hard, but yes.'

They arranged to meet and Emily went back to her other life, the one she would soon be finished with for good.

For three days Emily scrubbed and cleaned the house. The water was cold and her hands were soon even worse than before, but she was blissfully happy. On the fourth day she called on Renton and told him her news.

'I've found myself a man,' she explained, 'and we've bought a house. Will you help me furnish it?'

'Bless you, Emily! We'll have to have a double wedding.'

'No time for weddings just yet. There's a lot of work to be done and my man has a few business deals to settle before we get around to the officials,' she said with an air of pride. Cautious as always, she did not give him her address.

'Business deals? Buying a house? What have you found for yourself?'

'You'll meet him when I'm ready to receive visitors,' she said. 'Till then, will you help me or not?'

'If the cab is what you need, then it's at your service, my lady,' he teased.

Together they searched the market stalls and shops,

spending Emily's carefully saved money on a few good items of furniture. As a guide she imagined entertaining Jarvis's friends and went through what they would need. But she had a few embarrassing moments when she had to ask about china and cutlery, things that hardly existed in her world. Jarvis and Renton both at separate times explained their uses and she learned quickly, her observant mind soon completing her education. She hired a cart to collect her purchases and began to settle in.

Some men were engaged to cover the walls with paper that to Emily's eyes was so beautiful she kept touching it, feeling its smoothness even through her callused fingertips. The day she came back with a large mirror and a picture of fields, a river and some cows, she thought there was nothing else in the world needed for complete happiness. But Jarvis had one more surprise for her.

Every evening, instead of going back to the Nethersken, she slept at the house. First on the floor, then, when part of the shopping had been completed, on a soft bed. The first time she woke in it she had the sensation of floating and was unwilling to move and break the spell, but a loud knocking at the door jerked her up and she went down the curving stairs, straightening her clothes and smoothing her hair, her heart thumping anxiously.

A van stood at the kerb, with the name Willoughby's across its dark-blue side. Dressed in the same dark blue, a young man stood beside it holding a parcel.

'Name of Tilt?' he asked, touching his cap politely.

Emily's hand went up to repeat the gesture, unused to such respect, but she changed it to a slight movement and touched her chin.

'Oh, I wasn't expecting anything just at the moment,' she uttered in a strange new voice.

'Sign here if you would be so kind.' He offered her a small notebook and the stub of a pencil. She took the unaccustomed pencil and wrote her name with a flourish at the end, beginning to enjoy the encounter. She acknowledged the boy's parting salute with a more confident nod, and rushed inside to open the parcel.

When the final wrapping parted she shrieked with amazement. It was a clock, almost identical to the one she had admired in the borrowed room. Her first instinct was to hide it, afraid to put it on the mantelpiece for fear that someone would steal it. She clutched it to her chest and looked around for a likely hiding place. That was how Jarvis found her, tears in her eyes, fear and rapture both present in her expression.

'Are you pleased? Or not?' he asked.

'I love it so much, but where can I hide it? Someone might take it from me and I'd die if I lost it.'

Jarvis laughed and hugged both Emily and her clock. Then he took it from her, kissing her flushed face. He put the clock on the mantelpiece and touched the fringed tapestry valance that hung around the mantelshelf on a wire.

'There! The finishing touch to your furnishings. Emily, you have done me proud.'

'Will it be safe?' she said, wanting to nurse the treasure again and protect it.

'Of course. Haven't I had good locks put on all the doors and windows? As long as we are careful to lock up and take the key each time we go out, you can enjoy it without worry.'

She took it down again and, lifting her skirts, gave it a gentle rub. He took it from her and put it back in its place.

'And now, Miss Tilt, what about showing me our new bed?' He took her hand and led her up the curving staircase to the small landing. There were two doors and Emily gestured towards the largest room, which overlooked the street.

The floorboards were bare. A bed stood against one wall and along another a length of wood had been nailed, and on it were hooks on which to hang their clothes. Curtains hung at the window, heavy and ornate, crocheted in ecru cotton. She touched them proudly. 'These are new,' she said.

Jarvis began to undo the line of small buttons from her neck to her waist. Soon she became impatient and helped him and he was amused to see that now, she did not throw her clothes down with such abandon, but spent a moment folding them and, with her eyes, used the slight delays to glance at him and increase his desire.

He was fascinated by her paleness. He was reminded of the statues he saw in shop windows, of elegant women, draped with flowing robes. She lay back on the soft mattress and pulled him close, beginning to release his impatient body of the restricting clothes.

They lay for a while, relishing the comfort of the bed and the boneless sensation of after-love. He turned to look at her and said, 'You have the expression of a well fed cat.'

'Shall we have a kitten? Please. It would make sure we don't get troubled by mice.'

'Emily! You say the most unlikely things after loving!'

She was very lovely. Her hair, free and thick, lay around her head, radiating out in a golden-red sprawl. He felt desire move him but he turned away and stared up at the ceiling, a frown on his face. This would not do.

He rose from the bed and began to dress. He forced himself to look at her hands and feet which were unsightly. Sarah's hands and feet would be perfect. Emily's were discoloured and lumpy with chilblains. He must not become attached to her. He must not. She was useful, but for a while only and when her usefulness came to an end she would be discarded; one way or another.

His body demanded he returned to the bed but his head refused to submit. He thought of Sarah, whom he would marry one day. He imagined possessing her tiny body once he had succeeded in making his fortune and bought Weatherby for her. But, he reminded himself as he fastened the last buttons, he had no background to offer.

Yet, although her father was titled, her mother had been on the music hall stage, perhaps that would help him to be accepted. His imaginary past as an army officer was sufficiently impressive and the story of his bravery and subsequent wounding and discharge would hold good, he was sure of that. Hadn't he changed identity with a boy soldier all those years ago without causing a moment's suspicion? Luck was his inheritance and that was worth more than a title. Especially when Sir Jason would soon have little else!

His eyes roamed again to the bed and he saw that Emily had woken from a brief doze and was watching him, the catlike smile still on her face. One day he would possess Sarah, but that was still in the future, Emily was here, now. He moved towards the bed, removing his clothes again with increasing urgency.

The following day Emily rose early to go to buy her flowers. Jarvis ate a light breakfast with her and as she was leaving, said,

'Emily my love, I will be using this house as an address for business as well as a home. There will sometimes be messages arriving for me, in my real name and others. I want you to write them down with the greatest care.'

'Of course, Jarvis! Word for word.'

He smiled. 'I want you to promise not to enquire into my various dealings, but follow my instructions.' He kissed her as she promised. He had no specific intentions in mind but thought it best to cover any possibilities. He believed he could trust her, but reinforced her devotion with, 'We are a loving partnership, and we trust each other completely, don't we?'

Emily nodded, although she guessed the trust was one-sided. There was so little she knew about him, for all his apparent openness. There was nothing she couldn't tell him, but she doubted whether his thoughts would ever be shared with her.

She did have qualms about not explaining that Renton was her cousin and that he knew Sarah. If Jarvis was involved with Sir Jason, it might be an advantage for him to know, but her natural caution had not been completely erased, and she held the information back.

When she returned from the market she spent a while dressing her flowers, some with doilies and silver paper, others made into bunches and wrapped in coloured paper. The buttonhole for Jarvis she made with great care and stood it in a jar of water to stay fresh for him.

When her work was finished she dressed in some of the clothes she had bought, second-hand, in the market, and went out. She had decided to go to the coffee shop and mix with the ladies in the hope of learning how to behave in such places, ready for the time when Jarvis took her out. The idea frightened her, she knew she was walking dangerous ground, but she wanted to learn.

Away from the familiar places and out of reach of her old friends, should she get into trouble with the law, or the lawless, she would be without help. She decided to keep her fingers to herself and not be tempted to dip, even if the mark was asking to be robbed.

The day was chilly but the sun shone in the early spring sky as she stepped out and carefully locked her door. Walking along the road, where several of the householders were busy scrubbing their front doorsteps with scouring bricks, she felt she was gradually overcoming her fears. She was Emily Tilt who owned a house and had a handsome man to call her own. She held her head up and nodded politely at those she passed.

Reaching the main thoroughfare she faltered a little, and on coming in sight of the coffee shop she intended to visit, with its clientele so smart and so awfully confident, she lost her nerve and turned, to scurry back to the house at a very unladylike pace. For the rest of the day she cleaned her new home.

Chapter Twelve

The year did not start very well for Sir Jason. On three separate occasions, goods were found to be already taken when his customers went to claim them. Each time, the loss was a costly one, small packages of valuable glass and china or silk and satin, which Sir Jason's agents had bought to complete a cargo.

One morning he had a surprise visitor. Topham, his secretary, announced Mr Alfred Cummins.

When Alfred was seated near the fire and plied with biscuits and a glass of ale, Sir Jason waited for him to explain the reason for his visit.

'Sir Jason, forgive my impertinence in calling on you unannounced, but what I have to say will be of interest to you, I sincerely hope.'

Sir Jason held back a snort of impatience and wished the man would hurry up and say what he came to say.

'I have heard the regrettable news of your misfortunes through my friends,' Alfred began. 'Losing your valuable cargoes to such audacious thieves – well, it doesn't make any of us sleep easy. I think I can help.'

'How?' Sir Jason looked down his long nose and frowned, doubt clearly showing in his deep-set eyes.

'In my humble way I have a number of, er, contacts. I would wager that if you employed me to find guards for your goods, and allowed me to devise a slightly improved method of billing, changing the note by which goods are released, you would not lose another cargo.'

'Tell me what you would do.'

In his careful, slow way, Alfred made suggestions regarding the handing-over of goods which seemed so obvious, Sir Jason laughed. 'But I could do that! Why should I employ you?'

'Oh, please, Sir Jason! I fear you have misunderstood me. When I say employ me, I do not expect to be paid.' Alfred looked horrified at the idea. 'No, dear me, no. I only wish to help you. I think we men of business have to stick together and help one another in these wicked times. Oh, please, *no*, Sir Jason! I wish you to employ me to help you. No money is asked, or would be accepted.'

Over the next six weeks, five boatloads came into Sir Jason's warehouses and not a single item was mislaid. When Alfred again called at the office of Sir Jason, he was greeted with an enthusiasm that even he had not hoped for.

'My dear boy, you must dine with me. Tomorrow night?'

'Thank you, Sir Jason. Tell me, will your lovely daughter Sarah be present?'

Sir Jason thought for a moment, then said, 'I think not. I understand she will be at the house of Giles Hallam, a party for one of the boys, I believe. Sarah is needed to organise the games.'

'Tomorrow night, then, sir, and thank you.' Alfred was disappointed, but hoped that even if Sarah were not at dinner, she might arrive long before he had to leave.

Sarah and Caroline were shopping for the party. Their brothers were going back to school and college the following week and the party was a farewell.

'What a pity Reginald could not be home as well! But being a soldier makes it difficult for him to attend. It would have been wonderful to have all my handsome brothers at home at the same time.'

'I think the servants will have enough difficulty without Reginald, who usually brings half his regiment with him!' Sarah laughed. 'I hope Giles will put in an appearance,' she said with a sigh. 'But I suppose, even if he does, he will have little time for me.'

'I see little of him myself, but he promises that as soon as he has his new business underway, he will relax and begin to enjoy life a little more. He was left with a fearful burden when Father died, you know. The need to educate my four brothers, *and* there was my coming-out year. Now there's my wedding, to which we have invited half of London's society. Giles has been made to think like an old man before his time.' She looked at Sarah and, head close so the maids and Great-Aunt Milly could not hear, added, 'Sarah, it is still my dearest wish that you and Giles fall in love and marry. I mention it in every prayer.'

The two girls hugged each other, dark head against the fair one. Then an evening bag, covered with a pattern of seed pearls, caught Caroline's eye and she decided she must have it.

For a moment Sarah stood back, separated from the others and their excitement at finding something so pretty. She looked about her, wandering to the doorway to watch the activities in the busy street. They were in the middle of an area where shops attracted the richest of clients, yet only a few moments' walk from where she stood were the meanest streets in the city.

She had not been out at night for a while and now she had a strong desire to resume her search. The impulse overcame her as suddenly as the purse had caught the attention of Caroline, and she left the others, still discussing its suitability for use with the new clothes Caroline was choosing, and ran.

It may have been the determination to overcome the fear of meeting Arthur, it may have been a return of the pain of losing her sister; whatever the reason, she found herself heading for the alleyway behind the large store.

It was narrow and bounded on both sides by high walls in which doors gave access to yards and stabling inside. As she ran, she heard the shuffling of horses' feet and the occasional growl and bark of a dog left to guard an empty yard. Fear touched her shoulders like an invisible hand and she regretted her foolishness in leaving the safety of the thoroughfare. She lifted her skirts in a way that would have made Edith frown, and hurried on to where she could regain the shopping street.

The lane opened out into a narrow, shabby street where

gas lamps were broken and where, at night, she would never dare venture alone. She walked briskly as if with a clear destination in mind. When she came to the end of the semiderelict row, she saw another similar but better-kept line of houses.

She stood hesitantly, regaining her sense of direction and wondering which way she should turn. Left would bring her back eventually to the road in which she had parted from Caroline and the others. To the right? She did not know wher that would take her, but there were a few women about and she thought it safe to explore a little farther. At the next corner she stopped again and was thankful she did, for coming out of a house in the middle of the street she saw two people. One was Emily Tilt, and she was saying good-bye to a tall, well-dressed, bearded man.

She darted back into the shelter of the end house, hoping she had not been seen. What was Emily doing in a house like that? She thought she had her answer after a few minutes' observation and it was one she did not like. Almost as soon as the man had disappeared around a corner, Emily had a second caller. The man went inside and it was half an hour before he emerged. It was moments only before a third man came out.

Emily was startled to hear a knock within minutes of Jarvis's leaving. She was wary but, remembering the surprise when Jarvis had given her the beautiful marble and gold clock, she smiled as she opened the door. The man insisted on entering, having told her he had a message for the man of the house.

'I have to write it down,' the visitor explained. 'Got notepaper, have you?'

'Of course!' Emily replied haughtily and produced a leather-covered box of stationery.

He wrote diligently for a while, placed the notepaper in an envelope which he propped against Emily's precious clock, and left.

The second knock came only moments later and this time the visitor asked for a cup of tea.

'I'm not sure I want to offer you tea – ' Emily came close

to allowing her new accent to slip.

'I'm meeting someone here, on Jarvis's instructions,' the man explained. Emily prepared tea.

A sound from upstairs startled her and she was relieved to see Jarvis coming down the stairs.

'Don't worry, Emily.' He smiled reassuringly. 'I was just testing an emergency exit!' He left a few moments after her visitor, following a whispered discussion over the contents of the envelope.

She heard the name Sir Jason Lindhurst Ayres and wondered if she was being disloyal in not telling him about Sarah's activities.

Sarah left before the second man came out. She was unhappy and wished she had stayed with Caroline and the others. How could she tell Renton that his cousin was running a brothel?

She hurried back to the busy street, and the anxious faces searching for her made her feel guilty.

'I'm sorry I worried you,' she said. 'I was distracted by some people farther along the road and I wandered off without realising it. Come, I'll treat us all to coffee and cakes to apologise for my bad behaviour.'

Leaving Caroline's coachman to collect their purchases, the five ladies went to sip coffee and discuss their next call.

Knowing Sarah as she did, Caroline did not believe her lame excuse for leaving them. 'Where did you go?' she demanded. 'You shouldn't have left the safety of the street. What would your father say if he knew?'

'You won't tell, will you, dear Caroline? I can't help it, I find the city so fascinating and I long to learn more of its secret life.'

'You aren't still hoping to catch thieves that have evaded the whole of the police force?'

'Oh no,' Sarah lied. 'I admit I am not capable of facing such danger any more. I will leave it to the police. But other people's lives bring out a curiosity – '

Caroline shook her head impatiently. When Sarah talked like this she lost her patience. 'Let's talk of something else,' she said sharply. 'You talk of loving my brother and say you dream of being his wife, yet you wander in the roughest streets, mix with ragamuffins and play at being a detective! If you wander off again, Sarah, I will have to tell someone for your own safety. Perhaps Giles,' she warned.

Meekly, Sarah apologised and began discussing the games they would play at the evening party. 'Shall we go to the shop where we can choose some new games and perhaps a few tricks to play on your brothers?' she suggested.

The anger faded from her friend's face. Sarah knew Caroline would not tell, but she surmised that her friend was getting a little tired of hearing of her escapades and decided to tell her nothing more.

They discussed forthcoming social engagements and what they would wear. Sarah's brightness and enthusiasm were brittle as her thoughts kept returning to the disgrace Emily Tilt had brought on Renton and his family. She hoped he would never find out.

Emily had another knock at her door, this one at a time when light was fading and the lamp-lighter had not yet made his rounds. Before opening it, she took a firm hold of one of the pokers. A small, red-headed boy stood there holding the string of a home-made wheeled cart. On the cart was a delivery of wine, each bottle packed carefully in straw.

' *'E* sent this. *'E* said you was to pay me a tanner.'

'Clear off! Thievin' little – ' For a moment Emily forgot her new role. She raised the poker without further words and the threat was enough to persuade the boy he need not wait for payment.

'Tell 'im Carrots delivered as promised!' he called as he pulled his cart behind him and ran up the street.

'Carrots,' Jarvis explained later, 'is your new assistant. You can guard him and act as a decoy while he fills his pockets. That way there's no chance of my losing you to the prison, my dear. Carrots is expendable.' To prove that she was not, he led her up to their bedroom.

'What was all that knocking on my door and men coming to call?' Emily asked later.

'Nothing for you to worry your lovely head about,' he said firmly, and Emily knew he would not allow any further questions on the subject. 'But I do have something for you to do for me and this I will tell you about.' He asked for notepaper, and she watched with admiration as he penned a note to the editor of a local newspaper. It was an advertisement requesting enquiries about employment for men and their families in Australia. He explained the plan.

'I'm asking for five shillings to cover the cost of the advertisement and the replies, which is reasonable,' he said. 'Then, when we've had sufficient response, or we learn that someone is getting inquisitive, we disappear.'

'And collar the five bobs, you mean?' She looked horrified. 'No! Not here! We can't have the police coming here if something goes wrong!' She looked around in dismay. To risk all this was insane! She wanted to find bags, sacks and boxes and take up all the beautiful possessions and hide them away.

'Watch.' Under her anxious gaze, he added an address to the note and she sighed with relief. It was one unknown to her. 'This is the address of someone who has gone travelling on the Continent for a month. He always goes as far south as time will allow when the worst of the winter weather is upon us. You will go every day to this address to collect the letters. Carrots will go with you; at least, he'll be nearby in case of trouble.'

On the following morning, Emily, dressed in her respectable clothes, called on the address Jarvis had given her. She was nervous as she opened the metal gate and walked up the drive of the detached house, looking up at the curtained windows for fear that someone was inside. With the key she had held in her hand all the way, and which had marked her wet palm in her tight grip, she opened the door and stepped inside.

On the first morning there were only two replies. The following morning the envelopes increased to a flood, and she was glad of the shopping basket she had brought, in which she hid the letters on her walk back to her house.

When they finally gave up calling and the key had been replaced where the owner regularly hid it, they had received almost five hundred pounds.

'What shall we do with the money, Emily?' Jarvis asked as they counted the money and placed it in a tin box to hide in the loft. 'I thought we'd buy a few houses. How do you fancy being a landlady with a string of rents to collect?' He hugged her. 'Emily, we're going to be rich!'

'Can we eat out somewhere nice, to celebrate?' she asked.

'Soon we will, but I have to go away for a few days.'

'Alone?' If only he would suggest taking her with him.

'Regretfully, yes. I'm off to France, but before you complain, I must tell you it's business. I have to make sure some arrangements I have made for the downfall of Sir Jason are properly made. It will mean money, Emily! More marvellous money!'

'Seems we already have enough to make life perfect.'

The thought that she knew something about Sarah that might help him in whatever he was planning lay, a guilty deception, on her heart. If, at that moment, he had invited her to go with him to France, she would most certainly have told him. But he did not and the knowledge that she had something he needed, gave her a false sense of security. She held her tongue.

Jarvis stayed away for ten days and every one seemed like a month to Emily. As each day ended and she settled to sleep in the big bed, she felt hope drain from her with the last of the daylight. He was not coming back. Why should he? There were plenty of more beautiful women than she, ready to take him on. Each time she left the house, she almost ran the last few yards, afraid that while she had been away he had come and taken the furniture and the money he kept hidden in the loft.

She needed something to cheer herself, to boost her rapidly failing confidence, so, defying Jarvis's orders, she went once more to the house to collect envelopes. She had seen where Jarvis had placed the key and it was the work of a moment to slip inside and pick up the ten envelopes lying on the mat. She had dressed in her smartest dress and hat and forced herself to walk slowly as she closed the gate and headed back to her home.

At the corner she almost forgot her role and ran like the thief she was – a policeman was standing watching her. Her brief panic was halted and she nodded to him and said, 'Good afternoon,' then felt furiously embarrassed. She had added an aitch and said 'hafternoon', like the common woman she also was. She would *never* learn!

After burning all the envelopes and the letters that had been written with a hope of a better life, Emily went out again, this time to the shops, where she bought two dresses and an enormous hat. The hat was cinnamon, dressed with feathers in sage green, with touches of gold thread. Emily knew it would make heads turn and give a boost to her failing confidence. If, as seemed likely, Jarvis did not come back to her, then the new clothes would help her to find her place in the new life she was determined to have.

She unpacked her parcels and put the new clothes away. It was almost evening and the lonely hours stretched out before her. The beautiful clock on the mantelpiece told her there were at least five hours before she could expect to sleep. Perhaps she could give the kitchen floor another scrub? No, best not; if Jarvis did come he would not be pleased to see her acting the role of skivvy. She put on her second-best dress and made herself a cup of tea.

It was as she drained the last of the second cup that she heard Jarvis's key in the door. Replacing the cup hastily in the saucer, she stood up to greet him. He was dirty and looked tired, and she opened her welcoming arms to him with a sob.

'Jarvis! You're home!' She almost cried with relief. 'Oh, I'm so glad to have you back!'

'Emily, my dear, I missed you. Come on, get out your best clothes. We're going out to celebrate my return and a successful completion of my plans.'

'Where shall we go?' She was already lifted up by his excitement. Her thoughts teemed with places she had dreamed of seeing with him beside her. And what should she wear? It was hardly warm enough, but should she wear the dress with the layers of frilled lace over a skirt of hunting green? The colour suited her so well. And the bonnet with strings of the same green cloth and the flowers in dark orange? She flew upstairs and his long legs took him up behind her. 'I'll take you to the Cremorne Gardens and show you off to anyone who is there.'

Emily had often been to the pleasure gardens. The

Cremorne Gardens were a spectacle that delighted her although she had never been at ease among the smart crowds. She went there and joined those like herself who dawdled at the edge of things, content to watch others enjoying all the place had to offer. When the lighting came on the place had a magical air, with music emanating from the grandstand. The excitement seemed to Emily to lift her above everything that was ordinary.

She was tempted to wear her new clothes but did not want Jarvis to question her about where the money had come from. They would be for another day. She intuitively and regretfully felt he would not want her to be too noticeable. Especially in a place as popular as the Cremorne Gardens, where everyone went. He had been unwilling so far for her to meet his friends.

Late at night Cremorne Gardens was a different place. The atmosphere was without the gentility she knew from her afternoon and early-evening visits. The women were dressed more flashily, with lower necklines and skirts that exposed their ankles. Their expressions showed disregard for decorum and good taste. It had something to do with the way they stared at men without lowering their gaze until it was the men who looked away. But the men always looked again and frequently ended up walking arm in arm with them, whispering into a receptive ear.

Today Emily was one of the crowd, able to stare with slight disdain at those who stood back in the shadows looking on. Today she was walking with her man and happiness glowed in her blue eyes and added an extra lift to her young shoulders.

She was filled with such joy that she began to wonder what she could do to repay Jarvis. She thought of the only secret she had held from him; that her cousin and Sarah were still seeking after the men who had burgled and killed in Sir Jason's house. She wondered how to begin. He would surely value the information, having business deals in progress with Sir Jason, and she was excited at the prospect of helping him, imagining how pleased he would be. She did not consider that she would be putting Renton and Sarah at risk.

She did not want to confess the secret as if it were a crime, neither did she want to blurt it out without reference to anything, as a child sometimes will. No, she would wait for a suitable moment.

They sat at one of the small tables set around the grounds, partly concealed by bushes and trees, but in view of the most spectacular entertainments. She could see people standing looking down from the top of the bright tower. Flags of many countries were displayed, topped by the British crown and a sign announcing that 'All Nations Are Welcome To Cremorne'. Lights shone around a crystal circle, an orchestra played high above the throng. People danced and laughed, showing off their smart clothes, abandoning for a while the formalities of their social positions and relaxing. Garlands swooped up from the circling lights to touch the very top of the pagodalike building. Emily looked, and saw it as if for the first time.

She looked at Jarvis sitting beside her and was full of love for him. She felt as if he had personally arranged the display for her – a display she had walked past many times as an outsider.

The moment to tell him her secret came almost as she thought of the need to tell it. A figure walked across their path, looking up to where people on the tower roof waved and called down to their friends. A brief glance at the small face was sufficient for Emily to recognise Sarah. Sarah walked past, not seeing Emily or Jarvis, and unaware of danger.

The clothes were those of a boy and very shabby, and a large cap hid the long hair, but the figure had a lightness about its movements and was unmistakable to Emily's sharp eyes. Especially as she had been thinking of Sarah at the very moment she saw her. She pulled on Jarvis's arm.

'Jarvis, I want to tell you – '

Before she could finish, Jarvis pulled her up from her seat and pushed her roughly to one side. 'Hide!' he urged. As her life had been a constant flight from both the law and the more experienced thieves, she did so without hesitation. She crouched behind a thick, low-growing shrub and allowed a few moments to pass before daring to peep out to see the reason for his warning.

She stood up, crept slowly out of hiding and gradually mingled with the strolling, laughing revellers. Jarvis was talking to a beautifully dressed young woman whom he obviously knew well. Jealousy gnawed at Emily and she followed them for a while, wondering why he had not wanted her to be seen.

She pretended not to doubt that it had been for her own protection. But as time passed and he showed no sign of rejoining her, she faced the heart-rending truth. He did not want his friends to see him with her, Emily Tilt, flower girl. That was why he had chosen to take her in the late evening, when most respectable people would have gone home and the worst of the night people were yet to come.

Fine clothes or not, she would never be accepted as a fit companion for him. For all his generous words their relationship was a sham, a game of some sort. She was being used, and when she was no longer needed for this schemes she would be left to return to her own world.

As she walked home alone she tried to convince herself she was mistaken, that her overactive self-doubt had persuaded her wrong, but it was no use. She remembered the other times when he had hurriedly changed direction or pushed her into the doorway of a convenient shop. No, she had to face it if she wanted to survive; to Jarvis she was not his loving partner, just a dupe. With all her inbuilt wariness and street-learning, she, Emily Tilt the survivor, had been flattered and beguiled into believing that a man like Jarvis could love her.

She opened the door and went in. The room was faintly lit with the remaining glow from the fire. She stood for a moment, settling her mind and accepting what she had tried hard not to believe. Then she struck a lucifer and pulled on the chain of the gas light until the fragile mantle caught and filled the room with a friendly light.

There were some pieces of wood in the brass fender which she had bought from boys who came to the door selling what they had salvaged from a derelict building nearby. Emily watched as the flames, reluctant at first, began to lick around the edges of the new fuel. She took off the hat of which she was so proud, hung it on a hook and dropped into a chair.

She was still there when Jarvis returned, and her new marble clock told her it was five a.m. and time to go to the market to buy flowers.

She went upstairs to change her clothes. There was no hope of a bargain if she was dressed too well. The poor help the poor. She did not hear Jarvis coming up the stairs behind her, but as she dropped the last of her good petticoats, his arms wrapped around her and he lifted her onto the bed.

As she lay there for a luxurious few moments after his loving, listening to his sweet words she decided to stay with him and pretend nothing had changed, but begin to replace her savings which he had used. There would be a time when she needed money and the time might not be far off.

She did not sleep well. Jarvis had told her he would stay for one day only. He had to go back to France but would return on the following Friday. She thought she might go to meet the train and surprise him. If she saw him with another woman, respectability or not, she would scratch his beautiful eyes out.

Chapter Thirteen

Sarah ate breakfast late. Having been out during the evening of the previous day and again at night with Renton, she had found it difficult to persuade her brain that the day had begun. Great-Aunt Milly joined her and since this was unusual, the old lady normally eating in her bedroom, Sarah guessed she was to be asked a favour.

'Sarah, dear, I need some embroidery silks. Will you come with me to match them?' Great-Aunt Milly asked when the meal was finished. 'I need a young pair of eyes to make sure they are correct.'

'Of course, dear aunt. I will send the houseboy to find Renton. He shall take us, and perhaps, when we have finished your shopping and sat to eat some of your favourite cakes in Fortnum & Mason's tearooms, we can go to Father's office and travel home with him?'

'Yes, dear child, that will be a treat. But what a pity we have no coach of our own! You shouldn't have persuaded your father to get rid of the coachman before finding us another,' Great-Aunt Milly complained, referring to the recent outraged complaint from her niece which ended with the grumpy coachman being dismissed.

'How can I expect to persuade Father to take Renton back if he doesn't suffer some inconvenience?'

The old lady chuckled while shaking her head in disapproval of Sarah's tactics.

Sarah knew her aunt loved a day spent shopping but she also knew that the old lady's legs would not stand it. By breaking the hours with tea and a visit to her father's office,

Great-Aunt Milly would have a full and enjoyable day without becoming overtired. But Sarah's motives were not completely altruistic, she knew from Caroline that Giles was to call on her father that afternoon and she hoped to meet him there.

They had not spoken for several weeks and Sarah despaired of ever becoming more than just the friend of his sister. With Caroline's wedding set for Easter, the two girls often met to discuss arrangements and dream about that special day, but it was only rarely that Giles appeared.

When he did, he seemed pleased to see her and, for days after such a meeting, Sarah's hopes were raised and she waited for some communication from him that never came. She dreamed of being a bride with all the attendant splendour and with Giles as her handsome bridegroom. How wonderful if she and Caroline were to share a wedding day! But she seemed likely to end up like Great-Aunt Milly, a viewer from the sidelines of other people's romances.

The silks for her aunt's embroidery were soon chosen and they went to look at materials for some grey, purple and black dresses for the spring. When her aunt became bored, Sarah took her to the tearooms where she could sit in comfort and watch passers-by.

Acquaintances approached from time to time and the hours quickly passed.

'Shall we go to see if Father is there?' Sarah asked, when her boredom threatened to make her stand up and do a cartwheel just to see the reaction. 'It would be a pity if he had already left.'

Regretfully, the old lady rose and prepared to follow her niece to the hansom cab.

Sarah had always loved her father's office. It was large and smelled of wood, leather and dust. The floor was bare wood which, until the burglary arranged by Jarvis, had been covered with beautiful Eastern rugs of brilliant colours and intricate patterns. The wood in the desk was polished and in it, the reflections of the fire glowed redly. The walls were partly panelled in oak and above the panels was a flock wallpaper in a Chinese pattern that had always fascinated Sarah.

As a small child she had stretched up to follow the whirls of colour and trace the shapes on the strange creatures, beautiful birds and flowers of the surface. She still found pleasure in studying its complicated design. But today she hardly glanced at it; she was immediately aware of Giles, who stood beside her father, bending over the counter and following a line of figures down the page of a large, leather-bound accounts book.

For a moment they did not see her and she was able to look at Giles and wonder at the attraction he held for her that increased moment by moment until she thought he must surely see it written on her face. His hair was untidy at the nape and she smiled, knowing he had scratched idly with his pen in a moment of concentration. But his face wore a frown and when she tore her eyes away from him to glance at her father, the frown was repeated there.

'Put the book down, Topham, and get on with what you are doing,' her father said without looking up.

'I'm not Topham and look nothing like him,' Sarah protested with mock anger.

Both men looked up then, and it was Giles she watched as he saw her and smiled a welcome.

'Hello, Father dear; hello Giles,' she said, suddenly shy.

'My dear, I had quite forgotten you were coming,' Sir Jason confessed. He closed the book hurriedly but Sarah saw he held the page with a finger and sensed he was unhappy at being interrupted.

'You didn't forget. Great-Aunt Milly needed some silks and a view of the outside world so we thought, if you weren't working late, we could wait and ride home with you. But I need not stay if you and Giles are busy.'

Great-Aunt Milly came into the room, having taken her time and the assistance of three servants to climb up the steps from the pavement, and Giles found her a seat near the fire. After politenesses had been exchanged, Topham was sent to the shop for a tray of tea. But it was not a relaxed interlude. Sarah sensed that her father was anxious to get back to his books; he frowned, and she noticed how tense he looked. She wanted to go, but Great-Aunt Milly could not be rushed; she needed time to regain her breath after the flight of stairs.

Twice, while they talked, the secretary tried to interrupt, and each time Sir Jason brushed off the man's obvious concern. When he knocked and entered for the third time, Sir Jason sighed and asked, 'What *is* it, man?'

'It's this transfer-of-land form, I don't think we should – '

Apologising to the two ladies, Sir Jason followed the secretary out and they heard him say, 'I've explained, Topham. It's a procedure to save us time. The deeds will revert to me as soon as the building work has begun.'

'But, sir – '

'Just file it, Topham, and *do* stop fussing!'

'But is Mr Cummins a capable – '

'That is *all*, Topham.' The knowledge that what he was doing was not strictly usual made Sir Jason's voice louder than he intended, and Sarah glanced at Giles when she heard the name.

'Have you changed your mind about Alfred Cummins, Father?' she asked when Sir Jason returned, looking angry.

'He is experienced in things that are new to me. I am using his knowledge, that is all.'

'He is in Paris at present,' Giles added. 'And when he returns he is staying with me while his rooms are being redecorated.'

'I don't know what has come over Topham lately,' Sir Jason grumbled.

'Sarah, you are just the person I need,' Giles said, as much to ease the uneasiness in the air as for a need for assistance. 'Look at these drawings and tell me, what colour should I choose?' He picked up a folder which was tied at the opening with coloured tape and opened it in front of her. 'See? This is the main drawing room of my new gentlemen's club. I shall have leather chairs and tables in groups, bookshelves and places where men can sit in private, yet be a part of the rest. I have thought to furnish in red, with touches of gilt. What do you think?'

'Red, with touches of gilt,' she mused, staring into space and imagining the scene. 'Yes, that is what comes first to mind, but perhaps that is reason for reconsidering? Won't it be the likely choice among other such places? What about dark blue instead? With perhaps silver in very small touches? Wouldn't that be more elegant and unusual?' Enthusiasm grew and she went on, 'The linen would be purest white tablecloths of Indian cotton with an edge of blue – not too much, that would be vulgar. Silver cutlery, of course, and white china with a rim of blue and silver. Napkins blue with white edging. Yes, I think that would be better than red and gilt.'

Giles smiled at her, then looked at Sir Jason. 'I think your clever daughter has decided for us. Do you agree? I was not completely happy with red but could not think past it. Dark blue, yes, I think it will be perfect. Thank you, Sarah.' He took her hand and kissed it, his eyes staring into hers in a most disconcerting way.

'I agree,' her father said.

'You, Father? I did not know that you were involved in this enterprise with Giles?'

'Don't worry your pretty head about our businesses. We'll earn the money, it's your place to spend it and allow us the pleasure of seeing the results.'

He was smiling, but Sarah was not convinced. There was something worrying him.

'Father, I thought you did not like this Alfred Cummins? He is not involved in this, too, is he?'

'Sarah, I have no intention of discussing my affairs with you.'

'Sorry, Father, but – '

'Enough.'

'Come, I'll drive you home,' Giles said to ease the situation. 'My carriage should hold yourself, Great-Aunt Milly and your shopping.'

'Please, Sarah, be good enough to wait downstairs while I complete my discussion with Giles. We will not keep you more than a moment.'

'Very well, Father, and thank you, Giles.'

They woke the old lady, who had nodded off, still holding her teacup, and Sarah helped her down the stairs to where Topham sat in a room similar to her father's office but smaller. To Great-Aunt Milly's relief, the fire was as large as the one they had just left.

Sir Jason waited until the two ladies had gone, then said, 'Giles, I did not intend worrying you, but another cargo of mine has gone missing. This time, when the boxes were opened they were packed with rubbish. The goods had been spirited away.'

'So, you solve the thieving from the warehouses, and now this. Someone seems determined to beggar you, Sir Jason.'

'Nonsense! I can't be the only one singled out for fraud. I think I might ask Alfred for help. He stopped it last time. A thief to catch a thief, maybe?'

'Do you think Alfred is a thief?'

'No, certainly not! Heaven forbid, while I have so much of my capital tied in with his schemes! No, I think he knows some of the less savoury characters of the city, and sets some of those to catch the ones who affect us.'

Both men looked serious as they thought of how deeply involved they had become with Alfred Cummins. Given a second's thought that he might be dishonest was enough to make them shiver with fear of the consequences.

Giles shook off the worries and went down to escort Sarah and Great-Aunt Milly home.

It was what Sarah often dreamed about, sitting beside Giles on a leisurely ride through the London streets, able to talk with him. But the moment seemed certain to be spoilt.

'Giles, is there something not right with my father's affairs?' she asked in a whisper when Great-Aunt Milly's attention was elsewhere.

'Nothing for you to worry about, my dear.'

'Don't treat me like a child!' Her voice, forgetting her aunt in a flash of anger, came out louder than she intended and he touched her hand in a soothing manner.

'Hush, please don't alarm yourself. Your father is a clever man and if, I say *if* he found himself in any difficulties, he would quickly find a way through them.'

'There is something, I know it.'

His hand had not left hers, and slowly she turned her fingers around so they were holding hands. Her heart was beating rapidly as she looked up into his eyes.

'Oh, Sarah!' he breathed. 'If only – ' He stopped suddenly

as Great-Aunt Milly pointed at something in the street.

'Look at that!' she exclaimed. 'Women fighting in the road. What a disgrace! I do believe they are fighting for coins thrown by a passer-by.' Her old eyes were wide open and she bent her head to watch until the carriage had managed to pass the sprawling women, who had rolled almost under the horse's hooves.

Giles made a sympathetic murmur but his eyes did not leave Sarah's. 'Soon, my lovely Sarah, soon,' he whispered.

She was too elated to feel concern for the poor women, whose needs were so great they had to fight for a few coins thrown by young men who stayed to enjoy the spectacle. She sat with her small hand in Giles's large, powerful one and felt love and understanding flow between them. Soon, he had said. There was something holding them apart but the barrier would fall and . . .

The lips she loved parted and moved closer, temptingly close to her own. She heard his breath quicken and felt the sweetness of it on her cheek. Without consciously moving, and with the voice of Great-Aunt Milly still muttering as she stared disapprovingly out of the window, they kissed. Softly, lightly and for a moment only. For the rest of the cruelly short journey they sat wrapped in the joy of the brief contact and its tacit promise.

He helped her dismount from the carriage and stood while she went indoors, staring after her long after the heavy door had closed behind her. If only there were not so many ends to tie up! It seemed that the plans he was making to ensure the financial safety of his brothers were dragging on endlessly. Surely before the summer came he would be in a position to declare his love for her?

The opening of the gentlemen's club must be hurried along. He would tell Alfred to bring the delivery dates for the panelling and the furniture forward to Easter. Yes, he would give himself a completion date of Easter, when Caroline would be married and he would be relieved of his responsibilities for her. The decision eased his restlessness and he jumped back into his carriage and told the coachman to make haste.

Alfred was a difficult man to get hold of. He told no one

where he lived and when Giles did meet him, it was at several different addresses. At present he was in France and was not expected back until the overnight train from Paris on Wednesday. He would be at London Bridge Station to meet him.

Giles stood at the station and waited patiently for the train to arrive. Emily saw him but did not acknowledge him even by a slight nod. She hardly expected he would recognise her, not without a dozen shabby skirts and a basket full of flowers.

She saw him meet a tall, slim man. She heard the man greet Giles and in a deep voice say, 'Giles, what a surprise! I hope you are hungry, for the inn is the first place I intend to visit. Food on these trains consists of stale offerings from urchins and old hags on platforms and I swear the food is harder than the platforms themselves!'

She watched as the doors were opened and the train was emptied of weary passengers and their luggage. Of Jarvis there was no sign.

She turned away to leave when a man standing near the exit smiled and said, 'Surely no one has let *you* down, my dear? A beautiful lady like you? Perhaps I can offer you breakfast as compensation?'

Emily lingered, and allowed him to walk beside her. 'I must have made a mistake and met the wrong train,' she said.

'Then allow me to buy you a meal while you wait for the next one, eh?'

She did not realise it at the time, all she was intent on was reminding herself that she was young and not ugly, but the short walk with the stranger was the beginning of a new life. She was surprised how easy it was to persuade a man to pay for her company.

'Perhaps we can meet again, some time when you are not waiting for someone?' The man, who said his name was Ephram, smiled suggestively.

'I might,' Emily said. She loosened her beautiful hair from her collar and let it flow over her shoulders. She was beginning to enjoy herself and, if Jarvis chose to treat her badly, she would find someone with more consideration. She sighed with satisfaction later as Ephram helped her into a cab and paid the driver in advance. Confidence and good clothes were all a girl needed to better herself. She pocketed the piece of paper on which he had written 'I am to be found at Steinburg's Coffee House' and waved a polite goodbye as the cab took her away.

Ephram was obviously wealthy and he had done a great deal to increase Emily's confidence. As she sat in the cab, she felt a lady. Perhaps it wouldn't be difficult to become one? Clothes and confidence, she repeated to herself. Clothes and confidence.

Sir Jason was reading through the proposals for building a large boarding house on the land that he had cleared when he had needed storage for a cargo. In his neat writing he was making lists of possible expenses, taking the information from that gathered for him by his secretary and by Alfred Cummins. Of the two, those of Alfred Cummins were far lower.

The door of his office opened and he looked up irritably.

'What is it now?' he asked, as Topham approached his desk. 'More trivialities? What is the matter with you, Topham? You used not to pester me with small things. Deal with it, man, whatever it is!'

'It's these accounts sent for settlement, Sir Jason. I think you should look at them. There are several items that are for a – er – for ladies and I wondered – '

'Pay them.'

'A hat? Four guineas?'

'I don't remember every item I buy.'

'Very well, Sir Jason, but I don't think I should pay without you checking them, there are so many and . . . ' He hesitated as his employer looked up and glared at him. 'Yes, well, I'll pay them.' He backed out and had almost closed the door when Sir Jason called him back.

'Topham, I am expecting Mr Alfred Cummins. When he comes, will you show him straight in?'

Alfred arrived a few moments later with a sheaf of papers. He wore a new suit of burgundy with a cream cravat and boots and gloves of smooth black leather. His hat was also black, and around it was a trailing band of cream silk. The weather was bitterly cold and his face was red where the winds had whipped it before he had found a cab. His scar was blue and very noticeable.

'Good morning, Alfred,' Sir Jason greeted him, and offered warmed ale to thaw his visitor. 'You have the plans?'

'Yes, and I must say that what you are doing, Sir Jason, is philanthropic! No other word will do.'

Sir Jason looked pleased but shook his head. 'Nonsense, I'm just a businessman. This idea, for which you must take much of the credit, will bring in a steady income and, although it is a somewhat new field for me, I admit to being quite excited by it.'

'Lord Shaftesbury himself will no doubt hear of it.' Alfred lowered his voice. 'Honours come to those who serve and all that, eh?'

The two men studied the proposed buildings and discussed the various roadways and the size of the buildings until Topham once more appeared.

'Sir, if I could have a word? It's rather urgent.'

At that moment a nearby clock chimed twelve and Sir Jason stood up. 'I think it's time to stop and consider what we have discussed.' He politely saw Alfred on his way and went back to his office.

'Sir, may I ask if you have recently bought a large ruby?'

'A ruby? Most certainly not. Why?'

'Will you be kind enough to look at this, sir?' Topham handed Sir Jason an account headed with the crest of Willoughby's West End Emporium. Sir Jason ran a finger down the long list and shook his head. 'There has been a mistake. Go there and explain, will you? I have not bought any of these things. In fact, I do not know when I was in the place.'

'Will you now look at the other queries, sir?' Topham quickly handed him two other lists from different shops.

These, too, Sir Jason denied. 'Look into it.'

Later that day, Topham and Sir Jason totalled up all the money he had been charged for goods he had not received. The sum was a staggering eight hundred and seventy pounds. The accounts were paid but the shops were warned not to accept any further orders, even with the signature of Sir Jason.

By that time, Jarvis King had stopped using the name of Sir Jason for such things. Instinct had warned him it was time to destroy that disguise and forget shopping. His skills were needed for far larger dealings. He would soon be very rich, and would commiserate with Sarah on the misfortunes of her father. He smiled at the prospect of her appreciation of his help. Time then to say farewell to the delightful Emily and become the dependant and loving friend of Sarah Lindhurst Ayres. He sang softly as he headed for his next appointment.

A week after Sarah's visit to her father's office, Renton called and asked to speak to her. His young lady, Caroline's maid Lucy, was with him. Sarah sent for tea and invited them both into the small morning room; she knew that the drawing room would be uncomfortable for them.

'It may not be anything at all, Sarah,' Renton began. 'But I think you ought to see what Lucy found in the room used by occasional guests, friends of Giles – er, Mr Hallam, that is.'

Sarah took the piece of paper – a scrap saved from a burnt page – and smoothed it out carefully.

'I don't usually look, Miss Sarah,' Lucy explained, 'but there was a lot of paper in the grate and when I saw the writing I was curious. I couldn't help it.'

'It's a long line of names, my father's among them. What does it mean, Renton?'

'Not names, Miss Sarah, signatures.' Renton glanced at the door and lowered his voice as if afraid of being overheard.

'Signatures? You mean, someone has been practising using my father's name?'

'Forgery, I'd say.' Renton was grave. 'Your father's and others'.'

'What can we do? We ought to go to Henry Bannerman.'

'We ought to,' Renton agreed, 'but we won't.'

'I hope you don't think I'm the sort to snoop,' Lucy said

anxiously. 'It was only that – '

'Thank goodness you were quick enough to notice,' Sarah reassured her. 'I think you must search that room again. If he was that careless there might be some other small thing he overlooked.'

'There's nothing to find now. The room has been cleaned. I only found the burnt papers because I was helping the upstairs maid as she was ill. She has recovered now and will have thoroughly cleaned the guest room.'

'There might be something. Will you help us, Lucy?' Renton asked.

'Of course I will.'

It was easy for Sarah to arrange to call on her friend, and for her to arrange that Renton accompany her. It was natural, too, for Renton to go into the kitchen and spend the waiting time with his ladylove.

When Sarah went to find Renton to say she was ready to leave, he said, 'We have found something and you won't like it.'

'Tell me,' Sarah said firmly. 'If it's something unpleasant about one of Giles's unsavoury friends, then I must know.' The look of anxiety on Renton's face was alarming.

'Isn't this your father's cigar case? And aren't these his specially made cigars inside it?'

'Oh, Renton, you are silly? Father is a business partner of Giles. He must have left it here by mistake.'

'We found it hidden at the bottom of a wardrobe, and there were other things there too. Silver items, snuff boxes with jewelled lids, several wallets and some jewellery.'

'Put it back, Renton. There must be some mistake.' Sarah's face was drained of colour. Surely Giles couldn't be involved in robberies and thieving? She covered her face with her dainty hands and shuddered at the possibilities the discovery offered.

'Night houses are notorious places for thieves meeting thieves. It's possible that Giles – er, Mr Hallam – '

'No!' Sarah shouted. 'Put it all back. I'm sure there will be an explanation.'

Tears were not far away as she rode home. But by the time the cab had reached the gates of the house in Sallis

Close she had reached a decision. She would go out every night and follow Giles until she knew everything about him and the life he led.

Chapter Fourteen

Carrots slept in a derelict warehouse not far from St Katherine's Dock. It was in an area that was being rebuilt but he was able to move occasionally and keep ahead of the men who pulled the rickety buildings down.

He had been on the streets since he was two, sharing a home with others, gradually learning the art of survival until he was able to fend for himself. Drifting into casual relationships and drifting on when things became difficult, or when he or his partner became bored with the arrangement, he had settled more and more for being a loner.

Gathering pieces of wood, metal, sacks and, when he was fortunate, some tarpaulin, he made himself a reasonable shelter. Inside it he was safe from the wind and rain, he could keep his few possessions together and even, on occasions, light a fire to warm himself and dry out his clothes.

Whenever possible, he spent nights in the cheapest lodging houses. Once, when the snow was thick on the ground and he had only a penny to his name, he had spent a night at the Penny Hang, where ropes strung across a room allowed men and women to hang their arms over the ropes and relax and rest a little, if not sleep. He hated it and did not close his eyes but, to his surprise and profit, most others did. He had searched the pockets of the sleepers, but found nothing more than a few cigar ends. Small compensation for a night spent in the foul-smelling room, but it was a profit and that, to Carrots, meant survival for another day.

Recently he had been well paid. Jarvis kept him busy running errands and assisting now and then in burglaries. He was a remarkably good climber and could reach the open window of a bedroom swiftly and silently, before running down the dark corridors and staircases to open the door for Jarvis's partners. He helped Emily, too, when she was out for a dip. Together they worked the crowds and the proceeds were rushed to where one of Jarvis's men waited at the edge of the bustling shoppers, so if he and Emily were caught, they would have nothing on them to convict them of picking pockets.

He liked Emily, even now when she was changing from the flower girl to something of a lady. She treated him well enough. He thought her a fool and a flat though for allowing Jarvis to gammon her the way he did. A girl like Emily could earn a good life. She was an expert at tooling and if she would be persuaded to carry a small chiv to cut open pockets instead of slipping a hand in, she would be even faster. He handled his own small knife, feeling its sharp edge and the slim blade, which got smaller week by week with constant sharpening.

He stretched out for a while, enjoying the small puddle of sunshine that shone in through the old sacking onto his face. He felt under the pile of old clothes that served as a bed and found the paper bag. There were a few pieces of meat, a crust of bread and – a treat he had been saving – a piece of chocolate. He leaned against the wall of his shelter and ate hungrily, licking his filthy hands to savour every crumb.

Today he was working at the warehouse Jarvis rented a few streets away from the dock. The consignment of oak panelling was to be unpacked carefully, and the silver foil packing stacked onto a cart. The discarded packing was to be delivered to an address in the country, and Carrots guessed it was the same place he and Jarvis had visited and from where customers collected their supplies. He was curious about the importance of the packing and decided it would do no harm to find out why it was worthy of a hired cart and special treatment.

Emily returned from her visit to the market and put her flowers on the table ready to begin sorting them into bunches and posies. She hadn't seen Jarvis for two days, not since he had returned from France. The fact that he was in a temper was obvious when he burst in through the door and, without bothering to close it, asked:

'How did you know when I was returning from France? Who told you? Don't deny you were waiting for me. I was told!'

Emily was startled. 'What's so terrible about me knowing?' She was quick-witted enough not to tell him he had told her himself. If he thought he had relaxed into carelessness, letting her know his plans and movements, he might not stay.

'Who told you?' he demanded.

'I don't remember,' she said. 'I heard somewhere and thought to surprise you. Fine surprise *I* got, you not turning up an' all. Er . . . perhaps it was Carrots.'

'How would he know?'

'Does it matter? If you'd been with someone I'd have pretended to be meeting someone else. You know I'd never let you down, Jarvis. What are you complaining about if I missed you and wanted to surprise you?'

'I don't like my plans being known to half London.'

'Me and perhaps Carrots is hardly half of London!'

He said nothing more, but the anger simmered in him for the rest of the day. Even when she came back from delivering her flowers to Maggs's eldest to sell for her, he was still sitting brooding about she knew not what.

'Why not come to bed?' she said, knowing that was one way of relaxing him and making him leave his anger behind.

'I'm sorry, Emily,' he said then. 'I have so much depending on absolute secrecy that the thought of a careless word frightens me.'

'Come to bed,' she repeated. 'Common I might be but careless I'm not.'

Carrots made his way through the late-night streets to the warehouse. He stopped at one of the Tom and Jerry shops for a drink of beer, and bought a small loaf of bread to eat for his dinner. Then he began his night's work. The cargo he had to unpack and put aside was mostly panelling. It was to be used in the gentlemen's club shortly to be opened by

Giles Hallam, and his name was on each package.

It was easy work to open the individual packages and pile the oak panels against the wall, from where other hands took them and repacked them in thick, brown paper. The other pair of hands belonged to a large individual who, Carrots guessed from his battered face and ears, had once been a boxer. Neither spoke to the other. Carrots concentrated on keeping up with his part of the activity, afraid he would feel the punch from those huge hands if he caused any delay.

The sections of padded protection that had been on both sides of every piece of panelling were uniform in size and weight. It was impossible to see what was inside the strong silver foil. Then a corner snagged on a nail and Carrots, with one wary eye on the boxer, forced the packing down a little and discovered the reason for the concern over such a mundane item. Every section was filled with tobacco. He stopped and, in the silence, heard only the rough breathing of the boxer as air whistled down the distorted nose.

Every hour or so, the boxer would go out to buy beer. Carrots waited until he was safely out of sight, then removed three of the silver-covered squares to a different part of the warehouse and hid them under some old sacking. That lot would fetch a good sum. Enough to buy himself some translators – second-hand boots.

There were many things lacking in his life, but his thoughts and ambitions rarely went further than boots. He would be able to buy a pair that were almost new, and big enough to have room for stuffing with paper and straw to keep his feet warm. He whistled as he finished his day's work, unaware of the boxer staring at him.

He went back later that night with a sack to hold his treasure. The guard was easy to avoid and he went with confidence to where he had hidden the tobacco, not needing a light to find his way. He filled the sack and was lifting it up and onto his back when he was grabbed, a hand pressed over his mouth. He guessed it was the boxer, from the uneven breathing through the damaged nose and the strong smell of beer.

* * *

Sir Jason was out of the country. He had explained to Sarah that some difficulties with the deliveries of the furniture for Giles's new club made it necessary.

'Giles has decided he will open earlier than we at first thought, so there is a need to hurry things along.'

'When will you be back, Father?'

'When I am sure the delivery is on its way and there is no danger of any delay. Sorry, my dear, but I cannot tell you when to expect me. I may go straight to the office and, if I do, I'll send someone to tell you I am safely home.'

'Thank you, Father. I will be thankful to know that.'

Sir Jason laughed and patted her shoulder. 'Really, Sarah, there is nothing to fear. Thousands travel daily on the trains and ships. It is as simple as your getting into Renton's cab.'

'About Renton, Father – ' she began. But he shook his head.

'Not now, my dear.'

'If you know what I'm going to say, without my telling you, can I ask that you think of it while you are away? I would so dearly love to have Renton back.'

'I will think of it. But, perhaps, now he is a man of business, he might prefer things to stay that way?'

'Can I ask him?' she pleaded.

'We will discuss it when I return.'

'Thank you, dear Father.'

When he had gone it was easy for Sarah to go out at night. She was still frightened at the prospect of meeting the dangerous ex-boxer again, but hoped that a change of clothes would make her unnoticeable among all the boys searching for a few pennies on the dark streets.

Several times she saw Giles but failed to follow him. It was impossible for Renton to stay with her. Being on foot she could slip through the traffic that frequently blocked the streets, and it was sometimes as long as half an hour, judged by the many church clocks, before she met up with him again. Once she saw Giles and managed to follow his carriage for long enough to see that he was escorting the singer, Merry, back to her apartment with her dresser. She felt envy of the easy and relaxed manner of the woman as she allowed Giles to help her down and knock on her door, and wait with her until the maid opened the door and ushered her inside.

On the fifth night of Sir Jason's absence Sarah hesitated to go out. It was likely that her father would return soon, and she had learned that there was a train that left Paris at a quarter to midnight and would arrive at London Bridge Station at four-thirty in the morning. Knowing her father, she guessed he would travel overnight rather than waste a day on which he could work.

She decided it would be her last night on the streets. She was unhappy and the search had lost its excitement. She admitted to herself that she now did it more for the occasional brushes with danger than in a real hope of overhearing or seeing something to help Henry Bannerman find the men who had killed Margaret. Instead, she was unhappy that what she had learned led her to suspect that Giles was somehow involved.

She almost did not go. The lack of enthusiasm was increased by the sight, through the window of the warm room, of heavy rain. When people were out in such weather they did not linger and talk, but hurried through it to get to a place of comfort. It really was a waste of her time and, more importantly, of Renton's time. But, as it was almost certainly the final search, she went.

The clothes she wore were inadequate for the downpour and she was soon very wet. She shivered as she sidled along a high wall, taking the meagre shelter it offered. The woollen coat had let the rain soak through and her skin was tickled uncomfortably with rivulets of water that soaked into her underclothes.

'I think we should go home,' Renton said. He had left the cab in the care of a young boy and had walked with her through the streets not far from the house where Emily lived, although he was not aware of his cousin's new address.

'I agree. We could be the only people in the world,' Sarah said, looking around the deserted street. 'All sensible persons are safely locked up and enjoying a roaring fire.' Because they were apparently far from any listening ears, she did not disguise her voice, and the high sound reached the man standing, waiting for Jarvis, on the other side of the wall.

They heard the footsteps but did not feel any concern until they saw Arthur walking purposefully towards them.

'Run!' Renton said. 'I'll stay and hold him off.'

Sarah did as he said, but Renton's attempt to give her time was useless. Arthur savagely pushed the slim man aside, stepped over his fallen body and chased after Sarah. Painfully winded, Renton stood up and slowly went after them.

Sarah headed for the busier streets; other people were her only chance. Even in this awful weather, there would be some in the main streets. In the main thoroughfare that took people to the theatres and music halls, there was a chance of cabs passing, and surely someone would help her.

Arthur was close enogh for her to hear his tortuous breathing when she reached the corner and saw a cab approaching. She ran into its path and in her girl's voice called, 'Help me! Please help me!'

Sir Jason was already home from Paris. He had returned sooner than he had intended, dejected by his business failures and drawn to London by a desire to see Marie Mackworth. He had spent many evenings in her company since being introduced to her at Weatherby, and had admired her for several months before. The bad news he had met in France made him need her more.

She filled a need for laughter and light-hearted enjoyment that had been lacking in his life since the death of his wife. To face the criticism of family and friends again by marrying beneath him was something he was hesitating to experience. But now, knowing of her more conventional family, for whom she was an embarrassment, he felt cheered, encouraged, and was gradually allowing the loss of his lovely Audrey to be replaced by this charming and delightful singer.

He had already met her parents and soon he would take her to Sallis Close to meet Sarah again. Perhaps, he thought, it would be better to wait until the boys were home, the possible embarrassment for Sarah on meeting her mother's replacement would be more easily managed with more people present.

They had spent the evening at the theatre where Merry had performed twice, and had afterwards had supper in a small restaurant, where he had proposed marriage. Now they were in a hansom, taking her home.

'Before I give you my answer,' Merry had told him, 'I want to meet Sarah and your sons. I need to know if I can care for a complete family come upon me so suddenly.'

'My dear, you may have as long as you wish, but do not, I beg you, feel afraid of meeting my family. Sarah you have already met and as for little Isobelle, you know her sad story. The boys are almost grown and will be little at home. And they will love you at once, my dear. Your warmth will envelop them and make them yours from the moment you meet.' In the darkness he smiled at her.

She stretched out a hand and touched his cheek. 'I want to take the sadness from those eyes,' she said, smiling. 'If we marry, it will be my life's work.'

The carriage in which they were travelling suddenly pulled up with a jerk and a clatter of hooves. Sir Jason looked out to see the cause of the delay and saw a ragged child shouting for help. The child was looking at Merry and holding out her hand to be lifted inside. For a moment, the woman hesitated. Then the child said:

'Merry, please help me. I'm Sarah Lindhurst Ayres.'

The singer offered her a hand to get into the cab and thankfully Sarah climbed in, to see that Merry and her dresser were not alone. Sarah's father was sitting beside her.

'Father! I thought you were in France?'

'I thought you were in bed! Sarah! What is the meaning of such blatant disregard for my wishes and your safety?'

'Sorry, but there ain't room for more 'n three,' the cab driver shouted. ' 'E'll 'ave to get orf.'

'Drive on, man!' Sir Jason snapped, and such was the authority in his voice that the driver did so.

'Wait!' Sarah said, looking out anxiously. 'I have to make sure – someone else – is safe.'

At the corner, farther on from where Arthur had disappeared, Renton waved and ran along the main street back to his cab.

'And you really expect me to re-employ that irresponsible man?' Sir Jason muttered.

'He looks after me.' Sarah was defiant. 'And I would have been caught by that man, that terrifying, dangerous man, if Renton hadn't given me the few moments I needed to reach the main street!'

'He gains no credit for that! You shouldn't have been facing such dangers at all!'

'But Father – '

'Tomorrow you will be sent down to the country.'

From his voice, Sarah knew it was useless to argue. Merry put an arm around the shivering girl and held her until they reached Sallis Close.

Sir Jason was silent. For Sarah it was an ominous quiet before the storm of his anger broke, but Sir Jason was feeling defeated and ashamed. Since the death of one daughter and the maiming of another, he had been less than careful. His work had been half-heartedly carried out, and even when trustworthy and honest employees like Topham had tried to warn him, he had shouted them down and gone his own foolish way.

The visit to France to check on the men who worked for him there had revealed a shambles. The men he had originally chosen had long since gone, their places taken by people whom he would never have considered for even the most menial tasks. The arrangements, which he should have undertaken himself, had been left to others and the result was pilfering and fraud on a grand scale. He had been living out his grief and building up more.

As well as neglecting his business, he had let Sarah down. She had turned to a former servant for some comfort, and her wanderings, which could so easily have robbed him of another loved child, were a direct result of his lack of care.

'Would you like me to come in for a while?' Merry asked softly.

'Please, Father, may she?' Sarah pleaded.

'I would be grateful to you if you could spare us a few moments,' Sir Jason said. 'But Miss Mackworth's presence will not save you from hearing what I have to say about this.'

'No, Father. I deserve all you will give me as punishment.'

The shock of almost being caught by Arthur, closely followed by being caught by her father, made her feel sick. Remorse for the danger to Renton added to her unhappiness.

Merry and her dresser followed Sarah in and Sir Jason gestured to them to go into the drawing room.

'First, can I suggest Sarah is allowed to wash herself and change her clothes?' Merry said quietly. 'I think she and you, Sir Jason, would be more comfortable.'

Sir Jason nodded and Sarah and Merry went upstairs.

'Best not to wake your maid at such an hour. We'll manage between us, shall we?' Merry whispered. Her arm touched the girl's shoulder and Sarah felt an immense relief, knowing she had the woman's support.

Sir Jason looked up when they re-entered. All his anger and fear were gone, replaced by a great love. Sarah looked such a child. A beautiful child. Her face had been scrubbed clean and shone as brightly as her blue-grey eyes. She wore a nightdress that reached her ankles and over it a paisley shawl. Merry's arm was around her shoulders. Sir Jason opened his arms wide and walked to meet them. Instead of the angry words he had been planning while he waited for them, he hugged them both.

Sarah sat close to Merry on a couch and waited for her father to speak. When he did it was to surprise her.

'Sarah. My dear Sarah. I have something to tell you.' He looked at Merry and waited for her nod, then continued, 'I have asked Marie to be my wife.'

'And I have accepted, my dear.'

'Oh, Father! I couldn't be happier. I really couldn't!'

She hugged Merry, then her father, then cried. She cried because she *wasn't* happy. She had no one. Giles was a thief and possibly worse. Her life was a ruin. The happiness of her father and the lovely Merry only made that clearer.

Merry's dresser had found the kitchen and brought a tray of tea, which they sat and drank. Then it was again Merry who took Sarah up to bed. She sat beside the tired girl until she slept.

Sarah did not argue with her father's firm decision to send her to stay at Houghton Hall. She knew that there was no escaping from the man Arthur whom she had hunted and who now hunted her. But it would be several days before she left. Servants had to be sent to add to the slim staff always present. Stores would need to be replenished and her clothes sent ahead. It was decided that she would go in three days' time.

At Giles Hallam's country house, Weatherby, there were no permanent live-in staff. The grounds were tended by a trio of men who lived in the nearby village of Dymbank. Servants came from London when the family stayed, except for cleaning women and scullery maids hired by the day from the local cottages.

People were seen there on occasions but, as no one worked for the family closely enough to know what they were doing, little notice was taken of the coaches and wagons that called there. Apart from a few complaints that they had not been given the offer of a few days' work, little was said.

At the old farm, too, the visits of wagons and carts were considered unremarkable. Traders of all descriptions passed near the village and would find somewhere to rest the night before continuing their journey. It was supposed the callers were such as these.

Two people objected to these callers. Isobelle and Peter hid in the cupboard that opened out into what was the kitchen and glared angrily when men came, usually after dark, and disturbed their playing. Isobelle would shake her arm as if telling Peter to send them away, waving her fat first at him as well as at the unwelcome visitors. Peter spent a lot of time trying to evolve a plan to be rid of them.

The two they saw most were a tall, bearded gentleman who never stayed more than a few minutes and a thick-set, fierce-looking man whose face was battered and distorted. They could hear him breathing when everything else was quiet.

The idea when it came was quite simple to carry out. There were tools in plenty around the farm, some neglected and discarded, others in use and well cared for. Borrowing the best and repairing the worst, Peter set to work. With

Isobelle looking out for visitors, he worked with a saw and added pieces of wood for several nights.

They had found a new, secret entry into the farmhouse. Behind the dairy, the building was close against the hillside and it was here they had found the door. It led to a large, musty area below the main floor of the house and had once been used to house the cattle in times of extreme cold, Peter guessed. It was in this dark place that Peter worked at his plan. The entrance was masked by low-growing shrubs and a tall rowan, so they felt safe from discovery.

The children worked mostly in silence. Only when they stopped and went into the cupboard to eat their food in the pretence of greater warmth did Peter talk. Isobelle listened, nodding occasionally, but Peter knew she only half followed his words.

'The space between the secret door and the bank will have to be filled in,' he told her. 'Then we can stop those men bothering us and spoiling our game.'

Isobelle nodded, growled and, with a mouth full of bread, said, 'Bad men.'

The weather was bitterly cold. Snow fell and lightly covered the furrows in the fields. The sheep were brought close to the farm and fed on the stored fodder from the barn. It was too cold even for Mrs Brandon to insist Peter spend the time cleaning the plough and small tools in the shed, or whitewashing the barns and house. He was able to spend most of his time with Isobelle at the old farm.

They worked feverishly to complete their task. Carrying stones from the fields, where they had been piled at the side of the ploughed areas, they were soon ragged and blood-stained where the stones cut into their arms and hands. All feeling went from their fingers and their feet were stiff and torn in the heavy boots they wore. Even when darkness fell they laboured on.

From the farm, Peter wheeled a heavy wooden barrow and with this they travelled further afield to gather stones, throwing them into the space between the secret door and the rise of the hill behind the house.

They rested and went as usual into their cupboard to eat whatever food they had managed to bring with them.

'Bad men,' Isobelle said, as she tore off a corner of the loaf Peter had provided.

'Yes. But they won't come back after this.'

'Men gone.'

Peter laughed. 'They won't be gone! But once they've promised not to come again, we'll let them go.'

'Men promise. Not come. Any more.' Isobelle waved her arms up and down in the gesture for 'all gone' used by small children.

'Yes. They won't come and spoil your games again. Not after this.'

'More stones, Peer. Walk.' She stood up and they returned to their work.

Peter could hear her making small intakes of breath and after a while realised she was in pain. He looked at her hands and saw they were raw. Blisters had formed and then broken. Her nails were bruised and torn.

'Poor Isobelle,' he said, and the girl echoed his words.

He tore the tattered hem from her skirt and wound it around her hands to protect them.

'It's the best I can do,' he said. 'But from now on I will do three loads to your one.'

'One.'

'Just stand there and I'll tell you when it's your turn.'

The pile of stones reached high above the door before they were satisfied. Isobelle went back to Mrs Starkly's neat cottage and slept for a night and half of the next day, growling in her funny way when the old woman tried to rouse her.

Mrs Brandon was sent for to inspect the child, but could find nothing wrong.

'I think my precious has gone a-wandering and got herself lost. A good sleep is all she needs, and a bit of salve on them cuts, Mrs Starkly.' She searched in the basket she carried. 'Here, I've brought you some bacon bones. Make a good pot of broth. Warms a body up proper, that does, so's my cxperience.'

'Look at her clothes, Mrs Brandon. Ripped and shredded! She looks as if she's been in a fight with a wild animal.'

'Terrible child for climbing and the like. I reckon she's a changeling meself,' Mrs Brandon whispered. 'There's nothing of the lady in her, is there? There's a story behind this one. No doubt of it, Mrs Starkly.'

Leaving Isobelle still sleeping, and Mrs Starkly preparing vegetables for the broth, Mrs Brandon went home.

The day after being found by her father and Merry, Sarah refused to stay in bed. She was tired and aching, but she rose and ate breakfast with her father. The contrite expression on her face was, for once, genuine.

She had decided not to go out, but would wait quietly while arrangements were made for her journey to Houghton Hall. She would send her maid to find out if Renton was safe, though. That would be her first task this morning.

She sat in her room, playing with a piece of embroidery and doing an occasional stitch without any enthusiasm, when a visitor was announced. Edith had gone to find Renton, so Sarah went down alone.

'Mr Cummins! How nice of you to call.' She forced the politeness into her voice. 'Do sit down.'

'I hope you don't think it an impertinence, Miss Sarah, but I went to France recently and took the liberty of buying a bottle of wine for your father, and these sweetmeats for you.' He handed her a box covered in silver paper, decorated extravagantly with lace, ribbons and bows in pink.

'Thank you. Such a pretty parcel! It seems a pity to destroy it.'

She added little more, wanting him to be gone. She had to be polite, as he was one of her father's partners, but she did not have to like him. She wondered how Merry would handle a situation like this. She felt certain that she would learn a great deal from that lady. Things others had tried and failed to teach her.

Alfred sat a while talking amiably about people they both knew. Sarah guessed he was trying to assure her that he was well acquainted with the society in which she moved. She slid forwards on her chair as if she were about to rise, and the trick worked. He stood up, apologised for taking so much of her time, pleaded permission to call again, and left.

She had hardly reached the landing when the parlour maid again called her. She showed Sarah a note from Henry Bannerman, asking her to call.

'I can't,' she protested. 'I don't feel well enough.' She looked towards the door, which was closed. 'Is the messenger waiting for a reply?'

'No, my lady.' It was a polite but firm request to attend.

'Is Edith back from finding Renton yet?' Sarah asked.

'No, Lady Sarah.'

'Then send the boy to find him. I need him to take me to Mr Bannerman's office.' She shivered at the prospect of going into the streets. She needed Renton with her or she would not be able to cross the threshold of her home. After her recent foray through the back alleyways during which she had been chased by Arthur, she had suffered terrifying nightmares. And last night, when Merry had gone, she had woken and lain shaking with the fear of what might have happened. The streets in daylight were just as dangerous as at night.

It was almost lunchtime before both Edith and Renton were found and they set off to see the superintendent. Sarah had managed to tell Renton most of what had happened the previous night. He had assured her that nothing had threatened him on his way back to collect his cab.

'Do you think that is what Uncle Henry wants to talk to me about?' she asked, as he helped her to her seat and closed the doors of the cab.

'Would your father had told him?'

'I don't think so. He had Marie Mackworth with him and I think she would have persuaded him to let things lie. She is coming to dinner this evening and, I suspect, will try to persuade me to give up our search. She is a very sweet lady. It is too early for an announcement, but she will one day be my stepmother.'

'Do you mind?'

'No. She is enough like my own mother for me to warm to her and wish them as much happiness as they can find. I dread to imagine what my aunts and uncles will say, though. Mother used to tell me of the fearful quarrels that took place when Father announced that he wanted to marry her. Some members of the family have not spoken to him since.'

It was raining and the street less crowded because of it.

Only around the gatherings of stalls selling fresh food were the roads congested. In doorways Sarah saw bundles of rags that she knew were human beings trying to stay dry. Once their clothes were wet there was little chance of drying them unless they had the money for a shelter.

Sarah raised her head and displayed a haughty expression for the police constable who stepped forward and offered his hand to help her down. Renton had opened the low double doors at the front of the coach and waited while Edith and Sarah were escorted to the outer office. He threw a coin at a small boy waiting hopefully near to mind his cab, and followed Sarah inside.

Henry Bannerman sat behind his untidy desk but stood up to greet them, his coat and waistcoat littered with ash and strands of tobacco from his pipe, which he had been in the act of relighting. He brushed himself down and offered them a seat near the fire.

'Miss Sarah. Thank you for coming. And Edith. Would you like me to send out for something?'

'No thank you, Uncle Henry, but I am sure Renton would be glad of an ale.' As always, she made sure Renton was included in any politenesses offered. Edith, she knew, would not need anything. She preferred to drink her own cordials.

When the ale had been supplied, Bannerman opened a box and spread the contents on his desk over a piece of green baize cloth. Renton nudged Sarah sharing her alarm.

'I wondered if you recognise anything that belongs to your father,' Bannerman asked Sarah. 'I would have asked him, but I understand he is in France.'

'He is home again now and you will find him at his office.' She spoke quietly as her eyes absorbed what was in front of her. They were the objects Lucy had found hidden at the bottom of Giles's wardrobe. She pointed to the cigar case, wondering, as she did so, if she were sending Giles to prison. 'I think that might be Father's.' She could not be more emphatic, seeing pictures in her mind of the condition of men released from a term in prison. She could not give Giles up to such a fate.

'Can you be more specific?' Bannerman asked.

'Where did you find them?'

'Giles Hallam was given them in payment for debts at his gaming clubs. He usually shows me anything like this before selling them, in case it helps us find thieves. Some of the goods do not belong to those offering them. Of course, many are honestly come by. But in this case I think we have at least one item on our list of stolen property, and there's the cigar case. Can you tell me for certain if the case belongs to your father? Giles thinks it does.'

'Yes, I am sure. Those cigars are specially made for him.' Sarah raised her face to him, her eyes shining with relief. 'How good of Giles to be so observant and helpful!'

'Do you know who pledged it, sir?' Renton asked.

'Yes. Unfortunately we have learned that the man who offered it bought it at a street market. So, apart from a very thin lead, we have little hope of learning anything more.'

A disturbance in the outer office made them all turn. The door opened to reveal a sad tableau. Two men were holding a roughly made litter on which was the body of a thin, poorly dressed young boy. Mud streaked him from head to small, bare feet and almost hid his red hair.

'Found at the edge of the river by some mudlarks, sir, not far from St Katherine's Dock,' one of the men explained. 'It was no accident.' Then the man saw Sarah and hurriedly moved to block her view. 'Sorry, lady, I didn't see you there.'

'Put him in the morgue, constable,' Bannerman said. When the sad cortege had disappeared, he added, 'That was our thin lead. Gone now, I'm afraid. We've been watching him for weeks, hoping he would lead us to a gang who've been practising around here. Acted as crow, he did, and helped a few other schemes too, but we waited too long. Young Carrots can't help anyone now.'

Sarah, Edith and Renton left, stepping around the wet patch left by the dripping corpse. Sarah was white with shock.

'I'll go and see your father, Miss Sarah,' Bannerman said. 'Sorry you were upset. They forgot you were here.'

Sarah was glad of Renton's grip on her arm as they walked back to the cab. How could she tell Renton that the boy was an assistant of Emily Tilt? That he probably helped her procure clients for her sordid business? But Renton knew about his cousin's involvement with Carrots.

'That boy. He was always with Emily. I thought she did a bit of dipping to eke out her flower-money, and lately she is hardly on her stand. Do you think she has gone in for more profitable thievery?'

'I think she has bought a house, so her . . . business has obviously improved her situation.'

'Do you know where this house is?'

Sarah nodded.

'Why didn't you tell me?' He stared at her when she did not reply. 'What is her business, Sarah?'

'There she is! Why don't you ask her?'

At the moment they were talking about her, Emily stepped out of an omnibus and, seeing them, waved her gloved hands in a slow, ladylike manner. Sarah turned her head away in disgust.

'What's the matter with her today?' Emily asked as Renton reached her side. 'Toffee-nosed all of a sudden, ain't she?' She waved again at Sarah, who glared and looked through her icily. 'Please yerself!' Emily said, turning her back on Sarah.

'You're looking prosperous, Emily,' Renton said, touching the fur collar of her coat.

'Things is looking up for Emily Tilt. I've got meself a man.'

'Emily, you aren't – you don't have . . . ' He couldn't frame words to speak of his suspicions.

'I've got a man and as I told you it's all respectable. As soon as we're settled in and got everything nice, we'll be inviting you and that Lucy of yours for tea.'

'I'm glad, Emily.' He looked at her doubtfully, that coat was expensive. 'If you need me any time, you know where I am.'

Renton returned to Sarah, who still waited, looking away from Emily, accusation in her eyes.

'She's got herself a man. Seems he's wealthy by the look of her. I never dreamed our Emily could look so much a lady.'

'Ladies are far more than fine clothes, as you well know,

Renton.'

He was surprised at the sharpness of her tone, but decided there might be a bit of jealousy even between women as far apart as Sarah and his cousin Emily Tilt.

Chapter Fifteen

Emily was thrilled with owning a house. Every morning when she had attended to her flowers and prepared them for selling, she began cleaning. A neighbour, Peggy, whose husband was a coal merchant, had given her some polish and had shown her how to make it, and now she had everything shining like new.

She began scrubbing the stone floor with a large brush and a giant bar of soap. Her bucket was full of hot water which she had heated on the fire and to which soda had been added to soften the water and increase the lather. She could not imagine being happier.

Jarvis did not come home every night. She knew he sometimes had to go down to the country, and, at other times, business matters kept him late and he found a bed away from her. When he was home he regaled her with exciting tales of his adventures and they sat long into the night in front of their fire in comfortable chairs, sipping ale, until tiredness or desire sent them up the curved stairs to their bed. She was still in almost constant fear that one day it would all end, but she pushed the doubts aside and enjoyed each day he spent with her; one day, memories might be all she had.

As she worked, Emily smelled the aroma of the pies she had cooking in the oven beside the fire. Tonight she and Jarvis would enjoy a meal together. The pie contained meat, liver and oysters, which she knew were his favourites.

A loud knock at the door disturbed her reverie and she hurriedly removed the sacking apron and wiped her hands on the scrap of towel hanging behind the back door. She patted her hair as she had seen others do, and smoothed the skirt of the grey day-dress before opening the door.

'Rent!' The man standing outside announced as the door opened. 'Rent. It's overdue.' He was a short, thickset man with a pudgy face and had a green velour hat on his head decorated with a buckle at the front. His tight green trousers ended in boots of dark leather which were so old they curled up at the toes. He smelled of damp and staleness and Emily disliked him on sight. She put on her most haughty expression and in a carefully controlled voice asked:

'Who are you?'

'I am Harry Hatch, farmer.'

'You don't look like a farmer, Harry Hatch!'

'You don't look like a flower girl, Emily Tilt!' he said, admiration clear in his eyes.

She looked at him with disdain. The short-waisted jacket with tails looked as if it had been worn by several others before him, his yellow waistcoat with revers was snuff-stained and too large. Even the pin stuck proudly in the green cravat was bent and lacking a stone.

'You have made a mistake, my good man,' she lied – although with little hope of being believed. 'My name isn't Tilt and this house is not rented. We own it. Good day.' She went to close the door, but the man's foot shot out and the curled toe of his boot held it. The thought passed through Emily's mind that that must be how his boot had become such an odd shape.

'Name of Jarvis King?' he asked, almost casually.

'Never heard of him. The name is St Germain,' she added, inventing the name in an instant. 'And I've told you, there's been a mistake. This house is not rented.'

'Sorry, my dear lady.' His voice was heavy with sarcasm. 'But I don't make no mistakes. The name on my books is Jarvis King and he owes me for two weeks. Unless you pays me something now, you'll have your stuff out on the pavement before you can clap them poor hands of yours.'

Putting her hands behind her back, Emily began to tremble. Was it right? Did this horrible little man have the power to throw them out?

She held herself as tall as she could and said slowly, trying to disguise the quiver in her voice, 'You will have to come back tomorrow. I will have to speak to my – to Mr St Germain.'

'Tomorrow at midday. If you ain't here, or if you're unwilling to pay what you owes, out you go, you and your – 'usband.' He gave her a page from his book. 'Supposin' you can't find your rent book, here's a copy of all that's been paid.' He touched his foolishly large green hat and walked away.

Emily stood on her step, staring after him.

'Trouble, my dearie?' a voice asked. It was Peggy, her neighbour.

Emily smiled and shook her head. 'Just an enquiry about someone who moved away owing money. I couldn't help him. Really, it's disgusting the way some people carry on, isn't it?'

'Don't I know it. Why, if we were paid all we were owed I'd live in a palace.'

Having declared her respectability, Emily went inside.

She lifted the golden-crusted pie out of the oven and sat before the shining, black-leaded grate to stare at the page Harry Hatch had given her. She no longer doubted the horrid man. Jarvis had gammoned her. She, Emily Tilt, had been led into the oldest trap of all, that of believing someone like him could love her.

She did not cry but sat staring into the red, comforting glow of the fire and made her plans. Her first, brief impulse was to take what she could carry and leave, but where would she go? Not back to the Nethersken. She was under no delusions of how long she would keep her treasures if she slept there. Her gaze travelled to the mantelpiece and the beautiful clock. How could she go back to being the constantly drunk flower girl? There had to be a way forward.

She was thankful she had retained her flower pitch. At least that would ensure she did not starve. Then she remembered the stolen items that Jarvis sometimes hid upstairs and at the back of the coal store. She would stay and gradually take back what he owed her. Then, when the time was right for her, she would go.

She went upstairs to take off the dress she used for housework. Drawn by curiosity she had not before succumbed to, she began to examine his private boxes. Several of them held clothes, and on a closer examination she realised they were disguises to go with the variety of beards and wigs which she found in another, smaller box. She thought about them for a while before continuing her search. On a piece of paper, written in a neat hand, were two addresses. One she knew at once as the home of Sir Lindhurst Ayres, where Renton had once worked. The other was a place in the country, the house of Weatherby, three miles from the village of Dymbank.

A sound outside made her imagine Jarvis's rage if he discovered her searching through the boxes she had sworn not to touch. She made herself take time to put everything back where she had found it and then changed her dress and went downstairs.

Her mind whirled with thoughts of how she could leave and not go back to the life she had led before Jarvis. She had been more daring in her robbing and with Carrots to help her had entered new paths. She had been lucky, but it would have to stop. Then she thought of the disguise and fear struck her. Only *she* had been openly seen about when one of Jarvis's schemes was in progress. She had gone without disguise and very memorable with her fine clothes and her bright-red hair. He used disguises that made identification almost impossible, but he had allowed her to go openly as Emily Tilt to collect envelopes when he had set up the fraud. He had encouraged her to dress well and be noticed when she and Carrots went on one of their regular pickpocketing forays. If the police came, it would be her they took away.

She counted her cash and decided that, even with the need to save for a place of her own, she had to continue with the treatment on her hands. She went to the doctor's and then on to her flower pitch, sad, hurt, but determined not to fall back into the old, comfortless existence.

' 'Ere, Maggs,' she called to the chestnut-seller, who was already getting the brazier lit. 'Would your Eddy carry on working me pitch for a while? There's something I've got to do.'

‘ ’Course. ’E’s quite enjoyin’ it, is Eddy. Thinks ’e’ll get a spot of ’is own, ’e does.’

‘So long as it’s not too close to me!’

And so it was arranged, and Emily went back to the house and changed again into her newest and smartest outfit.

Her attitude to money had changed since knowing Jarvis, and she used some of her cash to buy a pair of French lace gloves and a handkerchief, to which she added some of the perfume Jarvis had brought her back from Paris. She observed that with spring lightening the sky and warming the air, ladies she passed were already wearing lighter clothes: muslins, cottons and fine woollens. And the gloves were longer, reaching the elbows. Beautiful gloves were a necessity with her hands, as well as a joy.

She found Ephram easily. She had discovered where the small, expensive coffee house called Steinburg’s was, and went in at the same time as a group of customers, laughing and chattering as if she were with them. Seeing him she stopped and gasped with surprise, and, with a pretence at nodding goodbye to the crowd, hesitated before the table where he sat alone.

‘Emily? My dear, what a surprise! Do sit. What will you have?’

To anyone watching it would seem that their meeting was arranged. Emily sat opposite him and smiled with a half-turned face, her hair down over her shoulders, her blue eyes glowing with pleasure.

‘A surprise indeed, Ephram. I was just intending to sit with my friends for a while before I brave the shops to buy myself a new outfit for the spring.’

It was so easy. They went to the most expensive shops and it was Ephram’s wallet that opened to settle each account. Emily fluttered her eyes with dismay as he refused to allow her to pay. They ate dinner in a popular restaurant where there were entertainers and lots of beautiful women, but Ephram’s eyes remained fully on her.

Going back to his rooms was unpleasant but necessary. Although she allowed him to touch her and undress her, it was hard not to run away. But she knew this was the only certain way of avoiding a return to the Nethersken and poverty. Clothes would deteriorate and she would soon become shabby; too shabby to attract the right sort of man.

When Harry Hatch called again the following day, Emily invited him inside. She handed him the paper and the money owing and demanded his signature to say it was paid. He signed it 'Harry Hatch, farmer'.

'What d'you mean, farmer?' she asked with a laugh.

Harry smiled and invited her to come and see. 'I have three cows all milking and a happy little family of pigs. Chickens, too. All living in the space beside my house. Now you and I are friends, I'll take you to see them if you wish. Fascinating it is to watch the creatures grow fatter and fatter.'

Emily pointed at the gilt-framed picture of cows on the wall and shook her head. 'That's as close as I need to get to cows!' she said emphatically.

They talked for a while about his farm, then Emily said, 'I won't be staying here for much longer.' She touched the side of her nose to suggest it was their secret. 'I might be moving on. Supposing I wanted to buy a house, I'm not as clever nor as smart as you, Harry Hatch, so how do I set about it?'

'Got the money, 'ave you?'

'Enough, or I soon will have. I'm not in desperate straits even if I do sell flowers. In fact,' she boasted, 'I have someone hired to look after it for me.'

'I could certainly 'elp you there.'

He nodded several times to show his willingness and Emily noticed how short his neck was, and how thick. She wondered curiously whether his body was fat too, or whether, under all the layers of clothes, it was graceful and slim like Jarvis's. She could see from the way he looked at her that she might soon have the opportunity to find out.

She hesitated at first, refusing to acknowledge the signs and respond to them, but as he talked of offers to assist her buy the property, and promises to steer her right, she began to weaken. As the heat reached his face and made his eyes sparkle and widen, she began to move sinuously in her chair. She placed her teacup on the edge of the brass fender in such a way that he could see the rise of her breasts under the embroidered muslin fichu at her neckline. There was a moment of coy hesitation then she allowed him to lead her up the stairs.

During the following weeks, Emily was anxious. She continued to steal when an opportunity was too good to be missed, but was afraid her luck would run out. Carrots had failed to make an appearance and she wondered whether he had been caught and imprisoned or gone into temporary hiding. Her clothes and luxuries were building up nicely and she knew that when she did move out of the house, Renton would have to be told. She did not want to go ignominiously pushing a handcart late at night.

When she thought the time was right and she had enough money and possessions to leave, she went to find Renton.

'My man – Mr St Germain – he's been cheating me,' she explained.

'Other women?' Renton asked sympathetically.

'No, worse than that, for someone like me. He took my money, hard saved, and told me the house was ours. Then I found out it's rented and he's spent my money.'

'You look very prosperous, Emily. He's treated you well.'

'Yes, and he's taught me a lot. But it's time I went. Will you help? Come and help me flit?'

'Flit? On the quiet, you mean? Why don't you just walk out? You're entitled to. If he's cheated on you he'll guess why, won't he?'

'I'm a bit afraid of him. I want to flit while he's away for a few days. I've got a place to hide. You won't tell no one where I am, will you, Renton?'

'What does he do, this mysterious man of yours?'

'Anything illegal he can think of that he can use others for. Took hundreds off of people who answered a note in the news-sheets asking for men and their families to go to Australia, he did. And it was *me* who went to pick up the letters from the address he'd given. *Me* who would have been caught if the Peelers had cottoned on.'

Renton listened while Emily told him of some of the other tricks Jarvis had thought up.

'You've found yourself a smart one there, Emily!' He looked at her and admired the quality of the clothes she wore: a light woollen outfit in cinnamon with touches of cream at the neck and around the edge of the layers on the skirt, and she carried a reticule made of leather and tortoiseshell. 'He's certainly done you no harm, by the look of you. Can't you persuade him to go into business legitimately?'

'I don't like being gammoned. And he's put me at risk and hidden behind me. I don't like that. If we'd been true partners like he promised, things would have been different. But now I want to get out. Will you help?'

'Just tell me when and where and I'll be there.'

'There's something big planned soon, I know that. It's something to do with ships and cargoes and I won't say no more so don't ask me! But I'm afraid that if things go wrong, it'll be me that gets nibbed. I ain't no glock!'

Emily went home and prepared for her departure. Jarvis was away again and she knew she had at least a full day, possibly more, before he returned. She took three hundred pounds from the stuff he had hidden, and left the rest of his money safely where he had concealed it on a shelf, a couple of feet up the chimney in a tin box. They never lit the fire in the small back bedroom and it was perfectly safe there.

When it was time for Renton to come for her, she had all her treasured possessions packed and ready to be moved. The clock was wrapped in several blankets and was her priority. It went into the cab first. The pictures followed, and the bed linen and curtains. Even some of the furniture was squeezed into the small vehicle. Emily followed behind it on foot, carrying the last of her clothes.

She had directed Renton to the 'farm' owned by Harry Hatch, who had promised to hide her temporarily until Jarvis's rage had worn off. When she arrived at the shabby dwelling, she saw that the cab was already being unloaded, Harry and Renton packing the boxes into a small shed beside the one in which the pigs dozed contentedly. She wondered sadly if the smell would ever fade from her beautiful things.

'I hope this bloke St Germain doesn't find you, Emily,' Renton said. 'He's bound to have friends who will help him get revenge for all this. Move on, *fast*.'

'Don't worry, I'll look after your cousin,' Harry Hatch promised, with a smile that in the light of the flickering candle made him look more like a villain than a friend. 'She'll be safe from – Mr *Germain* and friends.'

Renton noted the hesitation over the man's name but it hardly registered. He wished Emily good luck and went back to where he might get a final fare before finishing for the night.

On the following morning, Emily risked the streets, hoping that Jarvis was still absent or on his way home, and found an urchin willing to deliver a message for her. She had written a note in her childish handwriting which she asked the boy to take to the office of the Metropolitan Police.

It told them the address of Jarvis's house and where to find his store of stolen goods. It also gave a brief hint of some of his more daring activities. Bannerman was told and he arranged for a team of his detectives to surround the house, hiding in empty houses or standing idly near disguised as vagrants or out-of-work characters with nothing better to do.

Jarvis returned from France very early in the morning and went at once to a lodging house where he could eat breakfast and rest until the city came to life. He did not feel easy wandering about when there were few people on the move, he always tried to avoid being conspicuous. When activity in the streets was beginning to increase, he set off for home.

He took a cab for a part of the way, then left it, preferring to walk the short distance that separated the lively thoroughfare with the quiet area in which he and Emily had set up house. He turned a corner and slowed, on the pretext of changing the grip on his bags. Something was different.

A man leaning on the end wall of a row of old cottages, half hidden by a tree, was not an unusual sight. But the standing position was somehow wrong. He leaned, but stiffly, as if he would much prefer to be in a more upright stance. Another man, dressed in rags, sat on the edge of the road, his head bent as if he were examining his boots. Again the man's attitude was stiff and, to Jarvis's trained eye, unnatural. He turned and walked back the way he had come.

He took several turnings that brought him back to the house from a different direction. More men. He had been betrayed. Emily, he thought grimly. Carrots had been attended to; it must be Emily. He hesitated for a moment, thinking of the money hidden in the chimney. He was loath to go without that. But go he must. The time had come for him to go abroad.

He cursed his bad luck that meant leaving Sarah and any hope of marrying her. It would all have been straightforward if only he had been given time to complete the last stage of his plan. Now he would have to go north, or travel to another country, without her.

He made his way in a circle around the house he had shared with Emily, thanking his wits for not buying the place. He wondered vaguely if Emily had found out the house was only rented, and if that had caused her to leave him. She must have gone. If she told the Peelers, she would have made sure all evidence of her own criminal activities was removed. He felt a momentary regret for the loss of her. She was a delightful companion for certain things, but would never have satisfied his need for acceptance in higher social levels.

Sarah had been his dream, and now the dream was gone. Or was it? Perhaps he could take her with him? It might mean he took her with him by force, but he was sure he had detected in her some small attraction for him. His green eyes glittered as he thought the plan through. If he could only return to the house to collect his money, he would forget everything else and leave the country, taking Sarah with him. She would surely love him once they were together and there was no one else to help her. With her father penniless, she would appreciate how good he was to her.

He reached a shabby lodging house and arranged for a room. He stayed there until nightfall.

That night, as he went cautiously through the cellars of the street leading to his house, he felt a passing regret for Carrots. He could have done with the boy's nimbleness and skill at slipping through narrow spaces now. He would have to risk walking boldly to an adjoining house and hope the watchers were too rigidly following their instructions to watch for him entering another house.

He knew that the roof spaces of the row of houses all joined each other. He had checked every escape route as soon as the house had been chosen. So it was without any fear of disappointment that he went into the back entrance of a place farther along the row. He was bent over, one leg apparently twisted, and carried an advertising placard which announced:

Finest Fish delikasies at

Kelly's on the Strand.

Oisters all fresh

Jelly'd eels at their best.

He wore a dirty, straggling beard of grey and his clothes looked as if made for someone twice his weight.

He entered the empty house and went up into the roof space. It was difficult without a light, but determination made him persevere and he finally groped his way from access to access until he reached the end wall.

Working back again, he counted the faintly lit loft entrances and found his house. Slowly he lifted the flap and placed it to one side of the square opening. The house was silent and still. He lowered himself to within a few feet of the floor and allowed himself to drop. He felt the draught through the open space and hoped no one was there, for the movement of air would have made them curious.

He found a chair that Emily had left behind, and, standing on it, he took the tin containing his money and a cache of jewellery which had been kept secret from Emily. He hoisted himself up into the roof space and made his way back to the lodging house.

Sarah was sitting in the drawing room, staring out along the driveway, waiting for Giles's coach to arrive to take her to Houghton Hall. She was numb with shock. Houghton Hall was to be sold. A moment before, as he left for the office, Sir Jason had told her he needed to sell their country house in an effort to save their London home.

He looked ill. Lines of worry on his face made him look an old man. His eyes, reddened by long night hours poring over his books, were underlined with black smudges.

'Father?' she had asked. 'Can't you explain what has happened?'

'My new investments were ill advised and I have not watched to make sure they did not get out of hand.' He dropped his head to avoid her eyes and said, 'Dear child, I have beggared us.' He covered his face with his hands and sat, his shoulders bowed. Sarah could not run to him and comfort him in case he broke completely. Better to be strong and capable, if she could.

'Selling Houghton Hall is not so terrible. If that will save us, then good riddance.' She added more softly, 'But, of course, we'll have to bring Isobelle back. We cannot have her so far away from us without a chance of visiting her.'

Sir Jason raised his head and stared at her as if she were the most precious thing. 'My dear Sarah! You are so brave and pragmatic. So like your mother.'

'We will help you, Merry and I. You have many friends who will do what they can.'

'Alfred Cummins had been a help. He has stopped the thieving from my warehouses, although he was too late to prevent the insurers from penalising me and charging me a very high rate for the rest of my ships.' He looked sad. 'As for Merry, I have told her to find someone more deserving of her than I.'

'Surely she would not agree! Find this Alfred Cummins. He has helped you before so he clearly wishes you well. Perhaps he will think of a way to help you now?'

'I can't find the fellow. He seemed always reluctant to give his address. I hope he'll come to my office and have some advice to offer.'

After apologising for relieving all his worries onto her, he left her sitting at the window, surrounded by packed boxes and trunks, waiting for the coach to take her to Houghton

Hall for the last time.

She thought of the astonishing way her life had changed since she was last there.

All thought of marrying Giles must go. She would have to spend her youth caring for her father. Then she began to think about Merry. If she truly loved her father, surely she could not walk away from him now that he needed her more than ever? Dare she interfere? And dare she refuse to go to Houghton Hall, in order to stay with him and keep him company in his difficulties? Surely she would be more use here than shut away in the country?

'Edith?' she called. 'Will you take a note to Miss Marie Mackworth asking her to call on my father at his office?' She went over to the writing desk to write a short note, explaining that he was troubled and in need of comfort.

'At the office, Miss Sarah?'

'At the office. But remind her not to say I requested it.'

'Sarah, really it is not your place to interfere with your father's life . . . ' Edith guessed something of what the note contained. Servants were always first with news of changes and rumours below stairs had been circulating for days that Sir Jason might soon be in a serious predicament. Edith went on her errand, consoling herself with the thought that, should she have to leave Sir Jason's family, her new charge might be less wayward.

Sarah watched Edith leave, then settled to continue the wait for Giles's coach. She watched the street and was surprised to see Alfred Cummins approach the door and knock. She remembered how her father had praised him for his help, and stood up as the parlour maid showed him in.

'You have come from my father?' she asked.

'Indeed I have, Sarah. Please forgive me for this intrusion, just as you are leaving, but – ' he looked nervously towards the door – 'it is rather urgent and private.'

'Has something else happened? My father, is he – '

'It's from your father I come, Miss Sarah. He asked me to take you to a place near Houghton Hall, where he will meet you.' Alfred looked again at the door and lowered his voice as he added, 'Please, come with me and tell no one. His very life may depend on your cooperation and speed. Come with me now, this instant, and we can avoid further trouble.'

'Of course, the moment my maid returns.'

'Your maid? She is out?'

'On an errand, yes.'

'Then we have even less time. She will most certainly be followed. Come!' He took her small vanity case. 'We must go before she returns. Hurry, for your father's sake.'

All her instincts were against it, it was unthinkable that she should go with this man without even a maid to accompany her, but his voice was so persuasive and she did not want to cause more difficulties for her father by hesitating.

'But you must tell me *why* I have to go, and without a servant.'

His green eyes looked nervous. Sarah was afraid of what he would tell her. Some new misfortune must have overcome her father.

'What is it? Tell me, please.'

'He has had to – er – go away. He wants you to come with me. I will take you to him. There is a reason . . . ' He lowered his voice to a murmur and moved closer. 'I'm afraid your father has enemies. There is a chance, a strong one, that a ship coming into port tomorrow will be seized by Her Majesty's Customs. Illegal stores have been put aboard her. If your father can find the men who did it *before* the police arrest him, he may clear himself.' It was a good tale, well told.

'Arrest him? Take me to him at once! No, take me to Henry Bannerman. This is ridiculous! My father would not be thought guilty for one moment!'

'I'm afraid he already is, Sarah. You see, following on all his recent difficulties, it is not hard to believe he has taken the only way he can of recouping his enormous losses.'

As he talked, he took her hand and gradually coaxed her towards the door.

'We must hurry.'

'I have to wait for my maid.'

'There is no time, and secrecy is of the essence if we are to save him. He's depending on you, Sarah.'

Persuaded for her father's sake, Sarah went with him, unseen by the servants, into the hansom cab waiting for them.

Chapter Sixteen

When Giles's coach called to collect Sarah to take her to Houghton Hall, there was great consternation.

'Sir, Miss Sarah has vanished. That gentleman, Mr Cummins, called to speak with her urgently, and the next moment they had vanished.' Edith was wringing her hands and trying to hide her tears. 'I was out, Miss Sarah having sent me on a message, you see.'

Giles stared at the woman as if she were talking utter rubbish. 'Edith, pull yourself together! She can't have vanished! Have you looked in the grounds?'

'The garden isn't that large, sir. We've searched every inch.'

'I'll go for Bannerman.' Giles was afraid that Sarah's investigations had resulted in her being taken by someone who needed to silence her, and his limbs turned to water. 'Send for Renton, too!' he instructed. 'He knows Miss Sarah well. Perhaps he can guess where she has gone.'

Renton received the news of Sarah's disappearance as he was leaving home and at once went to find Emily. She was out on the streets regularly and might have news of Sarah. But he was disappointed. Maggs had not seen her and although he asked almost everyone he met, no one knew where the flower girl was to be found. It was by sheer good fortune that he saw her. In one of the meanest streets, he caught a glimpse of her standing at the door of a house that seemed to be surrounded by animal sheds. He reached her before she managed to close the door.

'Go away, Renton! I don't want to be seen.'

'Let me in!' he growled, pushing against her surprising strength to force an entrance.

'I'm hiding from – you know.'

'Sarah is missing. Someone is hiding *her* and, cousin or not, Emily, *she* is far more precious to me! Tell me where she is if you want to stay hidden! Or I'll find and tell your Mr Germain if it's the last thing I do!'

Emily stood back from the door and he almost fell inside.

'I haven't seen her. How am I to know what the likes of her get up to?'

'She was sitting waiting for Giles Hallam to collect her and take her to Houghton Hall, and she disappeared. Emily, I'm afraid for her. Please help if you can. No one knows the streets and what's going on like you.'

Since I scarpered from – him what I lived with, I haven't been on the streets much. Scared of Jarvis Ki– St Germain, I am.'

The slip of he tongue was slight but Renton recognised the name.

'Jarvis King? Jarvis St Germain and other names? Good God, Emily, d'you know who you're mixed up with? Imagine Sarah in his hands!' He grabbed her fiercely and demanded her help. 'Tell me all you know, Emily, or I'll drag you round to the police so fast your shoes'll catch fire! Did you tell him about Sarah and me? Did you?' He stood over her in a threatening manner and she was aware of the strength of his protective love for Sarah.

'I don't know anything about why she vanished. How could I? And no, I didn't tell Jarvis about your nightly escapades.'

'He knows Sarah. Can you think of *anything* to help us find her? Where could she have been taken? Think, girl!' He was becoming more and more furious with her reluctance to help, and in his face was a threat of violence.

Resentment against Sarah still rankled and with it her own unhappiness at the path she had chosen to tread. Prostitution was something she had determined never to begin. She had seen too many take that apparently easy way of surviving and ending up in a pauper's grave before they were past their youth and beauty.

Renton's face glared at her, his face drawing closer in a threatening manner. 'Help me, Emily, or I swear I'll – '

Emily remembered the item about ships and illegal cargoes. Sir Jason's name had been on it. She relented, forcing away the fear of Jarvis's revenge. Best to help Renton; he was a cousin, after all, and, more importantly, he had often helped her in the past and she might need his assistance in the future.

' 'E'll kill me if 'e knows I've blabbed.'

'Just tell!'

'I found some papers. Something to do with shipping, with Sir Jason's name on them. I didn't understand it proper, but I think Sir Jason's been set up for a charge of smuggling.'

'Anything else?'

She hesitated, glancing at the closed door as if expecting Jarvis suddenly to burst through it. 'He uses other names.' While Renton listened carefully, she told him all she could remember.

'Tell me where he keeps his stock. He must have a house somewhere. You must have heard some addresses. Tell me what you know, all of it, and I'll leave you in peace, but let me ever find out you've left something out of the telling and I'll – '

'There was the name of a place. Weatherby, I think it was, and a village. Something-bank – '

'Dymbank?' he suggested.

'Might have been.'

After pressing from her a few more scraps of information, he left her. She was frightened, he knew that and felt a momentary regret for the danger he had placed her in, but then he concentrated on finding Sarah. He pushed his way savagely through the streets, knocking people out of his path. He went to find Giles, who he knew was with Henry Bannerman. He quickly explained the implications of what he had learned and he and Giles set off at once for Weatherby.

'But why would this, er, Jarvis want to take her there?'

'I don't know. But with Bannerman and his men concentrated in London, I think it a strong enough suspicion for us to follow.'

'I hope you're right.' Giles was unhappy at risking going so far away from Sarah's haunts on the word of her ex-coachman, but trusted that, of all people, Renton would be most likely to understand the situation and act in Sarah's interests. But he was not fully convinced until Renton gave him a list of Jarvis King's other names. That and the warning that Sir Jason was being set up for a smuggling charge persuaded him, and they set off in the phaeton, the fastest of his coaches, to catch the stage.

Alfred and Sarah had almost reached Weatherby. It was an overcast day and she was not inclined to look out of the window but sat staring down into her lap, exhausting herself by wondering if she had been stupid not to wait for Giles or even Edith. If she had, would she have put her father at risk? If only Renton were here!

'Where is my father? Is he waiting at Houghton Hall?'

'No, but somewhere where he is relatively safe – for the moment. Don't worry, Sarah. You can leave everything to me. Just relax and enjoy the pleasant ride. The view is hardly perfect, but perhaps the company will compensate you, just a little?' He smiled to reassure her and Sarah returned his smile. He really was a most unusual man. She wondered if he were in love with her. Then he began to sing softly and the words were a declaration. One she did not want to hear, yet it was a pleasant diversion from her worries.

'My love, her eyes are glowing,
How lovely it would be
If her eyes that shine so brightly
Shone that way for me.

My love, her lips are roses,
How lovely it would be
If those lips that are so tempting
Were offered now to me.

My love's in love with dancing,
How lovely it would be

If instead of loving dancing
She'd fall in love with me.'

Sarah turned away in embarrassment, but his soft and pleasantly tuneful voice touched her. He was a very appealing man. But there was Giles and always would be.

'It was a song I heard once or twice at the music hall,' he said. 'Every time I hear it I think of you, Miss Sarah.'

Night had fallen, and she looked out and saw only their reflections. The intimacy was comforting. She felt that in the present calamitous, uncertain circumstances, he was someone to depend on.

The relaxed friendliness stayed with them. When they alighted from the coach which had been hired to take them on the final part of their journey, the open countryside and the darkness made it natural for Sarah to allow him to take her arm. She was still anxious about her father, but the intimacy of the long journey had made her more certain that Alfred was able to deal with the situation and bring them through it in safety. Hadn't her father told her how he had helped him?

He led her from the road through a narrow, rutted lane without lights. She had to ask him to wait a while for her eyes to accustom themselves to the darkness. Gradually, the sky seemed a shade lighter and the trees on either side stood out and began to take shape. She walked on beside him and he talked about how soon they would be comfortable and well fed, and sitting in front of a warm fire with Sir Jason. She held back the fear that now came over her in waves of near-panic and walked on, staring into the blackness, expecting every moment to see lights, but the track continued and seemed without end. Why hadn't she insisted on waiting for Giles?

When they eventually reached the house, it was in darkness.

'Surely they aren't all abed?' Alfred said. He went to the door and opened it. A smell of damp, neglect and decay met Sarah's nostrils and she stepped back.

'This can't be the place! We must have mistaken our way in the darkness.'

'Then we can at least shelter and rest a while to consider where we made the mistake.' He guided her to the door but Sarah again pulled back.

'I can't go inside. It smells foul!'

To her alarm he gripped her arms fiercely and forced her to step inside. She struggled and tried to scream as he pulled her through the door and pushed it closed.

'Let me go! How dare you handle me so roughly? I do not intend to stay here. Open the door!' Badly frightened, she used the method that usually worked, that of demanding with as much authority as she was capable. But Alfred ignored her insistent cries and held her more tightly.

When she paused for breath he said quietly, 'Sarah, my dear, I cannot allow you to run around in strange countryside unprotected. Forgive my mishandling of your dear self, but it was for your own protection. I have been fortunate enough to be able to assist your father out of several difficulties and hope to do so again. In this, he faces great danger from a man who has determined on his downfall. Have you heard the name Jarvis King?'

Confused and frightened, only half listening to his softly spoken words, she said, 'No. My father does not discuss his business affairs with me.'

'Jarvis King has cost your dear father a great deal of money. His intentions are to destroy your father completely, but don't worry, Sarah. You will have me to protect you, should the worst happen. I will always be your friend.'

'Why are we here?' she whispered. 'Please, take me to my father.' In a slightly stronger voice, she added, 'I demand it!'

From his pocket he produced a lucifer and began to light an oil lamp on the mantelpiece. He adjusted the wick and slowly revealed their shelter. As the light increased, Sarah's spirits diminished. She was chilled and more afraid than when she had been out on the London streets facing Arthur. There at least it had been on her own terms, her own choice, while here she was utterly dependent on this friend of her father's.

There was no fire and from the look of the grate there had not been one for years. What furniture there was had not been used either. If this room was a sample, there was certainly no comfortable, warm bed for her. In sudden panic she ran to the door. She had no idea where she was, but felt an urgent need to be outside, away from this awful place. Before her fingers could turn the knob and pull open the door, Alfred was there, standing against it, his eyes glittering brightly in the light from the oil lamp, the scar very prominent.

'I cannot stay here,' she said, bravely trying to hide her fears. 'There must be something better close by.'

'Did you see any lights? Any sign of habitation? No, Sarah, I'm afraid we must stay here until dawn, then we'll be able to get our bearings.'

She stifled a sob. As if to comfort her he put his arms around her; then, to her horror, his lips were searching for hers. She struggled and kicked wildly, trying to escape from his embrace.

'Come, Sarah, you know you feel something for me.'

'Let me go! A friend of my father's you might be but that doesn't give you the right to suppose . . . ' The words failed as she stared in horror at his face. The scar was gradually uncurling.

He sensed what had happened and slapped his hand to his cheek.

'Who are you?' she whispered.

'A friend.'

'Let me go, please let me go!'

'Your father is depending on you.'

'Who *are* you?'

He felt in his pocket and brought out what she gradually realised was a false beard and put it on. Then he removed it and pushed some cotton waste into his cheeks and added a grey wig and a moustache. Terrified, but mesmerised into watching, she saw him change character time and again. Only the eyes did not alter, but held her in a steady, hypnotising scrutiny. She realised in spite of her terror that he was waiting for her admiration. Frightened as she was, she did not give it.

'Take me to my father and stop playing stupid games!'

'I change my name as easily as I change my face,' he said

calmly. He replaced the beard and took off the small glasses of the most recent of his changes and said softly, 'Like this, I am Jarvis King the man your father would dearly love to meet.' He laughed and turned away.

She struggled to reach the door, calling out in the vain hope of someone hearing, but she was quickly overcome and forced to sit in a corner of the room. He sat near her, between her and the door.

There was no possibility of running, so she settled to rest on the floor of the chill room, the dampness seeping into her body and dropping her temperature alarmingly. She knew she would not sleep, should not sleep. She began flexing her feet and hands to keep stiffness at bay, watching Alfred, who was pretending to nap in a corner opposite. Twice she stirred and made as if to rise, and like a cat he leapt up in an instant and towered over her threateningly.

In the silence following the vain attempts he once again sat quietly, eyes closed and head lowered towards one shoulder, but she knew he did not sleep. His breathing was steady but not with the slowness and evenness of unconscious rest.

Then his breathing seemed to fill the room and echo around her. She blamed the utter quiet and her imagination, but fear clutched at her as she realised it was not Alfred's breathing she could now hear. Someone else was present.

The lamp had been lowered and the shadows seemed alien and full of imminent danger. Her heartbeat was loud and blended with the wheezing that came from somewhere outside the room. Her senses were alert and her mind grappled with the problem of what to do.

She felt the unmistakable sensation of being watched. Then she clutched her mouth to stifle a scream. The door began to open. A man was entering and as the breathing became harsher she knew the man was Arthur. The criminal she and Renton had been seeking since the death of Margaret, was only inches away from her.

'Alfred! Help!' she shouted and began to move towards him, seeking the lesser evil of his protection against the new threat. He stood up, but not to confront the intruder, only to stop her from leaving.

‘So you’re here.’ Alfred addressed the man who now stood in the doorway, his bulk blocking light from the lantern and throwing a huge shadow. Sarah knew then there was no escape. She was to die here in this old, dead building.

‘No trouble gettin’ ’er ’ere?’ Arthur asked, gesturing to Sarah.

‘She came like a lamb to the – ’

Sarah was unable to move. Alfred gripped her firmly and even should she escape from him there was no possibility of getting past Arthur. There was only one way that would give her a chance. She prayed that Alfred’s love for her was genuine. Forgive me, Giles, she breathed, moving closer.

‘Let me go, Alfred. I’m not running from you. Just promise to keep that man away from me. I don’t want to leave *you.* I know you are trying to help my father,’ she whispered, stretching up her face to his.

‘Lock her in the kichen,’ he said coldly. ‘You must learn to love me before trying such persuasions.’

‘*Please*, Alfred.’

‘My name,’ he repeated slowly, ‘is not Alfred Cummins. I am Jarvis King.’

Sarah screamed as she was lifted by the huge man and carried through the hallway and into the room beyond it. She was thrown roughly onto the floor and the man went out. She heard a key turn and a heavy bolt thrust home; footsteps crossed the hall and then there was a silence broken only by the occasional murmur of the men’s voices.

Dawn was showing a faint light so Sarah was able to examine the room in which she was now imprisoned. There was a large oven-range fireplace and two chairs were set beside it as if the occupants had just stood up and walked out for a moment. In a corner was a cupboard, but an examination revealed it to be empty. There were strong locks on the windows and apart from some fallen plaster there was nothing else to see, no weapon with which to arm herself, no way of escape.

She took off her travelling cloak and began to exercise. Wrists and ankles, arms and legs; bending, stretching, leaping and rolling, determined that should an opportunity to run offer itself, she would be prepared.

The voices rose as if the men were coming closer and she crouched, ready to run. Her whole body was taut, waiting for the slightest chance, and she felt her heart thumping, anticipating the burst of energy. She watched the door for the first movement, but instead of hearing the key and bolt, there was a groaning, crashing sound which began quietly but increased until the din reverberated through the building. She covered her head, convinced that the walls were about to collapse. The roaring sound and screaming of breaking wood went on for an age and were followed by groans and shouts for help. But these too faded and there was silence.

Sarah slowly uncurled her body and looked around her. The room was intact although filled with choking dust that seemed to rise from the floorboards and fall from the ceiling. The silence was more unnerving and eerie than the unexplained crashing sounds. What could have happened? After a while, she moved towards the door and listened. Then, as the silence continued, she tried to get out.

She struggled with the door but it would not budge. What had happened? Had someone else arrived? If so, were they people who would help, or more friends of the fearsome Arthur? She called several times but there was no reply. She sat again. It was best to wait until morning, then try to break a window and get away. She did not know why she delayed. It was fear that held her, but why should she want to stay in a place where she was unsafe? She decided it was the prospect of finding herself in a worse mess. Somehow the brief imprisonment had made this place a sanctuary and she was unwilling to leave it before making sure of her next move.

She was sitting tense and watchful, ears tuned for the slightest sound, trying to guess what had happened to the two men and planning what she would do when she succeeded in breaking out. Then, silently, the cupboard door opened and, to her utter disbelief, her sister Isobelle stood there.

'Isobelle!' Sarah held out her arms to her sister, but the strange child stood without a word or movement. Behind her stood Peter, the boy Sarah remembered from Mrs

Brandon's farm. 'Peter, what has happened?'

'We had to stop the men from coming. They were spoiling our games,' Peter said anxiously. 'Come on, through here. They can't get out.'

'But what happened? Where are they?'

'Walk,' Isobelle said. She and Peter re-entered the cupboard and Sarah followed.

The back of the cupboard opened out into the hall and when Sarah reached there she gave a gasp of shock. The hall floor was gone. Instead there was a gaping hole. Roughly sawn edges and splintered wood, tilted and wrenched, led her eyes down to the darkness below. She could just make out the sprawled figures of two men.

'Bad men,' Isobelle said with a growl.

'We had to stop them coming, see,' Peter began. 'We blocked the cellar door with stones, and weakened the floor. Then we only had to take out a few bits of wood and down it all went.'

'You did this? You and Isobelle?'

'We had to, see. Spoiling our games.'

It was dark when Giles and Renton arrived at Weatherby. There was no sign of anyone. Giles went inside and he and Renton looked in all the rooms, but it was not until they reached the servants' quarters that there was evidence of the place having been used by strangers. Rubbish littered the big kitchen and food was strewn about, clearly indicating that meals had been hastily prepared.

As dawn broke, evidence could be seen of many horses and carts having used the yard.

'I must talk to the servants,' Giles said. 'Will you fetch them?'

When Renton had been given directions and had ridden off across the fields to the houses in which most of the servants lived, Giles wished he had gone in his stead. He was in an agony of despair. Sarah must be in great danger and all he could do was sit and wait, depending on the actions of others, and hope that by some miracle she would be restored to him.

What should he do next? They had pinned their hopes on

this house and obviously something had happened here, but there was no sign of Sarah, so where should they look next? He felt useless. But one thing was certain, he would make the servants talk!

He thought of the old farm ruin. Was it possible that it too was being used by whoever held Sarah? He jumped up to go and investigate but sank down again. He had to wait until Renton returned. Then he would search every inch of every building for as far as he could walk.

Renton banged on the doors of the small cottages where men and women who worked for Giles lived, and demanded they open for him. They gathered together, some dressed, others wrapped in blankets dragged hastily from their beds. They all insisted they knew nothing of the goings-on at Weatherby.

'But surely you go there?' Renton insisted. 'You, I know you. You're one of the gardeners. You must be there every day. Surely you must know something?'

The man shook his grey head. 'Nothing, sir. I always have me head down, see, and I sees nothing but the soil I be working.'

'You, girl. You go daily and feed the hens. Who are the people who have been using the place in Mr Hallam's absence?'

'I feeds the 'ens, sir, and that's all. Seen no one.'

'You will all come with me. Now! Mr Hallam will want to hear how you can work at the house and see nothing when men and horses are using the place like an inn.'

Protestingly, the group followed him back, running behind his horse as he threatened them with the whip if they did not make haste. Most worked at Weatherby only when the family were in residence, but they must all have known what was happening. There was no doubt they had been frightened into saying nothing. He cracked the whip on the still morning air. If they were frightened, then he would frighten them more. Thoughts of Sarah in danger urged him on.

As they came in sight of the house, Renton slowed his horse and rode behind his unwilling flock as if they were sheep. Being higher, he saw the other figures before they did. He wheeled his mount to investigate. He found Sarah, bedraggled and blue with cold, walking through thick mud, followed by two shabby urchins whose sex he could not guess.

'Sarah!' He threw himself from his horse and ran to hug her. She was shaking with cold and fatigue. Mud splattered her skirts and completely covered her shoes and ankles. She looked as if she was unable to take many more steps. He picked her up and lifted her onto his horse.

'I was taken to the old farm. Alfred said we'd meet Father there,' she began. 'Instead *he* was there and I knew Alfred had tricked me. Now they are both hurt and – '

'Sarah, don't talk. Wait 'til we get back to the house. You'll only have to tell it all again for Giles – I mean, Mr Hallam.'

'Giles is here? But how did you know – ?'

'Hush, just rest. Tell us what happened to you and we'll tell our story. Frantic he is. I've been to gather the servants, as you see. Something's been going on here and Giles – Mr Hallam – will find out exactly what.' He went on talking to her, soothing her, telling her how much Giles worried and how quickly he had agreed to come when he, Renton, thought she might be here.

'We've got that Henry Bannerman and his men scouring London, and we're down here. Determined to find you we were, all of us. Thank God you're safe!'

'Where is Father?' Sarah whispered.

'Now we've found you, we'll soon get to Sir Jason. Don't worry.'

He spoke with such confidence, Sarah believed him.

The strange procession wended its way over the last field and into the grounds of Weatherby. As they were skirting the lake, Giles recognised Sarah with that sixth sense of those in love, and ran to greet her.

He lifted her from the weary horse and hugged her close.

'My darling Sarah, you're safe!' He called the servants to hurry. 'Fires,' he instructed. 'Hot water for her bath, and food. Quickly!'

'The men at the farm. They're injured. I don't know how

badly,' Sarah began. 'And Alfred Cummins is really – '

'They can wait! When you're fully recovered we shall talk,' Giles said firmly.

Bathed and with a light meal inside her, Sarah could not rest. The night without sleep had begun to show in her eyes, which were heavy and with dark patches underneath them, but she had to know what had happened to Alfred Cummins, or Jarvis King or whoever he really was.

'You stay here,' Giles insisted. 'Renton and I will go and we'll take the boy, Peter, with us. You rest. We'll soon be back with news.'

On foot, Giles and Renton headed for the old farm with Peter, who was becoming anxious about the work he should be doing for Mrs Brandon.

'Kill me she will,' he muttered, as they insisted he went with them.

'Not when we go back with you and tell her how you saved Miss Sarah and probably caught two criminals wanted by the London police' Renton assured him.

A scream from the house made their blood run like icy water and they all turned, but it was Isobelle fighting against being left behind. 'Peer!' she called.

'Best let 'er come,' Peter said resignedly. 'Likes 'er own way, that one.'

Renton had brought rope and, once they had seen the men locked in the cellar, he went down and, tying them like carcases of meat at the market, hauled them out.

'My arm, I think it's broken,' Jarvis said, and pain made sweat burst out on his grey-looking face.

'Oh, dear, what a shame, and it's your forgery arm too.' Renton pushed him remorselessly as he made him walk to the door.

'I can't walk, I feel sick,' Jarvis protested.

'You'll walk or be kicked every inch of the way,' Renton warned. 'If you die it'll save the hangman a job!'

Arthur was firmly tied and, with the other end of the rope held by Giles, and Jarvis led by Renton, who was hoping for an excuse to set on him, they walked back to the house.

Giles arranged for a messenger to be sent from the village to inform Henry Bannerman of the capture of Alfred, alias

Jarvis, and the fearsome Arthur. The two criminals were locked in a small pantry and the door padlocked and bolted. Food was passed through the small window, which was also kept barred and bolted. Giles was determined they would not escape from him and endanger Sarah again.

A servant went back to the farm to explain to Mrs Brandon, who shrieked with rage on seeing Peter and Isobelle.

'Where've you been, eh? Leavin' me to see to it all. Wicked boy! That girl's more important to you than your work and 'ome!'

'Steady, missus,' the servant, Gregory, explained. He had known Mrs Brandon all her life and knew her rage was on the surface and she would not harm the boy. 'Young Peter 'ere is a brave lad and he's caught two dangerous men for the police of London. Yes, 'im an' that young maid of yourn.'

The story was told with many additions. While Mrs Brandon and Gregory went through it again and again, Peter, helped by Isobelle, fed the pigs, collected the hens' eggs and made sure the goat had been milked.

When Gregory had gone and Peter and Isobelle had wandered off into the fields to look at the small herd of sheep, Mrs Brandon began to decorate the living room. She removed the rough covers from the chairs and replaced them with the flowery prints, and added cushions to the sofa. It was likely she and Isobelle would be having callers.

'Pays to be prepared, so's my experience,' she muttered as she worked. 'Oh, my!' she shouted then. 'Where's that young maid? I do 'opes as 'ow they 'aven't seen 'er in 'er present state o' dress! Isobelle!' she called. 'Pigpen? You come 'ere this instant. Got to 'ave you lookin' smart, and what a job that is for a poor farmer woman!'

Sarah slept all day and through the night. Giles and the maid sat with her, watching anxiously for signs of a fever, but she woke refreshed and unharmed by her frightening experiences.

'You will eat breakfast in your room,' Giles instructed. 'Then, when you're ready, Sarah dear, come down to assure

Renton that you are safely recovered.' He sent the servant temporarily acting as Sarah's maid to arrange for her meal, and left her to enjoy it.

Sarah spent the day sitting quietly near the fire in the elegant drawing room with Giles. She had no clothes of her own and was dressed in a swansdown-trimmed gown of palest green over which she had a lace stole. Both of which belonged to Caroline. Her dark hair had been washed and brushed and hung around her shoulders framing the face, still pale but already more relaxed and calm after the sleep. Giles thought he had never seen anything so beautiful, and he told her so.

He took her hand and they stayed, with only the temporary maid to listen, and talked, first about her adventures, which made the young country girl's eyes widen, then of their future together, which made her blush.

Towards evening, two coaches arrived. Sir Jason and Henry Bannerman were in the first one.

Sir Jason had been stopped at Dover, on his way to rescue a cargo which Alfred had warned him was in danger. He had intended travelling back on his own ship. He was taken to Bannerman's office, where he was told of Alfred's plan to have him arrested in charge of an illegal shipment.

When the message arrived from Weatherby, both men set off to join Sarah and take possession of the wanted men.

'First I will call in to tell Edith that Sarah is safe,' Sir Jason announced.

At the house in Sallis Close a visitor waited for him.

'Merry, my dear! But why are you here? How long have you been waiting?'

'No matter now I know she is safe. But I would like to come with you. Edith? Will you accompany me?' Ignoring further arguments, Merry sent the men on their urgent way and prepared to follow with Sarah's maid.

The journey had seemed interminable to Sir Jason. Knowing his daughter was safe was not enough, he needed to see her and hear from her own lips that she was unharmed. As the coach finally halted at the door of Weatherby, he jumped down and ran into the house.

'Sarah, my dear child! What has been happening? Are

you really unharmed?'

'Father, I am well. Giles has looked after me and I want for nothing now you are here.'

'Bannerman is with me and travelling behind us within a few hours are your maid and – ' he paused, and smiled at her – 'and Merry.'

Once all the arrivals had been fed and given rooms, they gathered in the drawing room and shared their information of everything that had happened. Faces began to look less strained and laughter gradually echoed around the large room.

The servants, having been reassured that Jarvis and Alfred could not escape, admitted that the house had been used for the collection of smuggled and stolen goods, which were sold there and taken away by customers who sometimes ordered in advance and other times came and chose from what was offered. The servants had been threatened with having their houses burnt and other punishments, even death, if they told of what they knew.

'Made to cook for them, I was, sir,' one little girl had admitted. 'Shamed I was, leaving the kitchen in such a state.'

'The smuggling and thieving of my cargoes will now stop,' Sir Jason told them with a sigh of relief. 'But I fear that the damage done by Jarvis and his men will take a long time to put right. The building scheme has drained my resources severely and I will have to sell much of what I own.'

'But how can that be?' Sarah asked. 'If you're building lodgings for the working-class city dwellers, surely you'll have an income from them?'

'The land I owned has been sold by that criminal. Using my name and forging the papers, he offered it for sale and has pocketed the very high profit he demanded for it. The money for materials and wages has also disappeared.'

'Now we have him in custody, I'm hopeful that some of the money will be returned,' Bannerman said. 'But much will be gone for ever.'

At the other side of the fire from Sarah and Giles, Sir Jason and Merry sat, also close together, hands touching.

'I refuse to allow this tragedy to spoil our lives, Sarah,' Merry said, smiling. 'Your father and I will marry in the month of December, when you're out of mourning. I hope you approve?'

'Father! Merry! I couldn't be better pleased.' She reached over and took both the singer's hands. 'I shall start at once to embroider a cushion for a personal wedding present.'

'Oh no!' her father moaned in dismay. 'Not another embroidered cushion! Poor Edith will be up for hours restitching it.'

Sarah joined in the laughter.

'Sarah,' Giles said then. 'You know that your father is selling Houghton Hall?'

'Yes, Giles, and I am sorry. I love it and will sorely miss the wonderful holidays, but I would rather it went if it will help Father through his present difficulties.'

'Giles is buying it,' Sir Jason said quietly.

Sarah looked at Giles in surprise, waiting for him to explain. 'But you already have this beautiful house?'

'Weatherby will be for my brothers,' he said. 'I want Houghton Hall, with its cottages and farms, the smithy and the mill, for us, Sarah. It was true when you told me you could happily leave town and settle here?'

He watched anxiously as she did not reply but began to search in the pocket of her gown.

'Sarah? I shall still have my businesses in London and you can visit your friends and the shops whenever you wish . . .?'

'Oh, Giles, what a *perfect* way to live! And here – ' she handed him a coin which she had taken from her pocket – 'here is the first ornament for our new home.'

'A penny?' Giles frowned.

'It was your first gift to me.'

'It was? It's a miserly gift for someone I love.'

'You threw it for a small urchin who found you a hansom cab, one night in London.'

'When Renton was so conveniently close at hand? You mean, it was you?'

She nodded, her smile widening as he showed the concern that made his expression so serious.

'Sarah, will you ever change?' He held her close.

Shaking her head, she asked, 'Do you want me to?'

'Not really, but I want you to keep yourself safe. I want us to grow old together.'

'I will. I really will.'